But Remember Their Names

Books by Hillary Bell Locke

But Remember Their Names

But Remember Their Names

A Cynthia Jakubek Legal Thriller

Hillary Bell Locke

Poisoned Pen Press

Copyright © 2011 by Hillary Bell Locke

First Edition 2011

10 9 8 7 6 5 4 3 2 1

Library of Congress Catalog Card Number: 2011920309

ISBN: 9781590589120   Hardcover
       9781590589144   Trade Paperback

Poisoned Pen Press
6962 E. First Ave., Ste. 103
Scottsdale, AZ 85251
www.poisonedpenpress.com
info@poisonedpenpress.com

Printed in the United States of America

For Laura Rose Sigmon, dona Dei

"Forgive your enemies—but remember their names."
—Robert F. Kennedy

Chapter One

AWWWKward!, Caitlin Bradshaw thought as she glimpsed her mother striding briskly toward her with a pack of cigarettes. Then she saw that the cigarettes were Caporals, which meant they weren't hers, which meant she *wasn't* busted after all. *Awkward!* became **WTF?** when Ariane took a cigarette from the pack. In the seventeen years and three months she had lived with Ariane Bradshaw, Caitlin had never seen her mother smoke.

Ariane shook the pack again and extended it toward her daughter. If Caitlin considered deceit or evasion, it was only for a millisecond. With a cautious half-smile, she drew a Caporal from the pack and leaned forward to accept a light that Ariane offered from a satiny black and gold tube. Caitlin's auburn bangs fluttered as, with practiced familiarity, she rocked her head back to blow smoke toward the ceiling. By the time Caitlin brought her eyes back down, Ariane had lit her own cigarette and sat down directly across the outside front corner of the computer desk from Caitlin.

Please don't let this be some gross peer-bonding thing, Caitlin prayed. *I'm not just your MOM anymore, I'm your FRIEND! We can talk about eVERYTHING!* Please not that.

Ariane brought her cigarette up for a contemplative pull, appreciative without being needy. At thirty-nine years old, she was no longer the stunning bride in the pictures taken thirteen months before Caitlin's birth, but she could still snap vertebrae anywhere in Pittsburgh. Unlined face almost perfectly oval, fine bone structure, chestnut hair with plenty of body, breasts notice-ably full even under the bulky beige sweater that protected her against late November chill—it made a nice package. Not long ago Caitlin thought she'd seen a few extra pounds accumulating uncharacteristically around her mom's waistline, but not now. Ariane looked like exactly the perfect weight for her five-five height.

"I didn't know you smoked," Caitlin said, not sure she was improving on the silence.

"I can't say *vice-versa*." Ariane smiled wryly. "But we have something more important to talk about. Soon, maybe as early as tomorrow, police officers will come to search the house. Do you have any drugs here?"

Ariane's studied calm was infectious. Caitlin gaped at the question, but didn't freak out.

"No."

"Before you tell me you don't smoke pot, remember that munchies go on the grocery tab, which I pay."

"I do weed sometimes with friends," Caitlin said, oddly unconcerned by what, five minutes ago, would have been an unthinkable confession. "But I've never held any."

"Any other drugs?"

"No." Caitlin flicked ash and puffed on her cigarette, trying to seem blasé but not quite bringing it off.

"Anything bad on your computer?"

"Not that I know of."

Ariane bent toward Caitlin and caught her daughter's eyes. She put her hand comfortingly on Caitlin's knee.

"Listen, honey. If you have something on your computer that's just embarrassing—say a picture of you shit-faced at a party or flashing your breasts or something—just leave it. Trying to delete it won't work and will make it look like you have some-thing to hide. But if there's something that might be criminal, we need to talk about it right away with Sam."

"Sam the Really Jewish Lawyer?" Samuel Schwartzchild did the tax and estate planning work for half the families Caitlin knew. Without waiting for a reprimand, Caitlin then contritely bowed her head and murmured, "Sorry."

"Save the apology. Let's focus."

Caitlin looked back up and again caught her mother's eyes.

"This is about dad, isn't it?"

"Yes."

"Has anything happened to him?"

Ariane glanced at a Phillipe Patek watch on her wrist.

"Not yet."

Chapter Two

I was on a roll when Pauline Denckla's peremptory rap on the side of my cubicle interrupted my dictation.

"Ms. Bradshaw is here, Ms. Jakubek." She didn't mean either "Ms."

"One second." I held up an index finger. "I'm about to win a case."

"This is the referral from Fletcher and Peck."

Referrals from the distinguished law firm of Fletcher & Peck command attention. On the other hand, the main thing I'd gotten from Luis Mendoza's seventy-two-second briefing an hour before was that Caitlin Bradshaw was a kid.

"Stash her in the library and get her a chocolate malt or something." I flicked my Dictaphone back on and resumed. "—certificate of the death of Tyrell Washington on November 18, 2010. Paragraph. Wherefore the undersigned counsel of record for defendant Washington respectfully moves the United States Court of Appeals for the Third Circuit for entry of an order vacating the judgment of conviction and remanding the case to the District Court with instructions to dismiss the indictment as moot."

I popped the minicassette out of the Dictaphone as I stood up and handed it to the formidable Pauline D, who hadn't moved a millimeter. She accepted it without enthusiasm.

"If Tyrell Washington is dead, this is a waste of time."

"Let's hope the Third Circuit sees it that way."

I headed for the reception area to fetch Bradshaw myself. In addition to potted plants and old magazines, it features a massive aquarium built into the wall. I think it's a nice touch, except when some of the fish die.

The Law Office of Luis Mendoza occupies half the fourth floor of a former warehouse now gentrified into a no-frills office building in downtown Pittsburgh. Eleven lawyers work there. Ten of them get paid. I'm the eleventh. Ten of them didn't go to Harvard Law School. I'm the eleventh. Ten of them work in offices. I draft briefs (for other lawyers to sign) and outline cross-examinations (for other lawyers to use) in a cubicle. But on the rare occasions when I see a client I get to use the library, which has a large maple table and four pine chairs and therefore qualifies as a conference room.

The Law Office of Luis Mendoza was not the plan. Harvard Law School *cum laude*, *Harvard Journal of Law and Public Policy* (not quite *Harvard Law Review*, but not bad), two-year clerkship with a federal district judge in Philadelphia—that résumé was supposed to park my cute little butt on Wall Street. It was working out just fine, too. By the end of interview season my third year in law school, I had an offer in hand from Calder & Bull, a solid Wall Street firm with lots of securities lawyers and even more litigators to get the securities lawyers out of trouble. Hundred-and-a-half starting salary with a twenty-five-thousand dollar signing bonus and a report date the September after my clerkship ended.

Then Lehman Brothers happened. Fall of 2008. End of the world as we know it. The letter from C & B came in June, 2009. New hires for the following September were being "deferred" until February 1, 2011. Fifty thousand dollars to tide us over, on the condition that we reaffirm our intention to go to work there and find some "non-competitive law-related activity" that would keep up our legal skills in the meantime. My personal theory was that they expected us all to go to Legal Aid and file class action suits against C & B clients. That way they could write the fifty thousand off to Business Development.

I've never been gut-punched, but I don't think it could hurt much worse than reading that letter. My fiancé, Paul Kaplan, actually took the news even harder than I did. I got some of my perspective back talking him down from his passionate artist's moral outrage. Paul is a budding postmodern novelist.

"That sucks!" he'd yelled around an f-bomb participle, startling several other pedestrians on Walnut Street in Philly. "That totally sucks! This is a tragedy!"

"Eight-year-old girls starving to death in Africa is a tragedy. This is a disappointment."

"But they're just blowing you off!" His perfect guardsman's moustache had quivered with indignation as his cobalt blue eyes flared in righteous anger at the bosses' perfidy.

"They're paying me roughly as much to loaf for a year-and-a-half as the average American family gets by working hard for twelve months. My dad would have loved to have someone blow him off like that when he was twenty-six."

With that, man-mountain Paul had whirled his six-foot-four-inch frame around and locked me in a bear hug that a few strollers probably thought was a mugging. He'd told me in a close-to-tears whisper how brave I was and how desperately he loved me. Paul did that kind of stuff regularly. It had given me a warm fuzzy, as it usually did. An artist's total empathy for the Other, combined with absolute devotion to yours truly. All that, and he was a hunk to boot.

"We'll make the best of it," he'd whispered then, intensely. Paul does almost everything intensely. "Maybe use the time to get settled properly in the City."

I'd hated to spoil the moment, but that crack called for a Cindy Jakubek specialty: the reality check. If you could somehow combine Paul's passionate impulsiveness with my analytic detachment and divide by two, you'd probably end up with a fairly normal human being. I figured our kids would become either Nobel laureates or serial killers.

"Uh, Paul?" I'd said in my patient, no-you-can't-have-a-pony voice. "Someone with student loans to repay does not live in

New York City for nineteen months on fifty thousand dollars. Not since the yuppies discovered Brooklyn."

Someone in that category didn't keep living in Philly, either, at least not in the apartment I'd leased when I had a nice, cushy, federal judicial clerk's salary. That basic economic reality brought me to Pittsburgh, which had two things going for it. The first was Luis Mendoza. He said that he could find a cubicle for me if I were willing to work as an unpaid legal intern at the Mendoza Foundation's Justice for All Project, which is one of several enterprises operating under the Law Office of Luis Mendoza umbrella. The second was my dad's house, where I could have room and board for three hundred a month plus help with the groceries. I could have had it for free, but I insisted.

Paul and I got to where we were moving through this little character-building experience with grudging acquiescence, if not contentment. I was learning some street law, maintaining legal skills, seeing Paul two or three weekends a month, talking once in a while with him about actually setting a date, and checking a snarky blog called "Above the Law" for rumors about Calder & Bull. Paul was writing a novel full of subtext and attitude, with occasional dialogue.

Anyway, that's how it came about that in late November, 2010, instead of helping out with abstruse motion practice in securities litigation of mind-boggling complexity in lower Manhattan, I was padding out to the lobby of a converted warehouse in Pittsburgh to shake hands with Caitlin Bradshaw. Mendoza had told me to do a preliminary interview so that he could deal with her problem, whatever it turned out to be, without wasting too much of his own time. Mendoza wasn't excessively scrupulous about the distinction between his non-profit foundation, which was *pro bono* and received lots of public and private grant money, and the emphatically *pro pecunio* side of his office: workers' comp, personal injury, small-time criminal work, divorce, bankruptcy—and referrals from Fletcher & Peck. He used me interchangeably between the two. In case you ever find yourself running a law firm, this is called "leverage."

The second I laid eyes on Caitlin I repented my chocolate malt crack. She wasn't a Valley girl airhead. A girl–woman, but more woman than girl. Her face, and especially her dove gray eyes, didn't look hard but they did look tempered, as if she'd had to take some knocks more serious than finding a zit on prom night. Only when we shook hands and I noticed the strength of her grip did it hit me: tennis. She'd been on a girls' varsity tennis team that had done something or other with "state" in it last spring. I didn't think much of jockettes when I was in high school—the feeling was mutual—but you have to give them one thing: winning, losing, and pumping your muscles even after they're throbbing and your gut is screaming at you to stop, puts one part of childhood in your rearview mirror pretty fast.

"Girls' Tennis State Championship, right?" I guessed on the way back to the library.

"Third place."

"Not bad."

"Better than fourth."

I got her a paper cup of water, sat her down at the table, and scrounged a half-used legal pad from one of the drawers. Then I asked her to tell me how Sam Schwartzchild at Fletcher & Peck had come to recommend that she see Mr. Mendoza. She walked me through the face-to-face with mom two days earlier. I'm pretty good at poker faces but my eyebrows arched when she mentioned calling Schwartzchild "Sam the Really Jewish Lawyer."

"I can't believe I said that." She noticed my reaction and veiled her eyes briefly with her right hand. "It was, like, I just regressed to mall-speak all of a sudden. Like when I was a sophomore and we were hanging out someone might say, 'We can chill at my house while the 'rents are downtown seeing Sam the Really Jewish Lawyer.' And mom is sharing with me and trusting me and I just blurted *that* out."

"Stress." I said this as if I knew what I was talking about. "Stress can do things like that. It acts in different ways on different people. Did the police come to search your house?"

My back-to-business follow-up drew a searching look from her. She saw 5 feet 6 inches and 117 rather well-distributed pounds of Slavic attitude now only a little over two months away from her Wall Street dream. I have an olive complexion and wear very little makeup. Jet black hair combed straight back from my forehead and parted in the middle, with no attempt at pie-crust curls or other nonsense at the ends. Small glasses with black half-frames perched an inch or so down my nose. The dress code at Mendoza's shop is business casual, but I was wearing a charcoal gray jacket and skirt, ivory blouse, hose, and black pumps. I was a lawyer, dammit, and I was going to dress like one.

"Yes," she finally said. "They came the next day. Sunday."

"Did they have a warrant?"

"Yes."

"What did it say?"

"I didn't see it. But they checked our two computers, the one Mom and I use in the great room and Dad's in his upstairs study. They asked Mom if there were any others. She told them about Dad's laptop but she was pretty sure he had it with him. They made a gross mess looking for it, but they didn't find it. They asked Mom where Dad kept his passport and she said it should be in his top dresser drawer. But they didn't find that either."

"Your dad was out of town?"

"He went to New York to a private show," Caitlin said. "Appraising art and antiques is one of the things he does. I thought he was coming back Sunday evening, but mom told the police that he'd called and said he'd be back tonight instead."

"Flying or driving?"

"What? Oh, I'm sorry. Driving."

"Did the police take anything else?"

"Three briefcases or attaché cases or something. They were all Dad's. Plus all our old check registers and bank statements. And there were a couple of mobile phones that I didn't know Dad used. They took those too."

In framing my questions I focused on this numbing detail deliberately. A good deal of the work done by Justice For All was on court appointments to handle criminal appeals for indigent defendants like Tyrell Washington. I'd seen plenty of criminal cases during my judicial clerkship as well. Between the two, I'd picked up enough to know that having your home searched even by well-behaved cops isn't like *Law and Order S.V.U.* It means drawers yanked out and turned upside down to dump their contents on the floor. It means guys wearing latex gloves throwing your bras and panties over their shoulders after they've pawed through them. It means couches pulled four feet away from walls and left sitting there in the middle of the room, with their cushions on the floor. It means books, CDs, and DVDs flung onto the carpet and ceiling panels in the basement pushed out of their frames. It had to be a searingly traumatic intrusion on Caitlin's white-bread life. I wanted to get her into the routine of talking about this stuff as though it were the French Open before I reached the elephant-in-the-corner issue: Who else in the house, if anyone, was in cahoots with Dad on whatever had caused a magistrate somewhere to sign off on a search warrant?

"We've been calling them 'police.'" I underlined the word in my notes. "Were they in uniform or civvies?"

"They were wearing suits. I thought they were FBI, but mom said they were some kind of state police."

I scribbled methodically on my legal pad to buy myself some time so I could figure out how to ask Caitlin whether her father might now be in, say, Brazil instead of driving back to Pittsburgh. Before I could come up with anything she set off on a ramble, almost as if she were talking to herself.

"I didn't know she smoked. I can't believe that."

"Excuse me?"

"I told you how Mom smoked a cigarette while she was telling me about how the police were going to come." Caitlin spoke over a catch in her voice. "I didn't have any idea she smoked. I remembered seeing her with a little extra weight a few months back and at first I thought maybe she'd started smoking to help her shed some pounds in a hurry, but that isn't Mom. It can't be a new thing. She must have hidden it all these years. So she wouldn't set a bad example for me, I suppose. Looking back, it seems so…I don't know, so *sweet*, somehow. So *Mom*."

She started to cry. I fished out a handkerchief and gave it to her, then patted her hand to show a little sympathy while she wiped her tears. While all this was going on, though, I didn't stop thinking—and what I thought was, *I'm not buying it.* The first thing my mom did after coming out of Mass every Sunday was light a cigarette, so I was going on intuition rather than firsthand experience; but I don't think you can live in the same house as a smoker for seventeen years and not know she smokes. I'd figured out that Caitlin had had at least one cigarette that day during our brief handshake and walk to the library.

Why would a mature and intelligent adult resume a smoking habit that she'd presumably dropped something like eighteen years before? Maybe because she was stressed out by knowing about her husband's illegal activities, whatever they were. If not that, what?

I put down my pen and took off my glasses. I leaned forward and put my hand close to Caitlin's without touching it. I reminded myself that I was talking to someone in serious pain, and made my voice as soft and sympathetic as I could.

"Caitlin, do you have any reason to believe that your mom and dad have been having problems in their marriage?"

She couldn't have looked any more wide-eyed if I'd asked whether she thought the pope might drop by for dinner.

"Oh, no. Dad is a lot older than Mom. Sixty-three. I guess some people called her kind of a trophy wife for him when they got married. But she's completely his. Absolutely devoted to him. I mean, he never threatens her or raises his voice, but he can get her to do anything he wants her to. Sometimes he'll just say, 'Ari, this is very important to me.' Or he'll act hurt and disappointed. And he gets what he wants. In the four or five years since I really started noticing it, he got her to stop seeing a friend that he didn't like and to drop her involvement with Greenpeace, which he called 'a bunch of eco-terrorists.' And to quit a woman's club he thought was 'skewing old' for her. Which is kind of funny, coming from him, but that's what he said. He said, 'Every time you walk in there you lower the average age by seven years.' So, I mean, like, no. She admires him and she really loves him. I don't think there's any way she could imagine living without him."

I didn't induce this massive data dump because I'm a master interviewer. I think Caitlin had just been holding that stuff in for a long time and aching to get it off her chest. I saw a kind of gnawing worry in her eyes when she talked about Ariane, the kind of feeling you have when you love someone so deeply that her pain really is your pain, and her joy exhilarates you. I'd already pegged Caitlin as a pretty tough cookie for a rich brat, but I decided that she and her mom had something special going on in the bonding department. Whatever. At least I had enough to fill Mendoza in about what was going on.

I asked her if she wanted some more water, or maybe some coffee. She said no, so I told her to sit tight while I went to see if Mr. Mendoza was ready for her. I found him leaning against the door of his office, chatting with Pauline D. He was holding a piece of paper and looking jovially dyspeptic.

"What's this I got here, Jake? We filing motions for the exercise now?"

"Hey, a win's a win."

"Sure, but how's this a win? It's just red tape for the clerks in Philly. Washington getting a shiv buried in him is tough luck for him, but it doesn't wipe out the jury's verdict."

"Yes it does."

"How you figure?"

"The presumption of innocence applies throughout the criminal process, including appeals. Thanks to us, Washington had a viable appeal pending. Because he's dead, that appeal is moot. Because of the presumption of innocence, the court can't just assume we would have lost. So the only thing the court can do is set the conviction aside and tell the lower court to throw out the indictment as moot. We win."

"That's one ugly win."

"There is such a thing as winning ugly. There is no such thing as an ugly win."

This was Mendoza's kind of language. Behind his forehead a scoreboard flashed

> Law Office of Luis Mendoza   1
> U.S. Attorney   0

His face lit up in a radiant beam. His eyes widened in delight. He raised his arms in a caricature gesture, as if he were an Anglo thespian in a high school production of *Man of La Mancha*. He rattled out something in Spanish, which I didn't understand a word of, except that I think *chica magnifica* showed up in it somewhere. Then he turned toward Pauline D, rolling her draft of my motion into a cylinder as if he were going to swat her with it.

"Get this puppy filed and served pronto."

He turned back to me, smile still on high beam, and offered me his right palm for a congratulatory slap. Then he stepped into his office and summoned me to follow him.

"So what's the deal with this *chica* Sam sent over here?"

I gave him a quick rundown, sticking to the essential facts. I knew he'd spot the issue without my spelling it out for him. He sat in profile to me while I talked, leaning back in his chair and looking at the ceiling. He's a quick study. He's never going to handle a triple-inverse merger or remove a case from state court to federal court under the embedded jurisdiction doctrine, but in his chosen areas of practice he's one helluva good lawyer. Even with the business casual dress code, he always wears suit and tie, including dress shirts with French cuffs. Sometimes the cufflinks have a scales-of-justice design embossed on them, and sometimes a skull-and-crossbones. Today was skull-and-crossbones.

"Okay." He jumped to his feet a second or two after the last syllable was out of my mouth. "Let's go."

He turned on the professional charm as he walked into the library and shook Caitlin's hand. No more macho swagger or sexist slang. He strolled in with a warm, reassuring smile and quietly confident body language that said, "No worries, I've been in tougher scrapes than this."

He picked a chair that let him sit facing Caitlin, about four non-threatening feet from her with a corner of the table in between them. I took one at the far end of his side of the table, where I'd be unobtrusively in the background.

"I've worked with Sam Schwartzchild on a lot of cases over the years." Mendoza carefully modulated his voice. "He is a very good lawyer. Did he tell you why he thought you should see me?"

"Not really. He just said there was a possible conflict of interest and he thought it would be better if I had my own lawyer."

Mendoza's grave nod acknowledged the Solomonic wisdom of Schwartzchild's view.

"Did the state troopers—that's what they were, by the way—ask you about your conversation with your mom on Saturday?"

"No. It's funny, Mr. Schwartzchild asked me that same question right before the conflict of interest thing came up."

I'll just bet he did, I thought. I kept my head down so that I could concentrate on my penmanship.

"Well," Mendoza said, "the first issue I would like to discuss with you is whether you have any legal obligation to report that conversation to the police."

"What? Why would I do that? Why is it their business?"

ASK HER! I telepathically willed Mendoza. *"Have you actually talked to your father since that conversation?" Ask her that!*

"Good questions," Mendoza said calmly, meaning Caitlin's audible ones rather than my mental one. "It would only be a concern for law enforcement if your father were in some danger. I take it you don't have any reason to think he is. Am I right?"

Caitlin's eyes went back and forth rapidly, as if she'd suddenly lost her bearings in the woods and was looking for a landmark. After a second or two, she seemed to recover. When she spoke her voice sounded confused but not panicky.

"No. No reason at all. I mean, I'm like, I don't even know why you'd ask that. I guess you have to, but I just don't see…. I mean, Dad is a curator and an art dealer. He spends volunteer time working as a docent. Why would anyone want to hurt him?"

"Very good point." Mendoza gave Caitlin a confident, affirming nod. "I'm not here to speculate about half-baked ideas some cop might have—or not. My job is to give you legal advice, and I'm going to give you some."

"What is it?" Caitlin seemed genuinely curious.

"You don't have any legal obligation at this time to go to the police and tell them about that talk you and your mom had. If the police ask you about that talk, you don't have to answer their questions. You can just say, 'That's private and I don't want to talk about it.' In fact, you can just say, 'Talk to my lawyer.' That's even better. You understand what I'm saying?"

"You mean I'm lawyered up, like the bad guys on TV."

"You're lawyered up like a smart girl in the real world. I'm not telling you *not* to talk to them. That's up to you. I'm just saying you don't have to if you don't want to. Right?"

"Sure, I guess."

"Okay. Now, Caitlin, do you have any questions for me?"

"No, I don't think so."

Mendoza stood up and took out three of his cards. Before handing them to her, he leaned over to put one of them on the table while he wrote an additional number on it.

"Caitlin, I want you to call me if any questions come up or if anything happens that you're concerned about. Call me anytime of the day or night. That number I wrote on the top card is my mobile phone, and I have that with me all the time. You can give the other cards to cops if they drop by to pass the time of day. Jake, you give her a card too, just in case."

Caitlin suddenly seemed to glow as I handed over one of my cards—and why shouldn't she? She'd just been treated like the most important client Mendoza had. I'd seen him do the same trick with restaurant owners and rock-hard hookers. It worked with them, too.

"I mean it, Caitlin. If anything comes up, give me a call. Ms. Jakubek here will show you out and get your parking ticket stamped."

He smiled. She beamed. They shook hands. Mendoza exited, basking in the glow of her esteem.

I showed her back to the reception area, and saw to it that the receptionist put a shiny yellow sticker on her parking stub. Then I walked her to the elevator.

"So if I, like, can't reach Mr. Mendoza, then I could call you?"

I felt the tiniest little surge of professional satisfaction. I wasn't exactly basking in the glow of her esteem, but apparently I'd made an impression.

"Sure."

She examined my card closely with a puzzled expression on her face. Then she looked back up at me with her charmingly ingenuous, tempered-but-not-hard-seventeen-year-old eyes.

"So, you're, like, you're a lawyer, too?"

Chapter Three

OHHH-kay, I told myself as I trekked back from the elevator bank. *Six months from now, while you're researching some tangled sale-and-purchase issue under section 16(b) of the Securities Act of 1933 and planning a trip to the bank to visit your money, you'll think back on that little incident—and you will laugh your ass off.*

It was pushing five o'clock by now, with Thanksgiving weekend on the horizon. Overtime? I don't think so. I headed back to my cubicle to log off for the day. On the way I stopped at Pauline D's desk to make sure she was preparing an intake and engagement letter for Caitlin Bradshaw. It was eight-to-one that Mendoza had gotten her on it while I was taking Caitlin to the elevator. One thing I'd learned in his shop, though, is that when it comes to legal paperwork it's better to check twice than blow it once.

Ms. Denckla frostily confirmed that she was indeed already handling the intake while she continued rattling her keyboard at ninety words a minute. Instead of stalking off, I took a deep breath. My next words stuck in my throat for a couple of seconds, but I managed to get them out.

"I'd like to apologize for the way I handled our discussion earlier. I shouldn't have been flippant with you."

If I'd gotten a picture of her face as she turned it toward me, I could have sold it to Webster's to put next to "flabbergasted." Her expression combined astonishment and suspicion, as if something as shocking as an apology from a lawyer had to mask a hidden agenda that would come back to bite her ample fanny if she didn't keep her guard up. For a long, long moment she was literally speechless. Then she recovered enough to respond.

"No apology is necessary. Mr. Mendoza agreed with you."

"He agreed with me about filing the motion, but that's no excuse for my copping an attitude with you. You were just doing your job. Anyway, I'm sorry."

Her face softened into a smile—somewhat confused, but still a smile.

"That's okay, Ms. Jakubek. Really. Please don't think anything more about it."

I trundled back to my cubicle, blitzed through the dozen emails that had accumulated since I'd left, and shut the machine down. I was just about to pull my coat on when Mendoza popped out of his office.

"Hey, Jake, you got a coupla minutes before you leave?"

"Sure."

I followed him into his office, but he only paused there long enough to take a long, thin cigar from a humidor on his desk. Then he led me out onto a balcony barely big enough to accommodate the two faux Adirondack chairs on it. He sank into one, and I took that as an invitation to perch on the other. The balcony is glassed in on its three exposed sides and has a jury-rigged space heater whose cord snakes back into Mendoza's office. The glass takes care of the wind, and the space heater takes care of the cold. In late November, unless you're a wimp from the sunbelt, it's actually fairly comfortable. This little arrangement is Mendoza's answer to the Clean Indoor Air Act adopted by some busybodies in Harrisburg a few years ago.

"This going to bother you?" He held up the cigar.

"Nope." He had the cigar in his mouth before I had that syllable completely out of mine, and he didn't waste any time lighting up.

"You think I made the wrong call on Caitlin, don't you?"

"Yep."

"Because when Caitlin asked mom whether anything had happened to dad, mom said 'not yet.'"

"Pretty much. If a client tells you he robbed a bank yesterday, that's privileged. If he tells you he's going to rob one tomorrow, that's an imminent crime. It not only isn't privileged, you're supposed to drop a dime on him."

He nodded in a way that implied understanding rather than agreement. He held the cigar in his mouth at a ninety-degree angle to his face as he lolled against the chair back. He was somewhere in his forties. I'm not sure exactly where. He wore his gray-streaked dark hair a little long, spilling over his shirt collar and curling up naturally at the ends. His bristly moustache was a distinguished charcoal gray and silver. He had a way of looking freshly groomed even at the end of the afternoon, as if a barber had finished with him less than two hours before.

"That was a righteous thing you did on the Washington case. His family won't understand the legal mumbo jumbo. Hell, *I* barely understand it. But it'll mean something to them that he won't have that conviction over his head when he goes to meet Jesus."

"Thanks."

"Why do you suppose he got killed?"

"I don't know. He was a thug. Thugs die young."

He closed his eyes and savored the rich, pungent smoke he was producing. His next question came from around the cigar.

"You see anything odd about a hard-core gangbanger like him getting sent to that Club Fed at Lewisburg instead of some more muscular pile of rocks?"

"Sounds like the government was negotiating an exchange of information for a recommendation to reduce his sentence. Risky business."

"Fatal in his case—if you're right."

I wondered where he was going with this. Wherever it was, he didn't seem to be in any hurry to get there. The smoke was getting a little thick by now in the semienclosed space, but I didn't mind. I'd actually gotten rather fond of cigar smoke. When I was a junior at Duquesne, the editor-in-chief of the student newspaper would host "cigar tastings" in his office every Friday. Undergraduate feminist paranoia being what it is, I suspected this was a ploy to have unofficial, male-dominated staff meetings. I showed *him*. I practiced until I could puff on a cigar without choking and attended three "tastings." No one discussed much of anything except NCAA basketball. I didn't acquire a taste for cigars, but I got to like the aroma. You never can tell when an eccentric taste like that might come in handy—and here I was.

"The thing is this," Mendoza said then. "Caitlin asked if anything had happened to dad. Before answering, 'Not yet,' mom looked at her watch."

So what?

"Point is," he continued, as if he were reading my mind, "why would she look at her *watch* on Saturday afternoon if she was planning to waste hubby Monday evening?"

"You're saying mom's statement to Caitlin doesn't imply that dad was still in danger by the time Caitlin spoke to us."

"Bingo."

"So by this afternoon, 'not yet' might be evidence that mom had already killed dad, but not that she was still planning to."

"And I don't think it was either one." He sounded pretty sure. "Personally, I think mom was expecting dad to get arrested and grilled by the constabulary. That's what hadn't happened to him 'yet.' Meaning he might be in danger from whoever was in cahoots with him about whatever the cops were looking into, because that would leave him in your basic Tyrell Washington situation. But that doesn't put mom's finger on the trigger for an *upcoming* murder."

"If you're right, then by this afternoon Caitlin had no legal duty to go to the cops. She might help to *solve* a crime by ratting out mom, but she could no longer *prevent* one."

"And even more important, *we* have no duty to go to the cops. Everything Caitlin said to us is covered by the attorney–client privilege. The imminent-crime exception doesn't apply."

"Which means you made the right call," I conceded.

"I get one right every once in awhile."

I turned it over in my mind while he contentedly sucked smoke into his lungs. Mendoza wasn't one of those puff-but-don't-inhale guys. He smoked like he meant it. After a minute or so he held the cigar up contemplatively and looked at the haze accumulating just above us.

"You sure this isn't bothering you?"

I wiggled the first two fingers of my right hand at him. With a surprised and intrigued smile, he handed the cigar to me. I took a respectable puff—a little awkward, but not bad—and contributed a decent stream of smoke to the ambient fog. The cigar left some interesting tastes rolling around my tongue: coffee, with a hint of...what? Chocolate? It was actually milder than I remembered cigarettes being, from my distant experience with them.

"I can handle it." I gave him back the cigar.

"You're something, you are." He shook his head. "You ever wonder why Fletcher and Peck partners with me on cases?"

The question blindsided me. Fletcher & Peck sent Mendoza something like a thousand hours of billable work every year. You can buy a lot of Cohiba panatelas with that kind of change. It did seem a little surprising, now that he mentioned it, and yet the truth was I hadn't wondered about it. I had unconsciously adopted a Wall Street associate's view of clients: you don't have to worry about where they come from; they're just *there*.

"I never really gave it any thought."

"Well, there's two reasons. The first is MBE. Not MB*A*, MB*E*. Minority-owned Business Enterprise."

"Such as the Law Office of Luis Mendoza."

He nodded. "Fletcher & Peck's clients are mostly Fortune 500 companies. The directors of these companies are enlightened, right-thinking people who believe in social justice. The boards tell their general counsels to send x-percent of their outside legal work to MBEs. If Fletcher & Peck partners with us on a case—say, has us research a couple of issues, add our name to the pleadings, show up in court for a hearing or two—the general counsel gets to count that case in his statistics. Or hers."

"An affirmative action scam."

"It's not a scam, Jake, it's a hustle. A scam means you're fooling someone. The directors know exactly what's going on. Their

PR departments report these statistics in self-congratulatory press releases. Minority interest groups all over the country pat the directors on their mostly Anglo heads and tell them how enlightened and right-thinking they are, and then don't make too much noise about how there aren't all that many black and brown and yellow faces among the directors themselves."

"Thanks. I feel a lot better."

"You should be taking notes, Jake. See, it's really not just MBE, it's *W*MBE. *Women* and Minority-Owned Business Enterprise. Women cut themselves in on this action a while ago. That's the way the game is played, Jake. Once you get to Wall Street you can afford to sit on your principles, polishing your halo. The rest of us have to dive in and try to get our share, any legal way we can."

I thought about asking for another puff on his cigar, just for the hell of it. I decided not to.

"So why is Fletcher & Peck partnering with you on the Bradshaw thing? There sure isn't any Fortune Five-hundred company involved here."

"That brings us to the second reason. They've worked with us enough to notice that we can walk and chew gum at the same time. We've become a known quantity. So now and then they actually refer cases to us just because we're good lawyers."

"Okay."

"Smart young lady like you, of course, by now you've noticed that it wouldn't be a bad idea for us to keep on being a known quantity for Fletcher & Peck."

"I'm not sure I would have put it that way."

"Which is true. I deeply value the good opinion of Sam Schwartzchild and his partners. But I still draw a line."

"And you draw it short of giving bad advice to clients."

"I said you were smart, didn't I?"

Chapter Four

The Monday *New York Times* crossword puzzle is waayyy too easy. I finished it about ten minutes into the thirty-five minute bus ride back to Dad's house that evening, which left me with nothing to do but think. There was no point in thinking about Caitlin Bradshaw's situation, because Mendoza was right: until the cops called, there was nothing to think about. I spent a couple of minutes thinking about whether I'd remembered to take the ground chuck out of the freezer and put it in the refrigerator before I left that morning. I had. My memory coughed up a distinct image of shrink-wrapped red meat slipping onto the top shelf of the refrigerator, next to the Promise margarine. I wouldn't have to squeeze in a trip to Sully's Grocery tonight.

I didn't have to look around the bus to know that I was the youngest person on it by close to twenty years. Pittsburgh is in Allegheny County, which has the second-oldest population in the United States—right after Miami–Dade, in *Golden Girls* country. Some of these people were poor, but most of them weren't. They were riding the bus from okay jobs downtown to decent houses in not-bad neighborhoods. They'd have meat loaf or macaroni and cheese or baked chicken for dinner, and then they'd spend the night watching the same TV programs the rest of America would. They'd make love with their spouses, or hit them, or ignore them, or remember what they were like before they died or walked out. Some of them would get drunk and some of them would read the Bible and some of them would fall asleep with Jay Leno flickering on their television screens.

Despising these people is one sin I'll never have to confess. I admire them. They pay America's taxes and raise America's children and fight America's wars. If they don't get up at six in the morning to catch the 7:20 bus downtown, America stops happening.

But is it also a sin to pity them? To shudder at lives that are all yesterdays and no tomorrows? To sit there with Kelly Clarkson throbbing in my iPod's earbuds, dreaming about how fast I could get out of their world?

I honestly don't know where this morbid introspection comes from. Class consciousness? *Puh-leese.* The only thing Karl Marx was worse at than economics is sociology. Everyone on that bus would have run for the same exit I did if they could have. Maybe it's some genetic-memory, Slavic guilt thing: *I don't DESERVE this. I'm supposed to be hoeing a wheat field in Silesia or somewhere, waiting to get raped by Prussians or Austrians or some other species of uniformed Germans.*

I got off the bus at 82nd and hiked two blocks uphill to Dad's three-bedroom brick-and-frame house on Hickory. I'm not kidding about the uphill part. You wanna know how hilly Pittsburgh is? The front half of the house is two stories and the back half is three stories—and that's not particularly unusual. Nothing from Calder & Bull in the mail and the rest was none of my business. Tool catalogues and bills, mostly. Nothing from either of my brothers, Sergeant Mike in Afghanistan or Father Ken in Erie. Dumped my briefcase on the kitchen table, moved the ground chuck from the fridge to the counter, and poured myself a goblet of Chablis to keep me company while I hiked upstairs to change into sweats and Nikes.

It was Monday, so dad wouldn't be home for over an hour— sometime between 7:30 and 8:00. I could have squeezed in a run, but I'd run twice over the weekend and I didn't feel like running in the dark so when I got back downstairs I found NPR on the radio. I put a skillet on one of the back burners on the stove-top, cut a two-tablespoon tranche off the end of a wrapped stick of margarine, and dropped that in the middle of the skillet so that it would slowly melt. Let's see, what else would I have to get ready? Quarter-cup of Worcestershire sauce, bottle of ketchup, bottle of barbecue sauce, small onion, slice of Kraft American cheese. With that stuff lined up on the counter I was set for Dad.

I dug out a mini-Wok that was my contribution to the cooking gear in the house and whipped up a little stir-fry for myself: most of the small onion, shallots, beans, carrots, garlic, sea salt, and some real butter. When I got that done I carried my plate into the dining room and put it down beside my laptop. By sitting on the interior side of the dining room table I could keep my eye on the driveway through the dining room window. While I nibbled veggies and sipped wine I booted up and checked *Above the Law*. Nothing about Calder & Bull. Good.

With my plate in the sink and a quarter of a glass of Chablis left I turned to my own blog, *Streetdreamer*. I didn't see any comments that merited a response, so I jumped right in:

> I took a puff on a cigar this evening—my first taste of tobacco in about six years. The good news is that it wasn't the highlight of my day. The bad news is that I can't write about what was. The worst news is that even if I could, I'm not sure anyone would be interested in reading it—including me. Oh well. One day closer to the Street.

I might have written more, but I heard the first four bars of "Hungry Heart" playing, which meant my mobile phone was ringing. Even better, Paul's number was showing on the screen.

Gut fluttering, I launched my musings into cyberspace and opened the phone. "Hey, lover, what's up?"

"Eight hundred words, dudette. Net."

"That's great, stud. So you're up to what, now—twelve thousand?"

"Almost thirteen."

I mentally ran through my nightly math exercise while Paul exchanged some billing and cooing with me. A respectable post-modern novel would have to run forty thousand words anyway, probably more like fifty thousand. So with eight hundred net today, Paul was averaging a little over five hundred net per day, which meant he was not quite two months away from having a first draft. I knew this was silly, that I couldn't compute fiction-writing productivity as if Paul were producing widgets, even if one of his characters is actually named Widget. But my bachelor's degree is in math; I had to find some way to deploy it in support of my lover's passion.

I can't tell you very well what Paul's novel is about, to the extent a postmodern novel is "about" anything. It's *not* about a subatomic particle. Start with that. The protagonist is a man who is *like* a subatomic particle in that you can't simultaneously know his location and his velocity. If he's driving on Frontier Street in downtown San Diego and you notice 38 on his speedometer, that means he might suddenly be on Eighth Avenue in New York. So he has to do things in motion of indeterminate speed, which works for sex but complicates going to the bathroom. Not to mention there's no telling where he might wake up on any given morning. Also, there's some really deep banter about confusing John Barth with Karl Barth and time (the concept) with *Time* (the magazine).

"So." Paul spoke in a mellow, serene voice that meant he was happy with what he'd written. "What *was* the highlight of your day?"

"What, you've been scoping out my blog while we're about three fingers short of phone sex?"

"Have to. Can't get too much CJ."

"That's sweet. Anyway, when I did the blog I was thinking about a client interview I conducted this afternoon. On further review, though, the real highlight was probably apologizing to someone."

"Not your boss, I hope."

"No, a secretary." I told him about Pauline D.

He whistled when I finished.

"You know what you are? You're the sixth proof, that's what you are."

"'Sixth proof of what?'"

"Wasn't it Augustine who had five proofs for the existence of God? Or was that Anselm?"

"Aquinas."

"Aquinas, right. I knew it was an A guy. Anyway, he had five proofs for the existence of God. You're the sixth. You couldn't possibly have happened by accident. Four more proofs and I'll start doubting my atheism. Maybe just three."

While I was feeling pretty good about that Paul ran in a light-hearted way through the joys of writing for four hours in his brother's basement after working the breakfast and lunch shifts at Mickey D's. I made sympathetic noises. He segued neatly into the perennial topic of us going up to New York together to check out housing possibilities.

"Not this week." I shook my head even though he couldn't see me. "I can't bail on Dad over Thanksgiving."

"He could come along. Thanksgiving weekend is perfect. You can have your turkey, then pop up to Newark on Friday. We'll find a couple of cheap hotel rooms there and take the train to Grand Central."

"Okay, Paul, let's play this out. I'm in my cheap hotel room at, say, seven fifteen Sunday morning. Let's say you're there too. You're fast asleep after a hard Saturday of checking out real estate. Suddenly, there's pounding on the door. Dad's voice: 'Cindy! Cindy! Wake up! We're gonna be late for Mass!'"

He started laughing, a little more than my crack called for. I figured I deserved the credit for that. Then I saw the headlights on an eighteen-foot step-van swing into the driveway. It would have been hard to miss them. They could've been used to spot enemy aircraft.

"Gotta go, tiger. My landlord just rolled in and he'll be hungry."

We exchanged phone kisses and hung up. By the time Dad—Vince Jakubek to you—walked through the back door, I had the butter sizzling in the skillet and ground chuck in a mixing bowl with chopped onion bits fluttering into it like pungent dandruff. He was wearing a baseball cap and a sateen baseball-style warm-up jacket, both electric blue and dominated by *PRO TOOLS*, in slanted script with speed lines behind it, as if the letters were racing. He was carrying his own computer in a leather bag and had a thick, grease-stained three-ring binder under his left arm.

I hustled over to give him a hug.

"What, you've taken up cigars now?" He'd caught a whiff of my breath.

"Oops, busted."

"No kidding, Buttercup, that is seriously addictive stuff. I oughta know. You'd better watch it."

I then missed an excellent opportunity to keep my mouth shut. "Am I just grounded, or are you going to turn me over your knee?"

Dad was supposed to chuckle at that, but instead he bridled. I'd forgotten how close we were to December 3rd. It would take some scrambling to save the moment. Fortunately, as soon as he opened his mouth I knew by heart what was coming next.

"I never hit you once the whole time you were growing up, Cynthia Jakubek—"

"Except that one time when I was eleven—"

"—except that one time when you were eleven—"

"—and I had that one coming."

"—and you had that one coming."

"You're the best, Vince." I hugged his neck and gave his cheek a quick peck.

Mission accomplished. He shrugged into a what-are-you-going-to-do laugh. Time to switch gears.

"How was life in the tool business today?"

"Not bad, actually. They're having a year-end promotion on large tool storage units. Priced under two thousand, markup protected, and dealer billing deferred to February."

"Sounds great." I'd actually understood most of what he said. A "tool storage unit" is a great big toolbox on wheels, with draw-ers and trays that have compartments perfectly fitted for every wrench, socket, screwdriver, drill bit, and other hand tool you could imagine. Also locks, I should mention that it has locks. Guys with grease under their fingernails who make fourteen-fifty to twenty-two dollars an hour will drop two grand on one of these things. Not with tools in it—empty. The promotion meant that, just in time for Christmas, Dad could offer these choice items at a price his customers couldn't resist, get his usual thirty-percent profit even though the price was reduced, and play the float on the bill for two months.

"Do I have time to change and take a shower?" He was already moving toward the stairs.

TAKE A SHOWER? Who are you and what have you done with Vince?

"Sure. You've got fifteen minutes, anyway."

We'd moved to the home on Hickory when Dad made foreman at Epsom Tools. I was nine. We'd lived in a duplex before that, so I know what crockery sounds like when it smashes against the other side of a party wall. I was sixteen and Dad was fifty when Epsom started offering early retirement packages. Not because of declining business. The dot-com bubble hadn't quite burst yet. I figured out later that Epsom was trying to buy its way out of a looming unfunded pension liability. Early retirement was a tough sell, because everyone there figured they'd have to relocate to someplace the Steelers didn't play to find jobs half as good as the ones they'd be giving up.

Dad had been taking shop when the clever kids were taking calculus at Kosciusko High, but he's no dummy. He has plenty of nonverbal smarts and a hardheaded peasant shrewdness. He took a long, careful look at the situation and accepted the early retirement package. Then, as he described it himself, he used most of his severance money to "buy a job" as an Authorized Pro Tools Dealer. A hundred-thousand-dollar investment got him an inventory of professional hand tools, a walk-in van big enough to drive the inventory around in, and a route list with eighty shops employing two hundred professional mechanics, give or take. Dad was sort of his own boss, sort of running his own business, but the best part was that he could make the adjusted gross income number on his tax return pretty much anything he wanted it to be. It worked. The mortgage and utility payments kept getting made and the groceries kept getting bought—yet I'd had no trouble qualifying for need-based financial aid at Duquesne and then at Harvard Law.

If you ever have to make a real, working class cheeseburger in the winter, when it's too cold and dark to barbecue, here's the way you do it: melt the margarine in the skillet; chop some onion into about half a pound of ground chuck; form the meat into a patty; poke a bunch of holes into one side of the patty with a fork; spread barbecue sauce over the patty, and then use a spatula to force the sauce into the holes; pour the Worcestershire sauce into the skillet; make sure the burner is on high; use a burger flipper to drop the patty into the middle of the skillet, standing well back so that you don't get spattered; give it about ten seconds to sear one side and then flip the patty; ten seconds for the other side and flip it again; turn the heat down to medium and fry the patty for about six more minutes per side; put the cheese on after you flip for the last time and put the top of the bun over the cheese while it finishes cooking.

Oh, yeah, the vent. I should mention that you need to have a vent over the stove, and it should be going on high from the moment you start heating the skillet.

By the time Dad came downstairs in jeans and a Pro Tools tee-shirt, I had the cheeseburger in a bun topped with lettuce and tomato, and some Lay's barbecue potato chips and a swatch of ketchup piled beside it on a plate. I had all of this sitting on the coffee table in the living room along with an open can of Schaeffer's on a coaster. The pregame show for Monday Night Football filled the TV screen.

"You're spoiling me rotten," he said as he sat down.

"That would make us even."

I went back into the kitchen to refill my wine glass. When I opened the refrigerator for the Chablis, though, I saw eight cans of Schaeffer's that were just sitting there. *What the hell.* I took out a can and popped the top. Dad's eyebrows went up when I landed beside him with my own beer.

"What are you trying to do—buff up your proletarian street cred?"

"You are the only male on this planet who could make that crack without getting beer-spritzed."

Halfway through the second quarter Dad was on his third beer. That wasn't anything like enough to make him drunk, but it didn't augur well for lighthearted gaiety as the evening moved along, either—especially if the game got dull. I didn't nag him about it, any more than I did about his pack or so of Marlboros every day or the twenty-five extra pounds around his gut. He was a grown-up and he had to make his own choices. But I decided to stay with him, instead of retreating to my room with my laptop.

Good choice. He started getting maudlin around the beginning of the third quarter, when he was on beer number four.

"I'm sorry about the street cred thing," he said. "I shouldn't of said that."

"It's okay, Dad. It was a joke."

He turned his head and focused his eyes on me with bleary intensity, if that's not an oxymoron.

"Don't give up."

"Don't worry. One kid to the army, one to the Church, and the third one a lawyer: you're hitting six-sixty-seven, and that ain't bad."

"I mean it. That kind of life for you is one of the things I worked for. One of the things we worked for. Your mom and me."

"I know."

"Mom" was the magic word. Ironic, really. Smoking hadn't shortened her life by a second. One kid in a Trans Am had accomplished in an eye-blink what thirty-five years of Salems couldn't. The cops said he'd hit her at sixty miles an hour when she was walking on the sidewalk at least three feet from the curb. Airbags saved the driver's life, but not hers. December 3rd would be the fourth anniversary.

Dad polished off the fourth beer and just sat there, holding the empty can in both hands between his legs, staring at the blowout on television. I knew what was coming. I looked around the room, searching for inspiration. I saw a small, framed painting of a French peasant couple stopping their labors at noon to pray the Angelus together as the church bell chimed. I saw the silver crucifix taken from Mom's casket.

"I shouldn't ever of hit your mom."

I only knew of one time that he'd hit her, during a rough patch in the Pro Tools dealership when he thought he might lose everything and she was nagging him to quit. There might have been other times, but I don't think so. Neither Mom nor Dad was all that much of a hitter even with us kids, at least by blue-collar standards. That one time Dad had smacked Mom, though, had come two weeks before the kid in the Trans Am. Mom had gotten past the anger and the hurt overnight, but Dad hadn't come close to getting rid of the guilt when the call from the cops came. Now he was beating himself up about it again. Why? Because my lame joke had triggered some Rube Goldberg chain reaction in his psyche? Because the calendar was careening ruthlessly toward December 3rd? Or was something else going on?

I clicked the TV off. I took the can out of his hands and set it on the coffee table. I squatted in front of him so that I could look up at him while I took his hands in both of mine. Time to play the Catholic sentimental piety card.

"You were a good husband, Dad. You loved Mom. She loved you. You gave her a good life and the kids she wanted. You're human. You made mistakes. You did things that were wrong. But she knew you were sorry and she forgave you. She's on her knees up in heaven right now, praying that you'll forgive yourself."

I saw a crafty gleam in Dad's eye. What I read in it was something like, *This ain't Sister Mary Second Grade you're talking to.* I sent an urgent telepathic message to Ken. *All right, bro. You're the goddamned priest. I need some help here.*

"Some sins," Dad said gravely, "are unforgivable."

I didn't get a telepathic response from Ken, but my memory did manage to spit out one of the Kenisms I'd heard over the years.

"That's blasphemy. God's power to forgive exceeds your power to sin."

He looked at me with a startled expression for about three seconds. Then, slowly, he started to smile.

"Blasphemy. That's pretty bad. I'd better get to confession."

"Right now," I said, standing up and tugging on his right arm, "you'd better get to bed."

After I hustled him upstairs and got everything turned off and locked up, I took a long, hot shower before bunking down myself. To Mendoza, Jake was taking that shower. To Paul, CJ was lathering herself up. Dad was dreamily thinking of Cindy, his baby, who had to be scolded about incipient bad habits. Pauline D would have figured that Ms. Jakubek was indulging herself by using up all the hot water in the tank. Calder & Bull didn't particularly care what Deferred New Hire Number Whatever was doing.

I couldn't waste a lot of energy stewing about which of those was the real me. That kind of thing was a luxury for people like Henry Widget in Paul's novel. I just had to hold them all together for a little over two more months.

Chapter Five

"Can anyone name a colonist who died in the Boston Massacre?"

Joan DeFillipo walked backwards through the Revolutionary War displays at the Pittsburgh Museum of American History. She led eighteen seventh-graders past paintings and exhibits depicting the run-up to the conflict: handwritten documents stamped in grudging compliance with the Stamp Act, pewter tea kettles, pamphlets printed with s's that looked like f's, and murals depicting the Boston Tea Party and what patriot propaganda had dubbed the Boston Massacre.

Silence greeted her question. A veteran educator, she was unsurprised by this.

"Can you name one, Josh?"

"Yeah," a mop-haired nerd-from-central-casting said, "but I'm saving it for Black History Month."

Titters piped through the group. They had no idea what the joke was, but they knew Josh had wised off. DeFillipo reacted with menacing blandness.

"It would be a very good thing, not just for you but for the entire class, if you would share the name with us right now."

Her warning produced icy dread in eighteen bellies. Eighteen preadolescent brains suddenly imagined reams of punitive homework being assigned over the Thanksgiving weekend. Josh shrugged eloquently in defeat.

"Crispus Attucks. African-American. Free person of color."

"Very good."

She gave them a little patter about the Boston Massacre while she led them toward the show's highlight.

"Can anyone tell me what happened at the Battle of Lexington?" She led the class through the door of a partition into a large room that seemed dark because almost all of its light was cast on a fifteen-by-twenty-foot stage.

"Yeah," Josh said. "The Brits kicked our butts."

"And how about the Battle of Concord a few hours later?"

"Upset win for the home team." Josh was on a roll.

DeFillipo stopped now before the stage and smiled in satisfaction at the gasps the scene evoked from the jaded twelve-year-olds. Amazing how kids raised on high-definition television and computer-generated special effects could be impressed by something as quaint as a life-size, waxworks diorama. But there it was, so close you could touch it—and *real*, not pixels on a screen. Lexington Common with what seemed like hundreds of colonists and redcoats, most painted on the backdrop and side flats but at least two dozen of them eerily lifelike wax figures coming right out to the edge of the stage. Bright red, wool uniforms, shiny leather belts, very real Brown Bess muskets, and an angry officer aiming a flintlock pistol at the rebels. Several of the colonists lay on the floor, bloody and either dead or in agony.

"No one knows for sure, but legend has it that an English officer with a pistol just like that one fired the first shot of the American Revolution," DeFillipo said. "Does anyone know how many colonists died on Lexington Common that morning?"

"Nine." A solemn, dark-haired girl spoke up before Josh could open his mouth.

"I think it was eight," DeFillipo said gently.

"Nine." The girl shook her head gravely and pointed at the scene. "I counted them."

DeFillipo turned toward the stage. She gasped. Less than a yard from her on the stage lay a corpse more real than Madame Tussaud herself could have produced. It lay on its side, with its face toward the front of the stage. Wax colonists hid its feet and lower legs. Its full, half-buttoned white shirt, dark, open vest, and dark trousers had come from Brooks Brothers, but in this setting actually looked vaguely colonial. Its eyes were now as sightless as those of the other figures on the stage. The dark brown blotch on the left side of the shirt was blood that a human heart had pumped in its final, defiant spasm.

Chapter Six

When I saw FEDRLBLDNG pop up on my caller i.d. screen just after 11:30 Tuesday morning, I figured Assistant United States Attorney Philip Schuyler was calling to bellyache about my dismissal-as-moot motion. I was right.

"This wasn't necessary," were the first, world-weary words out of his patrician mouth.

"'The history of freedom is the history of procedure.' Maitland."

I expected a peevish scolding for that crack, but instead his voice got serious.

"Do you have any information about why Washington was killed?"

"Not unless guesswork is passing for evidence over there these days."

"Guess for me."

"You were about to flip him and someone wanted to shut him up."

"If that were a good guess —and I'm not saying it is—then whoever it was might wonder if his lawyers were in the loop on the negotiations."

All of a sudden my snappy-patter switch clicked off. I felt a wet, cold drop in my diaphragm. A contract hit inside a federal prison is a huge deal. You're probably talking about a hundred thousand bucks to arrange it. You don't spend that kind of money to keep someone from talking about, say, where the DEA might find a rogue meth lab or a metric ton of coke. You're trying to cover up something like having a congressman or a federal judge on your payroll—and now you think that maybe Luis Mendoza and Cynthia Jakubek know what it is.

"Thanks for the warning."

"You're welcome, but this isn't just disinterested altruism. If Mr. Mendoza gets a feeler about a big retainer from someone who isn't on his regular client list and is a little vague about exactly what the work would be, it wouldn't be a terrible idea for him to give me a call."

"Noted." I exhaled noisily, and realized that I'd been holding my breath.

"You're a good lawyer. Watch out for strangers with candy."

"Thanks." I hung up, but before I could get all my fingers back on my desktop keyboard Mendoza came boiling down the corridor between the cubicles and the real offices.

"All hands on deck! My office! Now! Including you, Jake!"

I made it to his office in sixteen seconds flat, but even so Mendoza himself and three other people beat me there. When I completed the semicircle around his desk I joined Ricky Waters, who had only been practicing four years but had already notched three jury trial wins, which is a lot if you're representing defendants in criminal cases; Sal Brentano, who in ten years of handling consumer fraud and Lemon Law cases had gotten to know every civil service file clerk from Pittsburgh to Philly; and Becky the Techie, one of the firm's two investigators.

Mendoza stood behind his desk, looking at us, unsmiling. He was calm, as usual, but deadly serious. He drummed the eraser end of a pencil against a legal pad about four times before he started talking.

"About an hour ago, a seventh-grade class field trip stumbled over the body of T. Colfax Bradshaw in the Pittsburgh Museum of American History. Shot."

"From what range?" Waters asked.

"Too far away to leave powder burns on his clothing, so I think we can rule out suicide. Nothing official on time of death yet, but I'm betting on Monday night. It could have been as early as Sunday evening, because the museum is closed on Mondays and most of the so-called security cameras are dummies as a result of budget cuts, but eight-to-one it was Monday night."

Ouch! I thought. He looked straight into my eyes, challenging me to say out loud what he knew I was thinking. I kept my gaze level and my mouth shut.

"What this means," he said then, "is that we have a client in legal peril. Not sure yet what the peril is, but whatever it may be we're getting paid to get her out of it. So by three o'clock this afternoon I want to know every goddamn thing there is to know about what crime the state police were investigating Bradshaw for, what the cops think they know so far about his murder, and what he had for breakfast Saturday morning. I'll see you at three."

I went back to my cubicle to Google Bradshaw because I couldn't figure out what else I might bring to the party. It didn't take long. Thomas Colfax Bradshaw went to Groton which, for a white kid in the sixties, meant family money. He turned eighteen in '66, when 'Nam and the draft were both going strong, but he was too busy at Princeton (AB, Art History) and Yale (MA, Museum Management) to serve in the military. Nice little career in art and antiques, mostly flying below the media radar. Usual charitable and civic stuff. Cochair of the Steel Ring Arts Ball every other year, like clockwork, from '92 through '04. Quoted in the *New York Times* on the controversy over Italy trying to recover stuff from the Getty Art Museum in L.A.; got in a nice little shot about how something looted from a Roman galley that sank off the coast of Italy had presumably been looted from someplace else by the Italians who put it on the galley. Mendoza strode up to me just as I was retrieving my twelve pages of work product from the printer.

"Whatcha got, Jake?"

"Not much." I handed him the printout.

He gave it a skim, running an index finger down the middle of each page to help him speed-read.

"How do you suppose he got to be cochair of Steel Ring?"

"On a wild guess, Groton/Princeton/Yale."

"Necessary, perhaps, but not sufficient. He'd also have to write a check for something between twenty-five thousand and a hundred thousand dollars. The Steel Ring Arts Ball is a big league fund-raiser, and cochairs are expected to lead by example."

"So after 'oh-four, maybe he stopped writing those checks."

"Right. And the question is why."

"Case of the shorts?" I speculated. "Money trouble in paradise?"

"Not a bad guess."

Mendoza pursed his lips in a rare display of indecision. Then he seemed to make up his mind. When he spoke his voice sounded almost apologetic.

"How do you feel about driving me out to the Bradshaws' house? I'm not mistaking you for a chauffeur, but I need to get out there fast and I'll have to study this stuff *and* work my phone like a call girl all the way."

"I'm in." I grabbed my briefcase and we started quick-stepping it toward the elevators. "Are we taking your Citera?"

"No. We're taking the *Foundation's* Citera."

"Right."

"Flowers, you think?" We ducked into the elevator.

I rolled that over in my mind. Flowers seemed a little off-target somehow.

"You *send* flowers for a death in the family," I said then. "You bring food."

"No time for that."

"Give me five minutes in Elly's Deli while you're bringing the Foundation's Citera around and let me see what I can do."

He glanced at his watch as the elevator reached the ground floor.

"I'll give you eight minutes. I'll meet you outside Elly's at twelve-oh-five."

Delicatessen food is a little tacky for a bereavement visit, but I couldn't go home and whip up a pot roast in eight minutes. I elbowed my way through enough early lunch customers at Elly's to pick up a two-pound slab of meat loaf swimming in a promising pool of brown gravy in a shiny, tinfoil broiling pan. Replacing the shrink-wrapped cellophane over it with lovingly hand-folded aluminum foil to make it look a little homier took about thirty seconds, so I made it outside with a minute to spare. When Mendoza pulled up in the Citera, I stashed the meat loaf on the driver's side backseat floor while Mendoza was circling around to the front seat on the passenger side. I dumped my briefcase on the backseat as I slipped behind the wheel, which meant that the annoying little buzz-chime from the seat-belt cop in the dashboard stayed on even after I clicked my own seatbelt into place. I ignored it but Mendoza didn't. With a flash of irritation he reached laboriously into the backseat to retrieve the briefcase and haul it into the front to wedge next to his feet.

As I worked my way through downtown toward I-579, I mentioned Schuyler's admonitory phone call. He wasn't too impressed.

"We're court-appointed *pro bono* counsel for the appeal." He shook his head. "Strictly paper lawyers. No one thinks we'd be involved in any insider stuff. The operating assumption is that we barely know our client's name."

"Fair enough," I said. That sounded good, but I wasn't sure I was convinced.

"You know what I think? I think Schuyler has the hots for you and wants to be on your short list if you ever pull that engagement ring off your finger."

I actually blushed at that. Me, Cynthia Jakubek. Not much. Just a little pink creeping up the backs of my ears and across the top of my forehead. But enough to aggravate me.

Freeway driving in Pittsburgh is like performance art for sumo wrestlers. As you approach steep downgrades, and there are lots of them, you'll see signs telling you that a "Runaway Ramp" is a quarter-mile or a half-mile ahead. A runaway ramp is an unpaved lane that juts off about thirty yards from the edge of the freeway in a straight line and ends in sandbags and reinforced steel pilings. If you're driving a big rig, and you lose control on one of those grades, you're supposed to steer into the runaway ramp and for all practical purposes commit suicide rather than pile up three-dozen cars at the bottom of the hill and take their drivers along with you.

Mendoza worked his phone, just as he'd said he would. From his half of the first conversation, I gathered that the guy he reached was a cop acquaintance. After some convivial banter and a little Spanish, he got down to business.

"Listen, Hector, 'bout this rich Anglo just got his chest ventilated, I represent Caitlin Bradshaw....No, daughter....Since shortly after the *statzpolizei* tossed his mansion....Don't know what it was about. Neither does she....Anyway, reason I called, I don't want her getting the bad news about her *padre* from a detective when she's coming out of gym class. Just *por favor* ask whoever's running the case to call me and we'll set up a time to talk to her."

There was more Spanish after that, and then he ended the call. He immediately hit a speed-dial button and left a voice-message for someone he addressed as "Sam"—Sam Schwartzchild at Fletcher & Peck, I assumed—saying that we were on our way to the Bradshaws'. Then he gave the phone a rest for about ten minutes while he pored over my printout, now giving it careful examination instead of a quick-study skim.

"What's Becky's direct-dial?" This question came about the time I pulled off the freeway.

"Two-nine-seven-five-five-three-eight."

He started punching numbers instantly and was talking eight seconds later, which meant that Becky was at her desk and had answered on the first ring. I could easily imagine her sitting there at her computer, not saying a word except "Becky" at the beginning and "Got it" at the end, expressionless, listening on a headset while her fingers flew over the keys.

"Hey, Becky, this is Luis. Listen, Jake ran across something on Google about Bradshaw. He got quoted around three years ago in the *New York Times* on recovery of art that museums bought without being careful enough about how the seller got his hands on it. But there's nothing in the printout about any books or articles he's written, and he was living in Pittsburgh, so it's not like he had lunch once a month with the Living Arts editor of the *Times*. So what I want to know is, how did the reporter come to call him in the first place? He has to have a clipping file with contact information for half-a-dozen instant experts he could call on Manhattan Island, so how does he end up tabbing Mr. Bradshaw?"

By the time that call was over I had found Fleming Court—a local street, not an English manor—and was looking for the Bradshaws' house number.

We weren't the only ones who decided to pay respects to the surviving Bradshaws that afternoon. I automatically tallied the cars parked along the side of the street outside: Audi, Lexus, Escalade, BMW, Infiniti, Mercedes, Land Rover, with one telltale white Ford Crown Victoria, which I suspected meant the cops had beaten us there. Mendoza found a spot on a thirty-degree grade about forty feet beyond the driveway and eased into it. On the opposite side of the street was a green Prius. Not pale, washed-out mint green—you see a lot of Priuses that color—but honest-to-Pete, no-kidding, go-to-hell British racing green. Environmental statement, maybe: "When I talk about 'driving green,' I mean *driving green*." As we trekked back toward the driveway to head up to the house, Mendoza turned around and looked at the Prius for three or four seconds. "Notice anything about that car?"

"Little downscale for the market around here. And the color is unusual."

"It has New York plates. New York State and New York County."

New York County, *i.e.*, Manhattan. As in where Bradshaw was coming back from during his last weekend on earth.

"Do me a favor, Jake." He lowered his voice slightly because four people populated the front porch we were approaching. "When you get back to the shop, hop on the computer and see if it's possible to buy a Prius from the factory painted British racing green."

"Will do."

Three of the four people on the porch were men. The shortest of them was in his late fifties with a brocaded yarmulke fastened to thinning but still distinguished silver hair. I recognized him as Sam Schwartzchild. I'd never actually seen the other two men before but I figured them for cops, partly because their suits looked a lot more like the one Vince wears to Mass than the elegant number Schwartzchild sported. The fourth porch resident, a woman dressed in a navy blue pantsuit who looked like she was maybe ten years older than I was, confirmed this when the first word I heard her speak was "officers."

"Officers, we appreciate your concern. Ms. Bradshaw's personal physician has given her a tranquilizer. We will be in touch with you before the end of the day to discuss an appointment for an interview. In the meantime, if there is any information you would find useful in your investigation into this tragic business, please call me or Mr. Schwartzchild."

With that, she handed over two business cards.

One of the cops took the cards. He looked at the other cop. The other cop looked at him. Then they both gave for-the-record nods and started trudging down a flagstone walking path to the driveway. They didn't look too happy, but there was nothing they could do about it. You don't have to talk to cops if you don't want to, and no matter what the people who write the *Law and Order* scripts think, cops can't just run you downtown to improve your attitude. Still, I couldn't help wondering whether the encounter would have gone down quite this way if the little chat had taken place in front of a house on, say, Vince's block instead of in a neighborhood with half-acre minimum lot sizes.

"Sam, good to see you," Mendoza said, striding forward and extending his right hand, as soon as the cops were past us. "You can ignore the voice mail I left for you."

"Good afternoon, Luis. This is my partner, Sally Port. She handles some of our white collar crime work."

Mendoza shook hands, first with Schwartzchild and then with Port. Then he introduced me as his "colleague," which I thought was a definite improvement over "intern." Given the meat loaf and all, I just nodded.

"Food." Schwartzchild looked toward Port after glancing at my burden. "We should have brought food."

I'd never met Mrs. Bradshaw, of course, but the prim matron guarding the front door had to be someone else. She spent a couple of extra seconds on the once-over she gave Mendoza and me, for one thing, presumably because it was pretty clear neither of us had any ancestors on speaking terms with William Penn. That struck me as an awkward, protective impulse of a solicitous friend helping out in a time of need—a socially clumsy hesitation that the mistress of the house wouldn't have allowed herself. Fortunately, with Schwartzchild vouching for us, she quickly concluded that we weren't there to clean the pool and we stepped into the great room.

"Great room," not "living room" or "parlor." It's something you only see in newer houses, and more often in the West and Midwest than the East. Basically, except for a bathroom and maybe a laundry room, you have no inside walls on the first floor. There's an open kitchen defined by waist-high cabinets and counters taking up maybe an eighth of the floor space, and then a big open area broken up by nothing but the staircase. Put the dining table, the electronics, the computer station, and the couch, chairs, and coffee table anywhere you want to. You can make the whole thing one big dining room if you're having a dinner party, or one big den if you're having a cocktail party. Or, I suppose, one big bedroom if you're having an orgy.

I braced myself for the first scene of an imaginary ballet I'd like to compose someday based on John Cheever's short stories: *WASPS Closing Ranks.* Dry-eyed, stiff-upper-lipped, clipped-toned, stoic, they would be gathering protectively around one of their own the instant a breath of scandal whispered through the delicately scented atmosphere.

One good look around refuted this particular outbreak of my resentful class prejudice. True, one guy stood there in a navy blue suit with a dove gray vest and gold pocket watch, looking like T.S. Eliot getting ready for tea with Virginia Woolf, if T.S. Eliot had stood six-two and been rail thin with hair that was wedding-gown white; and the clergyman he was talking to looked like your basic, standard-issue Presbyterian who didn't overdo the blessed-are-the-poor stuff in his sermons. But there was also at least one yarmulke other than Sam's. One of the women was African-American and a man and woman just inside the door looked South Asian. Another woman had gotten her genes from someplace a lot closer to the Mediterranean Sea than the English Channel. This wasn't WASP, it was human. In a backhanded way, the gathering was the distilled essence of American equality: the only color that really mattered was green.

I spotted Ariane Bradshaw sitting at a writing table in the front corner of the room, down to the left from the front door. There was no mistaking her: Caitlin's face, matured by age and challenge. Another woman was sitting opposite her, taking notes on a mini legal pad, presumably making a list of shopping and various other chores she could take care of while Ariane dealt with the complications of a sudden death in the family. On the continuum running from prostrate-with-grief to merry-widow, I put Ariane right in the middle. She wore a sober expression, and I could see a puffiness at the corner of her right eye, sugges-tive of recent tears. But there was no distracted vacancy in her gaze. She didn't look like she was in denial, expecting all of this to disappear when she woke up from a bad dream. And there was no way she'd popped a Valium in the last two hours, which meant that Sally Port had been kidding the cops just now.

I made my way to the kitchen area and stowed the meat loaf in a black, top-of-the-line Sub-Zcro side-by-side that *no one* would think of calling a "fridge." Then I kept my back to the crowd so that I could check my Droid without seeming too insensitive. I didn't have to wait to get back to the office to answer Mendoza's little trivia question. He was on the far side of a generational line between people who associate the Internet with big-box, desk-top technology and people who grew up knowing that you can carry it around in a holster on your belt. It took me forty-two seconds to verify that British racing green isn't on the official Prius palette. Whoever drove that car here from New York had paid for a custom paint job. *Hmm.*

I figured that my job here, other than chauffeur, was to keep my eyes and ears open and my mouth shut. Anyone glancing at Mendoza would figure he was getting paid to be here, but I could pass myself off as part of the furniture. I was just about to start doing that when the Droid vibrated. I would have ignored it, but a quick look at the screen showed my lover's number. My pulse quickened, I got a major rush through my upper body, and I answered.

"Is this a good time for a quick question?"

"Absolutely," meaning that it was the worst possible time but that he could have basically anything he wanted. I started making my way toward the back door. Quickly checking the net is one thing, but a personal conversation in this setting would have been over-the-top rude.

"I'm looking for a cheap plot device. Would it make any sense for someone to time his death for just after the first of the year, to cut down on the death tax?"

"Depends on the year." I kept my voice low as I approached the clergyman and the guy in the gray vest on my way to the door. "This year it would be just the opposite. Thanks to President Bush there's no estate tax at all this year, but in 2011 it clicks back in unless Congress does something in a hurry—and right now you can get bets either way on that."

The guy in the gray vest looked at me in what I took to be reproof. I did my best to come up with an apologetic expression as I stepped out onto the driveway.

"Just the opposite!" Paul said. "That's perfect! And I can blame it on the Busher!"

"We aim to please. How are things otherwise?"

"Six hundred words. I'm in the zone."

"Fantastic."

We spent about five more minutes love-chatting. I glanced at the tiny, gold-mounted diamond on my right ring finger. It cost $225. Paul's first professional publication was a short story that he sold to an e-zine three years ago for $75. He cranked out three more submissions and a couple of reviews as fast as he could, but the e-zine didn't bite. So he spent a weekend whipping off a little piece of cheap porn that they snapped up for a hundred-and-a-half. He used those two checks—his first earnings as a writer—to buy the ring. I was feeling soft and dreamy when we ended the call so that he could return to the adventures of Henry Widget.

Just as I was turning to go back inside I heard tires whining on the driveway. I looked up to see a red Ford Focus rolling up with Caitlin behind the wheel. She pulled into the third port of a four-car garage.

I'm not obsessed with protocol, but I decided to take this one through channels. I did *not* hang around to chat up a vulnerable young woman who'd just become a semi-orphan. I hustled back in, wound my way through the crowd to Mendoza, and whispered to him that Caitlin had just gotten home. He murmured the news to Schwartzchild. Schwartzchild padded up to the writing table and quietly shared the information with Ariane Bradshaw. I read "thank you, Sam" on her lips as she stood up, offering a brave smile to him and a hand pat to the lady with the mini legal pad.

We all politely didn't notice her making her way out the back door. Pad lady began to work the room, apparently seeking volunteers for her three-page to-do list. I heard Sally Port explaining to the clergyman that she'd told the cops the doctor had *given* Ms. Bradshaw a tranquilizer, which was literally true, even though Bradshaw hadn't actually *ingested* it. She seemed way too pleased with this verbal sleight of hand, but I felt a twinge of grudging admiration for it.

I suddenly found my eyes focusing on a blond woman in a funereal black skirt and jacket who was coming in the front door—and I wasn't the only one; she was a head-turner. I felt a nudge on my elbow. I turned around to see the gray-vest dude bending slightly toward me with his hand extended, kind of like Mickey Mouse had the summer I was eight and we went to Disney World.

"Excuse me. My name is Walter Learned. I couldn't help noticing you bring in the covered dish. Are you a friend of the family?"

I shook hands with him while I thought about how to answer that. I had expected damp and limp in his handshake and got dry and firm instead.

"I'm Cynthia Jakubek. I've known Caitlin for a short time." I sensed Sally Port grinning at me a few feet away, but that may have been my imagination. "I feel a bit sheepish about taking that call a few minutes ago, but it was my fiancé. We expect to move to New York in a couple of months, and we've been talking about where to live."

"Quite forgivable."

I segued. "How long have you known the Bradshaws?"

"Tom and I go way, way back," Learned said. "Met during the summer he spent in Paris after his junior year at Princeton. I always thought I'd go first."

"Are you in the arts and antiquities field too?"

"Only on the fringes. An amateur basking in the reflected glow of the real professionals, like Tom."

"An amateur does something for love of the thing itself. So where art is concerned, 'amateur' is a pretty noble thing to be."

"What a captivating observation." He gave my right elbow a confiding brush with his left hand and pointed with his right at Schwartzchild. "Say, do you happen to know who that is?"

"Samuel Schwartzchild. Top trusts and estates lawyer in Pittsburgh."

"Excuse me for just a moment. Wonderful talking to you."

With that he loped off in Schwartzchild's direction. By the time I realized that I'd experienced a high-class brush off, he was towering over Schwartzchild's yarmulke.

"Mr. Schwartzchild? Walter Learned. You probably don't remember me, but it's good to see you again."

Schwartzchild looked blank for just a moment, then came up with a smile and shook Learned's hand. After that, Learned's voice dropped to a confidential, just-between-us-boys level, so I didn't hear the next part. I did see Schwartzchild glance suddenly and with apparent concern at the blonde in black who was now buttonholing Reverend Whoever in what looked like a won't-take-no-for-an-answer manner. Ten seconds later Schwartzchild was moving toward her in the steady but understated strides that I suppose you develop when you spend a lot of time going to your clients' funerals.

"Good afternoon, ma'am." He said this more firmly than you usually hear those words spoken. "I'm Samuel Schwartzchild, the Bradshaws' attorney. I don't believe I know you. Are you acquainted with Ms. Bradshaw?"

"I have to talk to her," she said. Someone who'd gone to, say, Stanford would have said she had a New York accent, as if there's a single New York accent instead of about six. I'd heard all six of them at Harvard, and hers sounded more like northern New Jersey which—trust me on this—isn't the same thing at all.

"That would be 'no,' then," Schwartzchild said. "And I'm given to understand that you're a private investigator."

"I'm an insurance recovery consultant, and I have to talk—"

"Thank you for that correction. My apologies to any private investigators whom my error offended. This is neither the time nor the place for deployment of insurance recovery consultant skills."

He held his hand out to one side and Port deftly put a business card into it, like an OR nurse slapping a clamp into a surgeon's hand. Schwartzchild tendered the card to blondie.

"Have your attorney call me."

"I don't have an attorney."

"Then I'd suggest that you engage one. Promptly. And I must insist that you leave the Bradshaws' home immediately."

It took her about five seconds and one survey of the unsympathetic expressions in the room to decide she had zero options.

"Fine." She spat this syllable. Then she spun around on one spike heel and headed for the front door. She didn't take the card.

Most of the room gravitated toward Schwartzchild to murmur low-key congratulations on the studly way he'd dispatched the blonde. I drifted toward the back door. Ariane and Caitlin hadn't appeared yet. That was good in a way, because things might have gotten a lot more interesting with the "insurance recovery consultant" if they had, but I couldn't help wondering what the hold-up was. A cathartic heart-to-heart with hugs and tears would have been a perfect psychological response, but I had trouble seeing those two doing kiss-and-cry in broad daylight.

As I got within peeping range of the kitchen window, I heard their voices approaching the back door. They both spoke in casual, no-drama tones, but I picked up a hint of tension in the words, as if keeping things low-key required a bit of effort from each of them. I stepped back, but still caught the last of the exchange, just before the back door opened.

"I came as fast as I could. As soon as organic chem was over."

"You might have left before it started."

"It's an AP, Mom. I want to go pre-med, and I missed Monday."

"He was your father."

"And he killed my brother."

The next thing I heard was the back door opening.

Chapter Seven

Caitlin surprised me. She dumped her backpack on the floor underneath some coat pegs just inside the back door and hung up her earth-tone suede jacket. Then, instead of flouncing upstairs to cocoon in her bedroom, she went methodically through the great room, greeting the guests group by group. Her voice was low and a little mechanical, and she used standard verbal formulas—"Thanks so much for coming"; "It means so much to Mom and me that you were able to come"; "Thanks for caring about Dad." Still, it struck me as a pretty impressive performance for a seventeen-year-old who'd just had her world turned upside down.

"I saved you for last," she said to Mendoza when she reached us. He started to respond, but she raised her hand and continued speaking. "I get that we have to talk. Let me change clothes and help Mom with our guests and then we'll sit down so you can ask me where I was whenever Dad was killed."

"No hurry." Mendoza had barely managed to get the words out before she headed upstairs, the hem of her black-and-yellow plaid uniform skirt sketching a brave little flutter as she reached the landing. That gave me a chance to share her "killed my brother" line with Mendoza.

Most of the guests seemed to take Caitlin's exit as a signal to start drifting toward the door, led by those who had accepted assignments from pad lady. I looked around for Learned, because I wanted to verify my sneaking suspicion that he matched up with the green Prius, but I didn't see him. Then I heard Mendoza asking me something in a near whisper.

"You got anything to write on?"

Yes, I came here prepared to practice law, even though I had to leave my briefcase in the car while I schlepped meat loaf in. I did *not* say that. What I said as I pulled out my PDA was, "Shoot."

"Okay. First, see if you can get the license number of that Prius without making a production out of it. Then call Becky and have her run the plate and while she's at it check out Walter Learned and Vera Sommers."

"Is Sommers the blonde that Sam booted out?"

"Yeah."

"And it was Learned who told Sam who she was, I'm guessing."

"You're guessing right."

I headed outside and strolled back toward Mendoza's Citera, trying to look like a put-upon young lawyer who had to fetch her briefcase. Crisp temperature, bright sunshine warm on my shoulders, no wind—stepping outside seemed like a real good idea. I had to take an unnatural angle on my supposed way to the Citera, but I did manage to spot the Prius' license plate and memorize the MEZ-558 on it. Then I fished my briefcase from the Citera, glanced inside it for effect, and closed the car door. I don't think I had Meryl Streep looking over her shoulder, but it seemed like a pretty fair acting job to me.

I leaned against the Citera's trunk while I called Becky the Techie to relay Mendoza's instructions. I had to leave them on her voice mail, which meant that I spent about forty seconds looking distractedly down the street so that I wouldn't bore myself to death with the sound of my own voice. That's why I happened to notice the blonde—excuse me, Vera Sommers—in a harvest gold Dodge Intrepid about ninety feet up the road. She was pointing an oversized telephoto lens through the windshield at me. Talk about clichés. All she needed was an unfiltered Camel dangling from the corner of her mouth and she could have stepped into some drag rip-off of hard-boiled pulp. I thought about flipping her off as I headed back into the house, but didn't. I made a mental note to ask Ken if that was a sin of omission.

I walked back in looking for Mendoza but I spotted Learned instead. He smiled at me and we exchanged friendly nods. Something about him seemed different, beyond the fact that he was now holding an oxblood leather attaché case, but I couldn't put my finger on it. It was like one of those can-you-find-five-differences-between-the-cartoon-on-the-left-and-the-cartoon-on-the-right things that newspapers sometimes put on their funny pages.

Pad lady was starting to shoo people out in a slightly less genteel way than she had been up to now, and Learned seemed to be taking the hint. I had the choice of tracking down Mendoza and breaking into the interview he was presumably conducting with Caitlin or chatting up Learned on his way out. I picked the second.

"In case you're interested," I said, "Vera Sommers is playing *paparazza* down the street."

"That doesn't come as a complete surprise. She's never been famous for either subtlety or finesse." If I'd impressed him by knowing her name he did a good job of hiding it.

"Have you known her for a while?"

"Known of her. She's been in the field for about seven years now. Not sure where she came from, but most people in insurance recovery are ex-cops of some kind."

"I wouldn't have thought you two moved in the same circles."

We had reached the driveway. He glanced at me with an avuncular smile.

"People like Sommers are hard to avoid in the fine arts market. A lot of sellers tend to offer intriguing pieces that they bought without being clear on the chain of title. That's an engraved invitation for Ms. Sommers and her ilk."

"You don't think very much of insurance recovery consultants, do you?"

"I 'don't think much' of people who sell heroin to school children. I *despise* insurance recovery consultants."

"Wow. Way harsh."

"Up to a point, I suppose." He stopped at the Prius—suspicion confirmed—and turned to look directly at me. "A lot depends on how it's done. The A-list consultants help insurance companies reduce payouts or get some of their money back, and that keeps premiums down for everyone. But the bottom-feeders are basically fences, trafficking in stolen goods."

He reached for his lower left vest pocket and looked surprised for an instant as he came up empty. Then he reached lower and pulled a silver pocket watch on a braided chain from his pants pocket, took a look, clicked it closed, and stowed it in the vest pocket. That's when my mind clicked on the something-different that I'd seen. When I first laid eyes on Learned, the pocket watch chain had curled from a belt loop up to the vest pocket. When I saw him again after my license plate quest, it had sagged downward into the pants pocket.

Looking at your watch is an infallible signal that a conversation should end, so I tried to think of some excuse for exchanging business cards. He beat me to it.

"I've enjoyed our conversations." He slipped into the Prius and tossed the attaché case on the passenger seat. "I can't promise anything, but I might be able to come up with a couple of leads when you and your fiancé start looking for quarters in the city. Can I get in touch with you at Mr. Mendoza's office?"

Fumbling a bit in surprise at this piece of luck, I dug out one of my cards and handed it to him.

"Thanks." He pulled a card of his own from his lower right vest pocket and handed it to me.

Handy things, vests. Maybe I'll start wearing them.

Learned pulled away and his Prius purred down the tree-lined street. Vaguely resentful that his seat belt buzzer hadn't sounded off about his case like Mendoza's had about mine, I took a quick look at the card:

WALTER LEARNED
Ars Longa LLC
New York, N.Y.

Oh well. Maybe he's in the book.

If Mendoza had wanted me to take notes while he talked to Caitlin he would have called me on my Droid. He hadn't, so I couldn't see crashing the party now. I thought I probably had half-an-hour to kill, and ordinarily I would have spent the time checking voice mails and e-mails. But I left the Droid in its holster. I spent the time thinking instead. It turned out I only had eighteen minutes instead of thirty, but that was plenty. When Mendoza waltzed back onto the porch and started leading me toward the Citera, I was blooming with the ripe fruit of cogitation. I decided to keep it to myself until after he'd given me the highlights of his Caitlin chat while he drove back downtown.

"'Killed my brother' got an interesting reaction," was his introduction to the debriefing as he pulled away from the curb. "Said she couldn't remember saying that and it didn't make any sense. But she admitted she was so strung out by Dad's murder and Mom's bitching at her that she could have said anything."

"Are we sure she's an only child?"

"No, but between now and sundown we're gonna get sure." Trying to get headed back in the direction we'd come from, Mendoza turned onto yet another placid, winding suburban lane. "I wonder what 'traffic calming' is."

I saw the sign that provoked his question—TRAFFIC CALMING in black on a yellow triangle—and said "Speed bump" a second too late. We took a belly-wrenching bounce over the thing.

"What else did Caitlin have to say?"

"Let's see. She was home alone Monday night. Did a load of homework and watched some tube."

"Did she do any of the homework on her computer?"

"Yes, but not until around nine. She was booking it before then. Says mom came in sometime after ten and she's not sure where she was before then. She offered to swear her mom was home with her if Ariane needs an alibi. I told her that would be a very bad idea."

"You're a role model for young lawyers."

"Goddamn right. Three phone calls to friends, but they were all on her mobile phone, so that proves nothing about her whereabouts."

"What about instant-messaging on her computer?"

"She said she's not allowed to use IM on school nights. Anyway she's felt a little funny about that since the cops searched the house on Sunday, so she hasn't climbed back in the saddle yet."

"So she doesn't have an alibi."

"She also doesn't have a motive," Mendoza pointed out.

"Unless we turn up a missing brother—or unless she knows more about estate taxes than my fiancé does."

"Where did *that* come from?"

"Any estate valued at more than a million and change will be worth fifty-five percent more up to December 31st than it will be starting the next day," I said. "Say Caitlin finds out over the weekend that dad's been swimming in the shark tank where she figures his survivability is low once stuff hits the fan. Since he's a goner anyway in her eyes, maybe she hurries things along a bit so that she and Ariane won't have to share with the IRS."

"That's cold." Mendoza whistled. "I'm not buying it. I'm not buying a word of it. But it is stone cold, I'll say that."

"That theory works for mom, too, by the way."

"Only if she happened to know that little piece of trivia about the estate tax springing back to life next year."

"Since she's a client of Sam Schwartzchild, I'd say her chance of knowing that is a lot better than Caitlin's."

"Do me a favor, willya?" Mendoza took his eyes off the road long enough to shoot me a pleading glance. "Use some of those IQ points of yours to come up with a suspect whose last name isn't Bradshaw."

"Walter Learned."

"What'd he do to get on your shit-list?"

"Toward the end of the bereavement visit this afternoon, he appeared with an attaché case he hadn't had before and his pocket watch in his pants pocket instead of his vest pocket."

"Jake, I'm pretty sure those are just misdemeanors."

"Why would a man move a watch on a chain from his vest to his pants?"

"I'll bite: why?"

"Because he had to pull down his pants—and then forgot to replace the watch when he pulled them back up."

"Don't get dirty on me, Jake."

"I'm just saying he went to the bathroom—and unless it's coincidence, he retrieved his attaché case while he was at it."

"Or maybe he just stashed his attaché case in the closet and got it back while you weren't looking."

"Maybe. But wherever he left it, someone took something out of it between the time he put it down and the time he picked it up."

"Why do you say that?"

"Because it had to be empty when he tossed it on the passenger seat of his Prius. Otherwise, the seat belt buzzer would have gone off when he turned the car on, and it didn't. And why would you carry an empty attaché case into someone's house?"

Mendoza bristled, which meant that he wanted to just blow this stuff away but couldn't quite bring himself to do it.

"If I didn't know you better," he muttered, "I'd say you were trying to promote yourself into a trip to New York City on the firm's dime."

"The Foundation's dime." I had him there.

Chapter Eight

"Okay, kids, it's showtime. Whattaya got?"

This question came from Mendoza at fifteen seconds after three o'clock. Same crowd as this morning, same configuration around his desk, except this time we were sitting down.

"Time of death was between five and nine Monday night." Waters spoke without notes and with minimal gestures in a dry, low-key voice. "They might refine that later on, but they're cutting themselves some slack for the moment because the museum keeps the temperature in that room down so the wax thingies won't melt. Body was not, say again, *not* moved after death. They're guessing forty-four or forty-five caliber on the bullet, but it somehow got beaten up something fierce penetrating all that soft tissue. Figure that out. No exit wound. Not sure what he had for breakfast, but his last meal was going to be lobster salad."

"So Bradshaw and his killer both got into the museum on a day when it was closed to the public?" Mendoza asked.

"Right. Probably means he knew the killer. Bradshaw had a key-card for the place and knew the security code because he was organizing an exhibit on something or other, and odds are he let the killer in."

"So think the cops?"

"Yep. And so thinks Ricky Waters."

Mendoza frowned. So did I. So did everybody else except Waters, who gazed with eerie calm into the middle distance and flicked a minute bead of perspiration form his deep brown face.

"Has the murder weapon turned up yet?" Mendoza asked him.

"If it has, they aren't saying."

"It would make sense for Bradshaw to chill at the museum for a while if he wasn't quite ready to be handcuffed by state troopers," Mendoza mused. "He couldn't expect that to last long, but maybe he just wanted to buy a couple of days."

"Makes sense."

"So have they found his car yet?"

"They have, actually—in a garage on East Thirty-ninth Street in Manhattan, just north of Park Avenue."

"How did he get home from New York?"

"Excellent question." Waters nodded just slightly. "First rate question. Really. He didn't come by plane unless he did it under an assumed name, and that's not easy to bring off these days. He doesn't sound to me like the Greyhound Bus type. Trains takes forever and they also require an i.d., for some damn reason. So I'm guessing he got a ride from someone."

"Okay." Mendoza sighed and sank back in his chair, then shifted his gaze to Sal Brentano. "You're on."

"The State Police are buttoned up pretty tight. The affidavit supporting the search warrant application, though, mentioned an intercepted conversation mentioning *l'aigle* finial."

"Who's Layla Finial?" Mendoza asked, approximating Brentano's pronunciation of the French word. "President of the Strippers With Funny Names Club?"

"Not who, what," Brentano said. "L-apostrophe-A-I-G-L-E. Object of art, apparently, and I'm guessing a pretty pricey one. Also, almost all strippers have funny names, so a specific club would be pretty redundant."

"*L'aigle* finial" rang a very faint bell deep in the recesses of my memory, somewhere between Torts and Civil Procedure from my first year in law school. I unholstered my Droid as discreetly as I could and Googled the term while Mendoza asked Brentano how he knew so much about strippers and Brentano said he believed in supporting single moms. I'd had about forty seconds on the web when Mendoza scowled in my direction.

"You got something for us Jake, or are you just checking out your boyfriend's tush?"

"A finial eagle—*l'aigle* finial—was one of the fine arts objects stolen from the Isabella Stewart Gardner Museum in Boston in 1995," I said. "Along with paintings by Vermeer and Rembrandt and some stuff by Degas and Manet."

Brentano whispered something blasphemous and whistled. "That was the biggest art heist in history. Five hundred million dollars. Never solved, and none of the stolen art has ever been recovered."

"What's a finial?" This was Mendoza's question, directed at me.

"A decorative ornament that you put on top of a flagstaff."

"What was this one made of—solid gold?"

"Don't know. But the flagstaff it came from belonged to Napoleon. The eagle was one of his symbols. And that eagle finial was probably designed by somebody famous. That's what makes it so valuable."

"Oh-kayyyy." Mendoza chewed that over for a second. "So maybe Bradshaw was fencing something from a real life *Topkapi* caper. It's a big deal. I get that. But why are state troopers taking time out from writing speeding tickets on the Pennsylvania Turnpike to dabble in an art theft fifteen years ago and two states north? Why wouldn't the Feds be walking point on this?"

"Maybe the Feds have other things to do these days." Brentano shrugged. "Nine-eleven and all that. Maybe they're more worried about Al Qaida than *l'aigle.*"

Mendoza took half-a-minute or so to digest that. Then he grinned and shook his head. He was smiling broadly when he looked over at Becky the Techie. "Top that."

"Wendy Sommers. Thirty-six. Divorced, no kids. Criminology degree from Penn State. Went through on an ROTC scholarship. Six years on active duty, four of them with the Criminal Investigation Division. Two tours in Iraq. Punched out with an honorable discharge. Made a run at the FBI based on the CID experience, but they rejected her. Caught on with Wackenhut for a couple of years, then went out on her own."

"What's Wackenhut?" My question drew stares telling me I was the only one in the room who didn't know.

"One of the biggest private investigation firms in the world," Becky said. "Offices everywhere."

"How's she doing as a PI?" Mendoza asked.

"Making a living, apparently. Works out of her house. Pays her bills. Leases a midsize car."

"Does she cheat on her taxes?"

"Not enough to draw an audit."

"Is she known to the police?"

"No record, except for a couple of speeding tickets."

Mendoza frowned thoughtfully. He did the thing where he leans back at about a forty-five-degree angle and examines the ceiling. He looked like he wanted a cigar.

"Okay. Check her out for boyfriends, especially long-term relationships with guys who are mobbed up. See if she's living beyond her means."

"Got it."

"By the way, did Jake tell you about our client's killed-my-brother crack?"

"Yeah," Becky said. "Bradshaw had two boys by his first wife. They're both in their thirties, alive and well. One is living in Chicago and the other in Dallas. No evidence that Ariane has had any other kids."

"So if we're gonna come up with a Caitlin sibling, even loosely speaking, we'll need a mistress or a hooker or at least a fling somewhere for Mr. B."

"Right. I'll add that to my to-do list."

"Okay." Mendoza slapped his hands on his desk. "Now how about Learned?"

"Born July 16, 1949 in Washington, D.C. Father was a diplomat, mom was a diplomat's wife. Apparently divided his childhood between D.C. and various posts in East Asia where dad was stationed. High school diploma from Gonzaga Prep in D.C., but he actually only studied there during his senior year. If he attended any universities he didn't hang around long enough to pick up a degree. According to a business card that Jake finagled from him, he's associated with a limited liability company called Ars Longa, which owns the Prius he was driving."

She stopped. Everyone waited. Nothing happened for probably ten seconds that seemed like sixty. Mendoza finally spoke up.

"What else?"

"That's it."

"That's *it?*"

"That's it."

"No jobs, no marriages, no divorces, no children, no lawsuits, no arrests, no convictions, no professional licenses, no residential address, no phone number, no bank accounts, no credit cards?"

"Nope."

"Where is Ars Longa registered?" This was still Mendoza asking the questions.

"Delaware."

"Is Learned a shareholder?" Waters asked.

"LLCs don't have shareholders, they have members," Mendoza said. "They aren't corporations. Neither their members nor their officers are public information."

"Right," Becky said. "The registered address for the LLC is a lawyer's office in Dover. The lawyer is the listed managing agent."

"So, bottom line, this is the invisible man we're talking about here." Mendoza's tone was incredulous. "He has lived for four decades since graduating from high school without leaving a footprint anywhere. I mean, you Google me you get, what, twelve-hundred hits anyway, and I'm nobody. But you Google him and you get nothing."

"Google Walter Learned and you get links to an architect in Palo Alto and a dentist in Nashville and a number of other gentlemen, but not to anyone with art or in New York City."

Mendoza swiveled toward me.

"You know what, Jake? If we can somehow find an address for this guy somewhere, you might get your butt sent to the Big Apple after all."

When I got to *Streetdreamer* around seven that night, I whiffed off eight lines about how driving a Cadillac Citera—"the Caddie with *zing!*"—had reminded me that I'm not ready to be fifty-two years old yet. I signed off with, "No way I'm even thinking about owning a car my first ten years in NYC."

I did all this to the aroma of roasting chicken breasts. Tuesday is Vince's short day—"short" being a relative term meaning that he finishes his route and gets home before five-thirty. So he always fixes dinner Tuesday nights, and it's always his one and only non-grill specialty: herb-roasted chicken breasts. He splits the breasts all by himself, brushes them with garlic butter, sprinkles on pepper, salt, and savory, pops them in the oven in a deep roasting pan, turns them over once while they're cooking, uses a turkey-spritzer to baste them twice with their own juice, and thinks he's Julia Child. Guys—you gotta love 'em.

I was setting the table when Paul called. Fortunately, I can set the table with one hand.

"Twelve hundred words."

"Twelve hundred in one day? That's, like, a record or something, isn't it?"

"Personal best. Any news from Calder & Bull?"

"Nope—and that's the way I like it. Nothing in the mail, and not a whisper on 'Above the Law.'"

"So how was your day?"

"Fantastic, actually. I was doing real, hands-on law with high stakes on a human scale. I was pumped all afternoon."

"Why would you want to trade that for reviewing thousands of pages of documents on a computer screen?"

"Hundred-and-a-half a year to start."

"That is *so* Harvard Law School."

"Well, lover," I pointed out, "that'd figure, wouldn't it?"

"I can't believe I said that. Actually, *I* didn't say that. I was channeling a Yalie I dated before I met you. She used to say that Harvard lawyers make money but Yale lawyers make history."

"She's right. Yale Law School produced Hillary Clinton, and she became the first Secretary of State in American history who'd flunked a bar exam."

"OUCH! *OWWWWEEEE!* Burn, baby, burn! Thank you, ma'am, may I have another?"

"Don't get kinky, Paul. This is a mobile phone. By the way, don't pack your bags yet but there's a chance I might be able to squeeze a trip to New York out of the thing I'm working on now and even tie our epic quest for housing into it."

"Are you kidding me? That's fantastic! How did you bring that off?"

"I haven't brought anything off yet. But save your chits for a couple of days off next week."

This chatter would probably have gone on for another half-hour, but Vince showed up in the doorway with two sizzling chicken breasts on a china platter.

"As the Meals-on-Wheels driver said when he skidded onto the sidewalk," Vince intoned solemnly, "'Dinner is swerved.'" The first time I heard that from Vince I was about eight years old. He was serving chicken breasts that time, too.

"Gotta go, tiger," I told Paul. "If your Yalie calls, feel free to drop my line on her. You don't even need to footnote me."

Less than three minutes later Vince was saying grace over the platter of chicken breasts, a bowl of mashed potatoes that ten minutes ago had been freeze dried flakes in a pouch, a bowl of yellow gravy, ditto, a margarine dish, and a small plate holding four slices of Wonder enriched white bread. Not even brown 'n serve dinner rolls. Vince doesn't believe in frills. Green vegetables are a frill. He'd gotten himself a Coke to drink, and I was sitting there with ice water. Not bottled water, straight from the tap. No matter how much money I make, I am *never* going to pay for something you can get for free out of a water fountain.

Vince finished grace, I said amen, and we dug into the meal.

"You sound like you're in a good mood, Dad." I said this to distract his attention as I unobtrusively cut the dark brown skin off my chicken and hid it near a mound of potatoes.

"This was a good day. You oughta see their eyes light up when they see that deluxe tool box. Like kids in a candy store. I got four or five good leads today alone. I bet I move half-a-dozen of the things by Christmas."

"Sounds great."

"You gonna eat that?" He pointed with his fork at the cholesterol-laden skin lurking behind my potatoes.

"No—and neither are you."

"Wanna bet?"

He had speared the thing and transferred it to his plate before I could flex a muscle.

Damn.

"Speaking of poultry," I said, "why don't you give me the keys to the Chevy right after dinner? I saw some eight-pound turkeys at Sully's over the weekend. If we get one of those in a pan of cold water in the fridge before bedtime tonight, it should be thawed in time for us to get it in the oven Thursday morning."

"Uh, yeah." He lowered his eyes. "That's something I've been meaning to talk to you about. I was, uh, thinking we might, uh, you know, have Thanksgiving dinner with Mrs. Banacek over on Gentry Street. I mean, neither of the guys can come home this year, and, uh, you know, I was just thinking."

"Does Mrs. Banacek know about this interesting thought?"

"She, uh, actually, she, uh, invited us."

"'Us?'"

"Well, me—but you'd be welcome. She'd love to have you."

"Vince!" The light finally dawned. "You've got a girl!"

"You pissed?" His voice was actually sheepish.

"Are you kidding? I'm thrilled." I put the puzzle pieces from last night together—the shower and the guilt-tripping about Mom and even the defensive sensitivity about me.

"You mean you'd, like, be okay with going?"

"No, Dad, I'd rather work my butt off in the kitchen all day so that I can serve a meal that won't be half as good as the ones Mom made. That'd be a lot more fun than sitting on someone else's couch and watching two football games while I surf the net on my laptop."

"So, that's a yes?"

I reached over and squeezed the big guy's hand.

"That's a yes, Dad. And if Mrs. Banacek would rather have you all to herself, I'll be totally fine having Chef Boyardee right here."

"That ain't gonna happen."

"One tip, Dad. After dinner, offer to help with the dishes. She'll say no, and you'll score like a gazillion points with her."

Chapter Nine

"So who we gonna *blame* for this?" The richly cadenced question, amplified by nothing but the Reverend Demetrius McKenzie's lungs, echoed with resonant depth off the church's white plaster and brown oak walls. "How 'bout the guards who didn't spot that shiv? We gonna blame them? Maybe the laws that treat crack like first degree murder and powder like a traffic ticket. Tell ya, there's a reason they call it *white* powder. We gonna blame them? How 'bout the judge who sentenced TIE-rell? Or the prosecutor who threw the book at him? Or the cops who arrested him, or the snitch who fingered him? Maybe we should blame them. Yeah, let's put this on *them*."

The rev wore a purple silk gown with a black velvet collar, which would have been a pretty bold fashion statement most places but fit right in here on Ohio Street at the First African-Methodist-Episcopal Church of Pittsburgh. Interesting to learn that my client's first name was pronounced TIE-rell, treating the y like a long I and stressing the first syllable. In the four months or so I'd represented him I'd always called him Tih-RELL.

Just for the record, going to Tyrell Washington's funeral wasn't my idea.

"It's called closing the file, Jake." That's the way Mendoza put it just before nine Wednesday morning when he told me someone should represent the office when Washington got his final send-off—and it couldn't be Mendoza, because he'd scheduled Caitlin Bradshaw's interview with the cops for later that morning. "He was a client of the firm when he cashed in his chips, so we'll be there when they sing "Dies Irae" for him—or whatever African-Methodist-Episcopals sing at funerals."

I doubt that even *Catholics* have sung "Dies Irae" at funerals since Vince was an altar boy, which suggested that Mendoza's liturgical record was a bit spotty. I didn't see any point in mentioning that, so I just agreed to go and he told me to put in a chit for the cab fare. The chit thing told me he was really serious. Mendoza doesn't get all sideways about writing off a client bill now and then, but he watches out-of-pocket disbursements like a hawk. He probably has PENNIES COUNT tattooed next to his navel.

So there I was at First A.M.E. Church at ten a.m. on Wednesday, one of a sprinkling of Caucasian faces in a swelling river of black ones. The pews shone and smelled of lemon Pledge, and someone had recently waxed the scarred maple floorboards. The casket looked like richly carved cherry, its red deep and lustrous. Mourners filled the first six pews and after that were scattered here and there throughout the rest of the church. Ten or twelve men among the hundred-plus adults. The number of kids surprised me, although I guess it shouldn't have. There must have been twenty of them, looking like they'd been scrubbed to within an inch of their lives and dressed to meet the president. Every now and then one of them would sneak a wide-eyed peek at me and then snap his head back around just in time to avoid a smack.

Somewhere around the second hymn, just after a reading from Isaiah, I'd started feeling guilty because I wasn't coming up with more in the way of deep emotion. Tyrell Washington was a pretty bad dude. He'd sold crack to school kids and carved up rivals who poached on his territory. When he died young, though, he left some hurting people behind him. I should have been sharing at least some of their ache, but instead I was counting the minutes until I could get back to the office and check my blog.

I'd had a brainstorm in the shower that morning, one of those *BAM!* things that stop you cold. Still dripping and without a stitch on I'd bent over my computer in my bedroom at 7:03 to zap out a quick entry on *Streetdreamer*:

> Sixty-six days and counting 'til I hit the Street and suddenly I'm thinking niche market. I heard yesterday about a New York outfit called Ars Longa that sounds like it plays to some of my strengths. How cool would it be to waltz on to the Street with a starter-client? Not one in a thousand new associates does that. Thing is, I can't track these people down. No website and they're not in the book. All I want is a fifteen-minute face-to-face with a decision-maker. Give me a lead and you've got a friend for life. Streetdreamer

I knew it was a million-to-one shot, but why not? I mean, go for it, right? Now I itched to see whether I'd provoked anything.

Once the pastor got into his gut-ripping blame eulogy, my cold detachment evaporated, at least for the thirty-five minutes or so that he spoke. Here was President Obama on steroids and blazing with passion instead of studied cool. I wasn't in tears or shouting *Amen!* like most of the women there, but he had me going.

"Tell ya who *I'm* gonna blame," he roared, smacking the chest of that purple robe with the heel of his right hand. "I'm gonna blame the man. That's right. I'm gonna blame *the man* who wasn't there. The man who made this beautiful baby named TIE-rell and then for eighteen years had more important things to do than help raise him. Jocanda Washington, you all know Jocanda. Yes you do. She's a fine woman. She's a *great* woman. She loves Jesus and she loved TIE-rell. She did everything she could. Everything she knew how. But ain't no woman can raise a son all by herself. A daughter, yes, that can be done. But a boy needs a man. And TIE-rell didn't have one. That man who wasn't there, he's the one killed TIE-rell, just as sure as if he'd stuck that knife in himself. You men here, you better be *there* when your boy needs you. 'Cause God is watching, children, oh yes he is. God is watching, you *know* he is. And if he doesn't like what he sees, he's liable to do somethin' about it *you* won't like much. Yes he is. Just ask pharaoh. Pharaoh didn't like what God did to him, now did he? Well you're not gonna like what happens to you, either, if you're not where you need to be and we end up like we are today with a young man oughta be workin' and playin' basketball lyin' in a *box* instead 'cause he didn't have a *man* when he needed one."

He went on for a while in that vein. He said that God sent angels on horseback to whip fathers who didn't guide their sons right, and he quoted something from the Old Testament to prove his point. A guy two pews in front of me looked around as if he suddenly heard hoofbeats thundering up the center aisle.

"I'll say one more thing," the pastor promised as my watch crept toward eleven. "One more thing. I want you to hear this now. When we lay TIE-rell to rest later this morning, we will be burying an *innocent* man. That's right. *IN-NO-CENT*. That's not me talking. That's not Reverend Demetrius. That's not Deacon Khalil. No sir. No, that's the *court* talking. That's what the *court* says."

He flourished a copy of my motion, which struck me as a bit optimistic but a real good bet all the same. This was a real crowd-pleaser. He had the congregation on its feet, whooping *Hallelujah!* and *Amen!* and *Thank you, Jesus!* I got to my feet to be polite, but I couldn't quite bring myself to yell. I felt like a Rotarian from Milwaukee at the premiere of *Rent*.

The service closed with two more hymns and a benediction. I hung back as the congregation filed out and then exited as inconspicuously as I could when the pallbearers began taking their posts around the casket. Just outside the door I found what looked like most of the congregation still there, lined up on both sides in rows going all the way down the steps and across the sidewalk, almost all the way to the hearse parked on the street. I had reached the sidewalk and was looking for a path to the rear of the group on the left when I felt a hand nudge my right elbow. Glancing over my right shoulder I found myself look-ing into the eyes of Reverend Demetrius, still robed. His snow white hair fringed a face the color and texture of saddle leather. He nodded at me and made a little gesture with his right hand toward the hearse.

A bespectacled woman who could have been anywhere from her late thirties to her early fifties walked over to me with a stately, deliberate pace.

"Is she the one?"

Rev D nodded.

Without warning she flung herself on me with a rib-cracking hug that pinned my arms to my sides. Sobbing, she laid her head on my shoulder.

"Oh bless you, child. God bless you, you sweet, sweet wonderful child." She choked the words out between sobs.

"Yes, ma'am," I murmured a couple of times.

"Can you come to the cemetery?" She stepped back, looking into my eyes with desperate longing. "You can ride with me."

"Now, Jocanda—" the reverend began.

"Sure." I said this on pure impulse. "Of course I can come. I'd be honored to come."

I followed her to the edge of the sidewalk and waited with her while the pallbearers brought the casket solemnly out and slid it into the back of the hearse. Then we climbed together into the backseat.

Even through light morning traffic and a bit north of the heart of downtown, the trip to the cemetery took a good twenty minutes. Jocanda Washington spent the journey telling me about Tyrell. He had a bad streak, she said, she knew that. Part of him had the devil in him and try as she might she couldn't beat it out of him. But he wasn't all bad. Part of him was good. Part of him was really, truly good, you know? He just loved his little nieces and nephews, loved them to pieces. Brought them things and liked to be around them. Hadn't been for that no-good girl he hooked up with…. I held her hands and listened and nodded and said *yes* every once in awhile, just for luck.

By the time we were graveside she had finished her catharsis and I slipped guiltlessly into the background again. The family group in the front row at the edge of the grave held hands while two guys from the funeral home who could have played defensive tackle for the Steelers lowered the casket snugly into place. Twenty-third psalm, naturally, then the thing from Romans about how if we have died with Christ we believe we are also to live with him. Ken had drafted me to read the New American Bible version of that one at Mom's funeral. After the readings Jocanda threw a trowel-full of soil into the grave to rattle dully against the casket.

At that point, a man stepped forward. He stopped and stood arrow-straight at the foot of the grave. Fifty if he was a day, thinner than day-old tea, and he could have talked eye-to-eye with Paul. He was wearing a maroon blazer with shiny brass buttons, but the rest of his clothing—shirt, tie, pants, socks, and shoes—was black. He carried a saxophone, supported by a strap over his left shoulder. No one introduced him, and he didn't say a word. Just raised that sax to his mouth and belted out something mournful and bluesy in a Dixieland sort of way. I didn't recognize it, but when I hummed an approximation of the tune for Vince that night he said it might have been "Beale Street Blues."

When the last note had died in the leaden November sky, people began to shuffle toward cars parked a hundred yards or so away. They'd be heading back to the church for a reception, so I figured I'd cadge a ride to within walking distance of a hotel with a cabstand. (This is Pittsburgh. This is not New York. You do not just stroll out onto the sidewalk and hail a cab.) Reverend Demetrius, now in a deep red clerical shirt with a white collar under a black cloak with white satin lining, intercepted me. He had another man with him whom I recognized as the deacon who had announced the hymns and read the first piece of scripture at the funeral.

"Deacon Khalil would be pleased to drive you back to your office, Miss Jakubek."

"Thank you. I appreciate that."

"Thank you for coming. 'You too are living stones, built as an edifice of the spirit.'"

"You're welcome. It was an honor to be here. I'm glad I came."

Khalil led me to an enormous Chevy Suburban, the kind of thing you could cram eight or nine kids into if you needed to get a Sunday School class to a church picnic or something. He made sure I could clamber into the front passenger seat without a boost—it was a pretty close question—and then pulled himself wordlessly behind the wheel.

During our half-hour trip downtown to Mendoza's shop Khalil handled the SUV like a Driver Education poster boy. He kept his hands in the ten-to-two position. He kept his eyes on the road. He stayed at the posted speed limit. He not only signaled turns, he signaled lane changes. He came to a full and complete stop at all red lights and stop signs. He drove, in other words, like a guy who did *not* want to give any cop an excuse to pull him over and check him out on the squad car computer. He radiated a zenlike calm throughout the journey, betraying a trace of nervousness only at the end, when he had to double-park for twenty seconds in front of Mendoza-land.

"Thanks for the ride," I said as I hopped out.

"You're welcome." Those were the only words he spoke to me the entire time. When I'd given him Mendoza's address he'd just nodded, and he'd done the same thing when I'd suggested a turn or a particular street. I'd taken one stab at starting a conversation, asking him how long he'd known Reverend Demetrius. He had shaken his head, not so much in negation, it seemed to me, but more as a suggestion that this question involved an impenetrable enigma far beyond the grasp of mortal discourse.

Riding the elevator up to the office I realized I was feeling something odd, a kind of warm, gauzy giddiness combined with a belly-tingling excitement. It was a rush, but with more texture than, say, a pot or margarita high. I'd played the usual legal game, danced the intricate gavotte with doctrine and prec-edent, but this was something new. This time I'd actually made a difference in the life of a human being. I hadn't just stroked my ego and flexed my intellectual muscles. I'd touched Jocanda

Washington's life. Neat. I realized that Mendoza had made me go to the funeral so that I could have this feeling.

I was ready to dive onto my computer as soon as I got to my cubicle, but I saw the red message-waiting light blinking on my phone. Odd how peremptory that seems, how compulsory. How many people can ignore it for a couple of minutes while they check their emails or sort papers? Not many that I've noticed. I punched the right buttons and retrieved the message.

"Walter Learned here. I feel a bit sheepish because I just realized that the card I gave you doesn't tell you how to contact me. That card is a marvelous cachet of exclusivity with insiders, but not much help to anyone else. In any event, if you do get to New York you can reach me at this number." He recited a telephone number with a 212 area code that matched the one on my caller i.d. screen.

I forgot all about checking my blog. I hustled over to Becky the Techie with the number. It took her less than a minute to tell me it was assigned to an off-the-shelf mobile phone with prepaid minutes, not associated with any address. That didn't surprise me. Instead of taking the edge off my mounting excitement, it ratcheted the feeling up a couple of notches.

I impatiently checked Mendoza's office and saw that he was just putting his London Fog on a coat hook after getting back from the Caitlin interview. I managed to contain myself until he'd gotten behind his desk and sat down. Then I knocked and barged in.

"How was the funeral?"

"Very special. Thanks for sending me."

"Glad you could cover it. Something else on your mind?"

"I just got a voice mail from Learned. We now have a phone number for him, but we can't track it to an address."

That got his attention. He looked up at me, frowning deeply.

"You are *really* hot to go to New York, aren't you?"

I shrugged casually and decided that two of us could play head games if that was what he wanted. "How did Caitlin's interview with the cops go?"

"That's a good answer, *chica*." He leaned back in his chair and pointed a pencil at me. "The killed-my-brother line didn't come up and neither did mom's 'not yet' crack, but they have more than a passing interest in Caitlin. After all, the odds say that a relative iced Bradshaw. I expect their working theory is that mom did it and Caitlin knows things she isn't saying."

"So we definitely want to get them interested in the art heist angle in order to bring some unrelated suspects on stage?"

"Yes. But this Walter Learned theory was one thing when he was a puttering art dabbler. It became a totally different matter when Becky found out that he's spent his entire adult life under the radar. You have to work at it to bring that off, and if someone is working that hard at something, there's a reason for it."

"I'm not planning on playing Mike Hammer in drag." I could see where he was going with this. "I'm not going to seduce him so that I can rifle his files while he snores away in postcoital contentment."

"Watch the dirty talk, Jake. This is a respectable establishment."

"I'm just going to see if I can somehow pin him to an address we can hand to the police."

"You're a lawyer, not an investigator."

"I'm a lawyer Learned knows and chose to call. Besides, I'll take Paul with me."

"A *novelist*? You'll have a *novelist* watching your back? Yeah, that'll scare the hoods, all right. They'll be wetting their pants."

"I met Paul at a fight outside Fenway Park." This happened to be true. "Punk from Southie said I 'looked like one fine lady' and wouldn't take no for an answer. Paul intervened, the punk insisted, push came to shove, two punches. Paul threw the second."

"Well, decking a south Boston punk at Fenway is more impressive than bitch-slapping an MIT student at Starbucks, I guess," Mendoza said. "Tell you what: I'll think about it."

I returned to my cubicle with the kind of feeling I've heard trial lawyers get when the jury is out and they really don't know which way it's going to go. Pulse racing a bit, I clicked up my blog to see if this morning's entry had provoked any useful responses. The first thing I read was *Four Comments*. Everything after that was a let-down.

"'Starter client?' You're not dreaming, Streetdreamer, you're delusional. No Wall Street firm would want the kind of client you could bring in." *GR8Lawyer*

"Quit kidding yourself, Streetdreamer. They didn't hire you to be a rainmaker. They hired you to spend 11 hours a day in front of a computer screen reviewing documents and researching Rule 10-b-5 and Sarbanes-Oxley." *Bntherednthat*

"Two points, Streetdreamer. One: If this potential client is worth having, someone already has it and no wet-behind-the-ears greenhorn who hasn't even knocked the felt off her antlers yet is going to take it away from him. Two: If, by some wild chance you did manage to bring a 'starter client' in, a partner would steal the credit for it before the ink was dry on the intake." *darrowIwish*.

"Tell me this, streetdreamer: If I had a lead on Ars Longa or whatever it is, why wouldn't I just go after it myself?" *2smart2dream*

I tried to restrain myself. I really did. After a valiant effort lasting fifteen seconds or so, I typed a reply to the third comment.

"To *darrowIwish*:

"Two points. One: Only male deer have antlers, so 'her antlers' is incoherent. Two: 'greenhorn who hasn't even knocked the felt off her antlers' is both incoherent and redundant. What makes a greenhorn's horns green is that there's still felt on the antlers because he (*see* point one) isn't mature enough yet to get sexually aroused and start banging his antlers against tree trunks to get rid of the felt and thereby impress chicks—excuse me, *does*."

I completed the post and was ready to click off the blog in frustration when Mendoza came strolling up. He was holding a sheet of paper tri-folded around something green.

"Okay, Jake, you win. Here's two hundred dollars for walking around money and a list of hotels where you can stay for under two-fifty a night. We'll cover your mileage at the IRS rate, which I think is over half-a-buck a mile now, so you should make out okay on that. No sense going up 'til Sunday because Thanksgiving weekend tourists will be filling every hotel room in the city through Saturday night."

"Got it." I took the page and the money from him.

"I want you goddamn back here by Tuesday morning and in one piece."

"Will do. Thanks."

He sighed and left. For the second time in thirty seconds I reached for the mouse to click off my blog. I heard a little *boink!*, indicating that I had just drawn another comment. Probably *darrowIwish* telling me that donkeys don't go to college because no one likes a smart ass, or something just as screamingly original. I glanced at the new message:

"Didn't anyone ever warn you about strangers with candy, Streetdreamer?" *demoticdiscretion.*

Chapter Ten

As soon as I tasted the gravy I figured Vince's second marriage was a done deal and the only question was when I could stop at Sully's to buy the rice. Lainie Banacek hadn't poured this stuff from a jar into a saucepan to heat it up on the stove. She'd made it from scratch, in-the-pan, with turkey broth, turkey drippings, flour, milk, salt, pepper, and butter (*not* margarine) that she'd left out on the counter overnight to soften. I couldn't believe the flavor. I closed my eyes to savor my first mouthful. I wondered if it would be too gauche not to bother using the turkey and potatoes as carriers and just pour a slug of the stuff into a coffee cup so I could drink it straight.

Seven of us gathered at 2:30 Thanksgiving afternoon around the Banacek table—strike that, *tables*, plural. To make room for seven, Lainie had had Vince and, unofficially, me hump the kitchen table into the dining room and put it end-to-end a tad unevenly with the dining room table. Lainie's oldest daughter, Barbara, and her husband, Stan, joined us along with their pair of rug rats whose names I didn't bother to remember. Lainie seated herself at the head, with Barbara to her right and Vince to her left. I sat between Barbara and her six-year-old boy, across from Stan, who was sandwiched by Vince and an eight-year-old girl. No one sat at the end, but a full place setting, including folded napkin, wine glass, and goblet filled with ice water, occupied the table space in front of an empty chair.

"Who's the plate at the end for?" the girl asked after her third mouthful of turkey.

"For family members who can't be here because they're serving with our armed forces," Lainie said. "Mr. Jakubek's son, Mike, is a sergeant with the Army in Afghanistan."

"Oh."

Stan and Barb exchanged glances.

"It's a family tradition," Lainie continued. "Your great-grandmother always set an extra place on Thanksgiving and Christmas when Mr. Banacek was serving in the Vietnam War."

"Oh." The girl took a second to digest that, then looked back at Lainie. "We've been in, like, lots of wars, haven't we?"

"Yes," I answered, after no one else seemed anxious to field that one. "Most of them someplace else—which beats the alternative."

"Oh." She took a stab—literally—at some stuffing, without moving her eyes from me. "That's a nice ring."

"Thank you."

"Does it mean that you're going steady with someone?"

"Something like that."

"Ms. Jakubek is engaged, dear," Barbara explained.

"You're getting married?" The girl's widening eyes left no doubt that I had just become a vastly more interesting person.

"That's the plan."

"Have you set a date yet?" Stan drew a glare from Barbara, who must have recognized this as a potentially delicate topic.

"Not yet. We're sort of at the L-O-I stage."

"I'm sorry." Barbara now turned her gaze to me. "L-O-I?"

"Letter of intent. Like for a business merger? It's like we have an agreement in principle, but we're still dotting i's and crossing t's and we're not ready to close yet."

"Law school humor," Vince said with a bemused head shake.

"I see." A millisecond after this response Barbara swiveled her head toward Lainie. "How do you always get the stuffing to come out so crisp on the outside and so moist on the inside?"

Vince picked that moment to ask Stan how business was.

"You know what, it's not all that bad. If you can turn a wrench and tell a differential from a brake pad you can make a living anywhere in this country, no matter what the economy is doing. Unemployment rate goes up, people figure they'd better nurse the old buggy through another winter and they bring 'em in to get 'em fixed."

"That's the gospel according to Pro Tools all right," Vince said.

"Well, they got that right. You know what's got the biggest enrollment at Allegheny County Community College, term after term?"

"I'm guessing automotive mechanics."

"Yep." Stan emphasized the syllable with an emphatic nod. "They got more than sixty students this term, and they've put out an RFP for eighty starter tool kits for next September. *Eighty!* Barb saw a copy of the paperwork."

"So cash for clunkers didn't hurt?"

"You kiddin'? At least half those clunkers never made it to the junkyard, and someone had to fix 'em. And I'll tell you something else. Any parts department manager who didn't knock down twenty thousand for himself on side deals during that little boondoggle just wasn't trying."

This is interesting, I thought. *I don't have the faintest idea what he's talking about, and I have a funny feeling I should.*

I was about to jump in with a probing question when Vince and Stan segued into the Steelers, which they could talk about in perfect sync. Stan would talk while Vince chewed and swallowed turkey or dressing, and then Stan would shove some dressing or turkey into his mouth while Vince said something. In its own way it was a thing of beauty, like a Rockettes routine.

I turned back toward Barbara, only to catch the tail end of her next question to Lainie.

"...love the way your yams always come out tender without being mushy. How do you do that?"

With a brief shrug, I shifted my attention to the six-year-old. "Looks like we have a date, tiger."

He looked at me for three seconds before making his opening gambit. "Have you ever been in a war?"

"No. I avoided detention once by knowing who won the Battle of Bemis Heights, but that's not really the same thing."

"Girls don't fight in wars, dummy," the eight-year-old told her brother scornfully.

"You'd get an argument from Sergeant Mike on that one," I said.

"*SEE?*" the boy gleefully retorted to his sister. "You're the dummy."

"All right, that's enough, you two," Stan snapped. "Less lip and more jaw. Clean your plates."

Given the shortage of conversational partners, I started doing a little arithmetic: .55 x 370. The distance from Pittsburgh to New York City is 370 miles, and .55 cents per mile is the current IRS car-travel reimbursement rate. I'd checked. So that meant that if I drove Vince's Chevy to New York and back I'd be able to give Mendoza a chit for $387, plus parking in the Big Apple. After taking out enough to cover the gas that I planned to pay for with my credit card, Vince would still net well north of $300 for letting me use the Chevy over the weekend.

This multiplication was part of my being totally pumped about going to New York. I mean totally. *Not* because I particularly gave two rips about stalking Walter Learned. That was fun and games, an interesting break from cubicle grunt work. No, I was totally pumped about going to New York because I saw this trip as a foretaste of my real legal career—my real *life*. I'd been held up at the terminal gate for sixteen months now. This little jaunt wasn't anything close to a takeoff, but at least I was taxiing toward the runway.

Let's see. Three-hundred-seventy miles at, let's be realistic here, sixty per. If I pull out of the driveway by nine a.m. Sunday and if Paul can cab it from Grand Central, we can be in a hotel room together by 3:30 Sunday afternoon. No, wait, I forgot about Mass. Nuts. Vince will freak out if I skip Mass. So, eight o'clock Mass, pull

out by nine fifteen, we're still in the room before four. Or I could go
to Mass at 5:00 Saturday evening and—No, wait.

At that point a very interesting idea starting taking shape. I
got a little tingle from it, and I definitely didn't need any more
conversation. The buzz carried me through the pumpkin pie.

The look on Stan's face when Vince offered to help with the
dishes was priceless. Lainie responded exactly as I had predicted.

"No, of course not, dear, you're our *guest*. Barbara and I can
handle it."

I suddenly found myself in a rather delicate position. Barbara
was as much Lainie's guest as Vince was. True, she was Lainie's
daughter, but just because someone gave you time-outs when
you were eight doesn't mean she can stick you with chores when
you're over thirty and have kids of your own. What really distinguished Barbara from Vince was that in Lainie's world women
did the Thanksgiving dishes and men watched the Detroit Lions
lose a football game on television. Way fifties, but so what? If I
shirked KP I'd still feel like a jerk. I decided not to feel like a jerk.
I loaded up an armful of dessert plates and squeezed through
the kitchen doorway with my burden.

"That's all right, dear." Lainie gasped audibly at the site of
a non-Banacek holding more than one piece of her best china.
"Barbara and I are used to this."

I suppose I could have taken that as a no and waltzed out, but
I'm stubborn. I knew that I wouldn't be trusted with anything
really important, like hand-washing the silver and the stemware
and putting them out to air-dry on dishtowels laid out on the
kitchen counter. I thought, though, that I might be allowed to
scour the broiling pan or load the dishwasher. Then I saw the
turkey carcass still sitting on the cutting board where Vince had
sliced off the breast meat and the drumsticks. Taking care of
that thing was a sloppy, greasy job that mom had always cajoled
Vince into doing.

"Tell you what. How about if I handle the leftover turkey?"

"Well, actually, that would be a help, Cindy, if you really
don't mind," Lainie said.

"Do you have any, like, Tupperware for the meat?"

Barbara, to her credit, managed not to show her undoubted disgust at my ignorance of elementary kitchen jargon. She brought out a china casserole dish and lined it deftly with wax paper. Then she got out of the way as I started making things happen with the carving knife and a long-handled fork.

This kind of thing takes about twenty minutes if you do it right. And you really should do it right. Cold turkey sandwiches for the rest of the weekend are even better than the roast turkey hot from the oven on Thanksgiving day itself.

While I was slicing away, I glanced a couple of times through the window at the backyard. The rug rats were throwing a football around, shyly joined by a kid from down the block who looked about seven. It was so genuine. So real. So American. *Yeah*, I thought, *this is what I really want. This is exactly what I want. I want to see kids playing in the yard of a single-family home. I want to see it once or twice a year, through a window in someone else's house. The rest of the year I want to look out my window and see smog and concrete.*

I folded the wax paper over the salvaged turkey meat and then covered the whole shebang with aluminum foil, just to make sure, before I slid it into the fridge. I felt thoroughly satisfied with my work. The turkey skeleton looked like the booby prize at a buzzards-and-jackals convention. Taking the top off the kitchen trash can, I dumped the remains into the garbage bag inside, which pretty much filled it up. I pulled the garbage bag out, tied it up, lugged it over to the kitchen door, and set it next to another bag that Lainie and Barbara had filled.

I thought of summoning the eight-year-old to carry the bags out to the garbage cans in the garage, just to raise her consciousness about stereotyping gender roles. But I didn't. I took the greasy things for their last walk myself. I returned to the kitchen ready to take the rest of the afternoon off with a clear conscience. Lainie and Barbara had things well in hand. The dishwasher was humming, the dish-drainer beside the sink was laden with assorted pots and pans, and the silver and stemware were soaking in clean, sudsy water.

"Let me know if I can do anything else." I said this with polite insincerity as I headed for the door. I already had one foot in the dining room when Lainie promised that she would.

I was checking my Droid when I joined Vince and Stan in the den, watching the Lions lose, albeit not quite as disgracefully as they usually do. They—Vince and Stan, not the Lions—took up rather more than two-thirds of the couch between them, so I dropped to the carpet.

"Stan's right about the request for proposal from ACCC, Dad. It's posted online. 'Highest scoring responsible bidder.' I'll print out a copy for you when we get home."

"Like I have a shot at that." Vince shook his head with world-weary disgust. "That's a central sales office thing, not something for independent distributors. Pro Tools, Matco, and Cornwell will all be bidding on it. When the elephants dance, the squirrels get crushed."

"Right." I switched my Droid to its PDA app and pecked in PRNT OUT RFP.

Okay, back to the weekend. The idea that sprouted while I was doing mileage-math had pretty much blossomed by now. I was so excited that I almost broke our rule and called Paul instead of waiting for him to call me. I held off, though. What if he was cranking out six, seven pages an hour when my ringtone distracted him and broke his concentration? How could I ever handle the guilt? Instead of speed-dialing him I gazed at the TV screen and wondered how much of professional football is passion and how much is habit. It could be worse, of course. We could be watching golf.

Paul's number finally showed up on my Droid screen a little after five. I had nodded off, but the ring galvanized me. I popped up and brought the phone to my ear as I sprinted for the porch.

"Two thousand words. Almost."

"Get out."

"Scout's honor. I did an entire chapter."

"That's fantastic, lover."

"So what's new in Pittsburgh?"

"I've had a fabulous idea about the New York trip I sprang on you last night."

"Tell me about it."

"Do you want the long version or the Cliff Notes?"

"All the gory details, please."

"Okay. Number one, I still have over thirteen thousand dollars out of the fifty thousand Calder & Bull sent me. Taxes took a bite, but my burn rate for the last six months has only been a little over a thousand a month, so with just two months to go and the last 10K CD maturing in mid-December, I'm feeling pretty flush."

"You realize, of course, that because you're both smart and beautiful, other women will have two reasons to hate you."

"That's a chance I'm willing to take. Number two is that US Air will fly me to New York and back for only a couple-hundred more than the mileage reimbursement I'll get from Mendoza. And number three is that the Hilton New York in midtown will charge me close to two hundred a night more than the hotels on the approved list Mendoza gave me, and I just realized that I don't care. I mean, I've got the money. I've only got two months left before I start earning a decent salary. Why not go ahead and drop, say, twenty-five hundred bucks doing New York right instead of cheaping out?"

"I love the premise. What's the plan?"

"We go up Saturday instead of Sunday. I'll fly in instead of driving. We can stay two nights. The Hilton still has rooms."

"You're a genius."

"Can you get off work?"

"Screw work. I mean, Cindy, this is just *so great*. It makes the whole thing seem so real."

"Exactly." No other adverb would do. My fiancé had just nailed it.

"Only thing is, being a kept man at a Holiday Inn on Seventh Avenue is one thing. Having that status at the Hilton will require some adjustment."

"Don't worry. You can pay off your share of the hotel bill by giving me back rubs."

Our conversation took a more intimate turn at that point. At that moment I felt deeply, truly happy in a way that I couldn't remember feeling for a long time. Which is kind of sad, when you think about it, but there it is.

Chapter Eleven

It's not like the Hilton New York is a luxury crib. Most lawyers with *AmLaw 100* firms would probably call it middle of the pack. A good, solid hotel with decently sized rooms, reliable plumbing, clean sheets, Wi-Fi, some premium cable channels, and waiters who can speak English.

When I finally got into my room around 3:10 Saturday afternoon, though, it seemed like a little piece of heaven. I'd had the usual aggravations negotiating the security checkpoint at the airport after shuffling through a long, snaking line to get there. My flight sat on the ground in Pittsburgh for forty-five minutes after boarding so that they could change a lightbulb in the control panel or something. After we finally took off, the pilot managed to find every patch of turbulence east of the Allegheny Mountains, and it must have taken us twenty minutes after we landed at LaGuardia to reach the gate. No courtesy van for the Hilton at the airport. My cabbie drove like a suicide bomber and scowled at a ten percent tip. The Hilton didn't have my room ready when I checked in, so I had to leave my TravelPro and its duct-taped handle with the concierge and kill two hours briskly striding along Broadway and Fifth Avenue in cold, late November weather. When I got to the discount ticket booth near Father Duffy's statue the cupboard was bare, at least for any show that was worth a damn.

And I didn't care. I was here. New York, where it was all going to start happening soon for Cindy Jakubek. I didn't care about the thread-count on the sheets or how thick the carpet pile was or whether I could get BBC World News on the radio. This place was just fine. As soon as I was unpacked and had left a voice mail at Learned's number I took a shower—not so much because I really needed a shower as because it gave me an excuse to wrap my squeaky-clean self in a decadently luxurious Hilton room robe while I swigged ice water and posted all the naïve exuberance you just read on my blog.

I had finished the post and was pulling my jeans back on when my mobile phone chirped. Paul's number blinked at me in the window. I had offered to buy Paul a plane ticket from Philly, but that didn't jibe with the live-by-his-wits, street-smart hustler narrative he's been writing for himself since Harvard cashed the last big check his grandfather's trust fund would ever write. Paul had cadged a ride from a buddy who could get him as far as Newark International, and figured he'd take a cab from there.

"What's up, tiger? Did Newark work out okay?"

"Perfect. Had to say no to some guy who offered to carry my computer bag and show me where the cabs are."

"Good move."

"He must've thought I was from Indiana or someplace instead of Philly." Paul sounded buoyant. "Anyway, I found the cabs all by myself and we've made it to Manhattan, but the cabbie is having trouble locating midtown."

"If he's a Newark cabbie you're lucky he found the George Washington Bridge. How hungry are you?"

"I'm starving. Hold on a sec." In my Technicolor imagination I saw Paul pressing his nose up against the Plexiglas screen between the front and back seats and addressing the cabbie with urgent exasperation. "Hilton Midtown….Hil-ton Mid-town. It's a hotel….No! Not *Lex. Sixth*! Just because they both have an x in them….Sixth *Avenue!*….Jesus!"

"Try Avenue of the Americas," I suggested.

"That's just for tourists."

"Doesn't sound like your guy is a native."

"Not far from Thirty Rock." Paul was addressing the cabbie again. "You know where Thirty Rock is, right?"

"How about Saint Patrick's Cathedral?" I offered this helpful suggestion just before I dimly heard a cabbie voice saying something that might have been *Allah Akbar!* "No, second thought, scratch St. Pat's."

"He's calling his dispatcher for directions. I'll bet Damon Runyon never had to put up with this kind of bullshit."

"Tell you what." I checked my watch. "It's pushing four thirty. How about if I order room service in ten minutes. You and the food should arrive about the same time. We can eat an early dinner and talk about what to do tonight."

"Deal. Ibn Saud here just found a street going uptown, so I might even have time to freshen up before they wheel the table in."

"New York strip medium rare, right?"

"Roger that," Paul confirmed. "See you sometime between now and midnight."

I clicked off my Droid and dug out the room service menu to see if I could find something tasty that had never had a mother. Waldorf salad. Close enough. When I punched the In-Room-Dining button on the room phone, I got someone who sounded like she was just a tiny bit tired of talking to people who speak louder and more slowly when they hear a Latina accent. I don't do that. I got the order placed, absorbed her promise that it would be up within twenty-five to forty-five minutes, cradled the phone—and suddenly saw a red light blinking.

Couldn't be Paul, because he would have called my mobile phone. Learned, maybe? Except I was sure I'd left my mobile phone number for him as well. I pushed a button above an exquisitely anachronistic envelope icon.

Not Learned. Turns out I'd gotten a fax—which didn't make a lot of sense. Hmm. Ordinarily I would have gone down to get the thing myself, but I didn't want to risk missing the room-service delivery if it came early. I asked the sort of nice person who was talking to me to have someone bring it up.

Then I went back to doing the hotel thing. Making the most of a hotel experience involves both art and science. I'd gotten a taste of it during recruiting season, when half-a-dozen firms had put me up overnight on callbacks, and I'd refined my technique while traveling a few times with Judge Mercado. By now I had it down pretty well: Two thick pillows plopped vertically against the headboard with Cindy's head and shoulders nestled in them; raspberry Snapple bought from a CVS during my walk (instead of bottled water taken from the grotesquely overpriced minibar) within reach on the nightstand; Kindle in my lap and TV remote beside me; tube on and flipping at my whim among WABC, CNN, and whatever college football contest ESPN had decided was this week's Game of the Century.

That's it. Unstructured time. Vastly more self-indulgent than dropping almost a hundred bucks on dinner for two, as I'd be doing within an hour. Pure me-time. For twenty minutes I was going to make Marie Antoinette look like a Calvinist.

Paul made it before the food. I gave him the room number when he called from the lobby, muted U.S.C. versus Washington or whatever it was, and bounded to the door when I heard his knock. He was wearing a Navy peacoat, an olive drab watch cap, and khaki pants, all while carrying a duffel bag with camouflage coloring. Military surplus by Benneton. The only thing he had that didn't look like he'd picked it up at a Pentagon rummage sale was his black leather computer bag.

I could have restrained myself but I didn't. With an elated yelp that would have scandalized Jane Austen I leaped on him to hug his neck with my arms and his hips with my legs as soon as I'd swung the door open. He barely had time to drop the duffel bag and computer satchel. He caught me with a game and delighted *OOF!*, wrapped his left arm around my back, and wedged his right arm underneath my fanny to hold me in place for a kiss full of passion and longing. I hungrily filled my nose with the scent of Dial soap, Old Spice, and Head and Shoulders, pressed my upper lip into the bristles of his moustache, and tasted the

McDonald's french fries that still lingered in his mouth despite the breath mint he'd popped.

"Someone is going to tell us to get a room," Paul whispered.

"We already have one."

"Race you there."

He carried me into the room and let me slide down his body to the floor.

"I win by a tush," I murmured, since my fanny had crossed the threshold before the rest of me and all of him. "Don't forget your bags."

It took Paul less than ten seconds to truck his modest luggage into the room. While he was doing that I checked the clock. We had a maximum of eighteen minutes left on the room service delivery window, and what Paul had in mind figured to take about seven of them. When we locked eyes after he closed the door behind him, the only question I had was whether he'd bother to shuck his coat first.

Paul peeled off the watch cap and started to remove his coat—you can always tell an Ivy Leaguer. He had the coat down to mid-bicep on both sides when a knock sounded and a lilting voice called, "*Roooom* service!"

Paul's face fell like a ten-year-old who'd just been served carrot cake at his birthday party. I went to get the door while he hustled out of the way. The room service guy wheeled in a linen-covered cart. He flashed me a suggestive little *I-was-young-once-myself* smile implying that he knew exactly what was going on. While Paul finished shedding his coat and got his computer plugged in, the waiter took half-dome covers off our entrées with a showy *voila* gesture, and then handed me a cute little leatherette folder.

I examined the bill, because that's the kind of thing you do if your dad was a machinist. $39.95 for the steak, natch. $23.95 for the salad. Ouch. On the plus side, they didn't charge us for the glasses of ice water. $11.50 for "Gratuity," thoughtfully computed for me by the In-Room Dining people at 18% so that I wouldn't have to do any math. (They'd left a blank space for "Tip" in case I wanted to improve on the "gratuity," but I figured 18% was plenty for taking off two plate covers.) Tax of $7.54. And $5.50 for a "Room Service Charge."

$88.47. Well over a week's groceries for the five of us when I was growing up. *Pang!* The thing that really griped me was the separate room service charge. I was paying the Hilton New York Hotel $5.50 to have a guy who probably wasn't bringing home $10.00 an hour take a five-minute elevator ride. It wasn't that I couldn't afford it or hadn't realized that it was part of the package. It just seemed *wrong*, a kind of greed-is-good excess for its own sake, like lighting a cigar with a ten-dollar bill.

Oh well, welcome to New York. I signed the chit with a flourish and smilingly returned it, as if spending the GDP of Botswana on dinner was the kind of thing I did every day.

The door closed. Paul looked directly at me. Then he turned his head thirty degrees and looked directly at twelve ounces of well-marbled beef on a plate. When he looked back at me, I had a pretty good idea of which way this one was going.

"Personally," he said, "I think steak at room temperature tastes great."

I felt waves of temptation pounding relentlessly against the leaky dike of my conscience. At that moment I wanted sexual intimacy with him more than I've ever wanted chocolate, and that's saying something. But I knew that Paul had been living on Big Macs and baloney sandwiches since our last meal together, and steak at room temperature sucks. Sex is important, but not as important as love.

"We're grown-ups." I hoped he'd recognize my primness as self-mockery. "We can prioritize our appetites."

He folded me in an embrace that took my breath away—that's a physical observation, not a metaphor.

"I love it when you talk dirty. Say it again.'"

"Pri*ori*tize our *ap*petites," I repeated in a breathy voice. Then I bit his earlobe.

"*Ow!*" He clapped his right hand over his ear. "I thought you were a vegetarian."

"I make exceptions. Let's eat while the meals are still fresh."

We sat down at the service cart with all the finesse of a couple of ninth-graders copping feels at a mixer behind the chaperones' backs. Paul swung a desk chair over to the salad end of the cart and gallantly took the corner of the bed as his own seat. I let him swallow three generous slices of steak before I introduced the next topic on my Paul agenda.

"So, after we've wallowed in carnal lust for a while, what would you like to do for the rest of the evening?"

"It wouldn't exactly break my heart to wallow in carnal lust until dawn."

"Interesting thought." I tried not to sound judgmental, but a novelist is an observer and Paul picked up the subtle cue.

"I know," he said, acknowledging my unspoken demurrer. "We're in New York City. We're within walking distance of Broadway and a subway ride from the Village. We shouldn't spend all night in a generic hotel room that could just as easily be in Philly or Cleveland. You're absolutely right."

"I couldn't find any tickets at the discount booth. But we could go online and see what's still available at full price. Everything on Broadway can't be SRO, even if it is Thanksgiving weekend."

"We could." Paul sliced some steak. " Or there's probably an indie-cult film festival going on in Tribeca or something where we could see some stuff that'll never show up at your local multi-plex. Or—what's that?"

"What's what?"

"Someone just slipped a white envelope under your door."

"Oh, that's gotta be the fax someone sent me. I told them to send it up."

"Should you check it out? I mean, could be from your boss or something, right?"

What he meant was, *check it now while I'm still eating steak instead of fifteen minutes from now when I'm planning on doing something else.* I grinned at him around a juicy bit of apple from the salad. Then I fetched the envelope. Inside I found a Hilton fax cover sheet and one other sheet of paper:

CYNTHIA JAKUBEK, ESQ.

GREETINGS!

YOU HAVE BEEN SELECTED—BY THE SELECTIVE
LEGAL SERVICES SYSTEM! BRING THIS PAPER TO 75
PARK AVENUE, 40TH FLOOR, AT 8:00 **TONIGHT**—
SATURDAY, NOVEMBER 27TH—FOR ADMISSION TO A
RECEPTION FOR NEW YORK'S NEXT GENERATION OF
LEGAL SUPERSTARS!

MEET, GREET, EAT, DRINK, AND NETWORK!

SPONSORED BY THE ASSOCIATION OF THE BAR OF
THE CITY OF NEW YORK, IN COOPERATION WITH THE
LEADING FIRMS LISTED BELOW:

A list of twelve law firms on anyone's A-List followed. Calder
& Bull was one of them.

I started to hand it to Paul, and then realized that that would
be inconsiderate. I laid it on the table where he could read it
without slowing up his knife-and-fork work. As a future Wall
Street associate, I could appreciate the value of multitasking.
He looked at it while he swallowed a piece of steak, speared
another piece, looked back at it while he chewed that one, and
then looked up at me.

"Command performance?"

I am deeply ashamed to admit that I didn't say no instantly.
For five long seconds I actually thought about whether I should
say yes, even though I'd hate myself in the morning. Then a little
blue-collar pride asserted itself. Okay, I was selling out. But I
was selling out for a hundred-and-a-half a year, not for a free
cosmopolitan. You want to give me three hours notice that I'll
be working all night on a preliminary injunction brief—fine.
But not for a cocktail party when you're not even paying my
health insurance premiums yet.

"No. Tonight belongs to you."

"God, I love it when you talk dirty."

"You already used that line."

"It keeps working." He polished off more steak. "I wonder how they tracked you down here."

"Good question. They have my numbers at Mendoza's office, and I left contact information there for this weekend. Maybe they faxed it there and it got forwarded automatically."

"You have an automatic forwarding app?"

"I have every app there is. I bet this Droid could shine my shoes if I told it to."

"If you'd been in charge of the D-Day invasion," he said gravely, "we would have captured St.-Lo at H-Hour plus six— and we wouldn't have shot any prisoners."

Warmed by that charming blarney, I returned to my salad. Sexual tension sharpens the senses. Have you ever noticed that? The lettuce tasted crisper, the silverware felt heftier, the incidental sounds in the corridor seemed clearer, and every morsel of the dead steer that Paul lifted to his mouth seemed sharply defined.

Also, deferral enhances desire. That's my second Searing Insight of the Day. You see a slice of chocolate cake and you think it would taste good. But make yourself put off eating it for half-an-hour. Watch it become an obsession. Feel yourself salivating at every thought of it. Notice with clinical interest as the minutes tick away how you get to the point where you'd kill for the thing. As I sat there nibbling my rabbit food and watching Paul savor every juicy bite of his steak, the sense of breathless urgency spreading through my body got hotter and more volatile with each passing second.

I laid my fork down beside the almost empty salad bowl.

I took a sip of ice water.

I stood up deliberately, trembling with the effort at self-control.

Turning feverish eyes toward me, Paul hacked at the rapidly diminishing steak with the ferocity of a medieval knight trying to slice through enemy armor.

"Take your time." I walked around the bed to its far side, shoved the pillows out of the way, and turned down the cover and the top sheet with decisive briskness, like a medical examiner whipping the sheet off a corpse in preparation for an autopsy.

Paul's silverware clattered on his plate.

I undid the top button on my blouse.

Paul stood up and turned around.

I undid the second button.

Paul clambered onto the bed and began knee-walking across it toward me.

The room phone rang.

A scream of primal frustration erupted from Paul as he snapped his head back and smacked his fists with punishing force on his thighs.

Savvier than Paul in hotel-craft, I knew the call would be from In-Room Dining, asking if we were ready to have someone come after our table. I held an unconcerned index finger up toward Paul in a just-one-minute gesture with one hand while I answered the phone with the other.

"Hello," a cultivated voice said. "This is Walter Learned. I'm in the lobby. Is this a good time?"

Chapter Twelve

So that's how I found out that the one thing on Earth Paul wanted even more than sex with me was a decent New York apartment. For Paul's benefit, I slowly and distinctly repeated "Mis…ter Learn…ed" into the phone, like a special education teacher on a lame sitcom. Paul stopped in mid-pant. He nodded vigorously and gave me two thumbs up.

"Uh, yeah…*sure*," I said. "This is a great time. Just finished dinner. Room eighteen-oh-five."

"Look for me in five minutes."

I hung up the phone and focused on Paul.

"Five minutes isn't enough for a cold shower. Think of something anerotic, like Sarah Palin gutting a moose."

After primly rebuttoning my blouse and flicking a few insubordinate strands of hair back into place, I got the room service table out into the hall. I accomplished that just in time to see Learned striding from the elevator corridor with his oxblood attaché case swinging slightly in his right hand. His outfit today bore no resemblance to the country squire look he'd been sporting on Tuesday. He was wearing caramel colored cargo pants, Nike cross-trainers, and a Pendleton black-and-red plaid shirt, all under a parka that looked suitable for above the timberline.

"Very nice of you to see me on such short notice." He shook my hand warmly as I showed him into the room. "I happened to be in the neighborhood when I picked up your message. I'm going out of town on Monday so I thought I'd just stop by and try my luck."

"Are you kidding? You're offering us twenty-four carat gold. We'd crawl over broken glass to talk to you."

His eyebrows went up a well-bred eighth of an inch when I said "we'd," so I thought this might be a good time to introduce Paul. I did. He got the same reaction from Learned as he did from most people. One good look and "Whoa!" Not that Learned did anything as vulgar or obvious as gape. Still, you could tell from his body language the impression Paul made. I basked in complacent satisfaction. *That's right, he's smart, he's passionate, he could model for GQ—and he's mine.*

"Paul's writing a novel."

I realized as soon as the words were out of my mouth how limp they had to sound. At any given moment, half the adults in Manhattan are writing novels. But apparently genuine interest flickered in the eyes Learned turned toward Paul.

"Really? Genre or mainstream?"

"Postmodern." Paul actually blushed at the compliment of an intelligent question about his work.

"Good for you. That's a field sorely in need of fresh blood."

Learned flipped his attaché case onto the bed and shrugged out of the parka. By the time I had the parka hung up, he was discreetly checking out the Wi-Fi switch on my laptop.

"You want to use a computer?" I asked.

"If I may. I don't have hard copies of the material I'd like to show you, but if you're on Wi-Fi I can get it for you in about five minutes."

"Easily done."

My ThinkPad had gone into screen saver mode while Paul and I were dining and flirting, and now it wanted a password before doing any computer stuff. I swiped the tip of my right index finger over a metal sensor below the keyboard. An oblong box appeared on the screen, but instead of an inviting green check mark it flashed "TOO FAST" at me.

I tried again. "TOO SHORT."

"It must be channeling my ex-wife," Learned muttered from over my left shoulder.

I gave up on the swipe and typed my password in. I had to pause to be sure I remembered it correctly, because I don't use it very often, but I got it on the first try.

"It's all yours." I vacated the chair so that he could slip into it.

It took him about thirty seconds to get the hang of my ThinkPad, which has a miniature red ball and a couple of click-bars instead of a mouse. It's not what you'd call intuitive. Once he got rolling, though, he hit links at high speed and soon my screen filled with a tiny picture and a bunch of data.

"I could print this out for you to pick up in the Business Center," he said, "but I don't want to risk someone else glomming onto it. This information isn't for just anyone. My contact has a passion for anonymity."

"I'll make notes."

Four screens and ten minutes later I took a legal page full of Cindy-scrawls over to Paul. As he read through the data his eyes lit up. Four one-bedroom apartments ranging from twenty-six hundred to thirty-eight hundred a month, including utilities. No parking, but who needs parking in New York? Well, lots of people, but not Cindy and Paul. One in Brooklyn, but convenient to the subway, and the other three actually in Manhattan. Pretty far uptown except for the most expensive one, but even so. Twenty-six hundred would be a breeze, and we could swing thirty-eight without breaking too much of a sweat. I sensed Paul salivating.

"You won't find those on craigslist," Learned said. "Before I leave on Monday morning I can make a couple of calls. Mention my name when you contact the landlords and you should be able to get a look that day."

"I can't believe how incredible this is." I beamed at Learned. "I can't thank you enough."

"Actually, you can." He took a pint bottle of Johnny Walker Red from the attaché case. "How about a drink? I'll provide the scotch if you'll provide the water and the glasses."

There was something deliciously, absurdly retro about the gesture—as if we'd time-warped into a *Mad Men* episode without the Winstons. I've never really gotten into the cocktail-hour thing. My judge liked a Manhattan after dinner when we were traveling, and I think my generation has made martinis more popular than they've been since Sean Connery was playing James Bond, but counting the minutes until five thirty so you could have a guilt-free mixed drink always struck me as prewar, somehow—like Bridget Jones using a cigarette holder. There were four other clerks that I'd go to O'Brien's Tap with at the end of the day sometimes during my clerkship, and we got to where we had a standing order: Tanqueray with a twist, whiskey sour, seven-and-seven, cosmopolitan, and chardonnay. I was the chardonnay.

Paul ran for ice, I scrounged the glasses—two tumblers and a bathroom glass that neither of us had used yet—and in a few minutes we were cozily sharing scotch and water on the rocks, for all the world as if we were waiting for Cary Grant to stroll in.

"What I'd like to discuss now, if you have a few minutes," Learned said once we were all comfortable, "is how you *can* thank me for helping out in your apartment-hunting efforts."

"Anything within a zip code of legal and you're on." I sipped diluted scotch and liked it.

"Have you wondered why I've been paying so much attention to you since our chance encounter?"

"Charm and good looks?"

Learned smiled at that. He swirled scotch around his glass, took a sip, and swirled it again.

"Not exactly. It was something I overheard you say about the estate tax kicking back in for people who die after the first of next year. At first, in fact, I wondered whether you intended for me to overhear it."

"I didn't."

"That's what I eventually concluded. Which made me very happy—because if you *had* wanted me to hear it, that would have suggested an implied threat."

"*Threat?*" Paul yelped. "To whom?"

"Ariane Bradshaw," I said as the dime dropped.

"Exactly," Learned said.

"Huh?" Paul asked.

"Estate tax," I said.

"Right," Learned said. "If someone worth, say, ten million dollars were to die just before Thanksgiving his heirs would get ten million dollars. Whereas if he kicks off during the Tournament of Roses Parade, they'd only get four-million-five-hundred-thousand. There were ways to avoid the tax, but you have to think about those things well in advance, and people got complacent."

For an awful moment I thought Paul was going to show us what a clever boy he was by spelling it all out: Ariane knows hubby is in deep with bad people; she figures they might kill him to shut him up unless he saves them the trouble by taking his own life to avoid the disgrace of a criminal prosecution; since he's toast before the Super Bowl either way, why not anticipate the inevitable with some forty-four caliber estate planning? But Paul kept his mouth shut. Apparently undergraduates learn *something* at Harvard, even in the English Department.

"What you need to know," Learned said, "is that Ariane Bradshaw did not kill her husband. All you have to understand is that unless I'm sitting here telling you a barefaced lie, she had no role in his murder."

The message came through loud and clear. If Ariane Bradshaw absolutely did not kill her husband, then I don't have to toss and turn at night agonizing over the ethical dilemma of whether my client—excuse me, Mendoza's client—should go to the police with her little tidbit about mom. I wasn't planning on agonizing over that, but now I was going to not agonize over it while pursuing four leads for great apartments. Plus, I was about half-an-hour away from bedding my fiancé. This was shaping up as one hell of a good day.

"You want me to share this with Mendoza, right?"

"Yes." He finished his scotch and water with a decisive gulp and stood up. "Now, I'm sure you don't plan on wasting a night in New York City sitting in a hotel room, so I'll get out of your hair."

"Actually," Paul said, "we've been discussing what to do tonight. The shows are all sold out. I guess it'll be a movie."

"No, no, no." Learned shook his head sadly with an appalled expression while he unholstered his mobile phone. "We can't have that. There's a show in previews at some downscale performance space in SoHo. *Saloon Singer.* Set at a place a lot like the Café Carlyle, featuring a lead who doesn't look much like Bobby Short but sings like an angel. A tenor angel. Eight o'clock. Definitely not sold out. There'll be two tickets waiting for you at the box office."

He thumbed a speed-dial number into his mobile phone. He gave whoever answered genial but firm instructions about tickets for Paul and me, while I fetched his parka. Only when seeing him through the door did I remember that the supposed rationale for my jaunt to the big city was to come up with some kind of physical address for him.

"My mom will come back from the grave to rap my knuckles if I don't write you a formal thank-you note for all your kindness. Where should I send it?"

He turned slowly and smiled at me. More than a hint of condescension at my amateur attempt to finesse information from him shone through the smile.

"Think nothing of it. The expression on your face is enough."

Chapter Thirteen

We didn't leave the Hilton until about 7:20, but we still made it to the Damp Squib Stage in SoHo before 8:00. I figured, no shot at an empty cab this close to Broadway, so we took the subway to Washington Square and hoofed it from there.

DSS occupied the second floor of an old warehouse that was apparently being rehabbed into lofts when the developers ran out of cash and their bankers ran out of guts. Its "box office" was two guys sitting behind a slotted, metal money box on a long folding table in the second floor hallway, right in front of the doors to the theater itself. I basked in the glow of you-aren't-in-Pittsburgh-anymore. In its own way, this kind of low-rent stuff stoked my New York high as much as the Nederlander or the Brooks Atkinson theaters would have. We joined the line of patrons about halfway up the stairs. Paul glanced appraisingly at the attendees ahead of us in line and milling around at the top of the stairs.

"We're on the high end of the age demographic here."

"Feeling old?"

"Not particularly. Just a fun fact."

He had a point. Dirt-cheap tickets for previews is a business model that skews young. A dude in a tux who looked like he hadn't been shaving all that long was sidling nimbly down the stairs, stopping about every three sidles or so to say something. By the third repetition we were close enough to make out his words.

"Stone Toad will not be appearing in this evening's performance."

"*Now* I'm feeling old." Paul offered me a bemused frown. "Do you have the faintest idea who Stone Toad is?"

"I know he's not on the management committee at Calder & Bull."

We moved up four steps before we had to stop again. From there we could see the door leading to the performance area and catch a glimpse of the space inside, which looked pretty skimpy. As we reached the top step, a woman in a circa-1948 black cocktail dress approached. She was smoking a cigarette in a short holder, presumably to suggest a Café Society ambience. Unfortunately, herbal cigarettes are all you can legally smoke indoors in New York these days, and they don't exactly scream "Toots Shor."

"Stone Toad will not be appearing in tonight's performance," she said.

I caught a cranky little pout sneaking across Paul's face, so I elbowed him in the ribs, just in case he was considering an appearance by the mischievous ten-year-old in his psyche.

We finally reached the table and cashbox, where I gave my name. One of the guys leered at Paul, but the other one lifted the coin tray and fished out two tickets paper-clipped to a Post-It note with CYNTHIA JAKUBEK scrawled on it. I thanked him.

"Stone Toad will not be appearing in tonight's performance," the leerer chirped.

"You still have the singing cats, though, right?" Paul asked.

"You're asking for it," I hissed in his ear as we made our way to the door.

"Third time's the harm. Plus, he was treating me as a sex object."

"Then you should have slapped his face."

"That would have looked like part of the performance—and I don't have an Equity card."

I couldn't help laughing. He can play me like a flute when he wants to.

"If I ask the chick passing out programs at the entrance whether Stone Toad is appearing in tonight's performance, are you going to hit me again? Not that a little subliminal S&M doesn't add spice to a relationship, but just so I know what to expect."

"You're in kind of a snarky mood all of a sudden. If I were feeling bitchy I might hint that you're a bit jealous of our benefactor, Mr. L."

Paul chortled. "Mr. L is gay. There is no straight guy over fourteen this side of the Atlantic Ocean who smokes Caporal cigarettes."

By now we had made our way into the darkened theater and found seats on metal folding chairs in the eighth—and last—row. I raised my eyebrows at Paul out of pure habit, even though he couldn't see them.

"What makes you think he smokes Caporals?"

"I noticed a carton of the things in his attaché case when he took the flask out."

"If he were gay wouldn't our tickets have been in an ivory parchment monogrammed envelope?"

"It was short notice."

The lights went from low to pitch black, a spotlight hit a pianist stage left, and the overture for *Saloon Singer* began tinkling through the room. What I remember of the first act was pretty good. They nailed the atmospherics and the songs had a smoky, nostalgic quality that caught me up and carried me along. The story line was just an excuse to pass time between songs, but that was okay. A preview for an Off-Off-Broadway play is barely above street performers in the show business food chain, but it was still wall-to-wall pros. That's New York.

Unfortunately, I couldn't give the performance the attention it deserved. "Caporals" and "short notice" kept distracting me. Caporals for obvious reasons, but I couldn't figure out why "short notice" was bugging me. It finally came to me at intermission. No, "came to me" doesn't quite get it. It hit me like Vince's palm had that time when I was eleven.

"I'm an idiot," I told Paul.

"'I'm an idiot' is the only non-brilliant thing you've ever said in your life. What are you talking about?"

"The fax. That stuff about a bar reception. What in the world was I thinking? Two hours in a decent midtown hotel room turned my brain to mush."

"Slow down." Paul gave me a baffled look. "Connect the dots."

"'Association of the Bar of the City of New York' my ass. You're talking about laying out fifty thousand bucks for an event like that fax described. That means you make damn good and sure people are going to show up. You send out save-the-date emails two months in advance, and follow up with electronic invitations that have RSVP response buttons. You don't count on faxing people a few hours before the thing is supposed to start. That fax was either a lame practical joke or a scam to get us out of the hotel room for awhile tonight."

"Doesn't bad guys planning their nights around us strike you as a little melodramatic and self-important?"

I winced. I'd just been called melodramatic and self-important *by a novelist*. That hurt.

"Trust me on this one, creative genius. We have to get back to the room. At least I do."

"No way you're leaving without me. I can't afford a cab and if I try to get back on the subway by myself I'll end up in the South Bronx and have to be identified from my tooth fillings."

Either we lucked out or my whispered prayers were answered. We got a cab less than two minutes after we hit the sidewalk and we were muscling our way through the Hilton's oversized and underpowered lobby door by nine fifteen. The elevator took its own sweet time but by now I realized that that didn't really matter. I'd done some math during the cab ride. Seventy-five Park Avenue is at most a half-hour walk from the Hilton, probably less. A cab ride would be even shorter. If there was no reception, we'd have found that out almost as soon as we got there, realized we'd been had, and presumably hurried back. This meant that whoever set this up couldn't have counted on having more than *maybe* forty-five minutes inside the room once they'd spotted us leaving the hotel. Therefore, they weren't there now, nearly two hours later.

The hallway on our floor looked normal. Perfect symmetry of colors and décor that seemed to go on to infinity. The only visual relief came from a room service cart down a bit from our room and on the opposite side of the hall. The guest who'd wheeled it back into the corridor after dining had *not* cleaned his plate.

I'm not sure what signs of forced entry look like, but if I saw any I didn't recognize them when we got to our door. I started to feel a little sheepish. If I had just reinforced some hysterical-female stereotype by letting my imagination run away with me, I'd be hearing about it from Paul for a long time. *Please let there be wanton destruction inside*, I prayed. *Please let the room be trashed—except for Paul's manuscript. Oh, and my computer.*

I slipped my key-card into the slot. The little green light stayed dark and a little red light came on. I checked the card to make sure I was putting the correct end into the slot and repeated the process. Same outcome. I tried the handle out of sheer cussedness, but of course it was locked tight. I tried my key-card a third time. Red light. First my laptop finger-swipe and now this. Apparently it just wasn't my day for cooperation from computer chips.

"Try your key," I told Paul as I stepped out of the way.

He did. Red light. A frown and six seconds of thought brought me to Plan B.

"The computer must have switched our keys off by mistake, or maybe we just got them wet or something. Why don't you take your key down to the front desk and have them restrip it, and I'll stay here and keep trying to make mine work?"

"You got it."

Insanity, according to Einstein, is doing the same thing over and over again and expecting different results. Embarrassment, according to Jakubek, would be having someone from Guest Services take the key I'd been futzing with and make it work the first time he tried it. I preferred insanity to embarrassment. I waited ten seconds, inserted my key-card into the slot, and slid it home again.

Green light!

I shoved the handle down and pushed the door open. I was about to charge into the dark room when something stopped me—namely, that the room was dark. I was sure I'd left the entryway light on when we took off earlier in the evening. Plus, I just wasn't getting an empty vibe from this room. Feeling conspicuously moronic, I stood there on the threshold for five or ten seconds, trying to imagine some way to slip my right hand in far enough to flip the light switch while still keeping the rest of my body anchored in the hall.

The door suddenly jerked all the way open and a startling black-and-white blur slammed into me. I'd reflexively retreated a step or two down the hall, and so instead of bouncing me off the opposite wall the blur knocked me fanny-over-shoulders onto and then quickly off of the room service cart. I smeared my hair abundantly with mayonnaise, barbecue sauce, and green beans. I stumbled to my feet just in time for the assailant to smash a muscular forearm across my nose and lips. Now, that was just unnecessary. No way was I going to give him or her any argument about leaving, which was apparently what the assailant had in mind.

That's when I heard a full-throated roar from Paul: "HOOOOO-RAWWWWW!" That probably wasn't what Hemingway yelled when he was defending James Joyce from bar bullies in 1920s Paris, but it sounded good to me.

Charging down the hall like the Rough Riders up San Juan Hill, Paul half tackled and half fell on my assailant, making up in ferocious enthusiasm what he lacked in pugilistic art. I only had a blurry view of what happened next. I saw both combatants scramble to their feet, and heard rather than saw something drop from one of the burglar's pockets. Paul took two or three punishing punches to his ribcage and I could tell they got to him, but he didn't give an inch. I had visions of Norman Mailer punching out Gore Vidal as Paul landed a jab of his own.

Then, the burglar backed up a couple of feet—and Paul took the bait. He launched into another bull rush, and the next thing I knew his feet were brushing the ceiling as the burglar flipped him over his (or her) shoulder and then let gravity take him ungently to the floor. In the quarter-second between the time Paul's butt landed and the moment his feet hit the carpet, the burglar had taken off in the opposite direction, without bothering to retrieve the dropped article. With a start I realized that it was my pink, digital camera. Why would anyone want that?

While we wait for Paul to get up, I will share with you the entire description of the burglar that I would have been able to give the police if we'd bothered to report this business: He or she—I really didn't have the first idea which—was wearing a black-and-white room service waiter's uniform and the *worst* black wig I have ever seen in my life. I mean worse than Donald Trump's. We're talking neo-Stalinist *crap*.

Paul bounced up, with obvious designs on pursuing the burglar. I figured that if he did there were two things that could happen, and both were bad. I managed a grunt suggestive of hideous pain. After an instant of agonized indecision, Paul decided that I should get priority.

He took me tenderly by the shoulders and scrutinized the mess where my face used to be.

"Are you okay?"

"A little wobbly, but I'll live."

What did we do about all the other guests who rushed out into the hall to see what the commotion was about? This is *New York*! No one came out. We would have had our rumble and its aftermath in total privacy if it hadn't been for a guy in workout gear coming back to his room. He got off the elevator just in time to see me wincing as Paul lovingly kissed my lumpy nose and swollen lip.

"Take it inside, kids," he said.

"Not a bad idea," I told Paul. "Let's see what's missing."

Chapter Fourteen

Nothing was missing. Neither of the computers, not a page of Paul's manuscript, none of the notes or other stuff from my backpack, no clothing or personal effects. Paul's macho Nikon camera, which was probably worth three times more than my smart little Minolta, was still there. My iPod and Kindle lay right where I'd left them. And if the burglar had searched the room, she (or he) had been pretty neat about it. Despite the fight-or-flight juice racing through our veins, we went over the room for a good ten minutes in an unhurried, methodical way. We checked and double-checked. Nada.

A question was nagging at me. I finally asked it about five minutes after we'd finished.

"How did you happen to come back just in the nick of time?"

Paul was standing about six inches from me, but I yelled the question so that he could hear me over the roar of the shower. I was washing green beans and barbecue sauce from my hair and he was soaping and rinsing my back. He was being a real gentleman about it, getting the job done without feeling me up.

"Well," he said, as he sent a delicious tingle down my back by squeezing a wash cloth full of hot water at the nape of my neck, "just as I got to the elevators, I realized something. Namely, that the desk clerk wasn't going to give me the time of day when I asked to have a key restripped for a room registered in somebody else's name."

"So you turned around and came back, with the idea of sending me downstairs."

"Right. I reached the corridor just in time to see you auditioning for *Cirque du Soleil*."

"Damn." I felt like slapping myself. "I should have thought of that key deal."

"Don't beat yourself up. You were right about the big thing, which is that someone wanted us out of the room."

"But I outsmarted myself on the timing. If the idea of the fax-scam was to get us out of the room, there's no way the burglar should still have been there when we got back."

"I can't figure out how the whole fax-scam was supposed to work in the first place," Paul said. "Calder & Bull could theoretically have gotten a fax to you here because it had contact information for you in Pittsburgh and it would have been automatically forwarded. But Calder & Bull apparently didn't send the fax. How did the *burglar* know you'd be at the Hilton New York tonight?"

"My blog." I shook my head at missing the obvious—again. "When I do the blog I'm living my life in public. I was so pumped about being in New York that I didn't even think about it. Anyone who knows I'm Streetdreamer could have known that I'd be in New York this weekend, staying at the Hilton in midtown Manhattan."

"That could be dozens of people."

"Over a hundred, if my computer isn't lying to me."

I turned off the shower and we stepped onto a terrycloth bathmat. Paul handed a big, fluffy towel to me.

"Do we call security?" He took a towel for himself.

"I can't see it. Especially with nothing missing. Worst case, they don't believe us. Best case we get some undocumented alien fired for renting out a uniform and a pass-key."

That was the end of our conversation for a while because Paul, being male, had already finished drying himself and was headed out of the bathroom. I toweled off vigorously and did some thinking while I was at it. I was playing with some pretty tough customers—like Vera Sommers, the "insurance recovery consultant" who'd been doing a gumshoe number at the Bradshaw place. Along with Learned, she was shaping up as a pretty good guess for who was behind tonight's little adventure.

I decided not to report to Mendoza until Sunday. I had one more thing I wanted to do in the room, but that figured to take about five minutes and the night would still be young. After the Damp Squib fiasco I was still hungry for a New York Saturday night. While I blew my hair dry, I came up with an idea: walk down Broadway until the Sunday *Times* came out, and then read it while we noshed on midnight pizza. I decided to try to sell it to Paul.

My inspired notion evaporated as soon as I stepped out of the bathroom. Paul was standing there barefoot, in jeans and a tee-shirt. He was sporting a goofy grin and holding out a bulky package that had been gift-wrapped either by a male or by a woman without opposable thumbs. Giving him a quizzical look followed by an expectant grin, I took the gift and set it on the bed to unwrap it.

Pajamas. Powder blue. Soft flannel. *The bottoms had feet.* A little big for me, but only a diva would quibble.

In my imagination I heard a disapproving cluck from Stacy Tarrant, my BFF from clerkship days. Stacy's a very together lady, but after bad experiences with guys she lapses into oral italics and tends to use words like *praxis* a lot.

"A gift from a male is his *projection* of his image *of you onto* you," the Stacy in my head lectured me. "That's the reality of the praxis at work here. He's infantilizing you, trying to turn you into Hillary Duff or something."

Right. I spent more weekends alone than I should have in high school and college because males were afraid I'd castrate them with my tongue. What Paul was projecting onto me was his image that I'm way too cute to be sleeping in sweatshirts and gym shorts.

I'll take it. I burst out laughing and jumped him for a hug.

All at once I knew what the rest of my New York Saturday night was going to be. I was going to climb into my new jammies and curl up to read the latest chapters in Paul's manuscript while he sat at his keyboard until after one a.m. doing his obsessed artist thing. Why? Because I could tell that that was what Paul really wanted, and he was my guy.

But I still had that one thing to do. After I put the new jammies on and did a little runway stroll so that Paul could admire them on me, I handed one of the room keys to him.

"Step outside the door," I told him. "I'll throw the deadbolt from inside. After I do, try the key in the door."

"Why?"

"To see if we get a red light instead of a green light."

"We will."

We did. The experiment took about thirty seconds, and it worked out the way I'd expected. If someone uses the key-card while the deadbolt is engaged, the key-card doesn't unlock anything—not even the main lock.

"So that's why you kept getting the red light," Paul said. "While the burglar is in here, she wants some privacy, so she throws the deadbolt."

"It's 'she' now?"

"We'll alternate, like in a law review article. I'll do 'she' and you do 'he.'"

"Works for me. And you're right. I got a red light until I sent you downstairs in a voice loud enough for the burglar to hear. When the burglar figured there was only one person left to worry about, he undid the bolt. Green light, open door, Cindy on her butt."

"So," Paul said, "we've figured out everything except who the burglar actually was."

"And why he went to all that trouble for a camera."

"And why she was still here long after she had to assume we'd be back."

"Maybe I should double-check that." I strode over to the wastebasket under the desk where I'd chucked the fax. "Maybe I just remembered the time wrong."

The fax wasn't there. I was certain that I hadn't thrown it away in the bathroom, but I checked the wastebasket there anyway. Nothing. I checked every other place I could think of where I might have thrown it or left it, and I didn't find it.

"Well," I said, "now we know what the burglar came for."

"The fax?"

"The fax. Taking my camera was just a blind."

"But that doesn't make any sense."

"It makes sense if having the fax might help identify the person who sent it."

"Even assuming that it could, the burglar couldn't cover her tracks by taking the hard copy. The Hilton has a record of receiving it. Any information we could get from the hard copy we could get from the Hilton itself. Or the police could, at least."

"Right," I said. "We could. But the burglar couldn't."

"I don't follow."

"I think two different people were interested in getting into this room tonight." I rattled the syllables out in staccato rhythm, like bullet points, as the theory took shape in my mind. "Why do I think that? Because there were two efforts to get us out of the room."

"The fax and the free tickets to *Saloon Singer.*"

"Right. And the tickets to *Saloon Singer* would have kept us out until well after ten thirty if your 'short notice' crack hadn't triggered my brainstorm during intermission."

"Which means that the second burglar was working for Learned," Paul said.

"And that Learned wanted the fax."

"But why?"

"Because he noticed the fax and realized that it had to be phony. He assumed that whoever sent it is competing with him and is after something from me."

"Which means the room got broken into twice tonight."

"Maybe yes, maybe no—but we have to assume that it was."

"Including by a first burglar who didn't take anything—not even a fax."

"Right."

"Hmm," Paul said. "So, what do we do about all this?"

"Nothing tonight."

"What do you want to do for the rest of the night, then? It's way too early to go to bed."

"Do you know what I'd *really* like to do?" I asked.

"What?"

"I'd like to sit down with your manuscript while you work on the next chapter."

He looked at me with wonder lighting his eyes.

"You are *amazing*," he said.

"I get that a lot."

Chapter Fifteen

His Paulness rolled over in bed and looked up groggily at me when I came back into the room around 9:25 Sunday morning. I found space on the desk for the tree-killer Sunday edition of the *New York Times*, a white sack holding a bagel and two croissants, and the Sunday bulletin from St. Patrick's Cathedral. Then I slid over to the in-room coffeemaker to try to figure out how to brew some of the packaged stuff that was included in the price of our room.

"Have you been up long?"

"Since the crack of 7:15."

"*7:15?*" He yelped the time, as if that were some unthinkable predawn hour. "*Why?*"

"So I could make eight o'clock mass at St. Pat's and pick up a little something to tide us over until we can go out somewhere for a real breakfast—because I am *not* going to pay the Hilton five dollars and fifty cents for the privilege of having someone charge me sixteen dollars for cold scrambled eggs."

"You went to Mass?"

"Mm hmm." I got the coffeemaker working. "Am I hearing an undertone of disapproval in your sexy baritone?"

"More like puzzlement. I mean isn't what we did last night like, a *serious* no-no in the eyes of the Church?"

"No. Working on postmodern novels is okay. I looked it up."

"No head games before I've had coffee," Paul groused. "You know what I meant."

"Oh, *that*: sharing sexual passion outside the bonds of holy matrimony. Yes, that is definitely against the rules."

"So couldn't you, like, burn in Hell forever for what we did?"

"No. Hell is for sins like blasphemy and eating meat on Good Friday. For fornication you spend eternity in Philadelphia."

He blinked. It took him close to a second to get it. One of the fun things about unbelievers is that they'll believe anything about Catholicism—anything. Then he jumped naked out of bed, hustled over to the table, and started scribbling in his notebook.

"Are you really going to work that little crack into your novel?"

"You bet. Just like your shot about Hillary Clinton flunking a bar exam."

"I read that last night. I noticed you gave the straight line to his girlfriend and let Widget have the snapper."

"That's why we call it fiction."

I didn't bother explaining why I went to Mass on Sunday with a Saturday's worth of sins on my unshriven soul. Probably eight hundred million adults on Planet Earth went to Mass that day, and all of them were sinners. To me, sharing love with my fiancé isn't in the same league as promiscuous, recreational sex—something that did come up once or twice in my occasional confessions back in the day. If I thought that was the worst sin I'd have to confess at my final judgment, I'd already have my harp and wings picked out.

"Okay." He turned around from the table. "What's on today's agenda?"

"Take your shower, get dressed, and enjoy your coffee and pastry while I e-mail Mendoza a report. Then we'll find some-place on this magnificent island where we can read the *Times* without getting frostbite."

The report took longer than I thought it would. By the time I hit SEND Paul was not only dressed, fed, and caffeinated but halfway through his weekly quota of disparaging snorts about the overrated hacks who somehow manage to get their fiction reviewed by the *Times* every Sunday. Just after 10:30, though, we were ready to go.

And go we did. We hiked up Broadway, found a non-chain diner-type place where Paul could get generous servings of pigs' bellies along with our eggs while we lingered over coffee and the *Times*, and then worked our way over toward Central Park. We weren't quite there yet when my mobile phone rang. Noting that it was Mendoza's number, I braced myself.

"Say it, Jake," were the first words out of his mouth. "'You were right, Mendoza.' Come on, I wanna hear you say it."

"You were right, Mendoza. You were absolutely right. There was danger here that I wasn't equipped to handle. You were right about everything except that crack about having a novelist watch my back. My novelist gave the burglar a dose of premodern muscle that sent the miscreant off with his or her tail between his or her legs."

Mendoza made an exasperated sound that didn't really qualify as a word. Then he said something in Spanish.

"We did get some useful information, though," I said, "even if we haven't tracked down a physical address for Learned yet."

"YET? YET?"

"That word may have been ill-chosen." I intended this concession as a tactical retreat. Mendoza took it as surrender.

"I want your butt on the next flight back to Pittsburgh, Jake. I should never have let you talk me into this. No more Agatha Marple stuff. We'll hand off that 'useful information' you stumbled over to a pro and he'll carry the ball from there."

"Look, Mendoza, it's two minutes to noon. We're stuck with the hotel bill for today anyway, and there'll be a change fee for an earlier airline ticket. I won't do anything adventurous, I promise. I'll head back Monday as scheduled and—"

"I DON'T CARE ABOUT NO STINKING HOTEL BILL! Screw the change fees! You get back here pronto! I haven't smacked an employee in ten years and I was married to that one, but I still remember how! *Andele, chica!*"

He punched out of the call. I gave Paul a quick blow-by-blow while I scrolled for the US Airways site on my Droid.

"He threatened to *hit* you?"

"That was just hyperbole. He and Sigmund Freud are working on sort of a daughter-he-never-had thing with me in Mendoza's superego."

"*Hyperbole?* You're rationalizing. Fathers don't hit their daughters."

I flashed him my how's-the-weather-on-Planet-Trustfund look and then quickly flicked my eyes back to my Droid because he *hates* that look. My discretion paid off. Instead of getting pissed off at me, Paul stayed pissed off at Mendoza.

"So now," he said disgustedly, "we have to hustle back to the hotel and kill the rest of Sunday afternoon trucking out to LaGuardia and looking for an earlier flight?"

"No. There's a three-oh-five, but we'd have to be in a cab in a little over half-an-hour to have a real shot at it, so screw that one. The seven thirty is more like it. Here's what we do. We take our own sweet time wending our way back to the Hilton. I'll use my magic little digital friend here to get the ticket switched while we're walking. Ten minutes in the Business Center to print out a boarding pass, fifteen minutes to pack, and we should still have more than three hours together before you give me a passionate kiss at the cabstand and send me on my way to the airport."

"I'm coming to the airport with you."

"That's sweet, but no. We'd only have two minutes together before I got in line for security, and then you'd have to head back to the hotel."

"The hotel?"

"Sure. We're stuck with the room charge for today anyway so you might as well enjoy the room tonight. I know, I know, it will seem empty without me—but you'll have the postmodern adventures of Henry Widget to keep you company."

"What about checking out tomorrow morning, though?"

"Piece of cake," I said. "They'll slip the bill under the door sometime tonight. PDF it to me so that I can get partial reimbursement from Mendoza and a tax write-off for what he doesn't reimburse. When you're ready to leave tomorrow morning, drop the two key-cards in the box they have near the desk and be on your way."

Paul's a smart guy—dummies don't get into Harvard unless they can play hockey—but he went from being too rich to have to do stuff like this for himself to being too poor even to think about it. His grandparents had set up a trust fund that threw off enough every year to cover Harvard's costs and provide comfortable walking around money. Then came the crash, and the trust fund portfolio took a dive even more nauseating than the one by Harvard's endowment. Now he's lucky to get $700 a month.

"You're really being incredibly wonderful about this, aren't you?" he said then, softly.

I turned toward him and caressed his stubbled cheek with the backs of my fingers.

"It's just a little money, Paul. It's not even very much money. Enjoy the room for an extra night instead of wandering around LaGuardia trying to cadge a ride back to Philly. Chisel eight hundred more carefully chosen words into your hard drive."

"Okay," he said. "But I won't do room service. I'll duck out for a burger or something."

"Bullshit. Dial yourself a steak."

Things went according to plan, except that the time I spent at the Hilton Business Center was closer to forty-five minutes than ten. I used the extra time laboriously talking the Hilton out of another copy of the infamous fax. First they claimed it was technically impossible to retrieve the transmission, which was a crock, and then they said they just couldn't find it, which even they didn't pretend to believe. Only after I played the trump card with an icy *I'd like to speak to your superior* did they finally manage to print out another copy and hand it over to me.

The time for the pseudo-event matched my recollection. I figured that retrieving a fax from a major hotel chain didn't qualify as "Agatha Marple stuff," so I scanned the thing into my laptop and emailed it to Mendoza with a suggestion that he have Becky the Techie do a reverse phonebook search on the transmission number. At 5:30 (I stole an extra half-hour) Paul gave me a bear hug and a love-pat on the fanny and saw me into a cab. Less than an hour later I was sitting at the gate, hoping and praying for an on-time departure.

Naturally, though, I couldn't let go of the eight-hundred-pound gorilla question looming like a near-term trial date over this weekend: two burglaries and nothing taken except a fax—what's the deal with that? As I methodically reconstructed everything printable from the time I hit the room until Paul and I left for Damp Squib, I came up with nothing. Then I decided that I might as well update my blog.

Update my blog. UPDATE MY BLOG!

It took me a few frenzied minutes to put it together. I was already in my seat on the plane when I punched Mendoza's number into my mobile phone.

"Jake," he answered, "this better not be a message saying you missed the last flight and are going to have to stay over 'til Monday anyway."

"The burglars didn't come to take anything." I was talking at two hundred words a minute to get the message out before they ordered me to turn the phone off. "They came to leave something. Or at least one of them did."

"Leave what?"

"Don't know. What I do know is this: Do *not* open that e-mail I sent you! Don't open another e-mail from my computer until Becky has checked it."

Chapter Sixteen

"Good catch on the computer, Jake," Mendoza said around a Monday-morning, death-warmed-over scowl. "Becky found the bug."

"He got into your computer and imported some pretty sophisticated spyware." Becky the Techie, sitting next to me in front of Mendoza's desk, shot me a glance through glasses in the kind of stainless steel frames that Mr. Spock on *Star Trek* wore before the Federation sprang for contacts. "Once you logged on with that thing in there, if anyone who was hooked up to the office network had opened an e-mail from you, whoever planted that bug could have taken every byte of data we have. No firewall this side of the Pentagon could have stopped it."

"Had to be Learned," I said.

"Do you know how he got in?" Mendoza asked.

"I had the computer open on the table when he came to our room. He probably spotted the password when I typed it in after my finger-swipe wouldn't work. I don't know how he managed to block the finger-swipe, but he obviously did."

"Dab of Vaseline on the bar would have done it," Becky said.

"If he got the password, all he needed was fifteen minutes alone with the computer and he could have installed anything he wanted." I hooded my eyes as I puzzled it through. "Especially after I obligingly showed him the wi-fi setting."

"So the question is why he went to all that trouble to penetrate our pleasant little shop here," Becky said.

"Let's think out loud about that." Mendoza pursed his lips. "Theory: Learned was up to his eyebrows with Thomas Bradshaw in whatever was happening to the loot from the Gardner Museum heist. Or maybe he was up to some other part of his anatomy with Ariane Bradshaw. Either way, he might want to find out if we know enough to put his neck in a noose."

"Heavy shit." This was Becky's idea of a compliment. She landed two knuckles as she tried to punch my bicep.

"Jake, give Cesario every scrap of information you wrote down about those apartments Learned touted to you." Mendoza was referring to Cesario Lopez, Becky's fellow investigator in the office. "Also everything we have on Vera Sommers. We'll see if Cesario can spend two or three days in the Big Apple without getting his face creased."

"Will do."

"Speaking of which, how's that nose and fat lip you brought back as souvenirs? And *don't* tell me your mother used to hit you harder than that for ditching school."

"No, mom never drew blood. It's nothing Tylenol can't handle."

"Good. Plastic surgery would raise the *hell* out of my group insurance premium."

Translation: "Welcome back, well done." Winning a fight was the best way to gain credibility in Mendoza-land, but taking a punch and then not quitting was a close second.

Chapter Seventeen

"I checked out all four of the apartments." Paul was telling me this a little after midnight Tuesday morning, and he was back in giddy-mode. "Sorry about calling at this ungodly time. Is it too late for you to talk?"

"Is that a trick question? Staying up 'til two a.m. is great practice for Calder & Bull."

"Anything new on that front, by the way?"

"Not really." I stood up to pace while I talked. "'Above the Law' is running with a rumor that C & B is expected to fall two places on the AmLaw one hundred profit-per-partner list when the new rankings come out in January. They'll still be in the top quartile, though, so that shouldn't be any big deal."

"Hmmmm." Paul followed this elongated syllable with a worried silence.

"Don't sweat it. Nothing to fret about."

"It's just that I've heard, I mean, people say that if a firm does a second deferral, that means it'll end up not hiring at all."

"What people are those, the Author's Guild? Look, you worry about dependent clauses and I'll handle the Greed-is-Good brigade. Tell me about the apartments."

"They are fan-*tas*-tic." Suddenly his voice was all bunnies-and-butterflies again. "Even the cheapy. Limited space, but I didn't see cockroach-one and the toilets flushed on the first try."

"Maybe we should go ahead and grab one."

"Something to think about, all right."

"You sound as happy as I've heard you on the phone in a long time, Paul."

"It's New York, baby. Writer's heaven. I'm in a New York state of mind."

Chapter Eighteen

I really believed my brave words to Paul about Calder & Bull, but even so I felt a belly-drop when I saw the e-mail from Humanresources@calderbull.com. I comforted myself with an axiom: bad news comes by snail mail. I closed my eyes and breathed a quick prayer. Then I clicked it open:

WELCOME TO THE CALDER & BULL CLASS OF 2011!

We hope you will be able to join us for a preorientation on the morning of Thursday, December 16, 2010, beginning at 10:00 a.m. Travel and overnight lodging for new hires living more than one hundred miles outside New York City will be covered by the Firm. Using the voting buttons above, please confirm your attendance.

The signature—Walter Lincecum, chair of the recruiting committee—required a suspension of disbelief: the e-mail had come from nonlegal staff, and Lincecum's well-manicured fingers hadn't contributed a keystroke to it. Who cares? I moved the cursor to ACCEPT up at the top and clicked. Then I warned myself not to gloat too much when I talked to Paul that night.

Chapter Nineteen

Ken drove in from Erie early on Friday morning to say Mom's memorial Mass. It wasn't anything special. Just the regular weekday morning Mass at eight o'clock, with a well-done-good-and-faithful-servant shout-out to Mom in his homily and a prayer for her added to the intercessions. It wasn't a student Mass, so there were only about forty non-Jakubeks there. Lainie Banacek came, and after a delicate little hesitation waltz, I managed to get Vince sandwiched between me and her.

After Mass we went to the cemetery to say familiar prayers under a leaden sky while a bitchy little wind whipped tears from my eyes. I added a silent prayer to Mom to figure out some way to get it through Vince's thick skull that the Lainie thing was okay. I'm a little shaky on the theology of how that works, but I figured that part was above my pay grade anyway.

Back home from the cemetery I put out some pastry and whipped up toast, bacon, and scrambled eggs. I stuck with toast except for nibbling on some Slavic delicacy that Lainie contributed to the pastry mound. Light frosting, with raisins inside. Not bad. I didn't think she stood much chance of weaning Vince off glazed donuts with it, but I gave her credit for trying.

As the post-breakfast talk got under way I policed up glasses and cups, trying not to make too much of a production out of it. Lainie gave up without too much of a fight when I shooed her out of the kitchen while I tackled the fifteen-minute cleanup job. Ten minutes into it, though, Ken joined me just in time to dry a couple of plates. I figured that meant he wanted to talk. I hoped it was about Lainie instead of Paul. It was.

"So this thing with Ms. Banacek looks pretty serious." He ran a dish towel sedulously over bone-dry china.

"Yep."

"I hope he has it in him."

I turned the faucet on full blast into the empty sink in case Vince or Lainie wandered past the kitchen door. "It'd be a great way for him to get past Mom's death."

"Do you think it might be the other way around?" This is priest-speak for, "It's the other way around, you moron."

I turned my head to look at him, half-a-foot taller than I am and radiating that mysterious calm that voluntary celibates often seem to have. The pale winter light streaming through the window four feet behind him emphasized his solidity by its evanescence. I noticed a chipped spot on the turquoise sash that I hadn't seen before.

"I'm not sure what you mean."

"Maybe Lainie Banacek isn't a way for Vince to reach closure. Maybe she's a sign that he already has."

"What I saw the Monday before Thanksgiving didn't look like closure to me." I gave him a quick recap of Vince's performance before and during Monday night football.

"What that sounds like to me is the last bad night before closure." Ken shot his left hand reflexively through his coal black crew cut. "He must have stumbled over a pretty talented counselor that night."

I felt my mouth puckering. I have a problem with compliments sometimes.

"All I did was make a joke and recycle some Sunday school bromides."

"Talented and modest on top of it." Ken said this as if he were musing to himself. "Are you taking the whole day off?"

"Just this morning. Vince plans on getting on his route by eleven, so I'll catch a bus for downtown around noon and get in an afternoon at my cubicle."

"That's okay, sis, I can give you a lift downtown."

"Thanks. That'd be great."

Like a mischievous eight-year-old who thinks he's fooling someone, Ken reached casually for a baggie with four leftover strips of bacon that I hadn't gotten into the fridge yet. I slapped the back of his hand.

"That's for Vince's BLT, and more concentrated sodium is about the last thing you need anyway. A stroke in your thirties would be a pretty harsh punishment for gluttony."

"You're absolutely right," he said with surprising mildness. "'Thou shalt not' is often just a way of saying, 'Bad things could happen if you do this.'"

Then he smiled. For close to an hour I actually thought he'd conceded a point.

I mean, talk about delayed reaction. I made Vince's BLT. I gave it to him in a brown paper bag with an apple so that he could eat lunch on the road as he drove from one stop to another. I helped see Lainie off. I waved to Vince as he pulled his step-van out of the driveway and headed down the street for a hard afternoon of hustling tools and shaking weekly installment payments out of mechanics. I rode downtown with Ken to Mendoza-land. He wasn't traveling in clerical garb and anyone who knew he was a priest would also know I was his sister, so there wasn't much risk of scandal. I got out of his car and walked across the sidewalk into the building. And I was all the way into the elevator, a good fifty minutes after his 'thou shalt not' line, when I finally got it.

"That sneaky little monk!" I sputtered at the elevator's ceiling. "That slick-talking Jesuit! He was busting my chops about Paul!" And I laughed.

Chapter Twenty

"Isn't chardonnay kind of wimpy for an after-work drink?" Sal Brentano aimed this gibe at me.

"Hey, at least I don't smoke Marlboro Lights."

"You don't smoke anything."

"When I smoked I didn't smoke Marlboro Lights—and I started at fifteen."

"These are for my girlfriend." Sal fingered the pack that the waitress had brought along with his Harvey Wallbanger.

"Likely story," Mendoza joshed.

"She might as well quit," I told Sal. "Marlboro Lights are the same thing as not smoking, except carcinogenic and more expensive."

"You better give up now, *chico*," Mendoza told Brentano. "You keep going back and forth with Jake here and you're gonna lose your amateur standing."

Meeting for drinks after work wasn't the usual thing with Mendoza's crew. Unlike the clerks' group in my Judge Mercado days, the Mendozistas weren't mainly single twenty-somethings. They had families or significant others they wanted to get home to, or in a couple of cases they were on the make for someone to share a bed with that night.

But this evening was out of the ordinary. Cesario was due back from New York. When word reached the office around 4:30 that his flight would be delayed, Mendoza had told him to meet us at The Bigger Jigger. The Bigger Jigger wasn't a sports bar or a gay bar or a theme bar. It was just a regular saloon. No televisions, no piano, and no line drawings of B-list celebrities on the white-painted walls in between its rough oak supports. Mendoza, Brentano, Becky, Ricky Waters, and now me.

Becky was the first to spot Cesario. He came strolling in, bundled up like a yeti but swinging a battered brown leather trial bag that, in addition to all of his private investigator stuff, no doubt carried the socks and underwear he'd gone through on his trip. Cesario travels light.

He milked the entrance. I mean *milked* it. He stopped at the empty chair by the table and dropped his trial bag on the floor with a solid thud. He took off a black Cossack hat and tried to smooth the wreck it had made of his dark, curly hair. He unbuttoned what looked to me like a Navy bridge coat—heavy and, from the musty-damp smell it gave off, wool. He loosened a gray muffler from around his throat. He got the waitress' attention and asked for a vodka gimlet. He took the coat off and draped it over the trial bag, then dropped the hat and muffler on top of it. He cupped his hands in front of his mouth and blew on them.

"For crying out loud, Cesario, it's twenty-eight degrees outside," Mendoza said. "That's not exactly arctic. Did you manage to get frostbite walking from the curb to the door?"

"I had to park *a block away*, man."

He took his sweet time sitting down. He shot the cuffs on what looked like a long-sleeved mechanic's shirt without the grease stains. He smiled. At last, he spoke

"The buildings the four apartments are in are owned by four separate corporations. The listed headquarters for each of those corporations is the same lawyer's office in Dover, Delaware that's also the official address for Ars Longa."

We all kept our mouths shut. After the buildup there had to be more. Cesario made eye contact with each of us, going methodically around the table and smiling benignly.

"The phony bar reception invitation was faxed from a Kinkos four blocks from the Hilton," he said then. "Which was very efficient because it was also composed, laid out, and printed there."

Mendoza perked up. "By Vera Sommers, by any wild chance?"

"No one there had ever heard of anyone called Vera Sommers," he said. "No one there could quite remember who had brought this little piece of business in, or what this cash-paying customer looked like or one single distinguishing physical characteristic."

"But what?" Brentano prompted.

"But when I showed Vera Sommers' picture to the counter-boy, he came in his pants. He had definitely seen her before, if you know what I mean."

The waitress hustled up with Cesario's drink. He sipped it, closed his eyes, and leaned back with the contentment of some-one who's enjoying a little bit of heaven.

"There's one more thing."

"Spill already," Mendoza said.

"Well, I got to thinking about how multitalented this Delaware lawyer is. Corporate, real estate—seems like sort of a legal mini-conglomerate. So I thought I should check her out."

"'Her'?" I shouldn't have bitten but I couldn't help myself.

"Seventy-three-year-old lady. Solo practitioner. Widow. Never goes to court. Not listed in *Martindale-Hubbel* or any of the other standard law office directories. No list of representative clients."

"Niche practice," Mendoza said. "Interesting."

"No, that's not interesting." Cesario shook his head and favored us with a broad grin. "I'll tell you what's interesting. What's interesting is that sixteen days ago this seventy-three-year-old shysterette became the registered owner of a military surplus Colt .45 automatic. First time in her life she's ever packed heat."

Now Cesario really had me. My sister attorney in Dover had chosen to acquire a piece of handheld artillery shortly after Tyrell Washington found himself with a shiv inserted between his second and third ribs.

"The bullet that killed Bradshaw was forty-four or forty-five caliber," Mendoza said.

"Yep," I said.

"Have the cops found the weapon yet?"

"Nope," Becky said. "Not as of four o'clock this afternoon."

Mendoza settled back. He took a nice, slow sip of bourbon and sweet. Then he looked directly at me.

"Drop by my office first thing tomorrow, Jake. Gotta job for you."

"Sure thing."

Everyone at the table knew what the job was: talk to Caitlin Bradshaw. And everyone understood why: in Mendoza's opinion, I had the confidence of our client.

Chapter Twenty-one

At 9:03 a.m. on the sixty-ninth anniversary of the attack on Pearl Harbor, I left a message on Caitlin's mobile phone, asking her to call me. At 12:17 she texted me back: "WHAT?" That pissed me off, but I swallowed hard and texted her back: "NEED2TLK. 4 TODAY?" It went back and forth like that through three more exchanges, raising my blood pressure each time, but I finally pinned her down to 4:30 Thursday afternoon at her place.

In between the fourth and fifth texts, Sal Brentano stopped by my cubicle. I wondered if I'd unintentionally cut a little too deep during our Monday evening banter, but he was bouncy and friendly. As he damn well should have been. After all, he'd started it.

"I was just thinking of something," he said. "Who does your dad's legal work?"

"His accountant." Sal laughed—all accountants think they're lawyers these days.

"Do you think he'd mind if I spent a day riding with him on his route? Just to wrap my arms around the business model?" Translation: *Hustle Dad as a client.*

"I'll ask him."

"Thanks. I'd really appreciate that."

A professional colleague had just asked me to help him get some potential business. In other words, after more than ten months, I was finally one of the boys.

Chapter Twenty-two

"An agent? You've got an agent?"

"I've got *a line* on an agent," Paul said. He was trying to be calm but I could tell he was even more excited than I was. "Bradley Nance. He's pretty well connected. He's the one who sold that account of the Lewinsky scandal that's coming out next year."

"I *heard* about that. *The Making of the President 1997.*"

"Or something like that." Even over the phone I could picture Paul's grin.

"So how did you manage this?" I pushed the quote Vince had prepared for Allegheny County Community College's starter tool set deal across the table. "I thought it took most writers years to come up with agents."

"Harvard College guarantees you two things: attitude and contacts. I used both of them. Hey, you aren't multitasking on me by any chance, are you? I just heard papers shuffling."

"That's a quote Vince wrote up for a government purchase. He asked me to look it over, but I've put it aside for the duration of our call."

"So you're billing your own father for legal work? That's cold."

"Yeah, but I'm giving him a rate: zero dollars per hour. I'll do the same for you when Bradley Nance gets you a contract with Random House."

"Remember, he's not on board with me yet. He liked the concept and the sample chapters, but I still have to meet him up in New York on Friday so that he knows I'm coachable and not a total closet case."

"Well watch your language, lover," I said. "If he's gay, slang like 'closet case' might offend him."

"Seriously? You think that might turn him off?"

"No, lover, *not* seriously. It was a joke."

"I *get* it!" By now Paul was approaching manic. "I absolutely *get it!* I'm gonna get that pun into Henry Widget's mouth if I have to write a whole extra chapter just to do it."

"Don't do that, honey. It wasn't that good, and even if it were, you can't write a whole chapter for a one-liner."

"Watch me," he said. "Just watch me."

He was no longer approaching manic. He was there. And I couldn't blame him.

Chapter Twenty-three

The first things I noticed in Caitlin's bedroom were the pillows. Three of them, one piled on top of the other two on her spacious queen-size bed, in perfectly-matched pillowcases that weren't fussy but somehow communicated that they'd cost a lot of money anyway. And I thought, *Why three? Why not two or four, instead of an odd number?* So I added that to the list of things I'd never understand about rich people. It's a long list.

Caitlin politely offered me the only real chair in the room, a sleek, comfortable, exposed steel and twill-fabric number at her desk. No, "desk" doesn't really do the thing justice. Try "work station." It had three shelves for books, a six-slot paper sorter, a plastic drum for CD-ROMs, and enough workspace to wargame the Battle of Stalingrad.

No computer though, I noticed. Caitlin must have been reading my mind.

"Dad wouldn't let me have a computer in my room." She parked herself on the corner of her bed. "And mom agreed with him. I guess they were afraid I'd get seduced by some creepy, bald fifty-year-old on the net pretending to be Justin Bieber."

"So you have to make do with the family computer downstairs?"

"Technically, *that's* my computer. Mom has her own laptop, and so did Dad. And to be fair, they were always pretty good about respecting my privacy."

"No PAW when you're on IM?"

"Not very often."

In instant-messaging code, "PAW" means "Parents Are Watching." Since most parents know that by now, I'm not sure that coding it accomplishes anything. But I thought that mentioning it might remind Caitlin that I was closer to her age than her mother's.

"So." Caitlin did a little hair-flick with her left hand. "What did you want to ask me?"

"Let's start with what I need to tell you."

I gave her a rundown of everything since her father's murder, hitting the highlights but skipping colorful details like my close encounter with a room service cart. I ended with Walter Learned's recent presumptive purchase of a .45 automatic, which is a lot more handgun than you'd need to plink tin cans on the back forty of your gentleman-farmer acreage.

The .45 got her attention. I could tell because she whispered the entire phrase *holy shit* instead of swearing in IM code. I gave her about six seconds, then used the same interviewing technique my mom had with me at fifteen after she noticed three Salems missing from her pack.

"So, Caitlin. Is there anything you'd like to tell me?"

"What do you mean?"

I managed to suppress a sigh before it passed my lips.

"I mean there's a good chance your father was killed because bad people thought he knew something about where the loot from the biggest art heist in history could be found. Walter Learned might be one of those people. Or not. Maybe he picked up the gun because he was afraid he was on the same list your father was. Whatever, other people might be in danger now—including your mom, and even you."

"You're right." Caitlin bowed her head for a moment, then raised it and looked directly at me with those tough-but-not-hard gray eyes of hers. "I was telling the truth when I told you that I didn't think there were any problems with my parents' marriage. But I figured something out on Thanksgiving Friday. I went out on the deck for a cigarette, and it came to me."

"What?"

"Mom and Learned were having an affair."

"You 'figured that out'?"

"It's not like I barged in on them when they were doing it or anything. But I was out there smoking, and that was my first week of smoking openly around the house without sneaking around or anything. And I was thinking about that whole business I'd told you about never seeing Mom smoke before. Which was true. I realized that that had to be because she *didn't* smoke before. I mean, maybe once in awhile at parties or something, but not an everyday thing where she bought her own cigarettes."

"I'm not following you."

"A change in smoking habits is one of the signs of an affair. I read that in *mademoiselleonline* or someplace. It said people will change brands or even go back to smoking after years of not doing it as a subconscious sign of intimacy if their lover is a smoker."

"I never heard that, but it makes sense, I guess. Still, even though Caporals aren't a common brand in this country, I'm not sure seeing a carton of them in Learned's attaché case is enough to convict him of adultery."

"Mr. Learned smokes a pipe. I figure he gets the Caporals for Mom because they're a lot easier to come by in New York than in Pittsburgh. But I'm thinking she went back to smoking because he smokes, which Dad never did. Which explains why I never noticed it before. But I'm not going just on that. I'm saying that's just what started my train of thought. I went back over things I'd seen when they were together, little snatches of conversation, vague talk about where she'd be on afternoons when he happened to be in town, and it all adds up. I know it sounds kind of dumb, but..."

"It doesn't sound dumb at all," I told her. "It makes all kinds of sense."

"But I don't want to tell this to the police. They might think it makes Mom look like the killer."

"Next to saying it to a priest in confession, telling it to me is as far as you can possibly get from telling it to the police. But here's the money question: Did you ever actually see Learned with any kind of a firearm?"

"Not exactly."

I did *not* ask her what "not exactly" was supposed to mean. I sat there, patient and expectant, just as I'd seen Mendoza do with a dozen clients. Finally, after she looked away and fidgeted so much that I halfway expected her to suggest a smoking break out on the deck, she spoke again.

"The last time Mr. Learned was here before Dad got killed, the first thing he did was go into the bathroom. Always before he'd just drop his attaché case by the computer desk in the great room, but this time he took it into the bathroom with him. When he left, same routine in reverse. I don't know why I was paying so much attention to it, but I was. When he was getting ready to leave that time, he went into the bathroom with the attaché case and still had it with him when he came out. Except when he came out I was looking right at him, and there was a bulge underneath his suit coat that could certainly have been big enough for a Colt."

I thought it would be pretty tactless to ask her to spell her theory out in greater detail, so I left it unspoken: Learned didn't want mom to notice that he was carrying a gun when he started doffing his squire-togs in the heat of passion, so he transferred the cannon from a shoulder holster to the attaché case when he got there, and then moved it back just before he left. In Judge Mercado's court, that would have been speculation and she wouldn't have let it into evidence. But then, Judge Mercado wouldn't have seen Learned's attaché case land on the passenger seat of his Prius without triggering the seat belt sensor. I had.

"I can see that," I said.

"So, is there, like, anything else?"

I had to think about that for a second. There was one other thing, all right. Mendoza hadn't gotten the truth about Caitlin's crack that her dad had killed her brother. No way that was some meaningless babble from a shock-addled adolescent. It would be nice to pin that one down. I looked at my client: cool, interested, impatient but not nervous. She wasn't going to tell me until she was ready, and I sensed that if I tried to force the issue now she might never be ready.

"Tell you what, Caitlin. If you think of anything else that might help, give me a call."

"You got it." She said this in a bright, captain-of-the-pep-squad voice. Also an if-that's-all-then-please-get-out voice. I might have the confidence of my client, but I was still hired help.

We both stood up and she walked me downstairs to the door. I did the goodbye thing on automatic pilot. I walked out to Vince's Chevy the same way. It wasn't deferring inquiry on the killed-my-brother crack that was bothering me. I was pretty sure I'd made the right call on that one. What was nagging at me was that I'd told Caitlin that Learned had acquired a .45 caliber pistol—not a Colt. She came up with the Colt part all by herself.

Chapter Twenty-four

That Friday, promptly after being advised by Assistant United States Attorney Phillip Schuyler that his boss couldn't be bothered to oppose my motion in the Tyrell Washington case, the honorable judges on the United States Court of Appeals for the Third Circuit granted it, just the way I had written it. The mandate was less than one page long, counting the caption.

Over my lunch hour I found a halfway decent frame for it at a place called The Great Frame-Up. I fit the mandate into place behind the glass, packed it in an envelope with lots of protective padding, and mailed it to my former client's mother. I guess it was a little like fishing for an encore bow, but it brought back warm memories and it made me feel good.

Chapter Twenty-five

Sal Brentano called me just after I got back from lunch on Monday. He was stage-whispering, and he sounded excited.

"I can't believe what I'm seeing. Your dad is about to sell a giant toolbox on wheels for eighteen hundred bucks to a guy who works in a bicycle shop!"

He had a point. Making a sale like that to a car mechanic is impressive enough, but at least a car mechanic could expect to use enough different tools in an average working quarter to fill the thing. A bicycle repairman, though? *That* was impressive.

This was the day I'd arranged for Brentano to take his ride with Vince. Actually getting the ride done required some complex logistics. Vince's route wasn't a geographic area; it was a list of business addresses. Wednesday's share had thirteen stops, with forty-one mechanics all told. So if Sal just met Dad somewhere on the route, say at his first or second stop, there'd be no convenient way for him to get back to his car whenever he figured he'd gotten enough face time with Vince.

The solution we worked out was for Sal to stop by *chez* Jakubek at 6:45 and ride with Vince right from the get-go. I would then drive Sal's car to work. Sal was to phone me when he was ready to call it a day, and I'd drive out to pick him up at the next stop on Vince's list. Sal would drive back to the office with me. Hence the early afternoon call.

"So, you know all about the door-to-door tool business now?" I asked.

"I know enough. Look, Vince's next stop is Cumonow's Hunting and Fishing at, like, sixtieth and Babcock. Can you meet me out there in forty-five minutes or so?"

"Sure."

I made it in a little over twenty-five minutes, so I had some time to kill. I wandered around the place, trying to figure out why anyone who worked here would have to buy high-end professional hand tools. I saw fishing rods for spin-casting and fishing rods for fly fishing and reels for both, but I couldn't figure out why you'd need anything more than a set of jeweler's screwdrivers to work on them. Outboard motors? Okay, yeah, maybe outboard motors. Still…

Then I came to the guns. I'm not a gun-wimp. Hunting is a huge deal in western Pennsylvania. Vince has a deer rifle—Remington thirty-ought-six. He made sure I went through hunter-safety classes when I was thirteen because anyone living in the same house as a firearm should have someone show them movies about what happens unless you "Keep the safety on until you have the target clearly in sight!" and "Keep your finger off the trigger until you're ready to fire!" and "Always maintain muzzle control!" After he finished Advanced Infantry Training, Sergeant Mike even took me to Howars Target Range a couple of times to shred paper targets with the current U.S. military sidearm, which is a nine-millimeter something-or-other. So I shouldn't have been overwhelmed.

But I was. I mean *damn!* Most of the back wall and half the intersecting wall were lined with long guns racked as close together as they'd fit: bolt-action, lever-action, and semiautomatic rifles in every caliber from twenty-two through forty-four/forty; pump action, semiautomatic, and double-barreled shotguns in twenty gauge and twelve gauge and even a couple in ten gauge.

In front of the rifle and shotgun racks were glass cases displaying handguns in an even more dazzling variety. I mean, okay, you're out there in the woods trying to blow away Bambi's dad, connecting with your hunter-gatherer DNA—fine, I get that. Count me out, but I get it. But what in the world are you going to do out there with a snub-nosed .38? Or, excuse me, a *derringer*? Not that that's all Cumonow's had. Not by a long shot, so to speak. You could buy all kinds of stuff with four-inch and six-inch barrels, not to mention a couple of toy cannons with eight-inch barrels.

That's when I got the first great marketing insight of my career: Men don't buy guns to go hunting or to get ready for the Olympic Biathalon. They buy guns for the sake of having guns, the same way women buy shoes, and then they invent a need to justify the purchase. And it's just a short step from there to *Men don't buy tools to fix things; they buy tools etc.*

I was shaking my head and muttering as I approached the end of the actual gun display, just before the telescopic sights and clay pigeon catapult. Cumonow's devoted the last section to replicas, starting with trap-door Springfields like Custer's men carried into their last fight at the Little Big Horn and going back through Civil War-era rifled muskets all the way to Kentucky rifles and Brown Bess muskets used in the American Revolution. I got all this from typewritten four-by-six index cards taped inside the tops of the display cases. Once you got past the Springfields the only difference I could see among the guns was that some had longer barrels than others. Naturally, there were replica handguns too. Same pattern: six-shooters like John Wayne used in all those movies on down to what I would call pirate pistols.

"Can I help you, miss?" The voice was simultaneously friendly and skeptical.

Startled, I looked up to see a guy only slightly taller than I was. He looked like he was in his sixties, and what was left of his hair was bright orange. I started to stammer that I was waiting for someone when a booming baritone from twenty feet away preempted me.

"Get that little lady a Smith and Wesson, Rusty!"

Rusty's brown eyes sparkled under arching eyebrows.

"You know Vince?" he asked me.

"He used to send me to my room."

Trailed by Sal, Vince strode up and warmly shook hands with Rusty.

"Can we make it fifteen instead of twenty-five this week?" Rusty pulled a thick wad of bills from his pocket as he asked the question. "Things are a little slow lately."

"Sure." Vince pocketed the money, set a tool bag he was carrying on the floor, and started printing out a receipt from a handheld thingie about the size of my Kindle. "But have you got five minutes? I've got something in the truck you can't live without."

"I've never gotten off your truck in less than twenty minutes in all the years you've been coming by."

"Five minutes. Scout's honor."

"All right." Rusty ostentatiously checked his watch. "You're on the clock."

I expected them to head for the front door, but Rusty turned around and strode briskly toward the stockroom entrance. I figured out later that Vince had parked his step-van by the loading dock in back in order to save curb space for customers. Sal and I looked at each other, shrugged, and followed them. I knew Vince was going to pitch Rusty one of those high-priced tool carriers and I wanted to see him in action.

I would have, too, if it hadn't been for the gunshot.

The sharp, reverberating roar came from my right. It was nothing like "gunshots" I'd heard on TV or in movies, and it was even louder than I remembered the live fire with Mike out at Howars being. I jumped out of my skin. So did Sal. Vince and Rusty just kept on walking toward the building's back door, as if they hadn't heard a thing.

My head had jerked reflexively toward the sound of the shot, so it only took me a second to realize what the deal was. On the other side of a half-glass, half-sheetrock wall I saw what I guess I'd call a shooting gallery. It was a room about thirty feet long, with space for maybe four people to stand side by side at the near end and plink targets at the far end. Right now one guy was in there. He wore a pair of ear protectors that looked like cheap stereo headphones. He hunched over a narrow, waist-high table, fussing with the weapon.

WTF? Was he firing a single-shot pistol?

"Let's go watch the master in action." Sal nudged my elbow toward the back door.

I couldn't take my eyes off the shooting gallery.

"You go ahead." I started walking toward the gallery entrance.

I stepped inside a little shyly. I'm sure my body language showed that I knew I didn't have any business there. I don't really remember much about the guy fussing with the gun, except that he could have been basically any white guy in late middle age: hedge-fund manager, college professor, insurance salesman, whatever. My eyes were on his gun. It looked vaguely like the pistol Johnny Depp had used in *Pirates of the Caribbean.* The guy glanced over at me, smiling, apparently pleased by my interest.

"Afternoon," he said.

"Good afternoon."

"You a shooter?"

"Not really. I've just never seen a gun like that actually fired before. I would have thought it was a movie prop."

"Functional replicas are actually the fastest growing segment of the recreational firearms market," the guy said. "Of course, some people would say that's like saying downhill skiing is the fastest growing sport in Somalia. Growth rates can look real impressive if you start with a low denominator. Hi, I'm Frank Cumonow, Rusty's partner."

He held out his right hand and I shook it.

"I'm Cindy Jakubek. I'm a lawyer."

"Vince's daughter? No kidding."

Right. Not 'a lawyer.' 'Vince's daughter.'

"Absolutely." I knew I was about to get a sales job, but I figured if I kept my ears open and my mouth shut I might learn something.

"This is actually pretty interesting." He carefully handled the gun so that the barrel was pointed at an upward angle away from the two of us. "It's a muzzle-loader, of course, so you start by putting this little packet of powder down the barrel."

He did what he'd just described, and then picked up a pocked gray sphere a little bigger than a large marble and a little smaller than a Jacks ball, packed into some paper wadding. He dropped it down the barrel. Then, very carefully, he picked up a small ramrod, stuck it down the barrel, and tamped the bullet home.

"So now you've got the load in place, but there's one more thing you need to do before you're ready to fire."

He sprinkled a dollop of powder on the plate under the gun's hammer. With that, he lifted the gun up in the air with both hands, rather like a bartender who'd just made an elaborate cocktail with an umbrella in it. He glanced over at me and grinned. He had me hooked and he knew it.

"Wanna try it?"

"Sure."

I used two hands to take the gun from him, terrified that I'd drop the thing and blow one of us to hell. It must have weighed eight pounds, and it felt heavier than that. Cumonow pointed his index finger at a target at the other end of the room. It was a lifesize, white-on-black outline of a human figure that already had one impressive hole in its paper chest.

Still using both hands, I started to lower the gun.

"First you have to cock the hammer."

Feeling like an idiot, I found the notch on top of the hammer with my thumb and pulled back. It was harder than I thought it would be, but I was determined that I wasn't going to ask the big strong man to handle this chore for the little lady. I put some muscle into it and pulled like I meant it. I heard a satisfying *CLICK!* as the hammer snapped into the cocked position.

"Ready to go," Cumonow said. "Ready on the left, ready on the right, ready on the firing line."

I switched the gun to my right hand and started to level it. I decided against using two hands on the grounds that I'd look like a dork if I did. I know how to sight a gun; so do you—it's intuitive. The barrel didn't have any bead on it, but I lined the front of the rim up with the cartoon valentine heart drawn on the outline. I found it hard to hold the thing steady, so I took a breath and let half of it out, which is one of the two things Mike taught me. Then I squeezed the trigger, which is the other one.

The hammer fell. I saw a bright orange spark and felt a slight burn on my right hand, like you might get if you're holding a sparkler at a July 4th celebration. But the gun's report wasn't instantaneous, as it had been when I shot with Mike. A moment's delay intervened between that spark and the explosive *BANG!* I wasn't ready for that. During that moment the barrel probably moved two inches.

I realized that I had unconsciously squeezed my eyes shut as the hammer fell. I opened them to discover that my right arm had jerked up to about a forty-five degree angle when the gun fired. I also felt a tingling little throb from my elbow to my shoulder. I squinted at the target through a blue-gray cloud of smoke to check my marksmanship. I saw a ragged hole above and just to the outside of the outlined body's right shoulder.

The next thing I heard was Vince's commentary from the doorway of the shooting gallery. He and Rusty and Sal must have watched most of my performance. They were all grinning like idiots.

"Not even a flesh wound," Vince said in mock disgust.

"It was a warning shot," I protested, which produced a couple of good-natured guffaws.

"So," Cumonow said to me, "what do you think?"

"You know what? I'm going to think about it. I'm actually going to think about it."

"What a coincidence," Rusty said. "That's what I told Vince about the toolbox."

Chapter Twenty-six

"Have you opened the attachments yet?" These were the first words of Paul's 9:00 call on Tuesday night.

"It's still loading. It must be a monster."

"It's worth it. Eight hundred words by the way."

My hard drive finally got ambitious enough to bring six thumbnail-sized, head-and-shoulder Pauls up on my screen. I clicked on the first one, which promptly turned into a screen-sized Paul. I caught my breath. This photo had *not* been taken by Paul's brother on his $400 Panasonic Lumix digital camera.

"Whoa. You look magnificent. I mean, you *always* look magnificent, but this thing is off the charts. Where'd you get the turtleneck and sport coat?"

"Wardrobe. The photographer had a closetful of cliché writer clothes in his studio."

I clicked on the second thumbnail. Same basic shot, except studied calm instead of intense glowering. The third and fourth replicated the first two but with a left profile instead of a right. I whistled.

"I can't tell which is your 'better side.' Left and right both look great."

"You don't really need to look at five and six," he said. "They added a prop. I'm a little embarrassed about them."

I instantly clicked on the fifth thumbnail.

"A pipe? A *pipe*? Have you ever smoked a pipe in your life? And bongs don't count."

"We were going for a Faulkner look." He had the grace to sound sheepish.

"So Widget is going to see a farm boy gratifying himself with cows?"

"You can't seriously be reducing William Faulkner to a handful of gothic southern stereotypes, Cindy, he—"

"I'm just goofing on you, lover. You actually look natural with the thing. So this is your agent's first step to marketing you?"

"It's kind of a preliminary thing. He's still thinking me over. But I'm starting to feel pretty good about it."

"Okay. Fingers crossed. And keep yours crossed for me. The preorientation at Calder & Bull is on Thursday. I'm flying to New York tomorrow. They're putting us up at the Sofitel. If you find your way there, look me up."

"If there's any way I can get there I will."

"Only if you can do it without hitchhiking. You have the great American novel to write. Henry Widget is a jealous mistress."

"You are the absolute best."

I went to sleep that night remembering the dreamy wistfulness in his voice and anticipating that unforgettable blend of carbon monoxide and ozone that blasts your nose the second you hit the sidewalk in New York City on a weekday morning.

Chapter Twenty-seven

I brought my TravelPro to the office Wednesday morning and caught a cab for the airport over the lunch hour. When Vince wished me good luck and Godspeed that morning he'd kept his tone light, but I could tell from his eyes that he felt like I was going away for good instead of for about thirty-six hours. And in a way, of course, I was.

The trip to New York was painless. As the plane moved away from Pittsburgh at five hundred miles an hour, my spirits rose at roughly the same rate. I spent the flight plowing through the *Times* and brushing up on the cheat sheet I'd made with all the dope I could find about everyone who was important at Calder & Bull. The cab ride was a breeze and the Sofitel had my room ready for me. The fact that it had been reserved by Calder & Bull instead of by The Law Office of Luis Mendoza probably had something to do with that.

The first thing I saw when I walked into the room was an array of white, yellow, and red roses set off prettily by baby's breath in a clear glass vase. I couldn't believe it. I caught my breath, realizing that I was looking at two days' wages at McDonald's. I ran over to bury my face in the rich scent and retrieve the card:

> *The Greeks sent a thousand ships to Troy over a woman who couldn't shine your shoes. Good luck tomorrow—and take no prisoners.*
> > *Love,*
> > *Paul*

By now, I was way, way up there. I didn't have a net, but I didn't think it mattered.

Chapter Twenty-eight

"There will be times when you feel absolutely overwhelmed. You're going to doubt yourself. You're going to wonder if you can do it. When that happens, just remember one thing: *we* have chosen *you*—and we are very good at what we do."

The speaker was Terry Dempster. He was fifty-nine years old. I'd checked. His brown eyebrows bristled, and if he'd had any hair it probably would have too. He wore a rumpled suit in a very muted green-brown plaid that looked like he'd deliberately chosen it to contradict pinstriped stereotypes about the way Manhattan lawyers dress. Within the giant horseshoe formed by long, mahogany tables in the Whistler Conference Room, seventy-six stories above Park Avenue, he took measured, confident strides, effortlessly managing to meet each of the twenty-seven pairs of eyes that followed him as he addressed Calder & Bull's Class of 2011.

Dempster was the sixth partner we heard from during our preorientation. The managing partner of the firm, the chair of the recruiting committee, and key players from major practice areas had each had their fifteen minutes with us. Also some lesser lights who'd told us how we'd be trained to use the phones and the computers and the security cards. Plus the head clerical assistant, my personal favorite, who told us to please not act like jerks with the secretaries because in most years, frankly, good secretaries were harder to come by than good associates. Dempster, though, was the one who commanded my attention. He chaired Calder & Bull's Litigation Department. Once I started he would be the most important person in my professional life until I made partner or left—and I didn't plan on leaving.

I was feeling warm and cozy. Buckets of cold rain pelted the outside of the building—almost Christmas, but it wasn't quite cold enough in New York to snow. All you could hear in this room, though, were Dempster's voice and the HVAC system's polite hum. After almost three hours in this mahogany cocoon, I felt insulated from rain, cold, and every other vicissitude of the outside world.

I was about to get bravely over *that*.

"When you open those big brown envelopes they passed out while Linda Stange was introducing me," Dempster went on, "you'll each find your presumptive report dates." *WTF? I thought we were reporting February 1st!* "We're staggering report dates by department, to reflect workload trends. Securities/ Mergers and Acquisitions attorneys report on one February; Commercial, Real Estate, and Labor on one June; Litigation on one September; and Regulatory and Tax on one December."

So close I could taste it, and now my Big Apple billet had been snatched away again.

I jumped up, muttering stuff that wouldn't be printed in the New York Times—or here. I ripped my big brown envelope in two, tearing expertly right through the middle of the adhesive label on the front that read JAKUBEK, CYNTHIA M. '11. I threw the two pieces at Dempster and stalked out with immense dignity. I deliberately knocked my chair over on the way.

Nah, I didn't do any of that stuff. I *wanted* to do it. I played out a lurid, three-second fantasy of doing it. But I didn't do it. I didn't clench my fists or stiffen my torso. I sat there with a polite, carefully neutral expression. I'm not against temper tantrums *per se*, but I'm a big girl and I pick my spots.

Dempster paused and gave us a knowing smile.

"I know." A gravelly voice that had captured numerous juries and, on one notable occasion, six justices of the United

States Supreme Court, rolled over us. "You're pissed off. You have a right to be. You feel like we're jerking you around. We are. I'm not happy about it. But we wouldn't be doing you any favors if we had you show up before we're ready to channel a coordinated work-flow to you. It costs this firm two hundred twenty-five thousand dollars for a new associate to sit down at a desk between the sixty-third and seventy-sixth floors in this building. That means we'll be looking for each and every one of you to produce at an annual rate of twenty-one hundred billable hours. It won't help either of us for you to sit here for three months or six months piddling around with six-point-two or seven-point-one billable hours per working day."

I did *not* gulp at those numbers. I knew exactly what I was signing on for when I accepted Calder & Bull's offer. Given all the time an associate has to invest in the job but can't bill to anyone, an average of nine billable hours per working day meant lots of late nights and Saturdays. I knew that. I wasn't afraid of working hard. But I was sick and tired of having rugs pulled out from under me—and I felt sick to my stomach when I thought about phoning Paul about this revolting development.

"Make no mistake," Dempster said. "You're not being deferred again, your report dates are being staggered. You have jobs here. You are going to work. For seniority and time-to-partnership purposes, your tenure will be measured from one February 2011 for each and every one of you."

He paused. He was good. I felt a little tiny bit better. Then he went on.

"One of the things you'll find in that envelope is a check in the amount of three thousand dollars for each month between February and your staggered report date. What's that? Ladies and gentlemen, that's a bribe. That's our way of saying, 'Please don't bail on us. Please give us one more chance. Because we don't want one of the hundreds of talented lawyers who've been sending outstanding résumés over our transom for the last two years. We want *you*.'"

From a purely professional standpoint, I had to admire his craft. He'd just told me I'd been screwed again, and yet I was ready to bust a gut working on a case with him. I knew that "staggered, not deferred" was bullshit, and I knew he knew it. That was like saying, "This isn't a contract, it's an agreement." I knew his assurance that I had a job for sure come September wasn't worth the powder it would take to blow it to hell. I knew Paul would read this as meaning that I'd never work at Calder & Bull and his New York state of mind was now officially brain-dead. And I *still* wanted to believe Dempster.

"Okay." Dempster checked his watch. "You've got a break before the tour of our offices—and *our* means yours as well as mine—so you can spend the next fifteen minutes twittering about what an asshole I am. I'll see you in September. And December. And June. And February."

He made a confident, smiling exit. Two-thirds of the suck-ups sitting around those tables applauded him. I swear they actually applauded him. If I ever stoop that low, please shoot me.

I left the conference room and found a fairly secluded spot about halfway between it and the lobby where I could lean against a streaming window and phone Paul. He answered on the first ring, which meant that whatever he was doing, he wasn't writing.

"Good news and bad news. I'm now supposed to show up for work on September first."

"What's the good news?"

"That is the good news. It's also the bad news."

I'll spare you the outraged string of obscenities, profanities, and vulgarities that was Paul's way of saying he felt my pain. Paul puts all his creativity into his fiction. When he swears he comes off like the average North Jersey seventh-grader. Blessedly, some static broke up the last three or four clauses.

"I hope you're about due for an upgrade on the phone of yours, lover," I said once I sensed that he'd run out of steam.

"It's this goddamn storm! Whoever heard of torrential rain like this so close to Christmas? I might as well be in Miami!"

"Hang in there, tiger. Look on the bright side. Once you turn Henry Widget into a million-dollar advance, we can move to New York together on your dime instead of mine."

Somewhere in the middle of the static, I heard him joking about how I'd just kicked him in the testicles, except he didn't say "testicles."

I still had nine minutes before the office tour started, which was plenty of time for call number two on my suddenly revised agenda. I had my thumb on the 4 that would speed-dial Stacy Tarrant when I sensed someone coming up behind me. Assuming it was one of my fellow deferred/staggered/new-hires, I put a this-is-*not*-a-good-time look on my face and swiveled my head around. I saw Terry Dempster standing twenty-two inches from me.

"Excuse me, Ms. Jakubek. Do you have plans for lunch?"

"Uh, no, actually, I don't."

"I'd appreciate it very much if you'd join Hank Braun and me and a couple of other new associates in the McReynolds room."

"Uh, *sure*. I mean, I'd be delighted, Mr. Dempster."

"See you noonish. And please call me Terry."

I couldn't spend too much time trying to figure what that might mean if I was going to call Stacy before the tour, so as Dempster strode off I turned back toward the window and speed-dialed her. When she answered she spoke in a tone that was clipped and efficient without quite seeming hurried.

"This is Cindy. Now they've bumped me to September first."

"Shit. That sucks. Lemme close my door." I imagined her low-maintenance blonde helmet-cut swinging as she scooted from around her desk to swing her office door shut.

"It does suck, but...." I paused awkwardly, searching for a silver lining. It took me about five seconds to come up with one. "...but at least I got invited to lunch."

"Well, that's something. Invited by someone cute?"

"No. Someone powerful."

"Even better than cute. That has to mean something."

"Yeah. But this reading tea leaves and telling myself every-thing is going to be all right someday if I'll just hold on crap is getting old."

"I hear ya, babe. But what's Plan B? Shopping your résumé around from scratch?"

"The thought has crossed my mind," I said. "I'm going to think about it long and hard before I deposit the latest check."

"I don't know, Cin. That means kissing Calder & Bull goodbye for sure. C & B is a bird in the hand, even if it's seven months farther off now."

"That's the question. If I'm patient, am I actually going to start my life in September, or am I just going to get another run-around six or seven months from now?"

"Yeah." She paused. "You're right. That is the question. Tell you what. Don't do anything drastic for the rest of the day. Don't get drunk and don't tear up the check and don't carve up any C & B partners with that rapier you have where most people keep their tongues. Let me ask around and see if anyone has heard anything more than rumors about Calder & Bull."

"Correct as usual, Queen Friday. You're incredible, Stace. But you knew that."

"Yeah, I did. And listen, there is a bright side. It's almost noon. I'm looking out my window at the JFK Parkway. I would love to spend my lunch hour taking a brisk, bracing two-mile walk from here to Ben Franklin's statue, soaking up a little winter sun. But instead I'll be sitting at my desk reviewing correspondence exchanged between our client and another firm's client about a software implementation project that cratered. A seven-month hiatus before you dive into that Serbonian bog isn't necessarily a horrible thing."

"Noted, Stace. Later."

I won't bore you with a recap of the tour. A law firm is basi-cally offices. There are corner offices for Dempster-class heavy-hitters, comfortable offices for regular partners, small offices for associates, cubicles for paralegals, and work stations for secretar-ies. They had a duplicating department that was pretty cool, a large windowless room with yellow walls, lots of machines, and a rich ink smell. That was the highlight. Now let's cut to lunch in the McReynolds Room.

In the middle of the room was an oblong table covered with a white linen tablecloth and set with china and crystal worthy of Smith & Wolensky if not Lutece. Six well-cushioned chairs sat around it. Atop a long credenza on the near side of the room, bowls and warming trays presented salad, rolls, sliced tenderloin in a rich, brown sauce, and a luscious-looking pasta swimming in cream and basil. I assumed it was a buffet and got ready to grab a plate and dive at the pasta. Fortunately, though, I held off, waiting for a signal from the host.

Good move. It was *not* a buffet.

Dempster came in about the same time as my fellow new-hires and ushered us to the table. He introduced us to Braun, chair of the Securities/M&A Department, who was basically Clark Kent in a three-piece suit but without the glasses and after aging not particularly well into his fifties. Suddenly two—not one, *two*— waitresses in black dresses with organdy aprons appeared. They took orders from each of us and then filled our plates.

Dempster waited until we were served. Then he glanced up and, somehow, just by glancing up, instantly had the attention of everyone else at the table.

"There is a plan. We're not just improvising and reacting and waiting for everything to be the way it used to be, like we were when we did the deferral. We're no longer guessing and hoping. We have a plan, we're implementing it, and the September report date is an integral part of that plan. That date is firm. It's hard. It's set in stone."

I nodded politely. One of the other new hires was bolder. Flicking through my mental Rolodex, I came up with the name Ephraim Pence for him. He had come in business casual, which I thought was a pretty edgy move. Plus, the open-necked dress shirt he wore had French cuffs and his cufflinks were embossed with the rainbow-globe icon from the Obama campaign. That was even edgier.

"That doesn't come as a surprise," he said, "but the confirmation is welcome."

HELLL-O, Mr. Smooth. Sharing pizza with this guy at ten p.m. during a time-crunch document review promised to be a real barrel of laughs.

"So," Braun said in a how-about-those-Mets tone, "how have you all been spending your time during your enforced hiatus?"

The other woman at the table, Melissa Drexler, jumped in to say she'd been interning with the Battered Women's Clemency Project, and gave a little rundown on the effort to spring women who'd killed husbands or boyfriends who beat them. Dempster and Braun nodded in approval, as they damn well should have in my less-than-humble opinion.

I try not to do edgy before my first paycheck, so I didn't mention helping out with a client in the middle of a murder investigation. I stuck with the *pro bono* stuff, mentioning my little Tyrell Washington commando raid. Braun met that with a challenging chuckle and a pointed comment.

"In other words, you got a dead drug dealer off on a technicality and pissed off an Assistant United States Attorney on the same day."

Stacy's admonition to watch my mouth with partners was still ringing in my ears, but then I remembered that Calder & Bull's Litigation Department had a White Collar Crime practice group—and that Dempster, not Braun, was the one who mattered to me. So I gave Braun the smile I used to use to try to get out of detention and spoke in my best approximation of a ladylike voice.

"Any day I don't piss off an Assistant United States Attorney is twenty-four wasted hours."

"Amen to that," Dempster said. "The difference between an Assistant United States Attorney and a terrorist is that it's easier to negotiate with a terrorist."

Braun turned toward Pence. "How about you, Ephraim?"

"I was lucky enough to catch a gig with Lawyers Without Borders."

"Do you mean Doctors Without Borders, the French orga-nization that got the Nobel Peace Prize awhile back?" Braun seemed genuinely puzzled.

"No. Lawyers Without Borders is inspired by Doctors Without Borders, but it has a legal mission instead of a medical one. Namely, to provide the benefits of American litigation tech-nology and trial tactics to mass-tort victims in the Third World."

Pence said this absolutely deadpan, in an anxious-to-please voice. For the first time since before my admission to Harvard Law I committed the sin of envy. At that moment, I wished I was Ephraim Pence. I wished I had enough guts to sit there and dump a load of unmitigated bullshit on these guys, and the flair to bring it off. The half-smile and the look I shot in his direction were intended to say, *That was beautiful, buddy.*

The fourth new-hire, Patrick Hoffman, was a little older than the rest of us, in his early thirties. He had a buzz cut and an undergraduate degree in electrical engineering, so he was tabbed for intellectual property litigation. I was smiling as I turned my head toward him, not to encourage him but because I'd just figured out what was going on here—what the real point of this impressive lunch was. We were auditioning for Braun. Securities/M&A was apparently coming up a little short in the new-hires who'd be showing up for it in February, and Braun was thinking of inviting one or two of us to switch from litiga-tion to his shop.

No, thank you. This was *not* going to happen to Cindy Jakubek. I intended to practice the kind of law that leaves blood on your knuckles, not paper cuts on your pinkie.

"Well, I can't top Eef," Hoffman said, referring to Pence. "I just pitched in with the Greater Oakland Performing Arts Council. Highlight was negotiating special benefit-royalties for a two-week run of sketches based on *It's Always Sunny in Philadelphia*, the TV show."

BOINNG! I suddenly felt an eerie detachment from the group, as if I were floating above it, watching a nice woman with black hair pretending to listen to these other people. A bunch of disembodied data fell into place in a coherent pattern in my mind. All at once I knew where Walter Learned was. And I knew something else.

I realized that Braun was talking again. It took a mental snap-out-of-it-Cindy slap for me to refocus and pick up what he was saying. I checked back in halfway through a sentence.

"…a little thought exercise. Let's say the firm wanted to establish a new office for a niche practice in an area where we've never operated geographically. You know…*suggestive pause*… penetrate a virgin territory. Say we have three talented partners under consideration to head this office up: a top-notch administrator, a proven business-getter, and a specialist in the practice area. Which one should we pick?"

"The business-getter." Pence looked Braun right in the eye as he spoke. "You can always hire an administrator." *Ouch. Well-played, Mr. Smooth.*

Hoffman's turn. "I'd ask for a business plan from all three and let those drive the choice. You're going to have to fill in gaps regardless of whom you pick, so you might as well make sure you have your ducks in a row on the fundamentals." *What, you went to law school because you couldn't spell 'MBA'?*

"I like the business plans," Drexler said. "But I'd factor in diversity concerns, given the importance that clients place on participation of women and non-whites." *That was subtle.*

After about five seconds of silence, Braun turned toward me.

"What about you, Cynthia? What do you think?"

I felt no pressure at all. I was in a zone where time moved more slowly for me than for everybody else. After what I'd just figured out, I simply did not care at that particular instant what happened to Calder & Bull, or to my job, or for that matter to me.

"Well, Hank, I think I'd offer three compensation alternatives. One would guarantee the new-office managing partner's current compensation for three years. The second would guarantee fifty percent of current compensation, plus ten percent of new-office net profit for the first five years. The third would have no guarantee but offer twenty-five percent of new-office net profit for the first seven years."

"Then, assuming each of the candidates picks one of the three, which partner would you choose?"

"The one with the biggest...*suggestive pause*...risk tolerance."

Dempster didn't actually do a spit-take, but he came close. He slapped the table with his right hand and laughed out loud. Then he pointed a mock-menacing finger at Braun.

"You make any pitch you like to anyone else, Henry, but leave this little lady alone." Then, turning toward me, he added, "I'm looking forward to September, Ms. Jakubek. You and I are going to get along just fine."

Chapter Twenty-nine

Unlike Calder & Bull, I didn't have a plan. I was improvising, scrambling, reacting, making it up as I went along. So far I'd only come up with step-one: the Hilton New York.

"Excuse me, Terry," I said to Dempster as we were making our way out of the room. "Is there a phone I can use for a few minutes? I need to change my travel plans and my Droid is about out of juice."

"Certainly."

I expected him to show me to a secretary's desk, but that was because I *still* hadn't come close to assimilating big-firm culture. He pointed me toward the far corner of the room, where I saw—a phone booth. I'm not kidding. Exactly the size of old-fashioned phone booths from the fifties like the ones Superman used to change clothes in on TV, it was enclosed in the same dark mahogany as the credenza and the wainscoting. Smiling my thanks to Dempster, I stepped in. A tiny light came on, and I had a telephone and complete privacy.

I got the Hilton's number from Information, but I turned down the offer to patch my call through. I dialed it myself instead. I wanted "CalderBull" to show up on the Hilton's caller-i.d. screen. In what seemed like a heartbeat I reached a woman with a winsome English accent who identified herself as Guest Reservations.

"Hi. This is Cindy at Calder & Bull. We have a client in the city this afternoon, and we need to get her a room for the night."

"Not a problem. Any special accommodations?"

"Preferred guest status."

"Not a problem. Name?"

"Jakubek." I spelled it for her. "Cynthia."

"Will Ms. Jakubek be paying herself or should we bill the firm?"

"She'll be responsible for her own bill."

"Not a problem. Done and done. Here's your confirmation number."

I wrote down a code that seemed long enough to launch nuclear missiles, thanked the Brit, and hung up.

Okay, what next? Get to the Hilton. I'd left my TravelPro in an ample closet off Calder & Bull's reception area, so I didn't have to circle back to the Sofitel. By pure good luck the closest thing I had to a dress winter coat was a raincoat with a liner, so I was actually prepared for the weather. Heavy rain meant no cabs, of course, but I'm not afraid of subways so when I got to the Hilton I was only wet instead of sodden.

The Calder & Bull juice worked like a charm. Less than an hour after stepping out of the phone booth I was ensconced in a room that made the one I'd occupied on Thanksgiving weekend seem like a closet. I thought seriously about pumping my brains out on an elliptical in the fitness center, on the grounds that that would slightly reduce the chances of my committing homicide in the next four hours, but I decided against it. I figured if I killed someone, I'd just take my chances with the jury. Instead I took a blistering hot shower, washed my hair, dried it, and pulled on my sweats only long enough to press my skirt, jacket, and blouse.

I dressed and did my hair as carefully as if I were going on a job interview. When I was through I stepped back and took a long, objective look in the full-length mirror: Not bad; borderline badass if you get right down to it and, frankly, that was the idea.

Okay. Droid—*not* low on juice, by the way—check; laptop, check; purse, check; attitude, check.

My Preferred Guest key-card persuaded the elevator to take me up to the top floor, and then it let me in to the Hilton

Club there. Just after two o'clock in the afternoon, not quite Christmas week, the Hilton Club had plenty of space. I took a table near the door and sat with my back to the window so that I'd have the best possible view of the corridor and the elevators. I opened my laptop up on the table, made sure the Wi-Fi switch was on, and put a legal pad beside it, with half-a-dozen pages folded over the top. That was my unsubtle way of telling any male who wandered in that I was working and no, he had *not* met me somewhere before.

A waiter came over, deferential and as whispery as if we were in church. Would I like anything to drink? Oh, yes, I would *really* like something to drink.

This was definitely not a chardonnay situation. Scotch was out; bad associations. A martini would have been an uptown choice but, frankly, I wasn't in a particularly uptown mood. I don't have much experience with vodka, so I didn't want to take a chance with it. Besides, a defiant streak of hard-core, blue collar cussedness had been rising in me since halfway through Dempster's talk this morning.

"Bourbon and sweet. Light on the sweet, plenty of ice."

He said "Yes, ma'am" in a deeply approving voice, as if this were the savviest drink order he'd taken that month. I brought a blank e-mail screen up on my computer and stared at it. After about thirty seconds of deep thought, I typed in Paul's e-mail address and stared at it for awhile. I had a pretty good idea of what I was going to say, but this was definitely one of those times when it was more important to do it right than to do it fast. The Hilton, coincidental meetings, complicated burglaries arranged at the speed of light, a superstar agent popping up out of nowhere for a wannabe novelist, pipes, sunshine and rain, pajamas and passion—that's what had all just fallen into place during lunch. I'd been running on cool fury ever since. Now was the time for a little more cool and a lot less fury.

I started to type:

My plans have changed. I'm going to stay in the City

overnight. Any chance you could run up from Philly?

Cindy

I hit SEND. The waiter brought me Jim Beam diluted with Coke. I took a sip. *Oh, yes! Yes, yes, indeed! I could get used to this, all right, oh yes I could.* And I waited. I finished the bourbon-and-sweet, switched to Snapple, and kept on waiting. I had been at it for about forty-five minutes when my Droid started vibrating on the table. I glanced at the number. Stacy.

"Hi, Stace."

"Hey, Cin. Good news. Calder & Bull has a plan."

"That's what the head of Litigation said."

"He was telling the truth," Stacy said. "In the last two months our modest little two-hundred lawyer firm here in Philadelphia has gotten résumés from six Securities-slash-M-and-A partners from Calder & Bull, and three from partners in Commercial Transactions."

"They're firing *partners*?"

"You bet. Thinning the herd. The fastest way to increase profit-per-partner is to cut the number of partners—as long as you can do it without losing any high-profit clients. Calder & Bull is slashing partners one department at a time, presumably to keep *The American Lawyer* from running a headline about 'Bloodbath at C & B.'"

"They've decimated Securities and Commercial, so the Litigation Department is next." I thought about the implications of that as I spoke the words. *I have a job because someone else is about to lose his.*

"That would figure. They're picking partners who don't control client relationships and throwing them to the wolves. Then they'll downstream the work those partners were doing to senior associates, and downstream the senior associates' work to junior associates."

"*E.g.*, me."

"*E.g.*, you. Come September, I would say you are in like an off-color simile."

It took me a good ten seconds to wrap my mind completely around this. The Calder & Bull job was real. It wasn't a mirage that would recede perpetually into the distance each time I thought I was getting close to it. In September, 2011 I was going to start getting a lot of money to practice law in New York City. When Stacy spoke again, her voice seemed far away.

"You still there?"

"Yeah, I'm just slowly processing the data. I mean, I have a job."

"Right. You have a job working for people who dump their partners overboard as soon as the sea gets a little choppy, but you have a job. So, congratulations—I think."

I heard a YOU'VE GOT MAIL! bing from my laptop, but resisted the urge to brush Stacy off.

"I didn't think I'd be working with an order of Franciscan nuns." I tried to sound lighthearted. "I knew the score coming in. Anyway, thanks, Stacy. This is exactly what I needed to hear right now."

"You're welcome, Cin. I just hope you feel the same way a year from today."

On that bracing note we said goodbye. Only then did I glance at my screen. The e-mail was from Paul. I closed my eyes and said a quick prayer: *Please let me somehow be wrong.* I opened Paul's response:

> WOW! No kidding? THAT'S GREAT! I'll try to cadge a ride from someone and see if I can meet you at the Sofitel at, like, 8:30 or 9.
>
> P

I answered immediately:

> AMTRAK leaves Philly at 4:30 and gets in just before 7. I could meet you at Grand Central.
>
> CJ

SEND. Wait. I didn't think I'd have to wait long. I slipped my legal pad back into the computer bag and signaled for the tab. I was feeling pretty confident. Also pretty berserk but, refined by the bourbon, it was a good berserk.

BING!

I didn't open Paul's response immediately. The waiter brought the check. Sixteen-seventy-five for one bourbon-and-sweet and one Snapple over ice. I added a two-fifty tip and charged it to my room. *Then* I opened Paul's e-mail:

> If I hustle, I can just barely make it. I'll call you if I miss the train.
>
> P

I closed my computer and shoved it in the bag as soon as I was sure my reply was hurtling through cyberspace. I walked out of the Hilton Club and straight down the corridor, past the elevator bank, toward the brace of Executive Suites at the far end. If my theory was right, Paul would hustle compulsively downstairs to check with the concierge about Amtrak's schedule. As I strode along the deep-pile carpet, I felt a tiny surge of doubt in my belly. *DOUBT IS GOOD! Let me be wrong!* Even assuming I was right, I might have a bit of a wait on my hands, but I figured the worst that could happen was that I'd waste some time and feel silly. Neither of those would be a new experience for me.

I was still walking when the last door on my right opened about twenty feet farther down the hall. I kept walking. *Please let it be Learned and not Paul.*

It was Paul.

I let him see me, and gape, and stop dead in his tracks. Then, almost on top of him, I spoke.

"Tell you what. Let's say your place instead."

Chapter Thirty

"That's a new look for you, isn't it, Tiger?" I brushed past Paul into the suite. "Goodbye proletarian chic, hello *GQ*."

Fair comment, if you ask me. He was wearing a French blue dress shirt and blue jeans that cost $400 if they cost a penny. Paul sputtered semicoherent clauses—I don't think any of them rose to the dignity of a full sentence—that all included "Cindy." I couldn't make out any of the other words, but then I didn't try very hard.

The suite was an eyeful. The foyer by itself—it had a foyer—was close to the size of a normal hotel room, and what I guess you'd call the living room looked at least twice as big as that. I'd describe the décor as early-modern Eurotrash, but by this point I had a pretty jaundiced attitude, so don't go by me. Dove gray leather furniture, shelving here and there bearing what looked like high-end art objects, and—I'm not kidding about this—a pale blue flag near the door with embroidered bumblebees on it.

My interior decorating survey didn't take long. I turned back to Paul.

"Thanks for the flowers."

"Look, Cindy, I'm not sure where you're going with this, but—"

"It's not always sunny in Philadelphia, Paul, but it's sunny there today, when you were blaming your phone's static on heavy rain. That's how I knew you were in New York. Which is okay.

You don't need my permission to come to New York. But you lied to me about it."

"I was hoping to surprise you." He managed an expression of utter and poignant sincerity that wouldn't have fooled a novice nun.

"No, Paul, you lied to me because you're doing something that you knew would piss me off and you didn't want me to know about it."

"You're jumping to conclusions."

"I would say that I stumbled to that particular conclusion, and none too nimbly. If I were jumping I would have figured out three weeks ago that you don't just happen to come upon someone at the Hilton the same afternoon she checks in and then arrange two burglaries from scratch in a couple of hours. You only manage that if you already have a network of useful relationships in place at the Hilton. That's the kind of thing you might develop over time if you live here permanently, like Eloise did at the Plaza. Clear as glass, but I didn't put it together until you rubbed my nose in it."

"Rubbed your nose in *what*?"

"In your association with me." The voice came from my right. Enter Learned, strolling around from behind the not-quite-ceiling-height wall separating the entryway from the dining area. "Now that you've demonstrated your belated deductive brilliance, Ms. Jakubek, please sit down. We have some serious things to talk about, and they directly implicate your client."

"Explain." I did *not* sit down.

"Assuming that Thomas Bradshaw was shot the Monday night before Thanksgiving," Learned said, "I was in bed with Ariane Bradshaw at the Monongahela Hotel at the time of the murder. Therefore, she didn't kill him and I didn't kill him. Because most murders are committed by relatives of the victim, that makes Caitlin Bradshaw the prime suspect."

"Only if you overlook the thugs who were afraid Bradshaw had a line on the Gardner Museum loot and might get too chatty with the cops once he was arrested."

"True. But cops are lazy. Some speculative group of anonymous criminals is a much less promising source of suspects than the victim's own family."

"Okay." I shrugged. "So what?"

"So. You figured out where I live. Congratulations. You can safely assume that the FBI already knows. If they have any business with me, they know where to find me. But the nasty people who killed Tom Bradshaw, assuming that Caitlin didn't, do *not* know where to find me. I'd like to keep it that way. If you spread my whereabouts around, you'll not only hurt your client—you could become complicit in another murder."

"Murder?" Paul yelped.

"Take notes." I gave him this instruction without bothering to look at him. "Maybe you can squeeze some of it into your next chapter."

"I take it you've got at least a general idea of what was going on," Learned said to me.

"Up to a point. You had been working with Bradshaw for a couple of years at least to follow some kind of a lead on the stuff swiped from the Gardner Museum. Or maybe to arrange to move a piece or two of it. You used your media connections to get him quoted for publication. A shady buyer who couldn't risk a legitimate appraisal might want some kind of authentication before dropping, say, twenty million dollars on a hot Monet. Media credentials would help. You were using Bradshaw as a cat's paw."

"No comment on any of that imaginative palaver." Learned spoke rather sharply, with a this-isn't-just-clever-banter edge to his voice. "But know this, Ms. Jakubek: Tom Bradshaw was a friend of mine. He was in serious trouble with nasty people. He came to me for help, and I did everything I could to help him. I drove him from New York to Pittsburgh because he was afraid that if he drove his own car he'd end up bullet-riddled at some rest stop along the way."

"Friend?" I raised my eyebrows—which is something I do rather well. "Do you always sleep with your friends' wives? What do you do to your enemies? Sodomize their children?"

Paul stepped toward me. He took very measured, deliberately nonthreatening paces, as if he were a grown-up. He seemed upset about getting caught, but not about anything else. I was looking for some kind of emotional reaction proportional to blowing up the last three years of my life. Instead I was getting Frat Boy of the Year. It was starting to piss me off—and I was already pretty hot when I walked in.

"Okay, Cindy." He used the kind of exaggeratedly calm tone that men have been using with angry women since about fifteen minutes after Adam and Eve left Eden. "Listen. I want you to just sit down for a few minutes and get a grip on things. Just think things over and calm yourself down a little."

I would like the record to show that, furious as I felt, I had been doing a pretty good job up to this point of keeping my temper. Not quite a self-control poster girl, but no over-the-top, Hell-hath-no-fury stuff either. That comment from Paul, though, pushed me right over the edge. I spun around and thrust my face at him so aggressively that he actually backed up a step, even though he could have put me in the hospital with one arm.

"Are you giving me a *time-out*, you pompous bastard?" I snorted. "Why don't you just go back in the closet, you weak, sniveling, chickenshit, supercilious, self-involved, egomaniacal *faggot*!"

"Now, Cindy, wait a minute," Paul said, retreating toward the shelving.

"If she throws something at you," Learned said, "for God's sake don't duck. The marble miniature bust of Napoleon on that shelf behind you is priceless."

Paul moved out from in front of the shelving to within reach of the pale blue flag, mostly furled around its pole in a polished brass flag stand on the floor. I took another step toward Paul, just because I got kind of a kick out of watching him back up.

"Don't tell *me* to 'wait a minute,' goddammit!" I spat the words, feeling my hair swish against my neck. "You *used* me! Every 'love' out of your mouth was pure bullshit! I was just your ticket to New York. I wasn't your lover, I was a fellowship—a *brunette fellowship.*" I flicked my hair with that last comment, in case Paul didn't get it.

"That's not fair." He got it.

I stretched my left arm out full-length to point at Learned.

"And you gave me up for a *white fellowship* because it came with an agent instead of just grocery money and a decent apartment."

"Now you're getting hysterical. This is just a lot of linear, left-brained thinking. You're letting yourself get trapped by your own logic."

I suddenly wanted to hurt him. No, something richer than that. Not just hurt. Not even mainly hurt. Hurt-plus. I wanted to *reach* him. I wanted to shred the cocoon of fatuous smugness that enclosed him, and rattle him. Really shake him up.

"I'm *pregnant*, you asshole!"

A barefaced lie, but it did the trick. I'd reached him, all right. The pregnancy worried him vastly more than being caught cheating on me did. His eyes snapped repeatedly in flustered confusion. He raised two finger on his right hand to his head as if he'd suddenly gotten dizzy. His nostrils flared and his chest swelled in what looked like the kind of rhythmic breathing exercise you learn in classes on panic attacks. Then he closed his eyes, took one deep, cleansing breath, and looked at me with his arms raised and his hands palms outward in a classic *calm down* signal.

"Cindy, I didn't know. I swear I had no idea."

"You were clueless? Well, there's a shock."

"Look, we can get through this. I'll be there for you. I'll help you arrange the procedure and I'll be there with you—"

"What 'procedure'?"

"You know. The abortion."

"There isn't going to be any abortion, you moral cretin! I'm not going to kill a baby just because his father is a prick!"

"Oh, God, Cindy," he said in a despairing plea. "Try to think rationally about this."

"It's a little late for rational. The time for rational was when you gave me pajamas that made me look like a twelve-year-old boy. But I wasn't 'thinking rationally' then, so why start now? You're looking at twenty-one years of child support, buddy. Seventeen percent of your gross. That hotshot agent of yours gets you a hundred thousand dollar advance, 17K goes straight to Cindy, right off the top. That's *before* the agent gets his fifteen percent commission, not after."

"Twenty percent," Paul mumbled in a deeply worried tone.

"Every royalty check, every advance, every honorarium from now until this little brat in my tummy finishes college—seventeen percent to me."

I was playing fast and loose with the law, but Paul didn't know that. Color drained from his face. His shoulders drooped. He sighed. He bowed his head and dropped his hands to his side. Even his moustache sagged. Then, suddenly, he brightened and brought his face back up with a tentatively hopeful expression.

"Wait a minute. What if—"

"Don't say it," Learned instructed him firmly.

Paul said it.

"—what if the baby isn't mine?"

"*YOU BASTARD!*"

I leaped at him like an Amazon with PMS, right fist cocked and eyes shining with feral fury. The veneer of Harvard Law School and Duquesne University evaporated in a heartbeat. I was back on a parochial school playground in a working class parish. There are certain things you don't say, and he'd just said one of them.

If he'd just stood there he could have taken my best shot without a whimper and then swatted me away like a bug. The pure savagery in my eyes, though, seemed to awaken some primitive terror in his soul, as if I were a wild animal attacking him instead of just a scorned lover. He retreated toward the foyer's near corner, making a panicky grab for the flag on his way. He held the thing horizontally in front of him, like a quarterstaff, ready to swing it or point it or thrust it or do whatever he had to do with it to keep me from making physical contact.

"Stop this idiocy!" Learned yelled, as I heard his feet hurrying toward us.

Two strides and a bound and I was on Paul. My left knee smashed his right thigh, not by design but because that was where it happened to land after I left my feet. I aimed a solid right fist at his face and landed it on his collarbone. Paul grunted, but that was about as much satisfaction as I got out of the exchange. Planting the flagpole against my ribcage and pivoting a bit to his left for leverage, he used his one-hundred-pound-plus weight advantage to shove me upward and brusquely away. I flew through the air for half-a-second or so before crashing into the shelving nearest the door.

Pain lanced through my kidneys and the back of my head. The sound of splintering wood and shattering porcelain would have filled my ears if the desperate keen of Learned's "NOOO!" hadn't drowned it out.

My butt hit the Oriental carpet before my feet did. Learned must have cheaped out on the padding, because *it hurt*. I saw stars for just a second. When my head cleared, Paul was still crouched in front of the door, flagpole ready. He looked genuinely worried that he might have hurt me, and at the same time terrified that I might jump up and come after him again. Learned was on his hands and knees, scampering away from us across the entryway floor.

I did *not* bounce up for a rematch with Paul. Decent punch, hard fall—catharsis. I may work that into a haiku some day. Anger still coursed through every fiber of my being, but at least for the moment my primal need for violence had spent itself.

Learned got up, a bit laboriously. He was clutching something shiny in his right hand. He turned worried eyes toward me, and for an instant I felt touched by his concern. But he wasn't worried about me.

"Napoleon?" He almost whimpered this question, in a little voice that was scared and hopeful at the same time. How deflating.

I felt around tentatively among the shards and splinters. My hand closed on something cold and hard under a slab of shattered pine. I picked it up and chanced a quick look at a palm-sized head-and-shoulders under a bicorne military hat in exquisitely blue-veined marble. The miniature size emphasized a striking precision of detail that made this lump of stone seem to throb with power and passion—a guy who'd kill a million Frenchmen for half of Europe without thinking twice about it. It was either Napoleon Bonaparte or his twin brother.

I held the thing up for Learned to see. He sighed with what I took to be a combination of relief and happiness. Then he walked over to Paul.

"Apologize to Ms. Jakubek. It was quite ungallant to insinuate that she has slept with someone else."

"Sorry," Paul tried to look contrite but it came off as sullen.

I choked back a two-syllable response and just looked at him with eyes colder than the ice in my bourbon-and-sweet earlier that afternoon.

"If you stay here much longer," Learned said then to Paul, "I think she really might kill you—and it's hell to get bloody brain tissue out of an oriental carpet. Go down to the bar and have a little Glenlivet on the rocks while Ms. Jakubek and I finish our stimulating conversation."

Paul looked confused for a couple of seconds. Then he dropped the flagpole, opened the suite door, and slipped out. The last thing I saw before the door closed behind him was a pipe in his back pocket. I swear on the Magna Carta that he had a pipe.

Learned picked up the flagpole and started fitting the shiny thing onto the top. It must have come flying off when Paul was muscling me around. Interesting that Learned had given that priority over the priceless miniature Napoleon I was holding. He gave me a controlled, unhurried look. When he spoke he used a soothing, sympathetic tone.

"I don't know if it helps, but I think he really does love you. Your line about the brunette fellowship and the white fellowship was inspired, but he wasn't *just* using you, the way he is me. He *was* using you. You were right about that. Artists use everybody. That's their nature. But that's not all there is to it. He loves you."

"Well he can take his 'love' and shove it up his ass."

I said this on automatic pilot. Ninety percent of my mind was somewhere else. Specifically on my little tirade about Paul's generous offer a few minutes ago to hold my hand during an abortion. I didn't know why I was thinking about it as I gazed at Learned, but I figured the reason would come to me.

"Are you hurt much?"

"Abortion," I muttered thoughtfully.

"Excuse me?"

"He killed my brother." Caitlin said that Ariane had looked like she was putting on a little weight a few months ago, but the extra weight was gone by the time of their dad's-in-trouble talk. Bradshaw somehow forced Ariane to get an abortion—at least Caitlin thought so. Why? Because she was pregnant with Learned's kid instead of Bradshaw's?

"Nothing." I gave him an *I-don't-have-any-more-time-for-you* headshake. "If you'll excuse me, I have to get an AIDS test."

Hurting like hell, I stood up and brushed myself off. I resisted the temptation to toss Napoleon at Learned, and instead politely handed it to him on my way to the door.

I had lots of things to do before going to bed that night: change my flight to the next morning; a little TLC for my bumps and bruises, which turned out to be not all that bad, considering; check in with Mendoza; forty blistering minutes on the elliptical in the fitness center; scorching shower; call Stacy after work to tell her I'd just joined the oldest women's club in the world; and get drunk.

But before doing any of that, I went to confession. I checked the Internet, figuring that even during Advent I'd have to go halfway across Manhattan to find a church where confessions were being heard on a weekday afternoon, but I lucked out: St. Pat's had them. After a bit of a wait in line I was slipping into a confessional by four thirty.

"Bless me, Father, for I have sinned. It's been about four years since my last confession. I just had a huge fight with my ex-fiancé. I called him a faggot. And I threw in a couple of god-damns while I was at it."

The priest behind the grill waited with the patience of someone who heard stuff worse than this from grade-schoolers every month. I could hear steady, quiet breaths before he finally responded.

"Are those the only sins you've committed in the last four years?"

I thought about that for a second.

"Those aren't even the only sins I've committed in the last four hours. But they're the only ones I'm sorry for."

Chapter Thirty-one

"You look like hell."

"Bad hangover, early flight," I told Mendoza. *Throbbing head* isn't an acronym for *laconic*, but it might as well be.

"I thought you weren't all that much of a drinker."

"I'm not. This is what happens when someone who isn't all that much of a drinker makes an exception, like I did last night."

"I hope you weren't drinking alone."

"Most of the time I had a friend from clerkship days on the phone with me."

"Must be a good friend."

"Yep."

We were at the Pittsburgh Airport's Three Rivers Café, drinking black coffee. It was just after 9:30 on the morning after—the morning after Paul became my ex-fiancé. When I'd checked in with Mendoza yesterday afternoon he'd insisted on picking me up at the airport this morning. I think he'd figured out that something pretty damn serious had gone down, and he wanted to spare me the humiliation of falling apart in front of the entire office if it came to that.

"Okay. Your getting drunk is none of my business, and why you got drunk is none of my business—"

"Actually, it is. As soon as I get through explaining why I got drunk I'm going to tell you some important stuff, and you'll need to figure out how much to discount it for bitterness and rage."

He shrugged eloquently. "Shoot."

I told him about Paul and Learned and then I told him about me and Learned. This was therapeutic. Trial lawyers will tell you that if you have some really shocking pictures or video to show a jury, you don't show it over and over. The first couple of times it makes an impact, but then it starts to numb the jury's reactions. The same thing works in reverse. By going over the trauma and betrayal again and again I was gradually reducing its power to keep on hurting me.

I had Mendoza's attention. He listened carefully, and he looked like he was getting not just the facts but the subtext and nuances as well. He nodded soberly when I finished.

"We've got a problem."

"We sure do."

"If half of what you say is right, Learned is up to his eyebrows in fertilizer, including a possible murder rap. If things get too tight for him, he'll do everything he can to pin Bradshaw's murder on our client, because the only other possibilities are him, or someone he's sleeping with, or people who are probably already trying to kill him."

"Yep."

"So here's the money question." Mendoza paused to make sure I was really focusing. "Do you think he's really trying to recover the Gardner Museum stuff?"

"I think he's trying to move it—or help whoever has the stuff move it. I think his effort to get it back is cover for trying to fence it."

"Or maybe the other way around," Mendoza said. "One way to get a line on the loot would be to put the word out that you could turn some of it into cash. After all, how do you fence art that's world famous for having been stolen? The thieves had to assume that they'd take the stuff and then quietly negotiate with an insurance company to return it for, say, twenty percent or twenty-five percent of its value. But it turns out the Gardner didn't have insurance."

"Which means that after this gang of Ocean's Eleven types pulled off the caper of the century, they were stuck with a ton of hot art and no way to unload it. So how does Learned convince them he could move it for them?"

"Maybe he invents some oil prince who can groove on having a Monet in his Saudi Arabian palace and showing it to his four wives and close friends."

"As long as we're making stuff up," I said, "let's say that the thieves buy Learned's line. He fakes a couple of relatively small sales to build confidence with the crooks, hoping to get to the point where he can tell cops enough to let them swoop in and recover the art. No insurance, but the Gardner has put up a five-million dollar reward, so he'd be in line for a nice payday."

"And if the bad guys catch on, he's in line for a forty-five caliber hole in his heart."

"Maybe with some collateral damage along the way—like Tom Bradshaw. In other words, you're right: we've got a problem."

Mendoza leaned back. He glanced at his watch. He surveyed the enlarged pictures of Ford Trimotors and Boeing 727s and Constellations that hung on the café walls. I couldn't figure out our next move so I asked him.

"What do we do?"

"Smoke out the Feds."

"Huh?"

"If Learned was doing this sting we're dreaming about, maybe he was doing it on spec, but it's more likely he was working with people who have badges—and money. The Feds are the most obvious choice."

"That fits in with them not being the cops involved in the search of Bradshaw's house. But 'smoke them out' how?"

"Give them enough dope to support a search warrant. If they don't bite, that means they're in bed with Learned. If they do, then at least the spotlight is on him and off of our client. Either way, we've diminished Learned as a credible source of testimony against Caitlin."

"The raw material for the search warrant has to come from me," I said.

"You're the only one who can sign an affidavit about what you've told me this morning."

"Great. I'm game. Let's get downtown and get to work."

That was *not* pseudo, ain't-I-a-trooper enthusiasm. I meant every word of it. I relished the idea of getting busy practicing law again. Banging out a statement detailing all my New York stuff—well, most of my New York stuff—and having coy telephone conversations with Phillip Schuyler at the U.S. Attorney's office were exactly what I needed. Twenty hours of hard work in the next two days would let me pour all of my hatred into constructive channels.

"Not so fast." Mendoza lifted his coffee cup halfway to his mouth and just held it there, as if we had all morning to sit around.

"What do you mean?"

"We can't go off half-cocked on this, and nothing important is going to happen at the U.S. Attorney's office between now and New Year's anyway. I have to talk things over with Sam Schwartzchild. I have to have someone other than you do some legal research. And then I have to prime the pump with Schuyler."

I bristled at that, but I kept my mouth shut long enough to think it through.

"You're right."

"Look, Jake, you've just been through a helluva bad trip. When you sit down with Schuyler, if that's what we end up doing, he can't think you're some psycho-ex-girlfriend-from-hell. You've been at the office for almost a year now, and you haven't had a vacation yet. I want you to take off until the Monday after New Year's. Go home and indulge yourself. Eat popcorn and vanilla ice cream with chocolate sauce on it, take long baths, watch old movies, lie in bed 'til ten a.m., track down some friends who'll go out drinking with you—whatever you have to do to start getting past the shitty way this low-rent, son-of-a-bitch, pretentious hack writer treated you."

"Thanks for the offer," I said. "I really appreciate it. But I think it'd actually be better for me to get to work on something."

"It might be better for you for the next six hours, but not in the long run. You can work seventeen hours a day. I know. I did it for close to a year after my divorce. But you can't work twenty-four hours a day. Sooner or later you wake up at two o'clock in the morning, and you have to be able to handle it then, too."

"Maybe, but—"

"No buts about it. I'm not asking, I'm telling. I'm the boss. You're on vacation for the duration of the holidays. C'mon, I'll get the bill and drive you home."

I came home to an empty house. I flipped on the living room switch so that the red and green lights on the Christmas tree would come on. I walked distractedly through the downstairs. I looked at the crèche on the dining room buffet. The shepherds and magi seemed to have mocking grins underneath their pious expressions. I glanced at a bright, cardboard Santa train about four feet long that I'd taped to the top of the wall in the downstairs hallway the night we put the tree up. I gave particular attention to the jolly, full-bearded Santa who was driving the thing from a perch on top of the locomotive. I decided that he needed to have his butt kicked.

Merry Christmas, Cindy.... No! Snap out of it! None of THAT crap! Self-pity is for losers!

Lugging my TravelPro upstairs to unpack gave me something to do. I got laundry down the chute and everything else put away except the pair of blue pajamas with feet that Paul had given me. I left those on the bed and just stood there, looking at them.

Could I have been wrong? No. There were too many facts, too clear a pattern. Besides, Learned had basically confirmed that he and Paul were sexually involved with each other, and Paul himself hadn't bothered to deny it. Some part of me deep inside, though, was whispering that maybe I'd gotten it wrong. Maybe

I'd jumped to conclusions. Maybe there was some non-betrayal explanation for what had happened.

I stripped and put on the pajamas. I walked slowly into the bathroom, turned on the light, and looked at myself as objectively as I could in the full-length mirror.

I'd made that crack to Paul about the pajamas making me look like a twelve-year-old boy because I was flailing around, searching for any piece of abuse to throw at him. But I'd nailed it. I mean bullseye. A twelve-year-old boy a little tall for his age. The jammies lent a grotesquely elfin cuteness to my figure while concealing every curve I had, including my breasts—and that's no mean trick. I thought for a second about what fantasies had been going through Paul's head when he made love with me in those jammies.

I would appreciate some credit for *not* vomiting, thank you very much. I wasn't feeling very tough right then, but I'm tougher than that. I trudged wearily back to my bedroom, took off the pajamas, and tossed them in front of the door so that I'd remember to put them in the bag of donations for Purple Heart Veterans. Then I climbed under the covers and curled myself up as tightly as I could.

If you'd been standing there you probably wouldn't even have noticed the first sob, a tiny little gasping, unimportant thing. Within seconds, though, I let go. The tears came in earnest, and I was crying like I hadn't cried since I got the news about Mom, sobbing and shaking like a punished child.

I ended up crying myself to sleep. The last thing I remember thinking through my convulsive sobs was *I hate you I hate you I hate you and if it's the last thing I ever do I'm going to kill you.*

Chapter Thirty-two

I didn't get out of bed until almost four o'clock in the afternoon. Crashing for five hours had done me some good. My headache was now aspirin-class instead of Advil-class, and I'd wrung some of the poor-little-me crap out of my system. I was still lower than Lindsay Lohan's voice after a pack of Camels, but at least I was functional. Even so, if the Christmas tree hadn't drawn my eye I probably would have ended up vegging out in front of the tube.

The tree, though, reminded me that Job-One was to hold it together through Christmas. I owed Vince that much. Vince had gotten the assignment of finding the tree and buying it and setting it up, because that involved going outside and using tools. I'd handled the substitute-mom stuff: finding the ornaments and lights and fixing popcorn and cocoa to keep us company while we decorated the tree; getting the Advent wreath and the crèche and all the Christmas decorations set up; digging up the thick red and white candles in their glass holders and putting them on the mantle and the buffet so we could light them on Christmas Eve before we left for Midnight Mass; and so forth. Until Vince took things to the next level with Lainie I was the closest thing to a companion he had on the premises. I couldn't crawl into a shell and let him go through the holidays with a basketcase on his hands.

Right about then I heard Vince's rig pulling into the driveway. I glanced at my watch to see if I'd somehow lost an extra hour after my Sleeping Beauty number. I hadn't. I hurried to the door to meet him as he walked in.

"You're home pretty early for a Friday, aren't you?"

"Yeah." He began shedding his parka, his body language as listless as his voice. "They closed Minelli's. Nine mechanics."

I blinked. Almost five percent of his customers gone, just like that. Nine guys who wouldn't be buying any more tools or, probably, making any more payments on the tools they'd already bought.

"Ouch."

"Yeah."

"At least you sold six of those big toolboxes. Maybe that'll tide you over until someone moves into Minelli's space."

He smiled indulgently at my naïveté. I got a Schaefer for him while he hauled the fleece-lined parka with its Pro-Tools logo over to the peg rack on the hallway wall.

"Thanks." He took the beer. "But if anything goes into Minelli's space, it'll probably be a self-service BP without a garage. And those big toolboxes aren't money in my pocket, just a credit on my tool bill. That credit turns into a charge-back if the buyers default on their installment payments. Meanwhile, *my* bill for those things comes due in February."

So I got a dose of perspective right between the eyes. Heartbreak at twenty-six versus bankruptcy at sixty. Yeah, that's close—not. I wanted to hug him and tell him everything would be all right, but I knew that would stop the conversation. I played it the other way.

"And that's not the worst of it. Turns out you're still gonna have an extra mouth to feed from February through August."

Vince blinked at that. It took him a couple of seconds to realize the implications. Once he had, though, he reacted fervently.

"What?" His eyes flashed with indignation. "They're jerking you around *again*?"

"Yep, they're jerking me around again. But I think that this time the deferred report date is gonna stick."

He turned his head away from me so that I wouldn't hear the obscenities that poured out under his breath. His fists clinched and his face turned purple. He was reliving vicariously, through me, the eternal working class curse: do everything right, obey the rules, pay your taxes (well, some of your taxes), work your ass off, study until your brain fries, turn in all your homework, show up for work every day even if you feel sick as a dog—and the suits will still find a way to shaft you. He turned back to me, contrition sketched eloquently across his face.

"I'm sorry, honey, I shouldn't of laid my stuff on you."

Now I hugged him, now that the weakness and vulnerability could be mine instead of his.

"It's gonna be okay, Vince. We're gonna make this work." I broke the clinch and got all businesslike. "Now, go grab a shower or catch some tube or something. I'll call for pizza."

He smiled, gave my shoulder a quick squeeze, and headed upstairs. Shower, yes—TV, no. That was a good sign. I decided to wait until later to tell him about Paul.

I managed to keep myself from falling apart for the next week. Then it was Christmas Eve and that cheered me up a bit. UPS dropped off a basket from Calder & Bull with more fruit in it than a platoon of vegetarian Marines could eat in a week. I had changed my Facebook status to UNCOMMITTED without further comment, and most of the reactions had "Right on, sister!" in them. I got three emails from Paul, which I took vast satisfaction in deleting without opening. I decided that I didn't really want to kill Paul. Vince and I spent fifteen minutes with Mike, live from Afghanistan, on Skype.

"Midnight" Mass started at 10:30. We got home in time to open one present each. Old family tradition. Vince opened a new set of deluxe barbecue tools that I'd gotten him. I opened a package that he'd slipped under the tree before we went to Mass without my noticing. It was small and light. It sure wasn't pajamas, thank God. I actually got a little excited as I undid the ribbons and pulled the wrapping paper off. I found a certificate for three free replica-gun rentals and shooting lessons at Cumonow's. I gaped at it for five seconds, then burst into laughter.

"I saw that look on your face when you fired that thing," he said.

"Vince, this is fantastic!"

Christmas Day I took a break from my broken heart and smoldering rage. My funk wasn't history, by a long shot. Closure wasn't even on my horizon. But for one day I just stepped outside of it. Just focused on Vince. Lainie was having Christmas dinner at her daughter's home and there was no way Ken could come over—priests are kind of busy on Christmas—so instead of a turkey I fixed a couple of Cornish game hens for Vince and me, with uncomplicated side dishes and chocolate cake for dessert. My vegetarianism is a personal preference, not a religious principle. I don't guilt-trip myself over an occasional exception.

Vince offered to help me clean the kitchen. Fortunately, I realized just before I would have shooed him out that I should let him pitch in, so I did. Ken called in the middle of our effort and between Vince's time on the phone and mine he stayed connected for an hour. With that interruption, it was dark by the time Vince put the last plate away and glanced over at me.

"Hey, you remember how we used to drive around during the holidays when you kids were young, and look at the lights?" He said this kind of shyly, in the voice he uses when he wants to make something he's been thinking about for three hours sound impulsive.

"Sure."

"Do you think it might be kind of a kick to do that tonight?"

That wasn't quite the last thing I wanted to do. It came ahead of root canal surgery and self-flagellation. But there was only one possible answer, and I made it sound peppy.

"I'll race you to the Chevy."

We spent forty-five minutes cruising around some neighborhoods that had always had a reputation for going a little over the top on holiday decorations. They didn't disappoint. Reindeer on rooftops, six-foot candy canes, lifesize nativity sets on front porches, Rudolph nuzzling nutcrackers, the whole nine yards. And lights, lights, lights. They started to blur together after awhile, but I suppose that's part of the point. All those bright lights, all those snowmen and Santas—a brave, brightly colored defiance of darkness and winter.

I could tell that this meant something special to Vince, something a lot more than it meant to me. I got a warm fuzzy remembering how we'd done this when I was eight and nine, but I wouldn't call my reaction transcendent. Vince was just plain sailing, with a little half-smile on this face and tears in the corners of his eyes. I wondered if maybe that was because he'd reached an age when you think about defying darkness and winter in more than a seasonal sense.

When we got home we watched some schmaltzy flick on TV—*not It's a Wonderful Life*—and had some more cake and went to bed. I'd gone an entire day, a good sixteen-plus waking hours, without thinking about myself. I fell asleep in a hurry.

Between Boxing Day and New Year's Eve, as I crashed from what passed for my Christmas high that year, I learned something. I learned that, at any hour of the day or night, some iteration of *Law and Order* is showing on some channel in Pittsburgh and, probably, anywhere else the English language is spoken. Which, all things considered, wasn't bad as shameless self-indulgence goes. I didn't binge on junk food, I didn't start doing cocktails at two in the afternoon, and I didn't quite waste *every* waking hour in front of the tube. I ran, read, and talked with Stacy. Also, four important things happened.

First, Ken called me on the 26th and left a message: "I don't know what's wrong, but if it would help to talk about it, please call me. God bless you."

Second, Paul drunk-dialed me at least three times and left messages that involved a lot of weepy pleading. I found guilty pleasure in it. I told myself that he was hurting more than I was—one of those lies you sometimes use to get you through the night.

I could have gotten past the cheating, I suppose. Maybe. You have to make allowances for human weakness. I could have gotten past the bisexuality. After all, if he loved me enough to forsake all others, why should I care if he was forsaking men as well as women? And maybe the pedophilia fantasies were just Cindy overanalyzing thin evidence. I never resolved that issue. I didn't have to, because what I *couldn't* get over was being used. I absolutely could not get past that. That was a deal-breaker. "I'm a passionate artist, so the rules that apply to ordinary people don't apply to me." Oh really? Well, screw that.

Third, on Tuesday, December 28th, at 3:37 p.m., I got a searing insight. I'd finished a punishing, three-mile run in thirty degree weather, taken a very hot shower, and gotten dressed in grubs. I was bluer than a midnight routine on Comedy Central, and I was right on the verge of moping. And then, with a little start, I looked up, eyes wide open, and the realization hit me: *I'm miserable, but not because my heart is broken. My heart is NOT broken. I was in love with someone who didn't exist, a fictional character invented by a novelist as the protagonist in a story called "Cindy's a Sap." Being brokenhearted over the Paul I'd been engaged to would be like being brokenhearted over Rhett Butler. I'm miserable because I got scammed and behaved like an idiot.*

Fourth, on December 30th, Mendoza called.

"Gotta dial back on that vacation, Jake. I need your butt in here tomorrow morning bright and early. The fish bit—and we've got some work to do hauling him in."

Chapter Thirty-three

I didn't meet with Schuyler until Monday. I spent Friday morning and part of the afternoon with Mendoza and Sally Port, the criminal law specialist I'd met with Schwartzchild the day after Bradshaw's murder. We had to do three things: (1) make absolutely sure I got the facts right; (2) decide whether I needed to tell Schuyler about Learned's claimed affair with Ariane Bradshaw; and (3) make absolutely sure I got the facts right. It took quite a while.

"You've gotta be comfortable with this, Jake," Mendoza said when we were hip-deep in the second. "The case law says you're okay, but case law is words in books. You're the one who might be up there on the stand someday, getting grilled about whether you willfully concealed information relevant to a murder investigation when you were talking to Schuyler."

I took a quick glance at Port. She was biting her tongue. *She* couldn't encourage me to keep my mouth shut about the adultery and she knew it. That might look like interfering with a witness. After all, her client wasn't my client. I thought it over. I thought long and hard. Calder & Bull or no Calder & Bull, a formal reprimand—or worse—from a judge wouldn't qualify as a very promising start to my legal career.

"I'm comfortable with it," I said at last, hoping I sounded more convincing than I felt. "The Feds aren't investigating Bradshaw's murder."

Port nodded and smiled without showing her teeth. Mendoza did not smile and he did not nod. He glanced at Port.

"We've been going close to two hours since our last break. You feel like a cigarette or something?"

She got it. I mean she caught the ball on the fly in full stride, without so much as a stutterstep.

"I don't smoke. But a breath of fresh air would be nice. Would it be okay if I stepped out on your balcony for a few minutes?"

"Of course."

"Okay, Jake," Mendoza said to me as soon as we had his office more or less to ourselves. "Sometimes a lawyer gives the right answer because it's the right answer, and sometimes she does it because it's an excuse to do something she wants to do whether it's right or not. I don't blame you for wanting the FBI to toss Mr. Learned's suite at the Hilton and generally turn his life upside down. If I were you I'd want that so bad I could taste it. But you can't let that foul up your thinking here. The Department of Justice keeps a naughty lawyers list, and if you get on it you'll be looking over your shoulder for the rest of your career."

"You're right. I'm no saint, and I'm not saying my motives are pure. But I'm not just doing a psycho-bitch revenge fantasy. I've thought this through."

"Why don't you share those thoughts with me?"

"The affair isn't just a possible motive for Ariane. If the cops start playing *what-if*, they could use it to focus some unpleasant attention on Caitlin as well. She's not just a spoiled rich girl. In her own way, she can be a pretty tough cookie. And don't forget her 'killed my brother' line. I don't have a legal duty to invite suspicion on my own client."

Now Mendoza nodded, and now he smiled.

It was still a grind after that—facts are always a grind—but it was just tedious, slogging work. No strategic issues. When Port left around two in the afternoon, she seemed confident that we were set for my appointment with Schuyler at eleven o'clock Monday morning.

After her exit, I told Mendoza that I needed to talk about a delicate subject with him.

"Delicate? You mean like more delicate than murder and obstruction of justice and playing look-but-don't-touch with the *federales?*"

"Much more delicate than that. Calder & Bull deferred me until September. I need a job through August."

"You got one. No brainer. I'm making so much money off you I should be ashamed of myself."

"Thanks. But when I say I need a job, I mean I have to start getting paid. I need to become a net producer in the Jakubek household."

You know that startled/dismayed look you sometimes get from a guy after you slap him for copping a feel? That *What was that? I can't believe that happened!* look? I got that from Mendoza. Two or three seconds later an agonized expression replaced it. My heart sank and my belly churned.

"Man, do I feel like a *schmuck* for that crack about all the money I'm making off you. What a way to start negotiations!"

"It won't be much of a negotiation. You have all the cards. Just make me an offer."

He folded his hands on his desk. He lowered his head and shook it. His body language screamed *I'm going to have to say something really, really HARD, and I HATE it!* I braced myself for bad news.

"Here it is, Jake. You're worth two thousand a month. Easy. But I can't pay you two thousand a month, because I got a kid I hired six months before you started and I'm only paying him twenty thousand a year. I can't give him a raise because he's not even worth what he's getting now, and I don't want to fire him until I've given him at least two years to make good."

"I don't want you to fire anyone."

"Of course you don't. I'm just saying. Anyway, I can't pay you what you're worth, but on the other hand, I don't want to insult you. So that's a problem."

"Insult me."

"Thousand a month."

I was about to say yes when he shook his head again, this time with a little body twist, as if he'd had a mini-spasm.

"No," he said then. "That's just not right. Not gonna do that. I'm better than that. How about fifteen hundred a month?"

"We've got a deal."

"You're one hell of a negotiator."

"A better one than I was when I walked in here," I said.

It took me until four o'clock to track down Sal Brentano. He'd pulled his sport coat on and was reaching for his overcoat. But I knew how to reverse that attitude in a heartbeat.

"How would you like to start 2011 with a new client?"

He stopped reaching for his overcoat. His eyebrows went up and a smile split his face. He pointed at a mate's chair in front of his desk.

"Who's the client?"

"My father. Or, actually, my father's tool business."

"So you're here with the consent of the client?"

"No."

"Well, that's kind of a technicality anyway. What's up?"

He sat down behind his desk and watched with obvious interest as I fished my checkbook and pen from the right-hand pocket of my jacket.

"I'm not looking for a professional courtesy," I said. "I want to give you a twenty-five hundred dollar retainer so you can charge your standard rate against it and work up an action plan to deal with a problem."

"What's the problem?"

I told him. He whistled.

"I'll dig up Dad's franchise agreement and bring it in on Monday so you can get started."

"No need to. I can pull up Pro Tools' UFOC online and get it out of that."

"What's a 'UFOC'? It sounds kind of dirty."

"Uniform Franchise Offering Circular. Most of them are indeed kind of dirty."

"Should I check in with you Monday afternoon then?"

"Sounds like a plan."

I wrote the check and handed it to him, giving him twelve-and-one-half percent of the bribe Calder & Bull had given me to hang loose until September. Interesting being on the client side of something like this. Handing him the money hurt. But when he accepted the check I felt a little thrill of relief. I had someone else on my side, and if he was taking my money it must mean he could help somehow. I wondered how I'd feel when I was the one getting the check and making that implied promise to the client.

Chapter Thirty-four

The room Phil Schuyler showed me into at 11:00 sharp Monday morning wasn't a conference room but a litigation workroom: Spartan trestle tables instead of polished mahogany, mismatched, straight-back chairs, and walls lined with metal shelves groaning under the weight of banker's boxes stuffed with documents. If you triple-billed the government for Medicaid work or put a little too much fiction into your application for a loan from a federally insured bank, this was where Schuyler came to put you in prison for forty-two months or sixty-seven months or whatever the pitiless sentencing matrix called for.

Waiting at the head of the table we found a man in his early forties whose hair was as black as mine except with tiny gray specks here and there. He was wearing a navy blue sport coat, charcoal gray slacks, and a dark green tie over a shirt with broad, blue stripes. When he stood up to shake my hand, I guessed his height at about five ten—well over mine and just under Schuyler's. If you'd seen him, you probably would have thought he was an accountant or maybe the kind of lawyer who handles loan closings and draws up an occasional will.

Schuyler introduced him as Ben Underhill, and said he was "a lawyer with DOJ in Washington." Schuyler is an old-school gentleman, and an old-school gentleman's blush tinges the tops of his ears when he makes a misleading statement. I spotted the pink, rather vivid against his straw-colored hair, as I shook hands with Underhill. I also saw the once-over Underhill gave me, focusing on my face and head, and looking like he absorbed every millimeter of them. His handshake was dry and formal. The vibe I got from wasn't hostile but firmly neutral: *We are not enemies; we are not friends; we are dealing with each other at arms' length.*

In other words, while Mr. Underhill presumably had a law degree and no doubt worked in D.C., Schuyler's technically accurate description of him was functional bullshit. Ben Underhill was a cop.

We sat down. I handed Schuyler two copies of my draft declaration. He gave one of them to Underhill. I sat there silently, trying to look serene and composed while they took their time reading through the draft. It described in full but deliberately non-vivid detail my adventure in Learned's suite. When Underhill looked up, I braced myself for probing questions into how I happened to find myself in the middle of a knock-down, drag-out fight with my then fiancé.

"You're sure the thing that came off the flagpole was gold?"

"It was gold-colored, and Learned acted as if it were very valuable."

"It was an eagle?"

"Yes. But not like the eagles you usually see on American flagpoles, with the wings folded. The wings were partially spread."

Underhill shifted his eyes toward Schuyler. If Schuyler responded in any way, I missed it. Then Underhill reached into a briefcase at his feet and pulled out a brown, civil-service routing envelope. He extracted three eight-by-ten pictures of sculpted eagles. He spread them out on the table in front of me.

"Did it look like one of these?"

"Definitely not this one." I put aside a picture of an eagle with its wings spread to full horizontal, like the one on the U.S. seal.

I took a while studying the other two. The wings on both were spread a bit, but with a fullness and roundness suggesting that the bird could spread them more if he wanted to. In different ways, they both looked a bit like the picture of the Gardner Museum's *L'Aigle* finial that I'd found on the web.

"It could have been either of these. More likely this one, on my left."

"'Could have been'?" Typical lawyer/cop follow-up.

"I'm not going to kid you. I saw the thing from about four feet away, and it's not all that big. I'd say there's a sixty to seventy percent chance that it was this one. If someone told me this wasn't it, then I'd put slightly better than even odds on the other one. But I'm not going to sit here and pretend to give you an absolutely positive identification." *Because you don't need one for a search warrant, so why should I?*

Underhill and Schuyler exchanged glances. Apparently I'd passed the picture test. Now what?

"If you don't mind, Ms. Jakubek," Underhill said, "why don't you just run over the whole incident in your own words? Just a little play-by-play."

I did. This was why we'd spent all that time slogging through facts on Friday. I had it cold, and I gave it to them with the kind of concrete details that someone who was making stuff up would trip over. I got as far as "...so then Paul grabbed that flag I'd seen" when Underhill interrupted.

"You'd noticed the flag when you came into the suite?"

"Pretty much."

"Because the finial drew your attention to it?"

"Not really. It was the flag itself. I mean, I'd swear it had bumblebees sewn on it."

"What was that?" Underhill posed the question with a trace of excitement. "Bumblebees? You're sure about that?"

"Yeah, I know it sounds odd, but—"

"Was something like that stolen from the Gardner?" Schuyler asked.

"No," Underhill said. "But the bumblebee was one of Napoleon's favorite symbols. It stood for industriousness and accumulation of wealth for the common good. It was fairly common to put bumblebee designs on Empire tapestries and furnishings."

"So this flag could be the real deal," Schuyler said. "Something authentic that Learned picked up from another source, and then he matched the finial up with it."

Underhill nodded. I shrugged. Schuyler hopped up to find a secretary to scan my draft into his computer so that the three of us could punch it up with some bumblebee stuff.

I was there for ninety minutes longer than I'd planned, but when I headed back to Mendoza-land I left behind me a declaration dated, witnessed, and signed under penalty of perjury. I'd done my bit for Caitlin Bradshaw and for the cause of law and justice. Also for Cindy Jakubek, who walked out of the Federal Building with a bloody knife and a clear conscience.

Chapter Thirty-five

I made my report to Mendoza a little after two. I set my plastic bowl of Stouffer's Lean Cuisine pasta and sauce on the corner of his desk. Now that I was getting paid I thought it would be bad form to talk to him with my mouth full.

"Underhill was almost panting while he waited for me to sign the revised version of my declaration. I wouldn't be surprised if the FBI drops by the Hilton sometime this week."

"Don't count on it. On fifteen-year-old cases, the United States Department of Justice moves at the speed of the average glacier. Underhill will have to get a sign-off from at least two layers of bureaucrats. Then he'll have to get a magistrate's attention. If he manages that much, his next job will be to beg the FBI's New York field office to pretty please find time for Learned. I'd be looking for a search more toward the end of this month than the end of this week."

"Even so, as long as Underhill even starts the process, doesn't that mean the Feds aren't working with Learned?"

"That was my bet when the game started," Mendoza said. "After this morning, I'm doubling down."

"So either they were working with Bradshaw before he passed away, or Learned and Bradshaw were working together and the Feds just lucked onto them."

"Feds sometimes just stumble over crooks, but that's not the way it usually happens. Bradshaw is the Pittsburgh connection in a case that doesn't have any others. If I had to guess, I'd speculate that he got a little bent somewhere along the line, hustling art from dubious sellers here and there. That made him vulnerable to federal persuasion. Let's say they set up a two-year operation with him—feeding him information, helping him with starter deals, and so forth."

"Then Bradshaw mentions *l'aigle* finial on a phone that state cops have tapped," I said.

"Right. Some bright state trooper makes the connection, sends it up the line, and the attorney general thinks, 'Man, this could make me governor!'"

His theory held together, except for one nagging coincidence.

"How did the state cops happen to have Bradshaw's line tapped in the first place? Why would they care about fine art stolen two states north of here?"

"They wouldn't. They care about taxes. Under-the-table deals mean under-the-table income that didn't show up on his tax returns. Pennsylvania cops will put a whole task force on some chain of service stations that's gypping them out of eighty thousand bucks. They could have suspected Bradshaw of being into them for half-a-million."

I nodded. I finished the Stouffer's. I caught Mendoza's eye and held it.

"Learned did it, didn't he? He killed Bradshaw. He figured out that Bradshaw was trying to trap him in a federal sting, and he blew his dear old friend away—conveniently making Ariane Bradshaw a rich widow in the process."

Mendoza looked at me like he had two pairs showing in seven-card stud.

"You remember that huge brouhaha several years ago about who leaked word to the media that Valerie Plame was a CIA agent? The one they just made a movie about?"

"Sure."

"Well, right in the middle of that, a *New York Times* columnist named Maureen Dowd took her Pulitzer Prize onto the *David Letterman Show* and pinned the leak on the vice president of the United States. Her exact words were, 'Cheney did it.'"

"But it turned out Cheney didn't do it."

"No, he didn't. And I don't have a Pulitzer Prize. So I'll hedge my bets until they find Learned's gun and a ballistics test matches it to the bullet that had Bradshaw's name on it."

I checked in with Brentano about an hour later. He had a grim-but-game expression.

"Pro Tools is pretty clean, as franchise operations go. One to two settlements over fifty thousand per year, and that ain't bad."

"Can we make them adjust Dad's territory?"

"Not just to make up for losing Minelli's. Businesses open and businesses close. That's a risk of going into the marketplace."

"It's not just Minelli's." I frowned, reminding myself not to shoot the messenger. "I spent most of the weekend going over Dad's books. He's had four other shops close in the last six months. The others were just two- and three-mechanic operations, but it adds up. Plus, over forty percent of his installment sale customers have been slow-pay or no-pay this year. Weekly installment payments are his basic cash flow. He's running a forty-thousand dollar balance with Pro Tools, and half of it is more than thirty days past due. For the last two quarters he's been living off his equity without realizing it. He's two big hits from being upside down."

Brentano nodded.

"If there's been significant shrinkage he can ask for a census of his route. Unless the territory is just flatlining, though, they don't have to give him more stops. After all, any shop they'd give him would have to be taken from some other Pro Tools dealer, and they're all in the same boat."

Ouch. Not a surprise, but still, *ouch.* I know, I know: 'Tough times don't last, tough people do.' But you can only take so many punches.

"Okay," I said in my best spunky-little-gamer voice. "Sounds like we need a game changer."

"I'll try to think of one. But game changers can be hard to come by."

Chapter Thirty-six

"Hello, this is Cynthia Jakubek. I will not be in the office this weekend because I have a life. Unless you're an insurance salesman or a broker making cold calls, though, I would like to speak with you. If you'll leave a number where you can be reached, I'll get back to you as promptly as I can."

Beep.

"Uh, hi, Ms. Jakubek? This is Caitlin? Caitlin Bradshaw? I was just—"

I picked up the phone with my left hand while I clicked Westlaw off my computer with my right.

"Hi, Caitlin. What's up?"

"Oh, you're there."

"I'm here. The voice mail prompt I recorded last night turned out to be a little optimistic."

"Oh. I guess you were, like, screening your calls."

"What's up?"

"Well, Mom had a couple of long calls with Sam Schwartz-child last week and earlier this week, so I was wondering if, like, maybe something was happening? On Dad's case?"

"Well, if the police are getting anywhere on the murder investigation they're keeping it to themselves. We know the FBI is now involved in the stolen art investigation that led to the search of your home by state police. They're not very chatty about what they're up to either."

"Do you think that, maybe, our house might be searched again?"

I frowned at the phone. Where did *that* come from?

"I guess I have no idea. I haven't heard anything about that. Has someone said something to you about another search?"

"Not, like, in so many words? But mom, after those calls, was doing the 'are you sure you don't have any pot' thing again."

"Lemme make a couple of notes here."

This was a stall. What I was really doing was trying to figure out how much I should tell our client. I had to assume that Caitlin would tell Ariane anything I said, and that Ariane would tell Learned. By spilling something to Caitlin that would end up helping Learned conceal evidence, I might only be buying her trouble.

"I'll put it this way," I said. "I can't rule out another search. Like I said, things are moving on the art investigation."

"Okay. Listen, is there any way we could, like, meet later today?"

"Sure." I glanced at 10:22 in the lower right-hand corner of my computer screen. "I'm planning on staying here until about noon. Can you get down here by then?"

"I suppose."

"You don't sound like a trip downtown was what you had in mind."

"Actually, I was hoping we could meet somewhere closer to home. Like, Berkshire Town Club, maybe? Where I play tennis? Would that be okay?"

I managed to keep my sigh inaudible. I mean, downtown Pittsburgh isn't exactly the South Bronx. This white-bread phobia about any place without manicured lawns and "traffic calmings" gets a little old. But Caitlin was a client, and travel time is billable.

"If they'll let someone wearing a sweat suit and Nikes into the club, I can be there by twelve thirty."

"Oh, they'll let you in all right. Thank you *sooo* much! I'll see you then."

She got the last words out fast and hung up quickly, as if she were afraid I'd back out if she gave me half a chance. I hung my phone up a little brusquely. Berkshire Town Club? Please. She might as well have suggested meeting at a mall. *'In the food court? Right outside Nordstroms?'* I'll bet Calder & Bull doesn't have valley girls on its client list.

At that point a little whisper of a doubt ruffled the handful of brain cells I wasn't wasting on condescension. I remembered deciding the first time I met her that Caitlin wasn't just a spoiled rich girl thinking about cutting class so she could buy some more lip gloss. In this call, though, she'd come off like an airhead who'd have trouble winning a debate with Paris Hilton. Had she somehow lost twenty IQ points since the last time I saw her, or was something else going on?

I don't know why, but Caitlin's call had started a convoluted free association sequence in my head: Search/cops/art/Feds/ Learned/strangers-with-candy/Schuyler/Tyrell-Washington. Schuyler had warned me about strangers with candy because I was representing Washington. Then it turned out Learned was the stranger—or one of them.

So did this mean Washington had caught a shiv because he was offering the Feds information about Learned and the loot heisted from the Gardner Museum? Where would a mean-streets punk like Washington come up with that? I mean, you wouldn't exactly talk to him about appraising Rembrandts, would you? No, what you'd be more likely to talk about with Washington is killing someone.

The phone rang. I ignored it, letting it ring through to my clever message prompt.

BEEP! I glanced up sharply as soon the voice started. Less voice than panicked whisper, really, choking as if it were on the verge of tears but also throbbing with urgency.

"Cindy, this is Paul! Please pick up! Your dad said you were at this number. Oh God, please be there! Something terrible is happening! The FBI came here. I let them in. I had to. Two of them. They're going through everything. I don't know what to do! Walt isn't here and I can't reach him. What do I do if—"

I picked up the phone.

"Paul, shut up."

"Cindy! Listen, I—"

"I said shut up." I wasn't being a bitch. This was purely professional. There were about seven incredibly stupid things Paul might do, and if I was very lucky I had thirty seconds to keep him from doing any of them. "Now listen."

"Okay."

"Number one: keep your mouth shut. Number two: do *not*, repeat *not*, call Learned until the Feds have left. Number three: stay out of their way. Number four: do *not* scurry around with your mobile phone taking pictures of what they're doing. Number five: if they ask you any question more complicated than your name, say you don't want to talk to them. Number six: when they offer you a copy of the search warrant—that's a piece of paper with a magistrate's signature on it—take the damn thing. Number seven: if they try to give you cash to 'cover any damages' or some crap like that, do *not*, repeat *not* take the money, because it's probably seized contraband with cocaine residue on it. Number eight: keep your mouth shut. Now pull yourself together and act like a man."

I almost hung up after that last one, but I didn't quite have it in me.

"What's happening?" His voice was higher pitched than normal but not quite a whimper.

"From the sound of things, the Federal Bureau of Investigation is executing a search warrant on Walter Learned's suite at the Hilton New York. Now did you understand what I just told you?"

"I had to let them in, Cindy. They had badges and a guy from the hotel with a pass-key, and—"

"I know you had to let them in."

"God, they're tearing everything apart!"

"Listen, Paul—God, I don't know why I'm doing this—just *listen* to me. DID-YOU-UNDERSTAND-WHAT-I-JUST-TOLD-YOU?"

I heard nothing for three seconds but a deep breath and an exhalation. Then Paul said, "Yes."

"Good. Now, don't say anything else. End this call. Turn your phone off. And just stand there like a mannequin at Bloomies until the not-so-nice gentlemen in the navy blue suits have left. Do *not*, repeat *not* give them an excuse to haul you down to Foley Square for some quality time in a squeal room."

"Okay. Okay." His breathing sounded like it was returning to normal, and his next words were fervent but calm. "Cindy, thank you."

"You're welcome."

"Listen, Cindy, I—"

I hung up. I immediately called Mendoza on my mobile phone and, after waiting impatiently through *his* voice mail prompt, I left a message telling him that the FBI was searching Learned's suite. I added Schwartzchild's number in case Mendoza didn't have it handy at home. The Feds had moved at the speed of light after getting my declaration, and I knew he'd want to be the one who got the news to Schwartzchild.

Then I dove back into the records for Vince's business that I'd brought down to the office so that I could go through them without him looking over my shoulder. I halfway expected Paul to ring back in thirty seconds, and when he did as far as I was concerned he could sob until he timed out on my voice mail recorder.

Forty minutes later, the office phone rang. I let it go all the way to *BEEP!* It was Paul. Some semblance of calm and control had returned to his voice.

"Okay, Cindy, they've left now. I think you'll want to know what happened, and I'm willing to tell you, but there's a catch. You have to listen to me for three minutes first. Just let me talk without interrupting and without hanging up for three minutes. Then I'll—"

I picked up the phone.

"Okay, you're on the clock. One hundred-eighty seconds. Go."

"Okay. Okay. Wow. Okay. All right, first, I'm a total shit. No argument. I have no excuse for what I did or what I said. You're the greatest thing that ever happened to me and you've been totally wonderful to me and then I treated you like shit. I cheated on you and I turned myself into a total whore. I'm worthless scum. I'm sorry. I really am. I wish I could wear a hair shirt for three hundred days or something to show you how sorry I am, but I guess even Catholics don't do that kind of stuff anymore. But I really am sorry. Anyway, the thing you have to know is this: I really do love you, Cin. I always did love you, all along. I wasn't just hitching a ride to New York with you. I love you to the depths of my soul. God this is bad prose, but it's the way I really feel. I panicked when it looked like New York wasn't going to happen for you. I admit that.

"I mean, you don't know what it's like, Cin. No one knows. I wake up in the morning in this blind panic that I'll pick up the *Times* and find a review of a postmodern novel with my premise. Something someone else has written and gotten published, because he's in New York and I'm not. There's no real shot for a first novel in Philadelphia, no matter how good it is. There's no real shot anywhere outside New York. So I panicked and I sold out and I did every goddamn gutless, phony, bullshit thing I despise when other people do them. I told myself it would just be a fling, 'til I got the novel placed or you got to New York. Which was a total bullshit rationalization that makes me sick to my stomach every time I think about it. I hate myself for doing that. And if you want to say you're through with me forever because of what I did, I don't blame you and I'll try to accept it. But don't walk away thinking I used you. Because I didn't. I loved you. I still love you. I'll always love you. Henry Widget and my love for you may be the only real things I'll ever have in my life, but they *are* real. So help me, God, they're real. Please give me one more chance. Please."

'So help me, God.' From an atheist. I love that.

"You have twenty-two seconds left. Anything else?"

"Cindy, isn't there something Catholic about forgiving as God forgives or something?"

"I'm pretty pissed off at God right now, so that may not be your best argument. Anyway, I held up my end. I listened to everything you had to say. I get it. I grasp the *I-acted-like-a-shit-and-now-I'm-sorry* thing. Now tell me what went down with the Feds."

He sighed.

"Right. The Feds. Well, like I said, they came here. They had a warrant. I had to let them in. I mean they would have come in anyway if I hadn't let them."

"Get to the stuff you haven't told me already."

"Well, they asked where the bumblebee flag was, and I said I didn't have any idea what they were talking about. And they didn't like that. So they just started tearing the place apart. They looked everywhere, inside everything. I mean, they were just pigs about it, like a couple of goddamn Ostrogoths sacking Rome."

"Did they find the flag and the flagpole?"

"I don't know." Paul sounded sincerely baffled by my question. "I mean, they didn't take anything like that with them. I didn't even know what they meant."

"They meant the thing that you knocked me halfway across the room with."

"Oh, that. No. Walt got that out of the suite the same day we had our blow-up."

Well isn't THAT interesting?

"Okay." I shifted the phone from my left ear to my right. "What else did they take?"

"Well, a little coke and some pot. And the gun."

"'And the gun.' What gun is that, Paul?"

"Great big honking automatic pistol. Taking that was illegal, right? 'Cause I looked at the search warrant, and it didn't say anything about guns or drugs."

"I'm not your lawyer, Paul. Did they ask you about the drugs?"

"Well, they asked if the stuff was mine, and I said no. I mean, the pot was, but I wasn't going to tell them that."

"What part of 'keep your mouth shut' was unclear to you, Paul? You've lied to the FBI. That's the same crime Martha Stewart did time for."

"Shit."

"Okay, Paul, now think carefully: Did they take anything else?"

"I don't think so. Not that I saw, anyway. I mean, I was pretty upset."

I did *not* manage to keep my sigh inaudible.

"Have you contacted Learned yet?"

Paul hesitated, which meant the answer was yes. He must have called Learned before he called me back—just in case I was wondering where I stood.

"Okay, you have contacted him. That means he won't be coming back to the suite. He may call you and ask you to gather a few things and bring them with you when you meet him someplace else. Do NOT do this. Do NOT fucking do it, Paul."

"Okay, okay. You don't have to swear."

"Gather up your own things. If your sugar daddy gave you a few bucks go ahead and keep them, but don't take anything else. Haul your worthless ass back to Philly. On Monday I'll text you contact information for three decent criminal lawyers in Philadelphia. Call one of them, and call whoever is managing your trust fund and tell him he needs to shake loose with however much you'll need for a retainer. Then go to that lawyer and tell him or her exactly what happened. Got that?"

"Listen, Cindy—"

"PAUL, DAMMIT TO HELL, FOCUS. Did you understand what I just told you?"

"Yeah, sure. But, Cindy, I just don't understand what's going on. I mean, this is crazy."

"What's going on is that you decided to start fucking someone who's the subject of criminal investigations by cops in three different jurisdictions. You're a material witness and you've handed the FBI a club to use on you if they want to beat compromising information out of you. If Learned is guilty of anything serious he's probably thinking about whether killing you would be worth the trouble. So you need two things: a good lawyer and lots of daylight between you and Learned. Just do what I said."

"Okay, I will." His voice softened and a pleading tone crept into it, like an eight-year-old begging not to be sent to bed early. "Cindy, will you think about what I said?"

"Sure, Paul." I sighed with infinite world-weariness. "I'll think about what you said."

"And Cindy? Just one more thing. Are you really pregnant?"

While I was gaping at the phone, I thought for a couple of seconds about how to answer that. I could have used the standard obscenity customary in these situations and then hung up, or just hung up and not bothered with the obscenity. But I came up with something even better.

"Keep guessing."

By now it was after 11:30. I tucked Vince's papers into my briefcase and clicked on Mapquest for directions to the Berkshire Town Club. While they were printing out, I was just about to start logging off when I remembered puzzling about the link between Tyrell Washington and Walter Learned. I googled "Pittsburgh African Methodist Episcopal Church." It came up right away, and its website said that its "Full Gospel Service" would begin at 9:15 on Sunday morning.

Chapter Thirty-seven

"I found some things while we were cleaning up the mess after the cops left." Caitlin told me this in a low-key, matter-of-fact voice.

"Anything important?"

"Not sure. Maybe."

We were in the lounge of the women's locker room at the Berkshire Town Club, standing at a round table—that's what I said: *standing*—that came to just below my diaphragm and just above Caitlin's belly. The lounge was a brightly painted open area with royal blue, all-weather carpeting that started about ten feet from the lockers themselves. We had red Gatorades in front of us. In sweats and Nikes I was, if anything, slightly overdressed for the venue.

"Did you go through the stuff you found?"

"Mm hmm. Sort of. I'm not sure I understood all of it. I mean, there was a prenup, for example. I always figured they had one of those, but I'd never seen it."

I took a long swig of Gatorade, thinking how much nicer my life would be at this moment if it were chardonnay. I had halfway expected her to pretend that she didn't know what a pre-nup was, and I was glad that she'd played it straight.

"Caitlin, I'm going to ask you a question. If you want to, you can tell me to go to hell. No hard feelings. Not my favorite answer, but I'd prefer it to a lie."

"Ask away."

Her voice was steady and her eyes met mine and held them. The mall rat/airhead on the telephone was suddenly nowhere to be found. I took a deep breath and asked my question.

"That stuff about how your dad had killed your brother—did you mean that he'd made your mom get an abortion?"

Caitlin bent over and lifted her purse from the floor to the tabletop. She wouldn't have surprised me in the slightest by taking out a cigarette and lighting it. I would've bet that the Berkshire Town Club took a laws-are-for-little-people attitude toward the Clean Indoor Air Act. But she didn't. Instead she pulled out a pacifier. I'm not kidding. She took a baby pacifier out of her purse and stuck the nipple between her lips. After a couple of pulls on the thing she took it out of her mouth, but she but kept it handy.

"The answer to your question is yes."

"Fallout from the cleanup, or had you already known?"

"I didn't know before. I found documentation for the abortion while we were cleaning." Caitlin looked away, and I could see her angrily blinking tears away from her eyes before she turned back to face me. "Mom knew it was going to be a boy, and she already had a name picked out. Geoffrey."

With that she popped the pacifier back into her mouth for two more tugs.

"Does Schwartzchild know?"

"Not from me. Mom may have told him."

I responded to that with something between a nod and a shrug.

"Now," Caitlin said, "can I ask you a question?"

"Sure."

"What if I went to the police and said that I killed Dad? You know, said he'd been molesting me or something and I shot him in self-defense. Maybe he called me from the museum to bring him some food and when I got down there he started coming on to me so I had to shoot him. Could I get off on that?"

I wanted to slap her. I really did. Her flippant presumption that she could just rearrange the universe to suit her own convenience exasperated me.

"No, Caitlin, you could *not* 'get off on that.' The police wouldn't believe that you just happened to have a high-caliber pistol with you when you made an after-hours food run to the Pittsburgh Museum of American History where your father had gone to ground. They'd rip your story apart before it was completely out of your mouth. They'd assume that you were trying to protect your mother, and focus their attention on her. They'd accuse you of obstruction of justice and try to use that to squeeze a confession out of your mother."

"Oh. Okay then." With a shrug she went back to work on the pacifier for a few seconds. "You're pissed off at me, aren't you?"

"Yeah, I am, actually."

"I didn't think it'd work, but I figured there was no harm in asking."

It seemed like a good time to find some noncontroversial territory to explore. Fortunately, a banal topic was staring me in the face.

"I take it the pacifier is a stop-smoking kind of deal."

"More like a control-smoking kind of deal. An oral crutch. I'm not going to stop smoking. I really enjoy it. But I want to be one of those people who smokes socially without making a habit of it. Like maybe ten cigarettes a week, three or four during the week and the rest on weekends. That'd be okay. But I've sort of stressed out since our house got searched, so I'm using this pacifier to keep cigarettes from owning me."

"I hope that works out for you."

"You sound skeptical."

"When I started smoking," I said, "my role model was Meg Ryan, the actress. I read that she might smoke a cigarette at a party and then not even think about smoking again for six months. I wanted to be the ultimate occasional smoker. But it got to be a daily habit, and when I finally decided to quit I went through three pretty damn tough months."

"That's funny." Caitlin shook her head. "I would have bet a thousand dollars that you'd never smoked a cigarette in your life. You're just not the type."

"That's exactly why I started: because I'm not the type."

"What do you mean?"

"Okay, I'm fifteen years old, right? Three weeks short of my sixteenth birthday, summer before my junior year at Kosciusko High. I'm not just an honor student with four APs on my schedule, I'm a classic grade-grubber, because I figure a full scholarship is the only shot I have. Now, Beth Fisher, a real cheerleader/prom-queen type, invites me to this end-of-summer thing at her house, because she's hoping that I'll 'help her with her homework.'"

"Meaning write some of her papers for her?"

"Right. I know that as soon as I walk in someone is going to offer me a cigarette, and everyone will expect me to say no because I'm 'not the type.' And I figure that if instead of saying no I take the thing and let someone light it and smoke it like I know what I'm doing, I'll knock their socks off. So I swipe three Salems from my mom's purse and teach myself how to smoke. By the time of the party I've learned how to inhale and how to hold the thing so I don't look like a dork and all that stuff. At the party I totally brought it off."

"That is so awesome." Caitlin squealed with apparently genuine delight.

"When I confessed to Mom about the missing Salems I got grounded for two weeks for stealing. But it was totally worth it. It was even worth the three months of purgatory when I decided to quit."

"You quit because it got to be a habit?"

"I was over a pack a week, which sure won't pass for occasional. But that's not why I quit. I was twenty years old and I figured I'd live forever. I quit because I realized during a summer job that in the business world, smoking is a badge. It's like walking around with a tool belt around your waist. Secretaries and keypunchers and salespeople smoke; lawyers and accountants and executives don't. I planned to end up in the group that didn't. So I quit."

"That's, I don't know, so *analytical*. I mean, you really thought it through."

"Analytical is one way to put it. Or you could just say that I started smoking because I was a phony and I quit because I was a snob."

Caitlin gave me a long, intrigued look. "You don't cut yourself much slack, do you?"

"You got me there."

Caitlin put the pacifier away—I figured that was a good sign—and drank some Gatorade. I felt a new connection with her. With a touch of amusement I wondered if some kind of bond between us had emerged from idle chatter about adolescent smoking adventures.

"Listen." She lowered the Gatorade bottle. "If I give you something, can you like, just store it in the file for my case down at your office?"

"Sure. But that doesn't mean the cops can't get it. Any tangible thing you give me they can subpoena, or if they're feeling really frisky they can just go after it with a search warrant."

"But they're less likely to do that than they are to search our house, right?"

"Probably true. Don't kid yourself, though. It happens. Lawyers get their offices searched every day."

Caitlin came up with a sealed, brown nine-by-twelve business envelope that she had retrieved from the yellow and black sports bag at her feet. It wasn't bulging, exactly, but it was nice and full.

"I'd like you to take this and keep it with my file. Will you do that for me?"

I thought about it for a second. I didn't like it, but I couldn't see a good reason to say no.

"Yes." I accepted the envelope. "I'll take it for now and talk this over with Mendoza on Monday. Bottom line, it'll be his call."

"Sure." Caitlin nodded. "I understand."

I'll just bet you do, princess. At fifteen hundred bucks a month, this isn't on my job description.

Chapter Thirty-eight

I figure if you go to a church on a Sunday morning you should expect a religious service, not an Apollo Theater stage show. I wasn't the only white at the AME Church of Pittsburgh that morning, by a long shot, but I was almost the only one who took this view of things. Most of the others looked dismayed to learn that the authentic African-American gospel singing they'd come for went along with a sixty-minute side dish of scripture and hellfire and brimstone.

The only other Caucasian exception I noticed was a woman about my height, maybe an inch taller, with hair almost as dark as mine. I would have guessed she was in her late thirties or early forties, but in your mid-twenties you can be comically wrong about age estimates so take that one with a grain of salt. She was into it. Not just the music, the whole thing. She followed the scriptural readings with what looked to me like pure joy, and I could tell it wasn't the first time she'd heard them. When she glanced over her shoulder once I saw the kind of luminous smile you remember all day. She didn't offer any shout-outs during the sermon, but I knew when she agreed and when she disagreed with Reverend Demetrius' take on things. About halfway through the service, I realized that if she stood out this much, I must be pretty conspicuous myself.

I had bargained for an hour and forty-five minutes of worship, with music and prose in roughly a one-to-two ratio. I pretty much nailed it. The sermon was a real hair-raiser. I mean old-school. In this church, Hell wasn't a metaphysical abstraction. Hell was a real place with real fire that really burned forever. It was just as real as, say, PNC Park, where the Pirates play, and it was a lot more real than, oh, Uzbekistan.

The rev said there were all kinds of ways to get to Hell. The road to Hell was an interstate highway with no speed limit and six lanes that all went just one way. That's right—SIX LANES! Abandoning babies you'd made was one lane. Using heroin or crack or just getting blind drunk every day was lane number two. Lane number three was joining a gang that made you kill your own brothers—Ku Klux Klanners kill black folks too, and they'll be there burning right along with you IN HELL! Abortion was lane number four—abortion might be a "choice" for white folks but for black folks it's "genocide on the *installment plan!*" Lane number five was lying with your own kind—"Homo-SEXU-*ality*," as the rev put it, unbridled disgust dripping from every syllable. And lane number six, the express lane, the fast-track to Hell—that was pimping: letting women do your work for you, beating them if they didn't peddle their flesh enough times every night.

The sermon took close to forty minutes all by itself, and I've gotta say, at the end of it I knew right where the rev stood. No focus group bet-hedging with him. No subtle distinctions, no on-the-one-hand-this-on-the-other-hand-that, no nuances and no finesse. Just your basic Absolute Truth, putting gays in the same basket as pimps and pushers and conflating problem pregnancies with complicity in a new Holocaust. I remembered screaming "moral cretin" at Paul when he just assumed I'd get an abortion, and I wondered whether I'd sounded as scarily dogmatic to him as the rev sounded to me just now. I kind of hoped so.

It took Reverend Demetrius and Deacon Khalid twenty minutes after the closing hymn and the last "AMEN! HALLELUJAH!" that followed it to press the flesh in the vestibule with all the congregants who lingered for a few more words and a hug or two. I hung back, figuring that people who came to this church every Sunday had priority over a papist interloper. The other white woman I'd noticed and an African-American woman whose bushy, gray hair framed a radiant face hung back as well. After the crowd thinned a bit, they gestured to me to go first. I shook my head and made a little after-you motion with my left hand. Given what I was there to talk about, I definitely wanted the last position.

"Sister Cecilia!" Demetrius boomed, warmly clasping the African-American woman's hand and then wrapping her in a hug. "How wonderful to see you this glorious Sunday morning!"

"Reverend, I want you to meet my good friend, Laurie Gramling. She's visiting from Milwaukee."

"Welcome to our church!" Demetrius took the white woman's hand. "And welcome to Pittsburgh. What brings you to our city?"

"I do antipoverty work in Milwaukee with a private group. I'm here for a meeting of coordinators from the eastern half of the country." I wouldn't call her voice lyrical, exactly, but it had a confiding, serene-but-not-complacent tone that drew me in. That's my excuse for eavesdropping.

"Wonderful. This must be your first time in our church."

"It is. Cecilia came to Mass with me last night, and was kind enough to bring me here with her this morning."

"Well, you're not seeing Pittsburgh at its best in this January gray, but if you visit us again during fruit-planting season, you'll find a completely different city."

"Careful, Reverend," Cecilia warned "If Laurie finds out you like raspberries, you'll be swimming in raspberry jam and coffee cake come July."

"I will watch myself," Demetrius said with mock gravity. "Thank you for coming."

The two women moved on to Deacon Khalil, which I took as my cue. Demetrius recognized me, but the warm hug he greeted me with came along with a wary smile. I could tell he figured I wasn't there to find Jesus.

"Reverend, I wonder if I could talk with you about something for five minutes or so."

"Certainly, child. Of course."

I paused awkwardly, expecting him to suggest that we meet in his office in ten minutes. He didn't move a muscle or say another word. I figured he needed a hint.

"Maybe somewhere inside the church, when you're through here."

"We are here together in the presence of God, my child," he said—or, rather, declaimed in a deep and resonant voice, spreading his arms wide and beaming. "He reads our thoughts and knows our hearts. Let us share with one another as we share with Him."

And so, a little late, I got it. He wasn't going behind closed doors alone with a white woman. Any business we had to do would get taken care of right here, in public, with freezing January air blowing through the church door to keep us from nodding off.

"Okay. It's about Tyrell." I remembered to pronounce the name 'TIE-rell.'

"I thought it might be."

"While I was still working on his case, I got a hint from the government that the reason Tyrell was killed was to keep him quiet about something."

"It would grieve me to hear that anyone thought Tyrell could be a snitch."

"I don't think he was a snitch." I focused on tiptoeing nimbly through the verbal minefield I'd just entered. "But you knew him much better than I ever could. If someone came to him about doing something very wrong that he wasn't willing to do, do you think he might have spoken up about it to save another person's life?"

The rev gave me a long, steady look. I won't pretend that I could read the calculation in his eyes, but he was thinking about something and it wasn't the Epistle to the Romans.

"It would depend on the life," he said finally. "Tyrell lived by a code instead of the Bible, but he had a part of Jesus in him."

"I'm not interested in helping the government," I said. "The government and I are on opposite sides. If the Feds were hoping that he'd open up about his source or people he worked with, I don't care. That's their problem."

"But…what?" the rev prompted.

"But if Tyrell's code told him to turn down money a satan offered him to kill someone who's still a target, I won't feel I've done everything I should for Tyrell unless I try to find out who that target is. I don't care who wanted the killing done. I just want to keep the target alive if I can."

He looked at me thoughtfully for what seemed like thirty seconds. I thought he might be waiting to see if I had anything else to say, so I gave him sort of a *that's it* head shake.

"I am sorry, Ms. Jakubek," he said. "I don't see how I can help you. But I will pray on what you have said."

I started to say *God's will be done*, but then I thought that might be a little too Catholic for the surroundings. I said the prayer mentally instead and took my leave.

I wasn't feeling any too chipper as I stepped outside, so I was grateful that the biting wind gave me an excuse to keep my head down. On the sidewalk I was surprised to hear Laurie Gramling's voice, along with footfalls fast-stepping on the sidewalk to catch up with me. I looked over my shoulder just in time to see her pull alongside. She stopped, and I did too. I relaxed a little. Her serenity was contagious.

"Wonderful sermon," she said.

That called for a tactful response, and I came up with one.

"I didn't necessarily agree with all of it, but it was stirring and he certainly got his point across."

"I don't mean the one Reverend Demetrius gave. I mean yours. As St. Francis said, 'The Gospel should be preached constantly. If necessary, use words.' I don't know exactly what you're doing, but I could tell you were witnessing in a way that went beyond words."

It was a sweet thing to say, but I'd just killed a weekend morning with nothing to show for it, so I was having trouble being upbeat. The best I could come up with was, "That's very generous. Thank you."

"He said he would pray on it." Gramling's tone seemed suddenly gentle. "And he sounded like someone who means what he says. Whatever 'it' is, keep your hopes up. God be with you."

We gripped hands in kind of a sister-solidarity sort of way. Then she and Cecilia waved and walked on. I followed them with my eyes for maybe twenty seconds before heading for Vince's Chevy. I wondered whether Gramling's encouragement would end up being the highlight of my January. Right then I would have given you roughly even odds on yes.

Chapter Thirty-nine

So what happened next? Well, for the better part of two weeks, aside from the Steelers making their third run for the Superbowl in the last six years, nothing much happened. Life went on. I went to work. I made a full report to Mendoza, who whistled and shook his head at the Feds getting their search warrant executed with such alacrity. With his okay I tossed Caitlin's sealed envelope in our file. He told me not to look inside it, so I didn't. I worked on Dad's problem. And I beavered away industriously at grunt work for other clients so that Mendoza wouldn't regret the fifteen hundred bucks a month he was now paying me.

I even found the heart now and then to update *Streetdreamer*. A lot of the comments on Calder & Bull's shift to a September report date were—how to put it?—less than supportive. "It's over, Streetdreamer, time to wake up." That kind of thing. I got to where I could shrug off the snarky cracks and even come up with a peppy retort once in awhile, the way I had before Paul cratered on me.

And speaking of Paul, I started reading his emails—well, skimming them—before deleting them, instead of just clicking DELETE without even bothering to open them. They were mostly variations on his telephone monologue. Eight days after my chat with the rev, I finally responded to one of the longer ones:

> Look, Paul, I need time and space, okay? When you say
> you weren't using me, what you mean is you weren't *just*

using me, as Learned put it. And maybe that should be enough. It's not like I've never done anything I'm ashamed of. But what I haven't figured out yet is whether the guy who was using me but not just using me is the same one I was really madly in love with, or whether *that* guy never existed in the first place except as a figment of my imagination. So just back off for now. Saying the same thing over and over again isn't helping.

As I read that missive over now, the ratio of self-important, superficial bullshit to constructive communication seems way too high. I'd be tempted to leave it out of the story altogether, just on ego grounds, except that sending it turned out to be the stupidest thing I ever did in my life.

But that's something I found out down the road. Right now we're coming to the day when the lull in the Thomas Bradshaw murder case ended. Namely, Thursday, January 13, 2011. Three things happened that day.

First, at 7:59 a.m., I was walking from the bus stop to Mendoza's building when I heard footsteps approaching rapidly behind me. Resisting the urge to look over my shoulder, I tensed a little and grabbed a fistful of purse strap with my right hand. I didn't really think I was about to be mugged, but I braced myself for a tussle, just in case. Next thing I knew, Deacon Khalid fell into step with me on my right, matching me stride for stride along the sidewalk. I swiveled my head and opened my mouth to say hello. He ignored all that. Without greeting me or so much as glancing at me, he just started talking, his voice barely loud enough for me to hear.

"Keep walking. Don't look at me. The reverend said to tell you that the person you are concerned about is no longer in danger. He has nothing on this Earth to fear."

"Thanks, but—"

"Have a blessed day." And before I could blink he was five yards beyond me.

The rev had said he'd pray about my question, and apparently he had. He'd given me an answer. The only way you can have nothing on this Earth to fear is if you're dead. So Khalid had told me that someone had approached Tyrell Washington about arranging a hit on Thomas Bradshaw. The Feds seemed to be royally pissed off about it, and doing the Learned search at warp speed told me they thought Learned was the perp. That fit Mendoza's theory that the G-men had been working with Bradshaw on an investigation aimed at Learned. In other words, I'd thrown my seduced-and-abandoned temper tantrum in the luxury lair of a prime murder suspect.

That seemed like a pretty good morning's work and I hadn't booted up my computer yet.

I thought Khalid's tidbit might be a little hot for an e-mail, so I decided to wait until I could give Mendoza an oral report. I kept checking his office every twenty minutes or so because I was bursting with my high-octane scoop. About three minutes after the 10:30 check he bustled past my cubicle with his coat over his arm and Becky the Techie in his wake.

"My office, right now, Jake," he said without slowing down. "You'd better hear this."

As I traipsed in I couldn't help wondering whether Becky could possibly have anything bigger than what I'd picked up.

Yes, she could.

"They've completed the ballistics test on the forty-five automatic seized from Learned's suite. It's consistent with the bullet that killed Bradshaw. Not a perfect match, but the only place you get perfect matches is TV. Any ballistics expert will tell you that the murder bullet came from Learned's gun."

"How did anyone get a ballistics test out of the State Crime Lab in less than two weeks?" I asked. "I thought the average turnaround for that outfit was closer to two months."

"Who said anything about the State Crime Lab? The FBI did the ballistics workup itself, in Quantico—and someone with clout obviously hung a 'Job-One' tag on it."

"Have the Feds told the local cops about the ballistics test?" Mendoza asked.

"Yeah. They were apparently in a good mood that day. That's how I found out about it."

"So Learned is looking at a murder charge under Pennsylvania law *and* an indictment for interfering with a federal investigation by killing a witness," Mendoza said. "The feds and the state cops must be drawing straws to see who gets to talk to him first."

"Good luck with that," Becky said. "The FBI hasn't come up with him. He apparently hasn't been back to the Hilton New York since his suite was searched. Five to two he's squatting on a different continent at the moment."

Becky and Mendoza had reached a lull, so I chipped in my morsel from Khalid. They both nodded sagely, and Mendoza promptly piped up.

"I'll call Sam Schwartzchild. Jake, you call Caitlin. Find out if she has any idea where Learned is—and tell her that you won't be the last one to ask her about that."

"Got it."

I almost called her on my way back to my cubicle. I was just about to punch SEND when I realized that it wouldn't be cool for Caitlin's mobile phone to ring in the middle of calculus class. She picked up on the first ring when I eventually called her over the lunch hour.

"No clue about Learned. Haven't seen him since the thing at our house after Dad died."

"Good enough. If any cops call with the same question, let us know right away, okay?"

"Sure."

"Also, if you or your mom do happen to hear from Learned."

"Right. Thanks. Later."

By the end of the afternoon, after I'd had a chance to absorb the day's bombshells, I mentally had the Bradshaw case halfway to the archives. Learned was on the run. As loose ends go, he was world-class. Even if the cops didn't think he'd killed Bradshaw they couldn't very well try to pin the murder on Ariane until they'd tied it up. Hence, at least for the moment, no danger of people wondering whether Mendoza had gotten Bradshaw killed by telling Caitlin at our first interview not to go to the cops with the mom-chat. Bradshaw's murder was still unsolved but no one was paying me to solve it, so who cared? As I walked through the January gloaming to the bus stop that night, it seemed to me that for the next six months Caitlin was going to need a tennis coach more than a lawyer. I climbed on the bus ready for thirty-five minutes of tunes and the *New York Times* Thursday crossword.

By the fourth stop I was concentrating on two problems. Neither of them was Caitlin. The first was finding a wedge for Dad to use with Pro Tools. The second was sixteen across in the puzzle: "Rupert nattering on?" The question mark meant the answer was a bad pun involving someone whose first name was Rupert. The only Rupert I could think of was Murdoch, the media mogul, and I was coming up with nothing for him.

I closed my eyes as the bus lurched to a stop, then opened them and refocused on the puzzle as we got under way again. A woman's voice from the aisle beside my seat, drilling right through my earbuds, startled me.

"Babbling Brooke. Mind if I sit here?"

She sat down without waiting for my answer, which was a good thing because I was going to be several seconds getting any coherent words out. I'd just gotten the answer to sixteen across from Vera Sommers.

"Rupert Brooke, the poet," she said. "'The sand of the desert is sodden red/Red with the wreck of a square that broke.' Great stuff for neoimperialists."

"Thanks."

"You're welcome."

While I was pulling the buds out of my ears I regained a semblance of composure and managed an intelligent question.

"Are you buying or selling?"

"I'm here because Learned asked me to tell you something."

"That would be selling, then. Shoot."

"He didn't kill Bradshaw."

"I think I've heard this one before." I heard an edge on my voice, and I decided to leave it there. "The version I got was that the night of Bradshaw's murder Learned was shacked up with Frau Bradshaw at the Monongahela Hotel."

"I don't know about shacked up, but they were in the same room until after nine o'clock that night."

"With the forty-five?"

"Yes," Sommers said. "I was his first line of defense against nasty people breaking into the room. The forty-five was Plan B."

"You've been working with Learned the whole time? On the Ars Longa organization chart you were bodyguard and vice president in charge of smashing noses?"

"You're a college girl. Figure it out."

I gave that one a shrug. Sommers quickly filled the silence.

"Learned was trying to work a deal on one piece from the Gardner Museum haul. Don't kid yourself. That stuff hasn't been sitting in a warehouse for fifteen years. They've moved at least two hundred million dollars worth of it at a dime on the dollar, and some of it has been through two or three buyers."

"Why did Learned go to all the trouble to get this information to me?"

"I'm not a shrink, but if I had to guess I'd say it's because he feels guilty about queering things between you and your boyfriend. He beats himself up about it, if that's any help. Anyway, he kind of likes you and he doesn't want you to get hurt. I mean 'hurt' as in a broken neck, not a broken heart."

"Ah, the faceless Gardner Museum gang again."

"You can believe it or not. No skin off my nose either way. But I'll tell you one thing. I've worked with him before and I never saw him with a gun until last fall. For some reason this thing started to break wrong, and he got worried about his own hide. He's supposed to be way offshore by now, and I hope to hell he is—because now that word of the search has gotten out, if he's anywhere in the United States he's a walking dead man."

I chewed that over for a couple of blocks. I wanted to believe her—but what about the ballistics test? And if the Gardner Museum gang was really part of what was going on, why hadn't it surfaced yet in this little adventure as anything more than a theory?

Unless it had surfaced. Unless right this minute I was sitting beside some of its hired muscle. Vera Sommers had been ostentatiously hip-deep in this mess since at least the Wednesday after Bradshaw's murder, but it had never occurred to me that she might be on the thieves' payroll. Why not? Because she was a woman? *Cynthia, you sexist pig.* 'Walking dead man.' If she *was* working for the Gardner gang instead of for Learned, then I was being warned off—hard. I shifted my fanny on the seat so that I could turn my whole body toward her.

"Have you heard about the Feds tying Learned's gun to Bradshaw's murder?"

"*Supposedly* tying it. The FBI isn't above throwing fairy dust at local cops."

"Okay." That struck me as way too pat, but what could I say? "Please tell Learned thanks. Tell him I got the message."

"He had one more message for you." She stood up and pulled the call-cord. "He said to tell you that Paul isn't evil, he's weak. And weakness is human."

"So is evil," I said.

"It's a good thing he put a woman on this job." She shook her head, smiling mordantly. "A man would have given up on you three blocks ago. This is my stop. Have a good life."

I didn't say goodbye or look at her as she moved toward the rear door. I forgot about the crossword and I didn't bother to rebud my ears. Something was stirring in my gut, and it flat out turned me on. A growing excitement jolted me like a double espresso. I couldn't wait to get to work tomorrow.

This was not because some not-quite-dead ember of love for Paul was bursting back into a brave little flame. It wasn't even because I had some more nuggets of information to serve Mendoza. I was getting psyched because I'd just figured out how to solve Vince's Pro Tools problem.

Chapter Forty

I've decided to think of the next Tuesday night as my first closing. The check had five figures instead of eight, and Vince's kitchen table wouldn't pass for the mammoth mahogany slab in the average Manhattan conference room, but if I could bring it off it would still be a closing. I'd discussed the concept with Vince on Thursday night, and he and Lainie and I had chatted about it over the weekend, but I could tell he was more than a little shaky with it. Tuesday night was showtime.

I squared the stack of paper that I had spent pretty much every waking hour on since Friday morning. Then I looked at Vince and Lainie.

"Okay, let me just go through these one by one." I held up a sheaf about a quarter-inch thick. "These are articles of organization and an operating agreement for a company called Jakubek Tools LLC."

"Incorporating me?" Vince's eyebrows almost reached his scalp. "Sounds kind of fancy-schmancy."

"Not exactly, big fella." I held up the second slab of paper. "Stay with me. This is an agreement selling me twenty-six percent of Jakubek Tools for twenty-thousand dollars. The thing paper-clipped to it is my twenty-thousand-dollar check."

"What, you're bailing me out? No way."

"I'm not 'bailing you out,' I'm buying into your company." I picked up the third chunk of pulp. "This is an agreement selling Lainie twenty-six percent of Jakubek tools for twenty thousand dollars."

"I don't have twenty thousand dollars, dear," Lainie said.

I held up the fourth item.

"That's why you'll sign this promissory note for twenty thousand dollars that Vince will accept for your share. It's non-recourse. That means if you don't pay he couldn't come after you for the money. He'd just get your share of the company back."

"Oh. Well, I guess that's all right, then."

"Wait a minute," Vince said. "That's fifty-two percent of my company."

"Right." I picked up the fifth sheet. "That makes Jakubek Tools LLC a women-owned business enterprise. Which means that its bid for the Allegheny County Community College starter tool set order will get a ten-point bonus when the bids are graded. And *that* means that if we submit a bid at your cost from Pro Tools, we've got a good shot at winning the order." All we had to do was put a woman—well, two women—on the job.

"But at cost I won't be making any money," Vince pointed out.

"If Pro Tools gives you a twenty-percent commission you'll make plenty."

"Why would they give me a commission?"

"Because otherwise they'll probably lose the order to Cornwell or Matco."

"That's right," Lainie said to Vince. "You're always telling me that their tools aren't as good so they buy business by underpricing."

"That's true." Vince nodded emphatically. I have no idea whether it actually was true. What mattered was that Vince thought it was. At that point, Lainie again chimed in helpfully.

"Would a commission that size be a help, dear?"

"Yeah, forty thousand or so straight to the bottom line would be a real big help. But the thing is, I've sold out of my own company."

"Actually, no, you haven't," I said.

"That's right." Lainie patted Vince's hand. "You can trust us."

"Just as important, you don't have to trust us," I said. "Lainie's promissory note is payable on demand. If she and I ganged up against you, all you'd have to do is demand payment from her. She wouldn't be able to pay, you could take back her shares, and suddenly you'd own seventy-four percent of the company instead of just forty-eight percent."

"Seems kinda slick." In Vince-speak, "slick" is not good.

"Well, you wouldn't want that corporations course I took in law school to go to waste, would you?"

"I think I know what's really bothering you, dear," Lainie said. "You don't like the idea of taking advantage of the government giving women special preference."

"You're right. I don't like that at all."

"Neither do I," I said. "But you and I didn't make the rules."

"It was the government that stacked the deck, dear," Lainie said.

"That's right." I liked the simile. "We just have to play the cards we're dealt. Think of it like Schedule C of your tax return. You lead a pretty good life, but year after year you show a net income not too far above poverty level."

"Arnie is good with the numbers," Vince agreed, referring to his accountant.

"Same thing here. We're being good with the numbers—they're just different numbers."

Vince picked up the pen.

The wall-to-wall work crunch required to turn Vince's tool business into a WMBE couldn't have come at a better time. It kept my mind off everything else—including Sommers' little number on the bus. At 10:02 Wednesday morning, right after I'd filed the Jackubek Tools LLC papers online, the bus chat once again intruded impolitely on my thoughts.

Assuming Learned actually had sent Sommers to me, I just couldn't figure out his angle. Sommers' main message was that neither Learned nor Ariane had killed Thomas Bradshaw. Why did Learned care what I thought about who killed Bradshaw?

What was I going to do—talk three levels of cops out of going after Learned? Or tell them something about him they didn't already know? What information did I even have, except maybe some stuff about Paul?

Some stuff about Paul. Oh shit. *Paul knows something. And Learned wants to protect him.* Hoo boy. This sucks. This really, really sucks. My mind started racing. Finding out that Paul was back living with his brother in Philly would be child's play for the FBI, so that couldn't be what Learned was afraid I'd spill. I couldn't think of anything else offhand. Maybe Learned would be afraid of things Paul *could have* told me, whether he actually had or not.

It would have been very dramatic and narratively convenient for Paul to call me at that moment, but of course he didn't, the inconsiderate shit. He called Ken. He called Ken just before 1:30 that afternoon—and an hour later Ken called me.

Chapter Forty-one

"I just finished talking to your ex-fiancé," Ken said when I answered his call. "And not because he wanted me to hear his confession."

"What did he have on his mind?"

"Atonement."

"I think atonement may be a low-percentage play for him."

"That's not really your call. Atonement is between him and God."

"Which in Paul's case means it's between him."

"I think he's serious about it, sis. Maybe he doesn't believe in God, but he has a deep need to make up somehow for what he did. At some level, he's genuinely sorry—and he wants to do something about it."

"It's a good thing he called you instead of me. Because I think the only thing he's really sorry about is getting caught —and being SOL now that Learned is out of the picture. When it comes to making up for what he did, I wouldn't have had a lot of ideas for him."

"He has some ideas of his own. That's why I thought I'd better talk to you."

Up to now I'd been leaning back in my chair with my ankles crossed, like a smart-ass undergraduate in a dorm lounge bull session. I sat up straight in a hurry.

"You have my undivided attention."

"He's sorry about being a phony. He reproaches himself bitterly for treating you in a way the man he thought he was wouldn't have. He wants to do something to prove that the Paul he's been holding out to himself and the world isn't a fake."

"'Do something' like what?"

Ken took a deep breath, suggesting that I was about to hear a biggie. With a panicky shiver, I wondered if Paul had played the suicide card with him.

"He told me he was going to find the real murder weapon—the gun that was actually used to kill Thomas Bradshaw."

"Last I heard, that was in an evidence locker in Quantico, Virginia."

"He apparently has a different opinion."

"Namely?"

"He didn't share his theory with me."

I bowed my head and closed my eyes. This put a new slant on things.

"Okay," I said then. "This is very bad. The only way what he said makes sense is if he knows something dangerous that he picked up from Learned—maybe something Learned told him to try to manipulate him into reckless behavior."

"You're right. This may be really bad."

I waited through a few seconds of silence, then got impatient and spoke up.

"Go ahead. Ask the obvious question."

"We have a bad situation. The obvious question is, what are you going to do about it?"

Obvious questions usually have obvious answers. Even so, my response was slow in coming and grudging when it arrived.

"I guess I'll give him a call. I guess I owe him that much."

"I don't think you owe him a thing, but I hope you call him. The reason to forgive our enemies isn't to liberate them from guilt; it's to liberate ourselves from hate."

"Paul was sweet to me and he got his butt kicked defending me from that burglar in New York," I said. "He's more of a disappointment than an enemy."

"Well, if Paul isn't your enemy, you'd better figure out who is—because *someone* is really beating you up over this."

"Got it." I sighed. "I'm my own enemy. I've been punishing myself for being a sap by getting all hard-case with everyone involved. I have to forgive myself."

"'Forgive your enemies—but remember their names.' God be with you, Sis."

I dialed Paul's number as soon as I'd hung up with Ken. I figured that it wasn't going to get any easier, so I might as well just get it over with. It's funny, after Paul's weeks of desperate efforts to get through to me, I somehow imagined that he'd be staring at his phone, ready to answer on the first ring if my number popped up on his caller i.d. He wasn't and he didn't. My call went through to voice mail.

"Paul, this is Cindy. We should talk. Soon." I recited my number and hung up.

I stayed at my desk until almost six thirty, doing document reviews that Mendoza could bill clients for—and waiting for Paul to return my call. Didn't happen. Interesting to get a taste of your own medicine. I buttoned things up, turned my computer off, and got ready to hustle downstairs for the last bus. As I headed for the door, I couldn't help wondering what in the world Paul even thought he was talking about with that "find the real murder weapon" stuff. Obviously, Learned could have handed him a load of crap and Paul would think it was gold dust, but science is science. The marks on the bullets match up or they don't. Like anything done in an honest lab. The numbers—

I froze with my hand on the door handle, ready to pull it closed. Lab. Caitlin had said that Bradshaw had killed her *brother*. Back into the office. I hurtled for the bank of file drawers where we had BRADSHAW, CAITLIN re: INVESTIGATION stashed. I pulled out the envelope Caitlin had given me. I ripped it open. By this point, I halfway expected to see a gun inside. I didn't, of course. Just paper—something that has killed a lot more people than guns have. I carried it over to my desk so that I could turn on my lamp and examine the contents carefully—the way I should have in the first place. *I should have pushed back on that one*, I thought, recalling my acquiescence in Mendoza's instruction to stow the thing without looking inside.

Prenup, check. No surprise. In case of adultery all bets were off and Ariane could theoretically end up with nothing but the house and half-a-million bucks. A laid-off steelworker praying for one more extension of unemployment benefits would have taken that in a heartbeat, but it would look like a catastrophe to Ariane. Caitlin was kidding herself if she thought she was going to hide that from anyone by giving it to me, but clients kid themselves all the time. Letter on Schwartzchild's stationery—presumably the cover note for the prenup. I put that aside without reading it. Then the document I'd really expected to find: a lab report. This one came from Boelter Laboratory Services. **CONFIDENTIAL** screamed at me from the top of page one.

It took me a good twenty minutes to read it through carefully, but I knew after thirty seconds that it was about more than the abortion. This was a report on a paternity test. Not a blood test. A comparative DNA analysis. No, wait, *two* DNA analyses.

The never-born male fetus whom Caitlin had called her brother and whose body had ended up in a MEDICAL WASTE bag was *not* the son of CANDIDATE A but of CANDIDATE B. No names, but unless Caitlin was full of it Bradshaw had bullied Ariane into aborting this baby. And if he'd paid several hundred dollars for the test I was looking at, it figured that the test had something to do with his decision. Which pretty much made Bradshaw CANDIDATE A. As to CANDIDATE B I was speculating, but my guess was Walter Learned. Because CANDIDATE B was also the father of a female child whose DNA was the subject of the second test report. That baby had been born a little over seventeen years ago. Had to be Caitlin.

I picked up the letter I'd discarded. It was addressed to Thomas Bradshaw alone, and it was *not* a cover letter for the prenup. Schwartzchild had sent it only a few months ago. I would have tried to remember whether the attorney–client privilege survives the death of the client, but I was going to read the damn thing anyway so I didn't bother:

Dear Tom:

Confirming the information that I provided to you during our telephone conversation, Fletcher & Peck will not be able to represent you in connection with the matter we discussed. Inasmuch as we have represented both you and Ariane on tax and estate planning matters over the years, providing the help you are asking for would represent a direct conflict of interest. If you decide to pursue the matter, I will be happy to provide you with contact information for several highly qualified attorneys in the Pittsburgh area who could assist you.

However you choose to proceed, I remind you that the impending return of the federal estate tax on January 1, 2011 makes it advisable for you to act promptly on this and on the other matters we have discussed. Measures that would continue the estate tax moratorium are now pending before Congress, but there can be no assurance that Congress will act on them between now and the end of the year.

Yours very truly and so forth.

I tapped the stiff, rich paper idly with the nail of my right index finger. This was your basic CYA letter, the kind that lawyers write to keep their malpractice insurers from getting cranky. Sam Schwartzchild was documenting the fact that he'd refused to help Tom Bradshaw with something bad for Ariane that had to do with estate planning—wills and trusts, for example. I couldn't blame Caitlin for trying to hide the thing. If I were Caitlin, and I loved my mom, I would have burned it.

Chapter Forty-two

"Okay." The Vintage Firearms rep at Cumonow's took a critical look at the flintlock pistol that I'd just loaded under his supervision and that I was now holding with both hands. "You're good to go. Just try to hold steady during that fraction of a second between the hammer falling and the shot."

I leveled the replica weapon that I'd rented with the gift certificate Vince had given me for Christmas. I aimed it at the chest of the human body outline thirty feet away. I took a breath and let half of it out. I squeezed the trigger and tried not flinch when the hammer fell. The shot sounded like a cannon, and the fragrant blue smoke I remembered from before blocked my view of the target for a second. The rep saw the result before I did.

"Gut shot him!" The rep seemed way too enthusiastic about this result. "Way to go!"

"I was aiming for his heart."

"Well, it's a smooth-bore weapon. You're not going to get the accuracy you'd have with a modern handgun that has rifling inside the barrel."

"Okay. I think I can take it from here for awhile."

The rep took my hint and wandered out of the shooting gallery, back into the main part of the store. It was exactly eleven o'clock Wednesday morning, some sixteen hours after I'd finished going over the stuff from Caitlin's envelope. If I'd had my way I would have been at Cumonow's two hours ago, but it took me a while to talk Mendoza into it. He'd pointed out that I was proposing to improvise a complicated plan on short notice. He'd added that if it was as important as I thought it was we ought to take the time to do it right. He was, of course, absolutely right on both counts. Unfortunately, time was the one thing we didn't have because my idiot ex-fiancé was threatening to run around like a cowboy on catnip. To his credit, when I reminded Mendoza of that he signed on for the little experiment I'd dreamed up the night before.

Which is why he waltzed through the door right about then with a Colt .45 semiautomatic pistol. Cumonow's rents weapons for thirty-five bucks an hour to people who just get a kick out of plinking with something heavy duty. I wasn't sure a .45 would be exotic enough for inclusion in the store's rental inventory, but Mendoza had come up with one. He took his place at the shooting stall next to mine while I favored my paper target with another ball in the short ribs. As the smoke cleared, Mendoza looked over at me.

"You billing this time?"

"Every minute."

"Let's see how your experiment turns out. Might have to take a write-off."

I dug a thick, square sofa pillow that I'd found in Vince's basement out of my backpack. I propped it up on the counter at Mendoza's slot on the firing line. Mendoza stepped as far back from it as he could—about eight feet, I guess—and I scurried to get behind him. Cumonow's had posted a **SHOOTING RANGE SAFETY PROTOCOL** on the wall and we were violating it by the numbers, so it's a good thing we had the place to ourselves. Mendoza took an FBI-guy stance—arms extended and slightly bent at the elbows, both hands on the gun, leaning forward with his hips back and his knees flexed—and squeezed off a shot into the pillow. It blew the thing a good three feet onto the target side of the firing line counter. I scrambled underneath the counter—another big protocol breach—and retrieved it.

We anxiously examined it. Major holes on both sides. This was not the plan.

"Hmm," Mendoza said.

"I really should have thought of that," I said.

"We're lawyers, not engineers."

The door to the shooting gallery slammed against the wall. Mendoza and I looked up, guilty as a couple of sophomores caught with pot under the bleachers. Sol Cumonow strode in.

"What in the *hell* are you people doing back here?"

It struck me as a reasonable question. If one of us managed to get our silly butts clipped by a ricochet, even if we were too embarrassed about it to file a lawsuit, the store's insurance rates would go through the roof.

"Well, basically," Mendoza said, "what we're doing back here is, we're trying to fire a bullet from this forty-five and then retrieve it."

"Oh." Cumonow nodded, as if this were a halfway sane remark. "Wait right here. But don't fire anything else until I get back."

He was gone a good fifteen minutes. When he came back he was wheeling a rolling picnic cooler behind him. He lowered the front end gingerly, and even so the lid popped up and water slopped over the edge and onto the floor. Then he opened the lid all the way, revealing a cooler sloshing to the brim with water. He looked at Mendoza

"You're buying the cooler, right?"

"I guess we are. How much?"

"Sixty-nine ninety-five. There's a special this week, just for you."

"This idea of yours better prove something, Jake," Mendoza said, glancing at me, "or we're going halvsies on this thing."

Cumonow gestured for the pillow and I handed it to him. He laid it on top of the cooler crosswise, with its ends supported by the cooler's sides. Then he stepped well away.

"You may fire when ready, Gridley."

Mendoza did the FBI-guy thing again, with the pistol aimed at the cushion. He fired. When he picked up the pillow, I saw a lump of lead resting on the bottom of the cooler under about two feet of water. Mendoza gave me a this-is-why-God-created-associates look. I took off my jacket, rolled up the sleeve of my blouse, and fished the thing out. Mendoza had pulled a baggie from one of the side pockets in his suit coat. I dropped the spent bullet into it.

"Now what?" Cumonow asked.

"Now we do it again," Mendoza explained.

We did it again. I fished the bullet out again. We didn't put this one in a baggie. Instead I took the thing over to the counter and started the ritual of loading the flintlock with it. I put the measured powder down the barrel. I picked up what was left of the bullet Mendoza had fired from the .45. It wasn't a sphere, that's for sure. It wasn't close to a sphere. I'd call it an ovoid lump, but I'm not sure that's a recognized geometric shape. The important thing, though, at least for the moment, was that it was smaller than the muzzle diameter of my pistol.

I shrugged. I dropped the lump down the barrel with some wadding. I picked the ramrod up, thrust it down the barrel, and seated the load solidly against the powder. I wondered why *Pirates of the Caribbean* hadn't used this as a phallic metaphor. I dolloped a little powder on the hammer plate. I took a deep breath. I carried the pistol over to the cooler. Then, pointing the barrel downward at the cushion in case there was a mishap, I cocked the hammer. I had to use the heel of my hand to rack it back two snaps to full cock.

"Can I shoot that, Jake? I've always wanted to fire one of these."

What Mendoza meant was that if the damn thing blew up he wanted it to take his hand with it instead of mine. Macho gallantry. I'll take it.

"It's all yours." I handed the pistol to him.

He took it in his left hand (he's right-handed), pointed it at the pillow, closed his eyes, and fired. When I opened my eyes

I saw a third hole in the pillow, which was still on top of the cooler. I grabbed the pillow and pulled it out of the way so that I could look for the slug in the bottom of the cooler. I couldn't see anything except water and cooler.

"Pillow." Mendoza snapped his fingers at me.

I traded it to him for the pistol. He checked the bottom of the pillow. Two exit holes instead of three. He flipped it over, dropped it on the floor, fell to his knees, put two fingers from each hand through the third hole, and ripped the pillowcase fabric. Then he started tearing and pawing through the batting underneath. Feathers, or whatever they were, flew into the air and floated around. He swatted through them, cussing a little manically in Spanish. He was suddenly more in love with my theory than I was.

"Hah! Gotcha, you stinking little sonofabitch!" Mendoza raised the lump triumphantly between the thumb and first two fingers of his right hand. Then he pulled a second sandwich bag out of his suit coat pocket and dropped the slug into it.

"So this would be about the Bradshaw killing a couple of months back, I'm guessing," Cumonow said.

"No comment. That's privileged information."

Mendoza was smiling. So was Cumonow.

After Mendoza had settled up I wheeled his brand new rolling cooler out to the parking lot, where he helped me dump gallons of water out of it. Then, shivering a bit but not hideously cold, we paused between his Citera and the Chevy I'd borrowed from Vince. (We'd driven separately because part of my brilliant plan was to pretend that Mendoza renting a .45 and me getting my first free session with a vintage flintlock had nothing to with each other.)

"If your theory is right," Mendoza told me, "Paul is on his way to Pittsburgh."

"For all I know, he may already be here."

"He hasn't gotten back to you?"

"Nope. He's playing if-you-can-be-a-bitch-I-can-be-a-bitch. But I doubt it would make any difference. Paul is on a mission.

He thinks Learned is being framed for Bradshaw's murder and that the real murder weapon is here."

"In theory, he could be right. Ariane has been cheating on Bradshaw with Learned—maybe for seventeen years, maybe off and on, who cares? Bradshaw finally finds out, threatens divorce, and she ices him to avoid downward social mobility."

I took a second to absorb the implications of Mendoza's snappy analysis. I let out a gust of breath that I didn't realize I'd been holding.

"So our demonstration might actually help make a case against Ariane."

"Which means it was a good thing we did it. If you could think of it, the cops could think of it, and now we're that much ahead. The next step is to have a chat with Sam Schwartzchild, so that he can have a chat with Ariane. Meanwhile, any steps short of imperiling your immortal soul that you can take to keep Paul from doing something conspicuously stupid in the City of Pittsburgh would be helpful."

"I'll try everything else first. If nothing works, we'll see if my immortal soul is negotiable."

Chapter Forty-three

I didn't try to reach Paul while I was driving back downtown. Instead I spent the drive-time thinking about what I was going to say. I figured he wouldn't answer, and I wanted to leave a message that would actually motivate him to respond. That argued against improvisation. Spontaneity is critical—it should be well-rehearsed.

By skipping lunch, I managed it. I sat in my cubicle at 1:02 p.m., glanced down at three-quarters of a page of bullet points, took a deep breath, and punched PAUL on my Droid's speed dial. Interesting that I still had him on speed dial. I'd been too damn busy for the last month to think about switching that slot to my dentist. Four rings and then a very nice lady who sounded like she was working in New Delhi suggested that I leave a message.

"Paul, this is Cindy. I'm sitting here at my desk, looking at the engagement ring you bought me with the first money you ever got for writing. I'm not going to pretend that I'm getting weepy, because you have an infallible bullshit detector and you'd know I was lying. But I do still have enough feelings for you that I haven't sold the thing to Josten's Jewelers yet. I'm worried about you and, even more important, I'm worried about me. We're in trouble. I need to talk to you about what it is and what we can do about it. I need a call and I need it soon. As in this afternoon. Sorry, that was bossy. Okay, bitchy. I'm a little on edge. Lemme try it again. This afternoon. Please. You know the number."

I hit the pound sign and punched off the call. Flattery works with most people and with males you should lay it on with a trowel. At that point it occurred to me that if he did return the call we could end up meeting that evening. I pulled open my top right-hand desk drawer and fingered through paper clips and rubber bands until I found the engagement ring, where I'd thrown it until I could hike over to Josten's. I stashed the ring in my jacket pocket next to the bags of measured black powder that I'd bought at Cumonow's and hadn't had to use. Then I put a reminder on my calendar to take Paul off speed-dial as soon as this circus was over.

I worked on other stuff over the next sixty-six minutes, but I ended up billing only eight-tenths of an hour. My mind kept drifting to Paul's crack about the "real murder weapon." Obviously, Learned had told him something about where this mythical firearm could be found, and that had to be someplace where Paul could conceivably get his hands on it. But where? Then, all at once, my mouth opened slightly and I looked up from my computer screen to stare straight ahead at a Dilbert cartoon taped to one wall of my cubicle.

Shit! Bradshaw's home! Learned stashed something there to frame Ariane when he was planning Tom Bradshaw's murder!

I jumped up and headed at a trot toward Mendoza's office. He was just coming out and moving rapidly in my direction. We both opened our mouths, but I got words out first.

"We have to talk to Ariane Bradshaw!"

"Then get your coat on. We're meeting her at Sam's office in ten minutes."

If you imagine Mendoza's office at one end of a law-firm décor continuum and Calder & Bull at the other, Fletcher & Peck would be closer to Calder & Bull, maybe ten clicks past the midpoint. The woodwork cheated toward the blond side, the carpeting was top-drawer stuff from North Carolina instead of eight-knot Persian, and the conference room they showed us into seemed designed to tell clients, "You're paying for oak, not marble."

On the brisk walk over I'd told Mendoza about my searing insight. He agreed that we should top the agenda with it. As soon as the four of us—Schwartzchild had Sally Port in tow—joined Ariane and Caitlin in the conference room, I zapped my theory out. Port nodded and unholstered her mobile phone.

"We've had two ops from Agincourt Security watching the house and grounds twenty-four/seven since the search of Learned's suite at the Hilton." She thumbed numbers as she spoke. "I'll give them a heads-up."

She strode toward the conference room door but someone answered before she reached it, so all of us heard her no-nonsense admonition:

"Okay, guys, just got word that you might have company in the next few hours. Strictly amateur hour, but he's a big SOB, so turn off *Adult Swim* and look alive."

"Okay," Schwartzchild said, "good start. Now tell us about the pirate pistol."

Mendoza provided a quick recap of our adventures at Cumonow's. He finished it off with a flourish by tossing the bullet-baggies on the table. I added one of the black powder bags—a nice bit of stage business that you wouldn't have gotten from, say, a securities lawyer. Schwartzchild looked a bit befuddled. He was too polite to say, "So what?" but his expression unmistakably conveyed that message. Port, the crime maven with most of her career on the government side, came to the rescue.

"Ballistics tests tie a bullet to a particular gun by matching up marks that the gun made on the bullet when it was fired. The rifling inside the barrel accounts for most of those marks. A flintlock doesn't have rifling. If you fire a bullet from a modern pistol, then retrieve the slug and fire it again from a smooth-bore flintlock, a ballistics test will probably tie the bullet to the contemporary weapon."

"So the FBI test on Learned's forty-five doesn't necessarily prove that it fired the bullet that killed Tom Bradshaw," Schwartzchild said.

"Right. And Ms. Jakubek's conjecture that Learned could have hidden the actual murder weapon at the Bradshaw home isn't completely implausible."

Gee, thanks.

Mendoza, Schwartzchild, and Port then began discussing whether we should go to the cops with this theory, or sit tight and hope for the best, or something in between. I tried to pay attention. I really did. But I had trouble focusing. Agincourt Security isn't mall cops with unloaded guns on their hips just for show. Agincourt is serious security for clients with serious money, most of whom have "Inc." in their names. Its operatives are all ex-military or ex-cop. They beat up Blackwater guys on the playground. The guns they carry have real bullets in them. Their job is *not* to observe and report. And if I was right, Paul was headed right for them.

Without staring, I glanced across the table now and then at Ariane. She sat there, poised but wound pretty tight from the looks of her thin lips and occasionally clenched jaw. Three months ago, I might have been asking myself, *Could she really have killed Tom Bradshaw? Really have stalked him to the museum with a cold-blooded plan worked out ahead of time, blown him away with her lover's gun, and then put the gun back in Learned's attaché case, knowing that that might get him convicted of a capital offense?*

Today, I'd dismiss such childish doubts out of hand. You bet she could.

"Okay," I remember Port saying at this point, "is there any place in the house where Learned could have hidden some kind of a smooth-bore pistol, where he could be reasonably sure you wouldn't find it?"

"I don't think so." Ariane's voice was calm and sure. "It's a big house, but it doesn't really have a lot of nooks and crannies. Tom had a pistol home this fall that he was working on for some exhibition, and the thing just stood out like a sore thumb. The case was too big and awkward to fit in his desk drawer, and he had to clear practically half a drawer in his filing cabinet just to lock the thing away when he wasn't working on it."

"How long ago was that?" Port asked this very casually, as if the answer were a trivial concern but she wanted to make sure her notes were complete.

"Mid-November is the last time I remember seeing it."

"Did Learned know it was there?"

"He could have," Ariane said. "It's the kind of thing Tom would have shown him if he got a chance."

"Learned did know," Caitlin said. "He commented to me about it once. I said something about how anything used for violence must be ugly, and he told me to ask Dad to show me that pistol. He called it 'breathtaking.'"

If you were watching carefully and knew what to look for, you could have spotted a flicker of alarm on Port's poker face as she framed her next question.

"Where is that pistol now?"

"I don't know," Ariane said. "I thought Tom returned it to the museum."

"I'm pretty sure that's right," Caitlin said. "He made some joke about having to borrow one of my tennis bags because he didn't have a briefcase big enough to hold the case, and he didn't want to walk from the parking lot with something under his arm that looked valuable."

"As soon as you get home," Port said then, very evenly, "perhaps you could check the file cabinet and everything in the study, for that matter, and make sure it isn't there."

Ariane sketched a brief nod.

"So," Mendoza said, "we send the bullets to Forensic-Tests-R-Us or someone so that they can do a workup on them, right?"

"I think so, yes." Port gave a deferential glance to Schwartz-child in case he wanted to countermand her directive, but he didn't.

Ariane and Caitlin looked like they couldn't understand why this was obvious, but I did. If the bullets were stashed in a lab somewhere, they wouldn't turn up if the cops dropped by Mendoza's office with a search warrant.

"For the moment, at least," Schwartzchild said then, "I take it our options are all on hold until we get the results of those tests."

"Amen," Mendoza said.

We all stood up, almost simultaneously. A quick round of goodbyes and the meeting was officially adjourned.

As I whipped through the handshakes I whispered to Mendoza that I'd meet him in the lobby in a few minutes. Then I retreated to the ladies' room and had Paul speed-dialed before I got the stall door closed.

"Hello?"

"Paul, this is Cindy. I *really* hope you get this message before you reach your destination. Listen—"

"Cindy? This is Paul. I answered. You aren't talking to voice mail."

"What? Oh." I ran my right hand through my hair, feeling like an airhead. "Sorry. I guess I'm just on automatic pilot."

"So. What's so urgent?" His voice had an oddly calm, I-know-something-you-don't-know quality to it that I couldn't remember hearing before. I halfway wondered if he was baked.

"I only have a minute, so I'll keep it simple. THERE ARE PEOPLE WITH GUNS AT THE BRADSHAW HOME. They know you're coming. Don't go there."

"Anything else?"

I took a deep breath. Lying through my teeth on a voice mail an hour ago was one thing, but I was about to ratchet things up a notch.

"How soon can I see you?"

"It depends. What are you doing tonight?"

So he was in Pittsburgh. Or pretty damn close to it.

"Tonight is wide open—*if* you promise me you won't go near Plantation Bradshaw. Because if you do go near it you won't be seeing anyone tonight except people with handcuffs—and I don't mean bondage mistresses."

"Cynthia, I solemnly swear to you that I will not come within a zip code of the Bradshaw place—wherever that may be. Where would you like to meet?"

Good question. One of the student dives near Duquesne? No. We'd stand out like a couple of narcs at a rave. I settled on The Bigger Jigger, near Mendoza's office. If anyone from his shop noticed us they'd know enough to keep their distance. I gave him the name and address, and started to provide him with directions.

"No sweat, I have a GPS. Eight o'clock?"

"Can't we make it six? How far away are you?"

"Not sure I can make it by six. Let's say eight, to be safe."

"You win." I sighed. "Remember your promise."

"I'll tattoo my promise on my right arm so that I can never forget it. Later…"

There was something really off about his half of our conversation. No intensity, no fervent passion, but instead this vague, well-meaning condescension, like a chess grandmaster who keeps asking you if you're sure you want to make that move. He smoked pot occasionally—he'd sometimes chided me for never indulging—but Paul on pot didn't sound like this. When he was high he came across as spacey and a little dizzy, not detached and two-moves-ahead-of-you.

My gut was churning with mixed feelings when I rejoined Mendoza in the Fletcher & Peck lobby. Because the love wasn't totally dead yet? No. As far as erotic love went, the cat was in the bag and the bag was in the river. But I didn't hate him anymore, either. I figured he was being used by Learned, and that if he didn't drop out of the game he'd probably end up dead or in prison. I didn't want that to happen.

Or maybe I thought that *I* could use *him*. Manipulate him into spilling enough about Learned to get that silky, sophisticated bastard behind bars where he couldn't threaten my client's mother—and therefore my client. Learned's sending Paul on a mission like this was a desperation play. I have a litigator's soul. I'm a predator. I smelled blood in the water, and I wanted to be in on the kill.

As Mendoza and I made our way back to the office, he started saying something about finding two or three private forensic labs and getting quotes from them. Nodding, I quickly looked both ways to make sure we wouldn't get creamed crossing Smallman Street. I saw a Prius painted British racing green. Before the car disappeared around a corner a block away, I knew where I was next going to see Paul—and it wasn't at any saloon.

Chapter Forty-four

They say it's easier to get forgiveness than permission. I knew I'd never get permission, so I decided to keep Mendoza in the dark and hope for forgiveness.

It took me about forty-five minutes to dig up three quotes for private lab ballistics tests and get them to Mendoza. He said that he'd take it from there, which was fine with me.

"I did finally reach Paul, by the way," I said then. "I warned him off the Bradshaw place and he promised not to go near it. But he's either in Pittsburgh or on his way."

"And he's still after 'the real murder weapon,' I suppose." Mendoza frowned. "That'd be my guess. I talked him into meeting me at eight tonight. Not alone. In a public place. The Bigger Jigger."

Mendoza grunted while he thought that over.

"Don't like it but I don't see any way around it. I'll have Cesario on-site, though."

He cupped his left hand around his chin and gave me his hard-as-nails look, daring me to challenge his decision. I answered that with an earnest, wide-eyed nod that has worked with every male I've ever known except Vince.

"Sure, if you think that's best."

"I think that's best."

"Okay. Great. Let me know if I can do anything else to help."

I returned to my cubicle and found other work to do until about three thirty. Then, leaving my computer on as a hint that I expected to come back to the office, I slipped into my coat and made a discreet exit. The Pittsburgh Museum of American History was thirteen blocks away, which is a little far for a comfortable walk in January, but the nearest cabstand was three blocks in the other direction. I just shrugged and hoofed it. I wanted to get there before four, and I made it with six minutes to spare.

I could have gone straight to the Museum Administration Office without paying admission, but I went ahead and laid out six bucks to get in anyway. You really had to want to get to the office to find the signs that directed you to it. I managed it. Eventually I stood in front of a desk occupied by a silver-haired, old-school secretary—the no-nonsense kind. No way anyone much below the mayor would have gotten past her—except that I knew a magic word.

"Excuse me. My name is Cindy Jakubek. I'm one of Caitlin Bradshaw's lawyers, and I wonder if I could speak for about ten minutes with the chief curator." The magic word in there was "Bradshaw."

"About what would you like to see him?" She didn't end her sentence with a preposition—like I said, old school.

"There's something that Mr. Bradshaw had withdrawn from the collection before his death, and I just wanted to make sure that it has been returned."

For just an instant I saw a *Whoa!* look on her face. Then she picked up her telephone receiver and dialed a three-digit extension without looking at the keypad.

Five minutes later I was one-on-one with an elderly gentleman in a navy blue, three-piece suit, white shirt, rep tie, and oxfords with the kind of gloss you only see on shoes that are shined every week. Just about my height, maybe a shade taller, he had little wisps of dove gray hair that fluttered like capricious confetti around the edges of pink and white blotted scalp. The secretary addressed him as "Dr. Wheatley," and he instructed me to call him Colin—short "o."

"Terrible, terrible thing about Tom." He took my hand in a damp, sympathetic grip, as if I were the grieving widow. "How is Mrs. Bradshaw doing?"

"Fairly well, under the circumstances, but of course it was a blow."

"I certainly hope they catch the cowardly murderer who killed Tom."

"I think they're making progress, but I'm afraid I can't talk about the case in detail."

"No, of course not. I understand. Now, what was it you wanted to check?"

I explained about the pistol Tom Bradshaw had taken home.

"Well, that doesn't ring a bell. Let's look."

He led me through a door behind the secretary's desk to an office with lime green walls and old-fashioned, heavy maple furnishings. Cabinets with shelves behind glass doors on top and drawers on the bottom lined three of the four walls. Wheatley trekked over to one of them. Bending slightly, he pulled open a long, wide drawer. He fussed out the top page of what looked like an inch-thick tranche of oversized, accordion-folded computer printout. I'm talking about the kind of printout you get from a main frame, not a desktop. It seemed anomalous, somehow, like an Amish mom pulling a functional light saber from her apron.

Apparently quite pleased with himself, he gestured me over to examine the printout with him. I followed the tip of his index finger as it traced down one line-item after another, finally stopping on the third line of the second page. I pushed my head closer to read the entry:

ELLIOT LIGHT DRAGOON PISTOL, 1 ea., cherry stock w/silver inlay, steel lock (w/o spr), steel barrel w/ bluing, cherry case w/fitted velvet interior, c. 1761 (?). 0099676148.

A handwritten note to the left of the entry read, "Temp. w/ drawn 10/12/10 TB."

"Oh dear," Wheatley said.

"What is it?"

"This notation says that Tom took the pistol out last October, but there's no entry saying that he returned it. Come with me, please."

Leading me through a door in the rear corner, behind his desk, he navigated through a warren of narrow hallways and corridors. We stepped out into a cool, dark room, where we startled a couple of people admiring the Battle of Lexington diorama. He led me brusquely onto the stage where bored middle-schoolers had found Tom Bradshaw's body just before Thanksgiving. He walked right up to a wax British officer with his pistol leveled at the menacing wax rebels. I followed him. Someone else in the room gasped.

After a few seconds of careful examination, he beamed with relief and, I think, pure joy.

"No question about it. That's no replica. That's a real Elliot. Our only one."

I caught my breath as I took a close look at the thing. Learned was right. It was magnificent, its nine-inch barrel resting in a stock that fit perfectly, its hammer coiled over on the flash-plate, begging to be cocked. The silver inlay in the stock winked at us. Some craftsman had given weeks of his life to creating this weapon, which wasn't for hunting, or plinking, or target shooting. The only thing it was good for was to kill another human being. I imagined the gunsmith laboring day after day, casting the parts, carving the stock and the grip, filing the spring, and then, one day, stepping back to gaze with deep pleasure on his handiwork, perhaps saying a prayer to thank God for giving him the skill to make something this beautiful.

Did he think about the widows and orphans his splendid pistol would make? Or did he tell himself, "Soldiers will fight and rich fools will duel over trifles if they choose, and nothing I can do will stop them. If they don't buy their pistols from me they'll buy them from someone else, and my children will go hungry"? Or did he think about it at all?

"Well," Wheatley said, "it's here after all. Thank God for that."

"Is it functional?"

"Oh, no. That little notation on the printout, 'w-slash-o s-p-r,' means that the lock doesn't have a spring. The only way you could damage a man with this would be to club him over the head with it."

"And there's no way to tell when it was returned?"

"No, unfortunately. Only that it was before Tom died, obviously."

Oh really?

"Thank you for helping me clear up this detail, Dr. Wheatley."

"'Colin,' please. Yes, yes, you're quite welcome."

We shook hands and exchanged casual goodbyes.

"They shouldn't have made you pay to get in," he said then, apparently noticing my VISITOR patch for the first time. "I'll call the front desk and tell them to give you a refund."

"That's all right. It's late in the day. As long as I'm here, I think I'll admire the display for awhile."

He beamed again, let me help him down from the stage, then gave me a courtly nod and ambled away. On my way to the office I'd made special note of the blue-shirted guards, who looked fat, bored, and sleepy, and the surveillance cameras that reminded me of Betamax antiques. I was feeling pretty cocky about bringing off what I had in mind.

I wandered to the back of the room, inconspicuous in semi-darkness about thirty feet from the stage. When the other visitors left and I had the room to myself I sat down cross-legged on the floor and waited.

I didn't have to wait all that long. At first I jumped a little at the random sounds of eleventh-hour visitors who wandered in for a last look at the diorama, but I got used to it pretty quickly. Then came the announcements that the museum was closing in fifteen minutes, then ten, then five, and all visitors should please leave. I stayed where I was. I assume a guard made a last round through the room—I heard unhurried steps after the lights went out—but he or she wasn't ambitious enough to spot me.

I got a little tense as time went by after that and nothing happened. I imagined how dumb I'd feel if it turned out my theory was wrong and I ended up having to make up a story about falling asleep in here and getting locked inside. Then I heard someone coming into the room and trying to be quiet about it. I instantly came alert. He walked toward the diorama and stepped onto the platform.

I counted slowly to ten. Then, in no particular hurry, I stood up and walked toward him as he worked the flintlock out of the wax officer's hand.

"Hi, Paul," I said.

Chapter Forty-five

"Cindy!" Paul hissed my name in a stage whisper, like a parent reprimanding his child in church. "What are you doing here?"

"Well, I'm not purloining antique firearms, am I?"

Striding forward as if I had some idea of what to do next, I stepped up onto the diorama stage. Paul just watched me come, not moving a muscle. This was the first time I'd laid eyes on him since the epic Battle of Learned's Suite. Yeah, there was a *poing!* all right—but its resonance had a bad side as well as a good one. Sure, the SOB could have made a living modeling men's briefs and posing for cologne ads. Some memories sparked a flare-up in my gut. But all the hatred came flooding back too. I remembered waking up feeling desolate inside, as if my soul were stuck in some perpetual winter twilight. I remembered eating food without tasting it. I remembered filling night after night with mind-numbing work so I wouldn't have to think or feel.

Paul apparently wasn't having this cuts-both-ways problem. His face lit up.

"How are you doing, Cindy?"

"I'm gnawed by existential doubt and seared by the tragic nature of the human condition, but aside from that I'm doing just fine, Paul. How are *you* doing?"

"Still little Miss Hardass." He gave me that melt-in-your-mouth smile of his.

"Were you planning on telling me about stealing the gun when we met at eight tonight?"

"I'm not stealing it. This is the murder weapon, Cindy. This gun that's been right under everybody's nose all the time. I'm just verifying that."

"Right. You're probably one of only seven adults in the country who know less about firearms than I do and you're going to do an expert analysis on this pistol."

"Walt is *innocent*." Paul transfixed me with the earnest expression of a middle-schooler talking about saving the rain forests. "They're framing him. What they did was, they—"

"Shot Bradshaw with a smooth-bore pistol using a spent bullet from Learned's forty-five," I snapped. "I field-tested that theory seven hours ago. But who's 'they'?"

"Wendy Sommers. She's working for the gang that has the Gardner Museum stuff. They thought Bradshaw and Walter were working together to help the Feds get them. So they killed Bradshaw and they're framing Walt for his murder. Two birds with one stone. It's brilliant."

"How did Sommers get her hands on Learned's gun?" In the excitement I forgot about tact. I shot questions at him as if he were on a witness stand. "How did she get in here while the museum was closed? How did she even know that Bradshaw would be in the museum, when the only reason he was here was that he wanted to chill someplace while he got himself psychologically ready to face the state police? How did she get close enough to him to shoot him with a weapon that's not accurate from much more than twelve feet?"

That wouldn't have been a bad closing argument. Unfortunately, Paul wasn't a jury of anyone's peers. He scowled, with a pitying expression on his face.

"You don't know Walt like I do. He couldn't have killed Bradshaw. He and Bradshaw were friends in a way that only certain kinds of men can be. You couldn't understand it."

"Paul, Bradshaw was killed by someone he knew and trusted. He let the killer into this museum himself. His body wasn't moved after death, so he must have let the killer come with him onto this display. That gun you're holding is one of the most valuable pieces the museum owns. There must be some kind of alarm that he could have tripped if he'd suspected anything. Up to the last second of his life he couldn't have imagined that he was in any danger."

Paul opened his mouth. I'll always wonder what would have come out if he'd spoken. The next thing that happened, though, wasn't Paul saying something. The next thing that happened was Cindy almost wetting her pants for the first time since the age of three.

A minuteman stepped out of the waxy crowd on this faux Lexington Common and walked stiffly toward us. He was carrying a musket in his right hand. I jumped at least a foot. Paul outdid me. He not only jumped, he dropped the bloody pistol. Only pure instinct and quick reflexes let me catch the two-hundred-fifty-year-old piece of custom-crafted artillery before it crashed to the stage.

"Walt!" he yelped. "You're supposed to be in Switzerland!"

Yep, the minuteman was Walter Learned, in heavy makeup and costume, but recognizable. He had to have been standing there that whole time, like some busker posing as a statue in a public square so that tourists will throw coins in his box.

"Hush." Learned spoke gently and offered Paul an encouraging smile. "I don't think Ms. Jakubek would snitch on you, but popping off with guilty knowledge is a bad habit."

"But you're in danger! You said—"

"Yes, I'm in danger, and the sooner I get out of here the better. So just listen. We don't have much time."

Learned turned toward me.

He heard every word I said, I thought. *He knows that I know everything. I am going to die. I am going to end my life holding this childish, dumbass relic of an eighteenth-century pistol in my hands.*

"Tom had decided to kill me," Learned said to me.

"Because of Ariane?"

"It's more complicated than that. Tom and I took a don't-ask-don't-tell approach. It was just a now-and-then thing with Ariane anyway. I hadn't been with her for years when circumstances sort of threw us together a few months ago. Anyway, Tom didn't have any standing to chastise Ariane for stepping out with me."

"Because he'd been cheating on her with you for years?"

"I suppose that's one way to put it." Learned sighed. "But don't get judgmental when I'm trying to give you information you want. What put me in Tom's crosshairs was Caitlin."

"You mean finding out that you were her father."

"Yes. That shattered his soul. He had no idea Ariane and I had gone back that long. The Feds were pressuring him. The state police were crawling up his rectum over some penny-ante tax thing. His patrimony was evaporating. All of that put him under inhuman stress. I should have been a better friend. I should have focused on that. But I didn't. When he found out about Caitlin, he snapped. He brought that gun home, replaced the spring, oiled it, and made sure the hammer and lock were in good working order."

"And then you turned the tables on him."

"If that's a conclusion, it's hasty, and if it's a question, it's pointless. You're going to believe I killed him regardless of what I say."

"But you *didn't* kill him," Paul hoarsely insisted. "You didn't kill anyone!"

"Never mind." Learned turned toward Paul. "She believes what she said. The police will believe it. Everyone except you will believe it. And there's no way to disprove it."

He kept on talking to Paul in a soothing voice, but I only caught the gist. I was feeling the coldest gut-chill I can ever remember. The look in his eyes when he spoke to me made me shudder. The last time I'd seen that look I was twelve years old, beside the bed where Vince's mom had been lying for two months. I hadn't realized what it meant until the next morning: it meant she knew she was going to die.

I'm three feet from a murderer. I'm standing three yards from where Tom Bradshaw was when that same soothing voice took him off his guard—fatally.

"The best way you can help me," Learned was saying to Paul, "is to forget about mock heroics. Sit tight here for half-an-hour. Then, get out and go to ground in Philadelphia."

As unobtrusively as I could manage, I fished the packet of black powder out of my jacket pocket. I didn't have any ammo for the pistol, but I figured I'd take it one step at a time. I tilted the gun's muzzle up as much as I dared, and poured the powder down the barrel. I probably didn't need to bother being sneaky about it. Learned had eyes for no one but Paul. I put a dab of powder on the flash-plate

"Do you understand, Paul?" Learned was saying.

Maybe he's just going to club me over the head with that musket. Okay, maybe if I just fired the gun, the blast and flash would shock him long enough for me to run.

Learned started to turn. I used the heel of my left hand to rack back the hammer.

"Later," he said to me, over his shoulder. "Good luck in New York."

Then, in three creaky strides he was off the stage and headed for the door.

"What's happening?" Paul swerved around to look at the doorway as Learned went through it.

"I don't know," I said. "Just shut up and do what he told you."

"But he's leaving!"

"Look, Paul, I know you're strung out. Just get a grip on it, okay? Two things I'm sure of are that Learned cares about you and he's smarter than you are. So stay here like he said. Whatever chance he has, it probably drops to zero if you go running after him."

Logic is no match for passion. "Like hell!"

Paul leaped at one of the redcoats to relieve him of the bayonet on his musket. He cussed and strained at the fitting where the bayonet joined the barrel. He was determined to gallop into a gunfight with cold steel, like El Cid in a time warp. I knew that, one way or another, he'd get the thing off before the night was a minute older.

"Paul, there are probably cops out there after him right now!"

"They'll be dead cops soon if they are."

I suppose I could have run over and tugged on his arm or something while I tried to yell some sense into him, but he would just have knocked me into the middle of next week with one paw. I dug into my pocket for the ring. Maybe that could grab his attention long enough to keep him from committing suicide. Holding the gun awkwardly in my left hand, I got the ring out.

"Look at this! Please look at it!"

He swiveled his head toward me. His eyes widened. I think it might actually have worked if I'd had another thirty seconds.

But I didn't. A strident clanging like an old-fashioned school fire alarm split the air. Lights suddenly came on. Paul went back to work on the bayonet, now with manic energy. I saw someone in a guard's uniform sprint past the doorway. Not slow, not fat, not sleepy, and holding a weapon that definitely wasn't a flintlock pistol. He glanced into the room on the way past. Couldn't possibly have missed us, and we were fiddling with the museum's crown jewel. But the guard kept right on running—clearly after something else.

I didn't waste any more words. I'd just gotten an idea and I didn't want to give myself time to think about it. I dropped the ring down the barrel of the gun. I pulled the ramrod out and pushed it down the barrel until the ring felt like it was seated tightly against the powder.

Paul yanked the bayonet off and jumped in one fluid motion to the floor.

Even over the clanging alarm I heard a burst of shots, way too fast for anything but a fully automatic gun.

I pulled the hammer back to full cock. Paul was halfway to the door by now. I took the monster pistol in both hands, extended my arms full length, and did my best to aim. Paul was one good stride from the doorway when I squeezed the trigger. The roar deafened me and my arms shot up from the kick. Backflash burned both of my hands and grains of half-burned powder buried themselves in my thumbs. All I could see was purple smoke. For a second, I didn't have any idea whether I'd hit him.

Then his piercing scream let me know.

"JESUS CHRIST, CINDY, WHAT HAVE YOU DONE? AAAGGHHH!"

I peered through the smoke. Paul was lying on his right side, screaming while he felt behind him with his left hand.

I aimed for his left thigh. I *swear* I aimed for the back of his left thigh. But it's a smooth-bore weapon and yada-yada-yada. I'd shot him right in the ass.

Chapter Forty-six

I laid the pistol down and sprinted over to Paul, pulling out my Droid on the way. Before I was halfway there, I heard five distinct shots—BANG! BANG!...BANG! BANG! BANG! I heard splintering glass, but no human screams. I hoped this meant that cops had arrived and were shooting at the rogue guard with the machine gun, because otherwise I figured Paul and I had no more chance than perch at a fish fry.

I had nine-one-one punched in and ready to send by the time I knelt next to Paul's writhing torso, but by then I heard something else: running steps approaching the room. If my prayers were answered a cop was coming, and he could get action a lot faster than I could. And if they weren't I'd be dead in about ten seconds, so there wasn't much point in complicating an operator's evening.

"God my ass hurts!" Paul squealed.

"As my sainted mother told me once or twice in that situation, 'Some day you'll thank me for this.'"

The footsteps slowed as whoever had been running decided to scope things out. A couple of seconds after I yelled, "In here! Gunshot wound!" a woman about my age came in. She was a cop: blue uniform trousers, regulation shoes, visored cap, and a big shiny badge on her leather jacket. And a gun. She held some kind of a semiautomatic pistol in her right hand. I wouldn't call the look in her eyes a thousand-yard stare, but it was in the neighborhood. Maybe six-hundred yards. Cops are pros about lots of things, but live fire at living, breathing targets isn't one of them.

"This man's been shot," I said. "Nonfatal, but he'll need an ambulance."

"Who shot him?"

"I did."

That surprised her but it also calmed her down. The training and drills she'd gone through clicked in and she went into triage mode: Take care of people who are injured or endangered first, and then worry about chasing bad guys and arresting people.

"Where's he hit?"

"Rear end."

She reholstered her gun and squatted to take a look. She probed the wound, and I could see that there wasn't too much bleeding. Then, in a surprisingly gentle way, she pried Paul's left eyelid as far up as she could with her left thumb—to check for signs of shock, I suppose.

She must not have found any. She spoke in clipped tones into a microphone mounted on her left epaulet. I didn't understand the code numbers she used but I picked up "ambulance" and "American History Museum." Calling for an ambulance meant there wasn't already an ambulance on the way. And *that* meant that all those shots I'd heard had either missed or produced a fatality. I don't think Paul had thought it through that carefully, but even he seemed to have some notion of what must have happened.

"That firing a couple of minutes ago," he said in a trembling voice. "Did someone…?"

The cop looked at him for a second before answering. When she finally spoke her voice was low and flat, as if she were making a report to a superior officer.

"One of the guards here heard voices and called it in. My partner and I had just gotten inside when someone tripped an alarm trying to go through a fire door. We spotted an armed white female in a guard's outfit running away. We shot at her, but we missed."

"What about the shots earlier?"

The cop shook her head and took a deep breath.

"We found a body—looked like he was dressed to do re-enactments here. Multiple gunshot wounds in the chest and heart. My guess is he was dead before he hit the floor."

"NOOOOOOO!" Paul's wail wrenched my gut. "No, God, he can't be dead! He can't be! He can't be!" Then he started sobbing.

The emptiness that came back to the pit of my stomach brought revelation along for company. I'd heard love from Paul during our time together. I'd heard lust, and I'd heard passion. But I'd never heard anything from the depths of his soul like this. Paul could never have felt for me what he felt for Walter Learned. It would have been criminal to ask him to try.

Then the cop remembered that the armed white female wasn't the only civilian shooter on the premises. With studious calm, she looked at me.

"So what went down here?"

I'd been working on an answer to that one, but Paul beat me to it.

"She *wanted* him dead." He glared at me, his eyes gleaming with white-hot fury. "She shot me to keep me from helping him."

"Who's 'him?'" the cop asked.

"Walter," Paul said.

"The guy whose body you found," I added. "Paul decided that someone was gunning for him, and he was running out there with that pigsticker to try to go after them."

The cop looked at Paul.

"You mean if she hadn't shot you, you were going to run around this museum waving that bayonet?"

"All he needed was someone on his side," Paul said before adding, as the pain flared, "OWWW! Goddammit!"

To her credit, the cop didn't roll her eyes or look at Paul as if he were an alien species. The guy had just been shot—embarrassingly, in the butt, but it still hurt. A lot.

"You realize," she said evenly, "that if you'd managed to get ten feet outside this room with that weapon, you'd probably have three or four bullets in you, right? If the murderer hadn't gotten you, my partner or I would have. And we don't aim for the ass when we shoot."

I thought about what to say. *Learned was dead meat from the moment he came here to save you after you attracted the attention of everyone who was looking for him by heading for Pittsburgh. He warned you and then he ran from this room to draw the killer away from you. When he realized someone was in hot pursuit inside the museum, he cut his already tiny chances of getting out alive by setting off an alarm to attract the police. Thug with machine gun or not, he might be alive right now if it weren't for you.*

Nah, I don't think so. "He told you to stay here because he knew he was in danger and he wanted to protect you. Getting yourself killed would've been a pretty shitty way of saying thanks."

The cop's microphone squawked to tell her the ambulance had arrived, so I didn't get a chance to hear Paul's reaction. Probably just as well.

After they loaded Paul onto the gurney the cop arrested me. After all, I'd shot someone from behind, in a place where I didn't have any business being after closing time, with an antique weapon that a suspicious soul might have thought I had designs on stealing.

Fortunately, Learned was a guy who'd been of interest to the FBI when he got himself hemstitched at a place in the process of being shot up by two Pittsburgh cops who had a story about an armed white female but no actual armed white female. My story backed up the cops, so they got a deputy DA to put in some overtime instead of making me spend the night in jail. Paul was a total mess during his hospital-bed interview, but he mentioned his own "dead cops" line and that made me look pretty good. By a little after eleven, Mendoza was driving me home, with the incident still under investigation but no charges pending—yet.

"Was that your first time in handcuffs?" he asked, referring to my arrest.

"Second. The first was foreplay during my I'll-try-anything-once phase."

He proceeded to chew me out royally in a mixture of English and Spanish, riffing on the obvious themes—I was lucky that DA didn't throw the book at me, if every Ivy League graduate was this goddamn dumb he was goddamn glad he'd gone to night school, I ought to be spanked, and so forth. I absorbed this stoically and with appropriate displays of contrition.

Finally he ran out of steam. After a few minutes of silence, he grudgingly growled something that I interpreted as a request that I sort the mess out for him. I looked up.

"All I have is a theory."

"That's more than I've got right now," he said.

"When Learned flew the coop we all assumed he went overseas somewhere. And that was definitely his plan. But he really cared for Paul. Paul lit out for Pittsburgh, so Learned abandoned his own escape plan. He had to know there was a 99 percent chance he was signing his own death warrant, but for the sake of love he settled for 1 percent. Paul's 'real murder weapon' chatter meant that he'd be coming to the museum, so Learned waited here, disguised as part of the scenery. The minuteman getup was a little baroque, but it let him hide in plain sight until Paul showed up. Maybe he figured that if he could just talk some sense into Paul he could make a run for it and hole up with Ariane Bradshaw while he worked out another off-shore exit strategy. And he might have pulled it off if not for us."

"It didn't occur to him to just have a chat over the phone?" Mendoza's tone was sarcastic, so I paid him in kind.

"Why not take out an ad in the *New York Times*? A mobile phone call is basically a radio transmission. Learned had to assume that inconvenient people would be listening in."

Mendoza chewed on that until he pulled into Vince's driveway. He gave me one of his sullen nods—the nod that means he got it, but he didn't have to like it.

"Well, at least it makes things simple. Learned killed Bradshaw, now he's permanently out of the picture, the cops are as far away from the Gardner Museum loot as they ever were, and the two female Bradshaws came through unscathed. Case closed."

"Right." I opened the door and climbed out of his Citera. "Case closed."

Neither of us believed it. Why should we?

Chapter Forty-seven

After thinking about it hard overnight, I told Phillip Schuyler the next morning that Wendy Sommers killed Learned. I told him this around 9:30 while we were strolling through Point State Park in downtown Pittsburgh, freezing our butts off because Schuyler didn't want my name to show up on the visitor's log for his office. I couldn't blame him for that.

"You can make a positive i.d.?"

"No way. I saw her face for two-tenths of a second, while she was running, and I had other things on my mind."

"Yet you're sure she did it."

"Yeah, but it's logic, not eyewitness identification." I stopped walking, half-turned and made eye contact with him, to be sure he'd get the message. "I didn't get it completely put together for myself until I was halfway through my shower last night."

"Put it together for me."

"She gave me an earful during a bus ride. Either she made a special trip to Pittsburgh to do a good deed or she was here stalking Learned and decided to warn me off to keep the body-count down. Learned's killer was an armed white female and there aren't a lot of other white females running around in this circus with access to automatic weapons. Seeing the perp sprint by in a guard's uniform last night reminded me of seeing a perp in a maid's uniform run away the night my hotel room was burgled, and Sommers is the most plausible candidate for the hotel thing. Plus, if the Gardner Museum thieves had had some other hired muscle on Learned's tail all this time, you'd probably have a line on them and you wouldn't be wasting your time on me."

Schuyler tilted his head first to the left and then to the right and then back again, the way you might do if you were considering some wacky theory that just might possibly be true. Then he started walking again, but he kept his face turned toward mine.

"So it basically comes down to the bus ride. If she was really relaying a message from Learned instead of trying to scare you off for her own purposes, then she actually was working with him and your theory falls apart."

"Oh, she was working with him, all right—but she was working against him at the same time." I panted a little as I picked up my pace to match his long-legged strides. "I think she was a plant, keeping an eye on him for the bad guys."

"Have you shared your conjectures with the Pittsburgh cops yet?"

"No. It's way too thin for an arrest warrant and if Sommers is going to run she's already done it. So there's no big hurry. I'll save it to use in case the DA presses charges against me."

"Why are you telling me, then?"

"Curiosity. Killing Learned wasn't a federal crime, so you don't have to do anything about Sommers if you don't want to. Of course, the only reason you wouldn't want to is that you think she's a possible link to the museum thieves, and you'd rather have her out there, so she can possibly lead you to them someday, than in a squeal room getting grilled by local cops. If you want her to stay on the outside, then *that* means you have the same theory I do, and you had it before I did."

It was Schuyler's turn to stop. I paused with him. He gave me a long, careful look. A little smile played at the corners of his lips, as if he were thinking back to a simpler time when women who came off sounding too smart got squelched. Then the smile disappeared and he got real, *real* serious. His expression told me he was speaking on the record, formally, with measured words, and I'd damn well better listen.

"I can't tell you not to give information to local law enforcement authorities."

"I haven't heard you say anything like that."

"Good." He hunched his shoulders, as if the raw weather were starting to get to him. "I don't think the DA is going to press charges."

"I don't think so either. Have a pleasant day."

◇◇◇

By mid-March, when Vince and I met with Pro Tools' Pittsburgh branch manager, the Commonwealth of Pennsylvania had officially decided not to charge me with any of the felonies that a mean-spirited prosecutor might have spun out of my museum escapade. The little insurance policy I'd bought with Schuyler probably had something to do with that and, to be fair, so did Paul. Being Paul, he got tagged as an uncooperative witness in a hurry, and even after he wasn't strung out on Percocet he repeated his dead-cops line and gave some helpful details about my pleading with him not to go in harm's way.

Maybe it's just sheer class prejudice, though, but I want to give most of the credit to an assistant DA making *maybe* fifty-five thousand bucks a year. I don't know his name, but it had to be one of four people and they're all guys. He came into the office and did a professional case assessment. After he'd read the reports, talked to the cops, and interviewed Paul one more time, he decided that I'd shot Paul to save his life and spare two police officers the inconvenience of blowing him away instead of to get back at him for jilting me. Paul still thought that I'd been trying to keep him from saving Learned—Paul can get plenty delusional without Percocet—but no one bought that.

So, like Mendoza said, case closed. I repackaged the papers Caitlin had sent to me and returned them to her, with a self-serving cover note for our Client Correspondence folder. In case it ever comes up for you, that's called "papering the file." We never bothered with the ballistics test on our bullets, of course. I've heard rumors that the FBI duplicated the experiment

Mendoza and I ran—but I've also heard rumors of alien corpses at Area 51. Believe whatever you like.

I won't bore you with a blow-by-blow account of Vince's negotiations with the Pro Tools branch manager, a shrewd, affable desk jockey named William Dhue. I figured we were at least halfway home before I ever saw the inside of Dhue's office, when Vince explained the unpainted pinewood coffin standing upright in the lobby of the branch warehouse. Twelve or thirteen nails studded its lid at various places. Vince nudged me and pointed at the coffin.

"Every time a Cornwell or Matco dealer goes out of business, the field manager for the area gets to pound a nail into that coffin."

Inference: no way Dhue was going to let either of those arch-rival companies grab the order that Allegheny County Community College was dangling. He played around with a 10 percent commission and then 15 percent just for pride, but we got to twenty before Vince was halfway through his first cup of coffee.

That wasn't the hard part. The hard part was parlaying that little wedge into more territory for Vince. Sal had come up with a promising negotiating ploy, but Vince had to make it work once Dhue provided the opening—which he did promptly after Vince explained why he needed a route census.

"Look, Vince, you're a solid dealer. Year after year. You want a route census, you get a route census. Period. But here's the thing. Milo Skerritt is bringing in his truck next week."

"Milo's cashing out?"

"Yep. Just can't make a go of it in this economy. So I've got an open territory on my hands until I can find someone who'll beg, borrow, or steal a hundred thousand bucks to become a Pro Tools dealer. Good luck on getting that done in less than six months. That means your field manager, who also happens to be Milo's field manager, is going to be spending half his time beating the bushes for dealer candidates and the other half collecting installment payments from Milo's old customers. So it's going to take a while for him to squeeze a census in."

Vince sprang the trap.

"Billy, you're right about everything but one. It's not gonna take you six months to fill that territory; it'll take you sixteen. Milo's territory is way light."

"Maybe, but what can I do?"

"Bust the damn thing up. Give me twenty of Milo's stops, and divide the rest between Tony and Phin. We'll take the customer accounts off your hands. That way you'll have dealers collecting them and your field manager can do field manager stuff. Meanwhile, you have Pro Tools guys servicing the stops, so Cornwell and Matco don't swoop in like vultures."

Dhue grinned, as if he actually appreciated the deft elegance of Vince stabbing him with his own sword. He took his Pro Tools baseball cap off, scratched scraggly brown hair, and put the cap back on.

"That might work. I'll have to run it by the suits, but I might be able to sell it. Just cool your jets for about three weeks, and then you'll get a note from Billy Dhue."

"I hope it's a love note." As we stood up I handed him my card, which included the scariest words most franchisors ever see—Attorney at Law. A little extra motivation.

Chapter Forty-eight

My Pittsburgh life began winding down. My Streetdreamer blogs got more confident. At the same time, now that it really did look like Wall-Street-here-I-come, I started having mixed feelings about it. I didn't understand them. Mendoza did.

"You helped a *client*, *chica*! You solved a *problem*! Gonna be a long time before you do that in New York. Associates in New York don't help clients, they help partners. That warm glow you got all over your body when you realized you'd saved your dad's business—you're gonna *miss* that, and the Metropolitan Opera won't make up for it."

"Are you saying I should think about staying in Pittsburgh?"

"No way, girl. You gotta get New York outta your system. You'll probably want to bail after three months, but don't do it. There is no one, no matter how smart she is, who can't learn something from an outfit like Calder & Bull. Give yourself a timeframe. Minimum two years, maximum four. Somewhere in that window, sit down and make a stay/go decision. Just don't stay there by default. New York is full of people who were going to be there five years and then move on to someplace sane but now they're fifty and it's too late. Don't be those people."

Made sense to me.

In mid-April, just after he'd filed his tax return, Vince proposed to Lainie. They set the date for mid-August.

In early May UPS delivered a small, brown package addressed to me at Vince's house. No return address, but I recognized Paul's handwriting on the label. I hadn't heard from him since the EMTs pulled him onto the gurney at the museum. I wondered whether I should soak the thing in cold water before opening it, but then I shrugged that off and just attacked the packing tape and cardboard with a butcher knife.

Inside I found a Lucite cube encasing the engagement ring that some ER surgeon had dug out of Paul's butt. Also a note saying it was all his fault, I was right, he was wrong, he'd been weak, he was sorry, and he'd always remember me.

The note was typewritten. Including the signature.

In late May I signed a lease on a generic apartment in an ice-cube tray building on the upper west side of Manhattan. Twenty-minute rush hour subway ride from Calder & Bull, and from spring through fall I could walk it in less than forty minutes if I wanted to. Occupancy September 1st, which would be tight, but I'd just have to find a way to make that work. I put this latest development on *Streetdreamer*.

That entry caught a comment that grabbed my attention: "Just remember, Streetdreamer, the only dangerous dreams are the ones that come true." The comment included a link. When I clicked on it, my screen filled with a brief story from the *New York Times*:

> Joseph Reynolds, until recently a partner in the litigation department at Calder & Bull, a prominent New York law firm, was found dead in his upper east-side apartment yesterday, the result of an apparently self-inflicted gunshot wound. Mr. Reynolds had left the firm a few weeks ago as part of a general thinning of partnership ranks that *The American Lawyer* has referred to as "a bloodbath." According to his wife, Jillian Welch, he had pursued various employment opportunities but had been unable to secure another position. He is survived by Ms. Welch and three children.

I made myself read it three times. Then I swallowed hard and went back to the list of things to do to prepare for my move to New York.

The note I got in early June was not typewritten. It was hand-written, with penmanship as perfect as any nun's. I opened the envelope to find engraved stationery, with "Ariane Bradshaw" embossed in black on cream paper, and the message in navy blue ink from a fountain pen:

Dear Ms. Jakubek,

I write first of all to thank you for the help and support which you provided to Caitlin on both a personal and a professional level in the aftermath of her father's tragic death last fall. Your empathy and commitment meant a great deal to her, and to me.

In addition, there is a matter that I hope to speak with you about in the near future. I wonder if you would find it convenient to visit me at our home this Saturday afternoon at two? In hope of a favorable reply I remain,

Very truly yours,

Ariane Bradshaw

Well isn't that interesting? A murderer with impeccable manners. Or not, to be fair. Learned gave Ariane an alibi for the night of Thomas Bradshaw's murder if he'd been telling the truth, and even if he was lying odds were that Sommers had killed Bradshaw and there was a gun-angle that I just hadn't figured out yet.

Anyhow, it didn't really matter whether the real killer was Ariane or Sommers or even Learned. It wouldn't make any sense for Ariane to kill me in her own home, so this meeting figured to be some kind of closure deal. Maybe even with a little monetary thank-you that I'd scrupulously turn over to Mendoza. Whatever. No way I was passing this up.

I called to accept the invitation, and sent her a confirming note. I didn't even have to check Emily Post to make sure that was the way to do it. I also made sure Mendoza knew where I'd be. I didn't have to check Emily Post for that, either.

After giving the matter a little thought, I went online to retrieve the official return the State Police had filed after their search of Bradshaw's house. Just pray that you never have to read one. Twenty-three hand-scrawled pages of mind-numbing cop-speak. The fourth line-item on the eleventh page rewarded my diligence: "Federal Tax Return, 2009 w/'FAFSA Worksheet.'" I happened to know what a FAFSA Worksheet was. FAFSA Worksheets had played a very important role in my life for seven years. They help you compute how much financial aid you can expect for college and post-graduate education, given your assets and annual income.

I didn't have access online to the actual worksheet found in the Bradshaw mansion, but I didn't need to look at it. The return told me that someone in the Bradshaw home had prepared one—and personal experience told me that with assets and income based on Ariane Bradshaw's prenup, the financial aid number was 0.

Chapter Forty-nine

I rang the bell on the Bradshaw front door promptly at two that Saturday. Ariane Bradshaw answered the door herself, wearing roughly what she would have for a state dinner at the White House. I doubted that was for my benefit, so I figured she had plans for later on.

"It's very good of you to come. Thank you so much."

"I'm delighted to be here. Thank you for inviting me."

Since her husband's death she'd put the first-floor great room through a world class makeover. An abstract piece had replaced the English fox hunting scene over the fireplace. A black, enameled escritoire with lots of pigeonholes and French curlicues stood where the maple writing table had been. She'd had the white walls repainted to feature alternating red and blue vertical stripes about two feet wide, set off with gold trim. She led me over to a conversation corner featuring a chintz armchair and sofa with rose petal upholstery—another new touch. A sterling silver tea service dominated the coffee table. I'm not huge on hot tea, but when she offered me some I said it would be wonderful. It seemed like the polite thing to do.

"I understand you're moving to New York soon." She served me and sat down with her own delicate cup.

"Yes. I have a job with a firm there named Calder & Bull." I realized later that I should have said "I've accepted a position" instead of "I have a job," but, hey, I'm new at this.

"Well we'll hate to see you leave Pittsburgh but it sounds like a wonderful opportunity."

'Thank you."

"The news about Walt Learned came as a terrible shock." She sipped some tea. "I know it must have been an awful trial for you. I hope you've been able to put it all behind you."

"I've moved on." I lapsed into cliché because the topic took me by surprise. "Mr. Learned was fascinating, but I never felt like I really got to know him."

"I thought that I did know him, but perhaps I was just fooling myself. No matter what the police think, though, I just can't bring myself to believe that Walt killed Tom."

"I can certainly understand your reservations."

As soon as these words were out of my mouth I realized that they might sound a little snarky if Ariane were the murderer. She didn't twitch a muscle. She put her cup down in its saucer, bent over, and pulled a dark brown wooden case from underneath the table. The thing had to be two-and-a-half feet long, and she needed some muscle to lift it up to the coffee table. We were now officially off-script.

"A lawyer in Delaware sent me this. It arrived about a week ago. Her cover letter said she was Walt's lawyer and his instructions were to get it to you through me, if possible, should anything happen to him. He wanted you to have it."

"That's very thoughtful of you." I hoped she could hear these serene words over the alarm bells going off in my head. "Did her note explain why she didn't send it directly to me?"

"Not really. She said that Mr. Learned thought it best not to suggest any association between himself and you."

I came within an electron of slopping hot tea all over my lap. Learned was trying to avoid attracting attention to me. The people whose attention he didn't want to attract already knew he'd been joined at the hip with the Bradshaws, though, so one more contact with Ariane wouldn't make any difference.

I opened the case. Lying inside on a custom-cut cushion covered with red satin were two flintlock pistols and the array of loading and cleaning apparatus that each required. They weren't antiques. They were replicas, like the one I'd fired at Cumonow's. Locks, stocks, and barrels had the gloss and shine of a professional buffer, not the patina of a couple of centuries. Plus, there were grains of black powder near the powder horn for the upper gun, and they looked like the kind of thing someone would have noticed if they'd been around for two hundred years or so.

The pistol on top had its barrel pointing to my left, with the one on the bottom pointing to my right. The barrels looked like they were eight or nine inches long. The lock and the grip on each added another four inches or so of horizontal length. I was looking at a replica set of matched dueling pistols.

I closed the lid and made eye contact with Ariane.

"I have no idea what I did to make Mr. Learned feel he should favor me with such a striking gift, but I can't tell you how much I appreciate your inviting me over to provide it to me."

"My pleasure. I'd love to be a fly on the wall when you regale dinner guests with the story behind these guns."

"Thank you." Associates at Calder & Bull don't have time to arrange many dinner parties, but why kill the buzz?

"I have to run to a planning meeting for a charity I'm involved with called SHIP," Ariane said. "Stop Hunger in Pittsburgh. If you have a few more minutes, though, I know Caitlin would like to say hello. She's down in the basement. The stairs are just off the kitchen."

"That's a wonderful idea. Thank you again for your hospitality."

We rose and exchanged damp handshakes. I picked up the gun case and followed Ariane to the kitchen area. She went out the back door and let me make my own way down the stairs.

I found Caitlin sitting in a brightly lit corner in the finished, uncluttered basement. She sat at a makeshift desk formed by putting burlap-covered plywood across a couple of two-drawer filing cabinets. She rocked minimally back and forth, presumably in time to the beat of whatever was pounding through the iPod buds in her ears. And she was managing to tweet with both thumbs while gripping a cigarette between the first two fingers of her left hand.

"Hi, Caitlin." I sketched a little wave with my free hand.

"Oh, hi." She glanced over at me wide-eyed, as if my appearance were a complete surprise. "Give me just a sec."

She finished whatever she'd been tweeting and put her phone down. She pulled the buds from her ears. One last puff on the cigarette and a languorous exhalation before she put the thing out in an ashtray.

"Mom has quit smoking again." Caitlin made this comment in the kind of exasperated tone that teenagers use to describe idiotically inconvenient parental behavior. "I come down here because I feel a little funny now smoking in front of her."

"Whatever works. Your mom said you wanted to talk."

"Sure. Thanks for sending those papers back, by the way."

"You're welcome."

"Did you happen to keep any copies?"

"Nope. The case is closed. Paper takes up space—and space costs money."

She nodded at the case under my arm. "Is that the thing Mom wanted to give you?"

"Mm hmm." I set it on the desk and opened it so that she could examine the pistols.

"Are these like the one you shot at the museum?"

"They're the same basic type of weapon. Flintlock pistol. But these are dueling pistols. The one at the museum was a cavalry gun."

"Do you mind if I pick one up?"

"Go ahead."

What, you're thinking that was the bonehead move of all time? Classic dumb brunette contriving to get herself in mortal peril through sheer stupidity? Come on. What was Caitlin going to do? Shoot her own lawyer in her own basement to protect her mother and then claim self-defense? That wouldn't be the most obvious move for someone who was planning anything. And if she weren't planning something, I didn't have much to worry about, did I? Besides, I had an agenda of my own.

Caitlin picked up the top gun, lifted it, and raised and lowered her hand a couple of times to get a feel for its weight.

"It's pretty heavy. Do you know how to load it?"

"The first thing you need is powder, which would be in that bulb thing there."

Exhibit B in the Caitlin-isn't-planning-anything file. If she were, at least one of the pistols would already be loaded.

Caitlin picked up the powder horn and in no time at all measured out two pinches and poured the powder down the barrel. She seemed quite pleased with herself.

"Nothing to it. I'll bet I can figure the next part out all by myself."

The case held six balls for each pistol. Big things—fifty caliber. Caitlin picked one of them up and dropped it down the muzzle. It made a little metallic rattle on the way down, with a barely perceptible *pock* as it hit the powder base. She pulled the ramrod from its holder under the barrel and thrust it down the muzzle. She didn't overdo it. Two measured pushes. She cocked the hammer first—full cock, in one motion, using the heel of her left hand. Then she deftly sprinkled a tiny mound of powder on the flash-plate.

Up to this point I'd felt completely confident that I could take her, if it came to that. Suddenly I felt dumb and a little scared.

"I wouldn't fire that in here," I said.

"No one is asking you to."

I decided I'd punch her in the throat if she turned on me. At close quarters, the gun would actually get in her way. I could block the thing with my left arm and jab short and hard with my right fist, just the way I'd learned to do it on the playground. I clenched my fist until my fingernails dug into my palm.

She didn't turn on me. With a nod she directed my attention across the room. One of her V-neck letter sweaters was draped over the back of a chair a good twenty feet away, hanging in a way that emphasized the blue and gold chenille D on the front.

Caitlin brought the pistol straight up in the air, then slowly leveled her right arm. She seemed not to be breathing at all, standing there with perfect poise, as close to motionless as a living human being can get. I was looking at the kind of natural athlete that I'd never be, someone with a fluid and effortless sense of her own physicality.

As if in slow motion I felt that I could see her finger squeezing the trigger, see the hammer falling toward the plate, see the spark as it struck the powder. The *BOOM!* from the gun didn't make me jump. I was used to that sound by now. Thick blue smoke fogged the air, but not thick enough to keep me from seeing an ugly, jagged hole marring the middle of the D.

"Nice shot."

"Thanks." She handed the pistol back to me, butt first.

"I don't think this is the first time you've ever fired a weapon like this."

"Maybe I'm just a natural."

"Anything is possible." I put the gun carefully back into the case. "Feel like a snack before I leave? I'll spring for lobster salad if you're up for it."

"Huh? Where did that come from?"

Pretty good, Princess, but not quite good enough. The "Huh" came a beat too slow, your eyes got wide, and the tops of your ears are crimson all of a sudden.

"Someone brought lobster salad to your father just before he was shot. Not the kind of thing you could pick up at McDonald's. I've had it on my mind."

"Oh." Caitlin had recovered completely. The crimson was all gone and her voice was normal. "I don't really care for it myself. Any other questions?"

"Questions wouldn't be a very good idea right now. There's a powerful subconscious urge to confess. Learned was counting on that when he sent me functional dueling pistols with everything necessary to fire them. You tried to confess to me once and I blew you off. If I ask questions now you might answer them—and that could get awkward."

"But then, you're my lawyer, aren't you?"

"Interesting issue. I frankly don't know offhand how much of this is privileged, Caitlin. I'd have to research that, and I don't do legal research for free."

"I don't blame you."

"In Scotland, a jury has a choice of three verdicts instead of just two: guilty, not guilty, and not proven. Scots lawyers say that 'not proven' means 'not guilty—but don't do it again.'"

"That's neat," Caitlin said. "Law is, like, really interesting, isn't it?"

"If you do it again, Caitlin, none of this is privileged."

Chapter Fifty

So that's my confession, Father. I'm sorry it took so long, but none of it seemed to make sense without the rest of it. There are plenty of sins in there. Pride, lust, greed and envy for sure. Even gluttony if you count my getting drunk after the breakup. And anger. Dear God, anger coming out of every pore. I think anger drove all the rest of it. So all of the biggies except sloth—and sloth is the one sin I'll probably never commit.

I traded the cased dueling pistols to Phillip Schuyler for a receipt from the U.S. Attorney's office. I thought there was a fifty-fifty chance they were stolen property and I didn't want to find out the hard way. I let him know they'd come from Learned but said I couldn't tell him how I'd gotten my hands on them. He said maybe I'd get a chance to tell a grand jury and I said, "Hit me with your best shot, kid." We both laughed, so that's not gonna happen. I'm not holding my breath 'til I get the pistols back, and I'm not sure I want them.

Caitlin killed Tom Bradshaw. She killed him to keep him from cutting her and her mother off with a measly half-million bucks because it turned out Learned was her real father. When she saw Schwartzchild's conflict-of-interest letter, she figured pitiless enforcement of the prenup and a change in the will and her trust were in play. Bradshaw bullied Ariane into an abortion of a child she'd already named, and I think Caitlin was pretty torn up about that for Ariane's sake. The love she has for her mother is deep and rich. But I don't think she would have murdered Bradshaw over that, even after she knew he wasn't her real father. I think the abortion told Caitlin that there was no way Ariane would have the guts to do anything about the financial punishment Bradshaw planned to administer.

So Caitlin did something about it herself. She had access to the museum's light dragoon pistol because Bradshaw hadn't returned it to the museum yet after bringing it home. She worked out the same bullet-switch trick I did and used it. She was out of school all day on the Monday Bradshaw was killed. She only needed Learned's .45 for ten minutes or so, and she could have gotten her hands on it while Learned and Ariane were otherwise engaged. She ruined one of her pillows by firing into it so she could get a bullet with .45-caliber ballistics to use in the flintlock. That's why the pillow was missing from her bedroom.

So I know she did it, I know why she did it, and I know how she did it. But the law says I can't tell anyone. I took an oath when I was called to the bar. I swore to preserve my clients' confidences and to defend them zealously within the bounds of the law. I was a big girl and I knew what I was doing. That oath pretty much defines who I am and who I've been trying to become since fourth grade. I'll be violating that oath if I rat Caitlin out.

I *could* do it anyway. I could break my oath and face the consequences. But I'm not going to. Let's be clear on that. I'm not saying *I can't*, I'm saying *I won't*. I won't clear Learned's name. I won't comfort Paul by telling him that maybe the only person he'll ever love wasn't a murderer after all. I won't bring a cold-blooded killer to justice. I take full moral responsibility for that choice. I'm pretty sure I'm making the right call. Right or wrong, though, it's my call and I'll live with it.

Bottom line, I guess, it's law versus justice and law wins. You go to law school to learn law—not justice.

To receive a free catalog of Poisoned Pen Press titles, please contact us in one of the following ways:

Phone: 1-800-421-3976
Facsimile: 1-480-949-1707
Email: info@poisonedpenpress.com
Website: www.poisonedpenpress.com

Poisoned Pen Press
6962 E. First Ave. Ste. 103
Scottsdale, AZ 85251